ALSO BY R.A. SALVATORE

THE LEGEND OF DRIZZT

THE DARK ELF TRILOGY
Homeland
Exile
Sojourn

THE ICEWIND DALE TRILOGY
The Crystal Shard
Streams of Silver
The Halfling's Gem

THE LEGACY OF THE DROW SERIES
The Legacy
Starless Night
Siege of Darkness
Passage to Dawn

THE PATHS OF DARKNESS TRILOGY
The Silent Blade
The Spine of the World
Sea of Swords

THE SELLSWORDS TRILOGY
Servant of the Shard
Promise of the Witch-King
Road of the Patriarch

THE HUNTER'S BLADES TRILOGY

The Thousand Orcs
The Lone Drow
The Two Swords

THE TRANSITIONS SERIES

The Orc King
The Pirate King
The Ghost King

THE NEVERWINTER SAGA

Gauntlgrym
Neverwinter
Charon's Claw
The Last Threshold

THE SUNDERING SERIES

The Companions

THE COMPANIONS CODEX

Night of the Hunter
Rise of the King
Vengeance of the Iron Dwarf

THE HOMECOMING TRILOGY

Archmage
Maestro
Hero

GENERATIONS

Timeless
Boundless
Relentless

THE WAY OF THE DROW

Starlight Enclave
Glacier's Edge
Lolth's Warrior

THE FINEST EDGE OF TWILIGHT

DUNGEONS & DRAGONS

THE FINEST EDGE OF TWILIGHT

R.A. SALVATORE

RANDOM HOUSE WORLDS
NEW YORK

Random House Worlds
An imprint of Random House
A division of Penguin Random House LLC
1745 Broadway, New York, NY 10019
randomhousebooks.com
penguinrandomhouse.com

2026 Random House Worlds Trade Paperback Edition

Originally published in hardcover in the United States by Random House Worlds, an imprint of Random House, a division of Penguin Random House LLC, in 2025.

ISBN: 978-0-593-87528-5
Ebook ISBN: 978-0-593-87527-8

Printed in the United States of America

1st Printing

Book Team: Production editor: Jocelyn Kiker • Managing editor: Susan Seeman • Production managers: Erin Korenko and Keila Sato • Copy editor: Jacob Reynold Jones • Proofreaders: Debbie Anderson, Emily Cutler, Judy Kiviat

Book design by Alexis Flynn

The authorized representative in the EU for product safety and compliance is Penguin Random House Ireland, Morrison Chambers, 32 Nassau Street, Dublin D02 YH68, Ireland. https://eu-contact.penguin.ie

To Diane, of course. What a journey, my love!

To my kids and kids-in-law, with joy and respect.

To my grandkids, with thanks for making this part
of life so amazing.

And to everyone in the world who's a bit
neurospicy, who dares to follow their truth and their
heart no matter what others might say.

We live once, and even for those who stretch it to
its limits, it's short.

Live true.

Live you.

—Bob

THE FINEST EDGE OF TWILIGHT

PROLOGUE
DALERECKONING 1504

Dahlia moaned with pleasure as she felt Bedorijay's fangs slipping through the skin on her neck. She closed her eyes and smiled at the warmth of her blood being sucked out of those punctures, and felt the darkness of Bedorijay's spittle entering her body. She had taken a vampire lover once before, a Thayan named Korvin Dor'crae, but she had never allowed him to bite her, and their lich masters, who were grooming Dahlia for their own designs, would have utterly destroyed him if he had.

Now, though, Dahlia held no such reservations regarding the vampiric infection. She ran her tongue over her canines. She carried still the teeth of an elf, yes, but Dahlia could feel that she was getting close now.

She wouldn't go out in the sunshine anymore, and even in the perpetual fog of this hilly and ancient forest called Kryptgarden, the daylight proved uncomfortable. In the dark of night her vision had sharpened, every shape distinct. She could smell the blood of any creature and even determine the type of animal—or if it was a person—from a long way away.

Almost there, she told herself, but she hoped that when the conversion was complete, when she was fully a vampire, these rituals would continue. This was lovemaking to her, more intimate and trusting than anything she had ever known.

The last decades of her life had proved to be a strange journey indeed for the former servant of the mighty lich Szass Tam. Dahlia had fallen in love—something she had never thought possible—not once, but twice.

Both times spurned.

Dahlia, the ambassador of the great Szass Tam.

Dahlia, the lover of Drizzt.

Dahlia, the proxy of Lolth, the Demon Queen of Spiders.

Dahlia, the lover of Entreri.

Dahlia, the forsaken.

Dahlia, the pirate.

Dahlia, the humbled, left for dead on the Docks of Baldur's Gate, all her possessions stolen.

Stolen, too, was Dahlia's will to fight back. She hadn't even gone looking for Captain Wildevane and his crew of thieves. They had taken Kozah's Needle, her magnificent tri-staff. They had taken her Cloak of the Crow, with which she could transform into a great black bird and glide on the winds. Her right ear had been torn, for they had ripped the nine diamonds from it, leaving jagged wounds. They had even cut off the single braid whose red and black strands had reached halfway down her back, leaving her bald, her blue-and-purple tattoo of a hunting cat seeming about to pounce from the right side of her head.

Truly, Dahlia had been a broken thing when she had wandered into the reclaimed and rebuilt town of Phandalin in the Lost Hills region of the Sword Mountains, halfway between Neverwinter and Waterdeep, and some seventy-five miles due south of Gauntlgrym. All she had wanted at that time, the summer of DR 1498, was to live simply, peacefully, keeping to herself.

Her ambition was gone, her sense of purpose lost. She wanted nothing more than to wake up, do whatever chores would suffice to feed, shelter, and get her intoxicated for the day, then stumble to her hovel apartment and fall down unconscious. Existence: just that, until there was no more of that.

That had all changed when she witnessed, quite by accident, a most shocking event. Every time Dahlia felt the fangs of Bedorijay, she thought of that night. As usual, she had been the last patron to leave her favored drinking hole in Phandalin. More than a bit drunk, more than a bit depressed, she had dallied on her way back to her tiny room, wandering the streets in an aimless and circuitous route that had coincidentally put her on an avenue some twenty paces behind the tavernkeeper, a too-pleasant halfling woman named Winnie Bean.

Her call to Winnie had been cut short when she noticed a giant bat flying down from a rooftop, flipping and transforming as it neared the ground. The halfling tavernkeeper's name caught in Dahlia's throat even as the vampire's fangs sank into Winnie's neck.

Spellbound, Dahlia had watched the creature's gentle caress of his chosen victim, had watched Winnie's obvious revulsion and rejection.

How wildly the halfling woman had fought!

But the diminutive Winnie had been completely overmatched, and the vampire soon had her caught fast once more. Winnie had met Dahlia's gaze in those last moments of her life, a helpless, terrified look on her face.

A pathetic look, Dahlia had mused, and Dahlia didn't cry out for help and didn't rush to Winnie's aid, for it occurred to her that Winnie should have given in, and thus this fate was borne of her own failing and panic.

Dahlia watched the frenzy of blood overwhelm the vampire. What had been a gentle bite, a sharing of fluids, became an insatiable hunger. The master of night tore out Winnie's throat, gulping at her spraying blood, then dropped her corpse unceremoniously to the cobblestones.

Dahlia met the gaze of the vampire when his feast was done, and she returned his toothy smile with a nod and a grin of her own.

Strangely, she had felt no fear of him.

And she knew that this vampire understood that truth.

A tenday later, after garnering as much information as she could, she had traveled to the dark and misty forest of Kryptgarden, to the ancient ruins of a long-abandoned monastery. Half-buried under the roots and soil, she had found a tunnel, a cracked and broken stairway into the mostly intact substructure of that rubble.

Upon her return to the small village, Dahlia again began to walk the streets of Phandalin in the dark, when all the folk were asleep.

He had been waiting for her, she knew, when he came down at her from on high that very first night.

But Dahlia was no halfling tavernkeeper. She was a seasoned warrior, a great veteran, and she fended the vampire's attacks long enough to convince him that she wouldn't resist him if their tryst meant undeath instead of death.

"I sought you out," she had told him in the midst of that initial meeting, a rolling battle along several alleyways and streets. "I know where rests your casket and could have destroyed you in the daytime were that my preference!"

That had given the vampire pause.

"You know I speak the truth," Dahlia pressed. "You saw the rose I left at the top of the stair."

She locked her blue-eyed stare on the vampire's dark orbs.

"You play dangerous games," he warned.

"They are worth the reward," Dahlia had huskily replied, and she craned her neck and lowered her weapon.

She remembered that first bite so clearly. She had stolen a magical dagger from the corpse of Winnie Bean and held it in her hand, ready to spin about and put it up through the vampire's jaw, through his mouth, and into his brain the instant she sensed that frenzy, that primal hunger overwhelming him. But as soon as those fangs had engaged, as soon as the warmth of blood and the mist of darkness had begun to mingle, Dahlia understood that she would do no such thing even if this magnificent creature had indeed begun to tear out her throat.

She would have accepted it.

He had been as her god in those first moments, his charm overwhelming her, this pleasure controlling her beyond anything her mind or her fears might argue.

That was a month ago, and the pleasure of this vampiric joining had not diminished.

Now, though, Dahlia had learned to keep her wits about her even in the thrall of the vampire's sensual feeding, of this intoxicating ecstasy. Now, Dahlia kept her focus on her true designs.

Bedorijay was her master, yes. She could not deny him.

Her master, but he was no longer her god.

As her own darkness increased, so too increased her personal agency, her free will. She was still here because she wanted to be, because she had embraced a promise of power and eternity. She had found purpose once more.

She could feel that her canines were ready to become true fangs.

She wondered if Bedorijay would soon accept her bite, if he would let her lead in their intimacy.

She wondered how long she would give him a choice. So she had believed in those first days, and so she had clung to that thought as the tendays passed, until finally the truth could not be denied.

She was not a vampire.

She was merely the child of a vampire, a vampire spawn.

She was a plaything of Bedorijay, nothing more—and to her horror, she had learned that she wasn't even the only one.

"This will be our last joining," the vampire master informed her when she climbed out of the dirt-filled wooden box he had given her as her bed, to find him standing over her, waiting. "You are fully mine now, but you cannot offer me the nourishment of true and pure living blood any longer."

"What am I to do?" Dahlia tried to keep the panic out of her voice.

"You are to serve me. You are to go out when I allow it, so that you can feed. But only when I allow it, and always discreetly."

Dahlia had no choice but to comply, and so she did as she was commanded through the tendays. She feasted mostly on goblins. But every now and then, she caught a human unawares, even drawing elven blood on one occasion, lamenting then that she could not do to the handsome elf traveler what Bedorijay had done for her.

No, she simply had to kill him, and what a waste of potential pleasure that was.

She longed for more, for her own spawn to feed upon and to command.

A few days after her encounter with the elf, Bedorijay again told her to go out and feed.

Shaking her head, Dahlia stepped over to him and put her hands tenderly on his shoulders, moving very close, though neither had any breath to share.

"I can be more," she whispered into his ear, and she lowered her lips to his neck.

Then she was flying away, hit by a tremendous blast of magical wind. She crashed into the stone wall of the crypt, but she hardly felt the impact.

She heard the other children of Bedorijay hustling off into the shadows.

She pulled herself to her feet, but he was there, suddenly, magically, and he grabbed her by the throat and lifted her up so easily with one hand to slam her and pin her against the wall.

"If ever your fangs near my neck again, I will stake you out in the sunlight and listen to your screams from below as the light of day curls the flesh from your bones."

The words stabbed into her thoughts and into her heart, filling her with unreasonable despair. There was magic behind them, she knew.

But she knew, too, that she was no match for Bedorijay, particularly not now, with her mind filled with bloodlust to the point of insanity, and her newfound vampiric powers far below those of her master.

She wanted to explain, to tell him that she could be so much more to him than just another of his spawns. She knew that he'd react badly, though, so she just lowered her gaze submissively and whispered, "I am hungry."

"Then go," Bedorijay told her, cupping her chin and lifting her face so that he could stare into her eyes, his expression somehow both charming and menacing.

"Go to the roads about Phandalin, but do not enter the town nor feast on anyone who is out and about. The weather has been warm and dry, and therefore many travelers are out, journeying from Waterdeep to Neverwinter and back. You are a highwayman, you see? Just do not leave evidence of the truth of your kills."

A very shaken Dahlia was more than happy to be out of the crypt and off across the mountains. The ruins were some fifteen miles southeast of Phandalin, and that over tall hills, and it would be another five miles west to the coastal road most traveled.

But Dahlia went east instead, running without tiring in her undead state. It was a longer journey through the area known as the Crooked Forest and out to the Long Road, but she would not tire, and she came in sight of the lights of the larger and more established village of Westbridge with hours to spare.

Dahlia grinned at her cleverness, for while her master had forbidden her from eating in Phandalin, Bedorijay had said nothing about going into Westbridge. She might pick a nice tall fellow for her meal, she mused.

Before she even started for the town, though, she saw the lights of a coach coming up from the south along the Long Road.

She ran up a tree and out onto a heavy branch overhanging the road.

This would be so easy.

She ran her tongue across her fangs eagerly when the coachmen came into view. Fools, she thought, for this inland road was more fraught with highwaymen than the High Road along the coast, and a mere pair of drivers, one fat and both old, surely didn't present an intimidating deterrence while driving what appeared to be a very expensive coach.

Dahlia dropped silently to the back of the coach, then climbed across the roof as the coach gained speed despite the driver's cries of "Whoa!"

"They've gone mad!" the other man on the right side of the bench cried, and he too tried to calm the team.

Dahlia slipped into the seat between them with such grace that the portly driver just tried to shrug her hand away, thinking it was his companion's.

"What, now, Bakerson! Calm them!" he said turning, the words sputtering through his lips and his eyes popping wide indeed when he saw Dahlia chewing on Bakerson's throat.

Blood dripping from her mouth, she so easily flung Bakerson off the right side of the speeding coach and turned her hiss, her demonic red eyes, and her clawed hands fully on the remaining driver.

He moved well for such a big man, Dahlia had to admit, though she thought he might have been more aware of his surroundings when he leaped from the coach to fly face-first into a rather large tree.

She'd go back and drink him later, she decided. She took up the reins and slowed the team—or tried to, for the horses obviously sensed her presence and were having none of that. Dahlia tugged with all her strength, finally breaking their stride. She immediately went back up on the roof away from the horses, then came down the back and around the side as the coach rolled to a stop.

She tore the door right off—so hungry!

Stepping up to move in, Dahlia hesitated at the unnatural darkness inside the vehicle.

"Bakerson?" came a voice from within that magical globe, which winked out then, revealing the speaker.

Dahlia froze in place, shocked. "Effron?" she whispered and gasped.

"Mother?" asked the small, twisted man inside as he presented his bone staff before him. A pair of eyes on the tiny skull topping it lit up with powerful magical energy.

Dahlia no longer drew breath, but even if she hadn't been an undead thing, she'd not have drawn any there, certainly.

"Three days!" Bedorijay fumed. "I had thought you lost, destroyed."

"Are you not pleased that I have returned, my master?" Dahlia asked, properly whimpering and groveling.

"How?" Bedorijay demanded. "How have you managed this? Your coffin is here! The dirt to which I bound you is here. You could not be away for so long." He paused and stared at her slyly. "Unless you planned this disappearance and took some of that sacred unhallowed earth with you. And that I will not tolerate!" Bedorijay roared, and he stepped forward, lifting a clawed hand above Dahlia's bowed head.

"She was freed of your binding through a ceremony, great Lord Bedorijay," came a feeble and scratchy voice from the dark stairwell of the crypt, and out walked a small and twisted man, one shoulder so far back that his left arm hung limply behind him. The man who appeared was not much above five feet tall and could not have weighed ten stones.

He wore a smug grin and carried a staff, capped with a small skull, which he tapped on the ground. The skull's eyes glowed a bright enough light for Bedorijay to note that this one was a tiefling, or half-tiefling, at least, for the ears that stuck out from his black hair seemed more those of an elf. Most striking, other than perhaps the location of his left shoulder, were his eyes, one blue, one red, and the ram-like horns on his forehead.

Bedorijay yanked Dahlia upright by the hair and pulled her very close, her head tilted in such a way that would allow him to bite out her throat with ease.

"Who are you who dares come to this place?" To accentuate the point, Bedorijay summoned several other vampire spawn from the shadows.

"I am Effron Alegni," the intruder replied. "I met your wayward child on the Long Road. She would not ever have returned here, for the sun was soon to rise, except for the ceremony of desecration I performed in a dark hole to keep her sheltered."

"She was not yours to save, and this place is not yours to visit!"

"Once I learned of the great Lord Bedorijay, I had to witness your beauty for myself. I am no commoner, and I carry the blood of Shadovar Lord Herzgo Alegni within me. There is much I can do to assist you."

"This child of mine will die for leading you here." He hissed and bared his fangs, turning for Dahlia's throat.

"No!" Effron roared, magical energy flowing forth.

Bedorijay stopped as if slapped, glaring at him.

The vampire spawn reacted at once and began moving in toward Effron.

"Tell them to stop," Effron commanded Bedorijay.

"Stop!" Bedorijay insisted, and the lesser vampires froze in place. Bedorijay's eyes widened in surprise.

"Let her go," Effron said. "Let my mother go!"

Bedorijay understood then the danger, understood the weight of compulsion slamming him.

He let Dahlia go.

He didn't want to, but he did.

"Warlock," the vampire managed to say, his mouth fighting against every syllable. Vampires like Bedorijay survived and thrived by dominating others, but he, too, had been dominated once, centuries before, when he had become the child of another vampire. He knew this feeling. He understood the magic that was now washing through him.

His mind just couldn't fathom that he was actually in the thrall of such a spell, powerful as it was.

The skull's eyes flared brighter, but the light narrowed, becoming beams that locked onto Bedorijay's eyes, blinding him. He knew that he should turn into a bat and fly away, or into mist and float from this crypt . . .

But he could not.

He felt hands upon the back of his shoulders. Then fangs—Dahlia's fangs!—stabbing into his neck.

Bedorijay flailed his head, wailing, cursing. Dahlia's arms went around him in a tight hug, and he could feel her strengthening. For she was drinking the blood of a true vampire.

She was becoming a true vampire.

He would have broken free, but the domination continued to confuse his movements too long.

"No!" he screamed, finally, and he burst away from Dahlia, throwing her aside. One step toward the warlock, though, and Bedorijay was struck by a black bolt of energy from that infernal bone staff. He continued forward for just a moment, until he realized that something strange was in the air before him, as if the planes of existence had been torn, the rip of planar fabric taking the shape of a . . . sword?

It stabbed at him, once, twice, and oh, the pain!

He staggered back, fending, and felt a stab in his back. Reflexively, he glanced over his shoulder, to see Dahlia rising and coming in again, leaping onto his back and sinking her fangs into the side of his throat, tearing and ripping the skin.

Bedorijay's eyes went wide with disbelief and at the stunning, burning pain, when that conjured sword struck again, plunging into his chest, into his dark heart.

Bedorijay stood there, arms splayed out, mouth loose in a silent scream, eyes peeled open in pure shock. Shaking, shaking, trying to fight through the paralyzing wound of the magical sword and of Dahlia's tearing fangs. Perhaps he could find the strength . . .

But the warlock's rain of Eldritch Blasts continued to batter him, and that rift sword, a conjured Blade of Disaster, struck again and again, tearing him apart.

In the shadows all about the room, the vampire spawn wailed and whimpered, confused and helpless, leaderless yet still held in thrall by the dying vampire—and surely in fear of the bared power of the mighty warlock that had walked into their home.

Bedorijay heard it all. He tried to call to them to come to his aid.

But it was too late. Everything around him began to fade. His memories, two centuries of memories, spun through his thoughts and flew out from him, vanishing into the ether.

Perhaps it was freedom, came his very last denial, though deep in that last flicker of consciousness, he realized it to be damnation.

Dahlia let the melting vampire fall to the floor before her and watched, licking the blood from her lips and fangs, as Bedorijay's form curled and decomposed, as the held-back decay of centuries came free to eat, as he became a skeleton, as he was reduced to dust.

"You are mine now!" she shouted at the spawn. "Go to your rest!"

They did. They scrabbled out of this entry hall to the various chambers nearby, and Dahlia smiled her extra-toothy grin of satisfaction when she heard their wooden coffins closing one by one.

"His arrogance destroyed him," Effron said. "He let me walk in here because he could not fathom that you would dare to betray him. Remember that, Dahlia. Look at the pile of dust before you and remember that always."

"Few would expect or understand your power, my child," Dahlia replied.

"Do not ever call me that."

"You named yourself as Effron Alegni to Bedorijay, but you have taken my surname, Syn'dalay," Dahlia countered.

"Perhaps I hate Herzgo Alegni more than I hate you. Perhaps."

"You have freed me. I am in your debt."

"Take heart that you cannot see yourself in a mirror, Dahlia, for you are a hideous thing."

"Can you not even call me mother?"

"No."

"You did so at the coach when first we met."

"I was surprised."

"Do you have to hate me so?"

Effron sighed and shook his head. "Here," he said. "Allow this spell into your mind."

He cast an illusion then of Dahlia, and worked it until it approximated her appearance. Her hair had grown thin, covering her tattoo, but it was merely a shag of snarls and wayward strands. Her face was sunken and hollow, her muscles slack.

She had been so beautiful once, and so powerful.

No, she couldn't lament the second, for she could feel an even greater power growing now within her.

But the loss of her beauty she could not abide.

She closed her eyes and ran her fingers over her head like a comb.

"I can already see you changing," Effron said. "I recognize you now more easily."

"As I was?"

Effron nodded, the action making his useless arm swing back and forth behind him.

"I am not even alive, but I feel . . . health."

"A vampire now, not a mere spawn."

"I will be beautiful again, my s . . . Effron," she quickly corrected. "I will wear the finest clothes and bedeck myself in jewels."

"Here? In this ruined crypt?"

Dahlia slowly shook her head.

"I must warn you," said Effron. "They are looking for you, or at least, they were when last I saw them a year ago."

"'They'?"

"Artemis Entreri, and likely Jarlaxle. They found Kozah's Needle at the bottom of the sea, but the stubborn Entreri refuses to believe that you are dead."

Dahlia shrugged. "He is half right, I suppose."

"If they find you like this, they'll not likely suffer you to survive."

"Artemis Entreri would make a fine companion in this existence." She knew as soon as she said it that it was a fool's hope. Surely Entreri was too dangerous a creature for her to attempt such a partnering. No, if he found her, it seemed likely that she would have to kill him and be done with it.

"Go to your rest, Dahlia." Effron turned for the door.

"I know where to find you."

"Please don't."

"Discreetly."

Effron spun around and glared at her. "Never. Should you come to my residence, well . . ." He looked down at the dust.

"Then you come to me," Dahlia begged. "Don't abandon me. You are all I have, all I ever truly had."

"You threw me off a cliff," he reminded her.

"In hatred of Herzgo Alegni, not of you. I thought we were long past that day of your birth, my son."

He grimaced when she called him that, but he did not retort.

In that moment, Dahlia knew, and she was happy.

"I have powerful enemies hunting me, and bills to pay," Dahlia said. "I need your help."

"Bills?"

Dahlia showed him the ragged tears on her right ear. "I have someone I want you to find for me. Just find them, likely in Baldur's Gate. Then I can properly repay them for their generosity."

Effron stood there, transfixed, too many emotions flowing through him to be able to sort them out.

"I want to be respectable," Dahlia said, and Effron winced because he believed her. "I want to pay them back, and I want to live in the station to which I belong."

To almost anyone else, that would have sounded ridiculous, of course, for Dahlia was *undead,* a vampire. But Effron the warlock, with his powerful, necromantic bone staff, knew many such creatures, from simple skeletons and zombies to specters and vampires and liches. He knew of vampires who walked among the courts of kings, discreetly, in the major cities of Faerûn.

The thought of Dahlia, of his mother—and she was, or had been, indeed physically beautiful—living in high station did not repulse him.

Far from it.

"I will return to you in a tenday," he promised.

Dahlia said no more and let him go.

She went to her coffin then, and moved the dirt to Bedorijay's beautiful casket, taking it as her new bed.

Before she settled in for the day, though, she did something she hadn't even considered since her days as Matron Darthiir Do'Urden in Menzoberranzan:

She prayed to Lolth.

PART ONE

THE OTHER SIDE OF THE CHASM
AUTUMN, DALERECKONING 1508

My name is not "Drizzt's daughter."

My name is Brie, but not in honor of my mother, Catti-brie. You've heard of her, I expect, heard of both of my parents.

Drizzt is the hero of Menzoberranzan, the slayer of the white dragon Ingeloakastimizilian, the man who forged peace between the barbarian tribes and the settlers of Ten-Towns. He is the legend of those in Menzoberranzan who forsook the ways of the Demon Queen of Spiders, Lady Lolth, and he is the bane of those who follow her diabolical plans. He helped the dwarfs retake Mithral Hall, then brought Bruenor Battlehammer to Gauntlgrym, where King Bruenor now reigns as the center point of the proud Delzoun dwarfs.

So many adventures he has walked, doing good as he believed, helping as he may. He is among the finest swords-men in Faerûn, and skilled enough in the Way of the Open Palm to take the title of Grandmaster of Flowers in the Monastery of the Yellow Rose if he so chose—and if he had not promised the late Grandmaster Kane that he would not.

So of course he will not, for Drizzt Do'Urden is ever true to his word.

He is admired, he is loved, he is feared, and he is loathed.

I admire him. I love him. He is my father. I am Drizzt's daughter.

But my name is not "Drizzt's daughter."

Catti-brie is the most unlikely of heroes. An orphaned human child, raised by dwarfs in a cave in the frozen tundra of Icewind Dale, where few would have survived into adulthood. But she did. Survived and thrived. She became a fine warrior—so skilled with her bow, Taulmaril the Heartseeker—as a member of the Companions of the Hall, the five adventurers who have etched their names into the songs of bards across the northern realms. And when she was injured, she found a new course—two, actually: one as a wizard and one as a priestess of Mielikki. And surely she was not just any wizard, for she was scarred by the disaster known as the Spellplague. And she was surely no ordinary priestess, either, for she became the Chosen of the goddess Mielikki, a hero who passed through death back to life, fighting as Mielikki's avatar against the Avatar of Lolth.

And she won. She always wins. She always finds a way. She is no less a hero than my father, and I am Catti-brie's daughter.

But my name is not "Catti-brie's daughter."

In truth, my name is not even Brie. It is Briennelle Zaharina Do'Urden, and I am given that name not for Catti-brie. Only the surname matches that of my parents.

My name comes from my grandfathers, with Briennelle a play on the feminine version of Bruenor, and Zaharina the drow feminine name for Zaknafein.

Yes, Bruenor, King Bruenor, with the wealth of a

dwarven lord and three armies at his command, and Zaknafein Do'Urden, considered still the greatest weapons master ever to wage battle in Menzoberranzan, and now a two-time champion in Cazzcalci, the great bloodsport, fighting for the Biancorso Whitebears of the Scellobel borough in frigid, faraway Callidae.

"Hail, King Bruenor!" they shout whenever my maternal grandfather walks the ways of any city in the north.

"Perte miye, Zaknafein!" the aevendrow cry whenever the great Zaknafein walks onto the icy arena under the lights of the Merry Dancers.

I am their granddaughter, and though I bear a derivative of their names, my name is my own.

I am Brie. Brie Do'Urden.

I have heard all the tales of my parents and their friends, recounted breathlessly by people who tell me how blessed I am and how lucky I must be and how wondrous my life must be.

I have heard all the tales, too many times.

My name is Brie.

I answer to Brie, I take responsibility for Brie, and for Brie alone.

Well, or to Breezy. I rather like that.

Pleased to meet you. Hope you learn my name.

But when you meet my children, should there be any and should you meet them, learn their name, the one they forge on their own, and it will not be "Breezy's daughter."

—Brie "Breezy" Do'Urden

1

UNCLE WULFGAR

"Many shadows," Wulfgar whispered to Breezy. He shook his head. The sun hadn't broken the eastern horizon before them, but the snowy mountaintops were beginning to glisten, and the sky beyond them was brightening.

"I prefer the shadows," Breezy replied. She reached for the buckle of her belt, a very special buckle, and uttered a simple command word while pressing a button just underneath its clasp. With a few clicks and a whooshing sound, the buckle sprang into shape, producing a polished compound bow, ready and strung with a bowstring that shimmered with lightning energy.

Wulfgar glanced back at her. "Do you know how to use that?" he asked, nodding his chin toward that bow, a fabulous weapon called Taulmaril the Heartseeker.

"Pull back the string," she answered with a noncommittal shrug.

The giant man, standing nearer to seven feet than six, his arms as thick as Breezy's thighs, brushed long wavy blond hair back from his stubbled face, narrowing eyes the color of a cloudless Icewind Dale sky to offer a look both sour and intimidating. "Shoot at nothing that I am fighting," he quietly instructed. "Shoot at nothing that is near to me. Shoot at nothing at all unless you must."

"You've killed three of the savage beasts in the week we've been out of Kelvin's Cairn," she reminded, giggling at Uncle Wulfgar's sorry attempt to cow her. "You said you'd take me hunting, not sitting to the side cheering you on."

"Then you've seen how formidable the yetis are."

"I have and remain unimpressed. Give me one fight. You said we were heading back tomorrow." She meant every word, for Breezy knew that she needed the experience and the trial of this battle. The most important fight of her young life was fast approaching, mere months away, and its outcome would determine her reality for the next decade or more, likely, as she climbed the monastic ranks in the far-distant Monastery of the Yellow Rose.

Wulfgar looked around. The two had come far to the south and east of Ten-Towns in their pursuit of the tundra yetis, venturing into the boulder tumbles that comprised the northern foothills of the Spine of the World mountain range. Out here lay many hiding places—and many monsters, no doubt, not limited to the yetis.

But Wulfgar thought that this monster he had spotted in the crevice between the boulders across the way was indeed a yeti, for the four-toed tracks of the heavy creature that had led him here were unmistakable and almost unique to the hulking creatures.

"I'll consider it, but not for this one," he said, and Breezy gave a low growl. "There are too many hidey-holes about, perhaps concealing other yetis. We must be done with this fight quickly."

"Together, then."

Wulfgar shook his head and shuffled uneasily. "Too many caves and shallows." He glanced back the way they had come, and it seemed clear to Breezy that he was thinking of retreating.

"If there are two, we can defeat them," Breezy insisted. "If there are three, I will call in a friend."

"And if there are four?"

"We fight harder," the young woman said with an impish grin. She couldn't let him change his mind and turn them about. She just couldn't. She needed this, and not simply as a training exercise for her considerable fighting skills—indeed, she would battle here with weapons that would not be available to her when she fought for the rank of Master of Dragons. What she needed was the experience of the stress, the very edge of catastrophe, the forced movements and reactions with her life on the line.

For even though her physical life would not be in great jeopardy in her coming trial, her identity, her pride, her growing sense of independence surely would.

Wulfgar shook his head, but he was looking back at the dark crevice ahead, his warhammer Aegis-fang in hand, his fingers flexing eagerly.

"If I tell you to run, just run," he whispered.

"Of course." Breezy stared at him and sensed his uneasiness. There was evil about—she could feel it, too, a quiet hush. Too quiet.

But she wanted her fight.

She had watched Wulfgar put that powerful warhammer to swift and deadly use, dispatching each of the three yetis they had come upon in their earlier days out from Ten-Towns with seeming ease.

There was more than one here, she believed.

And hoped.

"Don't shoot me in the back," Wulfgar said, not turning to regard her and instead beginning a low skulk toward the pair of giant boulders. He veered to the left, the northernmost giant stone and the one with the most open ground around it.

Breezy nodded knowingly. If others were coming, they would be farther from him, emerging from the larger boulder tumbles south of their position, giving Wulfgar and her a fine head start. She didn't want to flee, but she understood and appreciated the caution. Despite her earlier declaration, Breezy understood the truth of their enemies. Tundra yetis were huge beasts, resembling large white-and-light-brown gorillas, but more upright, like a gnoll. They had huge curving claws on ten fingers and smaller, thicker triangular daggers on the four toes of each foot. Their flat apish faces were dominated by huge mouths with long, massive canines. As much as she said she wanted to fight one, Breezy understood that it was nothing to be trite about. Tundra yetis were all muscle and natural weapons, which they regularly and efficiently put to deadly use.

Wulfgar stopped and turned about. "They aren't animals," he said to Breezy, perhaps the tenth time he'd told her that on this hunting excursion.

Breezy nodded. She understood his emphasis, as she had made it quite clear to him that she had no desire to hunt animals for anything other than food, and even for that necessity, she really didn't want to kill them.

But these weren't animals. They were malignant monsters. Hateful and savage and living only to inflict pain and death.

She told herself that repeatedly. There would be no hesitance here, no pang of guilt. For indeed, Breezy knew guilt. Her thoughts catapulted back to the journey that had taken her and the others to Icewind Dale. They had traveled the pass through the mountains and had been assaulted by a small army of orcs under the command of drow. Lolthian drow from the city of her father's birth.

Breezy winced as she recalled what she had been forced to do.

"Not now!" she scolded herself under her breath, and she shook the troubling memories, the distractions, away. She stared at the darkness between the boulders. Her thoughts reached into the shadows, into the tangible swirl of darkness she now knew them to be. She felt the movements of the air within them. She felt . . .

The yeti.

No, two yetis. She was surprised by how clearly she knew that, as if the shadows were translucent to her. She thought to call out a warning to Wulfgar but held her tongue, instead swinging her gaze to the south, scanning the other shallows and caves and crevices.

A third yeti. A fourth.

A fifth.

It was an ambush—the clever monsters had led them to this place!

Breezy did speak out then, but not to Wulfgar. She pulled an onyx figurine from her pouch and called to Guenhwyvar, the spirit panther from the Astral Plane, the longtime companion, longtime friend, to her father.

The first yeti exited the nearest crevice, veering straight for the enormous Wulfgar. Breezy didn't watch, focusing instead on the second creature in the crevice. She did hear the first yeti's roar, though, and out of the corner of her eye, she caught a silvery flicker in the air before the rampaging beast. How that yeti's roar changed so suddenly into something less ominous.

Aegis-fang, she knew, and she nodded, lifting and leveling Taulmaril. Yetis were broad-shouldered behemoths, and the crevice wasn't much wider than the beast that had exited it.

The shadows told Breezy that another yeti was in that crevice. All she had to do was shoot at the center of the darkness.

She let fly.

WULFGAR KNEW HE HAD BEEN seen in his move to the side—in fact, he had counted on it, flushing the yeti out of the darkness and right in line.

The beast went up high, arms above its head in a powerful display, adding a roar as it attacked.

Wulfgar brought Aegis-fang right up over his head, both hands low on the handle, and launched it into a spinning throw. It struck the yeti square in the chest, blasting out its breath, turning its roar into a gasp.

It didn't down the yeti, though, the tough beast stumbling through the shock and pain, then coming on again.

Seeing an unarmed human standing before it—a huge human, but still puny next to the yeti—drove the murderous monster on.

It closed and sent a clawed hand slashing across at Wulfgar's face. The veteran warrior turned and spun away before it, magically summoning Aegis-fang back to his hand with a mere thought as he continued his pirouette, then came around with the hammer in his grasp, swinging it in above the dipped shoulder of the overbalanced yeti, its arm still out to Wulfgar's right. With all his momentum and spinning weight behind the strike, Wulfgar deftly re-angled the heavy head of Aegis-fang to come in just above that shoulder, cracking it against the side of the yeti's head, sending the beast stumbling to the side and to the ground.

The warrior set himself to charge, then fell back with a start as a silver streak creased the air before him. A magical lightning arrow from Taulmaril, he realized, speeding toward the crevice from which the yeti had come.

"No!" he cried, looking to Breezy, his eyes widening as he heard the pained growl from within that crevice.

Breezy would need a perfect shot to bring down a tundra yeti with Taulmaril alone.

"By the gods," he muttered, understanding the ambush, and all he could think about was the possibility that he had just led his best friend's daughter to her death.

BREEZY WINCED WHEN THE MAGICAL arrow flew away, both from the blinding suddenness of its lightning flash and her slight tremble as she let go of the string. She saw the streak shooting too far to the right of her mark, clipping the southernmost boulder instead of disappearing into the shadows—or, hopefully, into the yeti she knew to be within that darkness.

Good luck was with her, though, for the arrow skipped off the stone, scarring the rock with its lightning energy and showering the area with sparks, deflecting left and into the shadows, affording Breezy a quick glance at the yeti within, at the look of surprise on its monstrous face, as the lightning shot into it.

She knew she hadn't killed it, certainly, and suddenly doubted her plan.

But no, she resolutely rejected the fear. And besides, now her companion Guenhwyvar, a six-hundred-pound black panther, was there beside her, awaiting her orders.

"My Guen," she told the panther and pointed to Wulfgar and his battle. Guenhwyvar understood and bounded away, while Breezy swung south and fired off three more shots in quick order, hoping to draw out the remaining ambushers.

And she did, three more furious tundra yetis emerging from the holes nearer the foothills, all charging toward her. "Brother Gregory is waiting for me," she told herself. "I need this!"

She smiled and nodded, but swallowed hard, not quite sure if she was being clever, or *too* clever.

WULFGAR KNEW THAT HE HAD hurt the monster writhing on the ground before him but hadn't finished it—a truth confirmed when the beast sprang right back up, its face bloody, its broken jaw hanging awkwardly. He had to fight through this behemoth, but he had to do so quickly, before the second one came forth and got to Breezy.

His concern turned to panic when he saw more arrows flying off for the southern areas, and more yetis emerging.

"What are you doing?" he yelled, whipping Aegis-fang across and nearly stumbling from the desperation behind that swing—a swipe that hit nothing but air as the yeti dodged back.

Wulfgar braced, recovering, expecting the yeti to leap upon him. And it did start to do just that, until a flying ball of panther slammed into its side, throwing it to the ground.

"Tempus bless you, Guen!" he muttered, leaping forward to intercept the monster emerging from the crevice.

He yelled for Breezy to run, even managed to glance back that way after his next swing stopped the second yeti, its chest still smoldering from the lightning arrow.

She wasn't there.

That confused Wulfgar, but he thought it a good thing, and thought, too, that he should quickly get away from this yeti and flee before the three newcomers could join in. He ducked back from a slashing clawed hand, started forward to strike, then jumped back again in surprise when the yeti's head simply exploded before him, its face tearing asunder and a bolt of lightning—no, a lightning arrow, shooting forth.

Wulfgar's jaw dropped open as the yeti dropped dead to the ground, for out of the crevice that had held these first two monsters came Breezy—and how she had possibly gotten in there, he could not begin to imagine.

"Run!" Wulfgar yelled at Breezy when he recovered from his shock.

"We've got them!" she insisted.

"We're outnumbered!" he roared.

But another roar, Guenhwyvar's roar, argued the point.

"No we're not! Three against three," Breezy said, leading Wulfgar's gaze to the southeast. "And one of them is hurt." The yetis she had flushed out had changed course, no longer targeting Breezy's previous location, now heading straight for them. Fearless Guenhwyvar bounded to intercept.

Wulfgar saw no wounds on the approaching monsters—until Breezy's next arrow flew out and clipped one on the shoulder.

"See?" she said as he turned to regard her. With a flick of her wrist, a press of a button, and a whisper of command, she rolled the magical bow back into its magical holster in her belt buckle, while drawing Icingdeath with her other hand.

"Anything to get your fight, eh, you stubborn girl?" Wulfgar asked.

"Just making you keep your promise, Uncle," she replied.

Ahead of them, Guenhwyvar closed on the nearest yeti, ending in a great leap that sent her soaring up at the beast's head. The yeti responded with flailing arms, trying to grab the cat, but Guen came in with hind legs kicking, front paws scrabbling wildly, and as soon as she connected, she leaped away, pulling free of the yeti's tentative grasp and launching the beast to the ground.

Guen landed cleanly, and at the very last moment as the other two yetis lunged for her, she turned into a sideways run.

"Smart cat," Wulfgar remarked, charging for the enemies. He lifted his warhammer, cried out to his god Tempus, and sent it flying away toward the distracted yetis.

Breezy regarded him curiously as she ran to keep up with him, for she realized something then that she had not before. Wulfgar's tone when he called to his god was one of habit, she thought, and not faith.

Did he believe? Did he care? Did it matter?

She tucked the thought away and focused on the battle at hand, realizing then that Wulfgar had aimed for, and struck solidly, the yeti nearest her. Breezy blew a frustrated sigh at the thought that he was putting her safety ahead of his own, at the realization that she was, in his mind and therefore in truth, a burden here.

Determined to change that perception, she put her head down

and sprinted ahead, her monk training propelling her faster than Wulfgar could possibly pace.

And faster than the yeti had expected, she realized to her satisfaction. It had caught the warhammer after the weapon had slammed it in the chest, and it was now confused, desperately looking for the weapon. For when Wulfgar called it back, Aegis-fang had simply disappeared from the beast's hands.

Breezy's first attack was free of any defense the yeti might offer. She made it count, leaping past the yeti and stabbing it in the side of its neck with her father's heavily enchanted scimitar. Icingdeath was a blade made as bane to creatures of fire, which a tundra yeti was not, of course, but even without its special properties eating the life force of the yeti, its fine edge bit deep, easily cutting through the yeti's tough hide and coarse hair.

With a roar of pain and rage, the monster swung about, its long arm flying wide. Breezy ducked back, but not enough, for she underestimated the length of a tundra yeti's arm.

Fortunately for her, the yeti hit her with a backhand, still a stinging and crunching blow that sent her flying away. But at least its long claws hadn't dug into her face!

Dazed and disoriented, Breezy stumbled and could only hope she was doing so in a direction away from the monster. She shook her head, clearing her thoughts enough to realize that the monster was close, just behind her and to the left. She pivoted about, cutting Icingdeath across, desperately hoping to keep the beast at bay long enough for her to find some balance and center.

She missed badly.

The yeti roared, towering above her.

She gasped.

Aegis-fang hit the yeti in the cheek, snapping its head to the side violently and sending it into an off-balance stumble.

The warhammer had barely disappeared, recalled to Wulfgar's grasp, when Guen leaped in and drove the stunned monster to the ground, the panther landing heavily atop it, paws scrabbling, claws raking and clawing.

Breezy half turned to see Wulfgar engaged with a fourth monster, a fifth dead beside him on the ground. She felt relief only briefly, before recognizing that her uncle had put himself into a terrible position with his current foe. His hammer was out horizontally before him, the yeti grasping it with one hand, trying to tear it away—and worse, trying to get in closer so that it could claw at him with its other hand, which it had already done at least once judging from the blood on Wulfgar's face, neck, and shoulder.

The relief became rage.

Rage that Wulfgar had helped her at his own expense.

Rage that Guen had come to her aid instead of to Wulfgar's.

Rage that they thought of her as one to be protected and not as a fighting peer.

Rage mostly at herself for needing them in this critical moment.

Out from the buckle and up came Taulmaril, Breezy's hand repeatedly snapping to the magical quiver strapped to her back. One after another, bolts of streaking lightning shot forth.

The first hit the yeti and broke its hold on the warhammer—and broke, too, any thoughts it had of slashing at the man before it again.

The second knocked it to the side as it tried to turn.

The third, the fourth, the fifth, the sixth all hit the beast center-mass, right in the chest, blowing holes, smoking holes, almost as if its life force were wafting forth.

The beast fell dead.

Behind Breezy, the first yeti stopped roaring, and a moment later, a blood-covered Guenhwyvar sidled up to her, rubbing her face on Breezy's shoulder.

Wulfgar, too, came over, his face a mask of anger.

"I told you not to shoot at anything I was fighting!" he scolded.

"You told me I could have a fight of my own," Breezy snapped back. "I just figured we weren't speaking to each other truthfully."

"You were losing!" Wulfgar sputtered, shaking his head, fighting to find every word through the emotions so obviously overwhelming him.

"So were you!"

"I would have won!"

"So would I!"

"Girl . . ."

"Don't call me that! I am a woman. I am a warrior, a Superior Master of the Order of Saint Sollars in the Monastery of the Yellow Rose—and soon to be one of the three Masters of Dragons. You are my uncle, but you are not my keeper. You are my companion, but you are not my protector."

Wulfgar started to respond, but he stopped short and just blew out his breath, shaking his head, his expression grim and full of doubt. "You are the daughter . . ." he started to say, but he just snorted and shook his head again.

"Why did you even take me out here?" Breezy asked.

"I thought . . ." Again, the big man stopped and shook his head. "Come, let us be far away before the smell of these rotting beasts brings a hundred more upon us."

"Five," Breezy said as Wulfgar started to turn.

"Five?" Wulfgar echoed, looking curiously for just a moment before managing a helpless chuckle as he looked about to the five dead tundra yetis.

"And I claim half the kills as my own," Breezy declared.

"Your parents will have my hide when they learn that we fought five."

"No doubt to make of it some armor that they can wrap about their little girl," Breezy spat and started away.

2

UNCLE JAX

"IF YOU WERE GOING TO COME UP HERE ANYWAY, WHY DIDN'T YOU JUST SIT IN with the caravan?" Breezy asked Jarlaxle when she caught up to him along the main boulevard in the town of Bryn Shander, the seat of power in the confederation called Ten-Towns, in the brutal land of Icewind Dale.

Jarlaxle gave the young woman—and he could see so very clearly that she was indeed a young woman now and no more a girl—one of his know-it-all grins. "I had business to attend. Running the city of Luskan is no easy—"

"You just figured that we would do the difficult job of traveling through the mountain passes with the primordial essence and the other items for the teleportation gate. Why work when you can have others do it for you, yes Uncle Jax?"

Jarlaxle just smiled.

"No denial? My grandda Zaknafein says you are a deadly warrior, but I've never seen you lift a blade. Why is that?"

"Because I haven't had to, my dear Breezy."

"You make sure you don't have to."

"Then I win."

"My father had to. My mother had to put her most powerful

spells to use. Grandfather Bruenor and Thibbledorf Pwent had to. I had . . ." Her voice trailed off.

Jarlaxle's smile went away, and he fixed the young woman with a somber look.

"Battlehammer dwarfs died transporting that primordial essence and the other parts," Breezy went on, her voice growing husky, her purple eyes showing moisture.

"I know what you had to do in that battle," Jarlaxle said quietly. "You, in particular. You saved the day, Breezy."

Breezy took a deep breath and nodded. She didn't want to talk about the journey to Icewind Dale. Not now, and maybe not ever, she believed.

"Uncle Wulfgar took me hunting yetis," she said.

"So I have heard."

"Must you hear everything about me before I can tell you?"

"Haven't you more important things to discuss? Events in front of you instead of behind."

Breezy started to argue, but quickly changed her mind, because Uncle Jax was, as usual, quite right.

"Now," Jarlaxle said when she gave him a nod, "I am told that you have changed your tradition, your Way, at the monastery. You are a Superior Master of the Way of the Open Palm and now entering the ranks where you must defeat a monk above you to climb to the next rank."

"To become one of the three Masters of Dragons," Breezy said.

"The first of the ranks earned by duel."

"Yes."

"And so against a monk who is already a Master of Dragons."

Breezy nodded. "He is formidable." She hid a little grin as the conversation inspired a memory of Brother Gregory from two years previous. He was formidable, that was true, but this particular mental image of the powerful monk wasn't about combat. She had been studying an old tome in the monastery's library, when she caught the normally buttoned-up Gregory staring at her from across the room, rather hungrily.

As soon as he realized that she was looking back, the handsome man blushed so fiercely that Breezy thought his nose would start bleeding, or perhaps even his eyes, for that matter.

Yes, the memory was quite pleasant.

She blinked it away and noted the wry grin of Uncle Jax. Was he reading her mind through the power of that strange eyepatch he wore?

Suddenly, Breezy feared that *her* nose or eyes might start bleeding.

"I will fight soon," she said, clearing her throat. "I will take the master's rank." She offered a wide smile. "I wonder how Tazmikella and Ilnezhara will feel when I hold that particular title."

"I wouldn't dwell on it around either of them, were I you."

"Master of Dragons," Breezy firmly stated. "And then only nine people will stand between me and the ultimate title as Grandmaster of Flowers, and I'm sure that I could defeat half of them in single combat already. "Almost all are very old—"

"And yet, with that ascension right before you, you chose this time to change the focus of your study?" Jarlaxle interrupted. "Why?"

Breezy blinked repeatedly as if she had been slapped. "I follow my heart. It guides my choices. This is no lesser . . ."

"It is a new discipline to you."

"The monk tradition called the Way of Shadow is formidable in ways most clever and quick," Breezy replied. "And I do not know why I changed my focus. It just . . . it calls to me. The shadows call to me. The idea that they are more than an absence of light, that they have substance simply in the way they affect the mind . . ."

She stopped and stared hard at Jarlaxle, whose smile was suddenly back and wider than ever.

"They do indeed," he said.

"I didn't choose it," Breezy tried to explain. "It chose me. And already I have found great benefit. In the battle with the five yetis. I stepped from the light of the open field into the darkness of a cave's shadows some ten strides away. A single step into the gloom, behind the yeti I had already shot without its awareness."

"I am sure there are great benefits and powers in all the monk traditions," Jarlaxle replied, but he didn't seem pleased by Breezy's decision—at least in terms of her switching traditions so near to the upcoming challenge.

She wanted to tell him of another time she had utilized her new skills, and to amazing effect, but her pained sensibilities choked out the words before she could begin the tale. She didn't want to talk about it. Not now, perhaps not ever.

She noticed that Jarlaxle was looking past her, then, and swiveled her head to see his most trusted scout, Braelin Janquay, approaching. With the death of Jarlaxle's most valuable asset and perhaps his dearest friend, Kimmuriel Oblodra, Braelin was fast ascending the ranks of Jarlaxle's Bregan D'aerthe mercenary band.

"You have felt the blood of an enemy flowing over your hand," Jarlaxle said to her, "an enemy who would have quite happily killed you. Has the master you challenge for the rank ever felt that very particular type of warmth?"

"I . . . I don't think Master Gregory has ever been out of the monastery," Breezy stammered, for she wasn't sure if, and indeed doubted that, Jarlaxle was speaking of the yeti fight.

"That is your advantage, then," Jarlaxle told her, his inflection and outstretched arm inviting her to leave so that he could speak with Braelin.

Braelin smiled, nodded, and patted Breezy on the shoulder as she walked past. She looked back more than once before she exited the room, and each time met the looks of Jarlaxle and Braelin, who obviously weren't about to begin their private discussion until she had closed the door behind her.

"SHE WAS BRILLIANT IN THAT cave coming through the mountains," Braelin said to Jarlaxle when they were alone. "From all that I have gleaned, it seems that she would have probably escaped with the coffer even if Guenhwyvar hadn't come in to finish off the Menzoberranzan agents."

"Using cavern jumping and this Way of Shadow?"

"So it would seem," said Braelin. "But mostly the latter, whatever it is, I would guess. She has a lot to learn of cavern jumping. Her training has only just begun, after all."

"She'll learn it," Jarlaxle said. "She moves with the grace of her grandfather and the determination of her father. She will run and leap through the heights and along the walls as if on a level field of grass. Her monk training combined with—"

"Take care, my friend," Braelin warned. "You are turning the daughter of Drizzt and Catti-brie into a weapon, and if it ends badly for her, how do you think they will make it end for you?"

Around the next corner, Breezy turned her walk into a run, doubling back around the small houses, then coming up in a shadowed alleyway between a pair of small structures, affording her a view of the two drow and keeping her near enough to hear. She only caught the last part of that exchange, and Jarlaxle's compliments brought a smile to her face. Of course, she realized, this was Jarlaxle, so he probably knew exactly where she was eavesdropping.

No matter. She understood confidently that Jarlaxle thought highly of her.

She crouched lower and listened intently as the conversation continued.

It seemed to her that Jarlaxle remained unshaken by Braelin's warning.

"What are you hearing?" Jarlaxle asked.

"Word of King Bruenor's intent with the portal has indeed leaked and spread far and wide in the towns and the dale."

"And?"

"As you predicted," Braelin replied. "And no more than a trio of the councilors of Ten-Towns are pleased with the news of King Bruenor's return."

"Ah, they're all happy that he's here," Jarlaxle countered. "Bruenor is well loved in Icewind Dale. The others are simply not happy with the reason he has come north."

"The installation of the teleportation gate to Gauntlgrym," Braelin said, nodding.

"But only three support him, you say?"

Braelin nodded again, and Breezy noted his sour expression.

"Lonelywood, of course, with their ties to Regis," Jarlaxle said. "Many halflings have come to that town ever since the heroics of Regis, and the scrimshaw of Regis are now well known throughout the lands south of the Spine of the World. The councilor from Bremen offers support for the gate, I would expect, as the town was founded by dwarfs, and they were the closest to King Bruenor when he lived here. And the third? Possibly Good Mead, as they depend the most on trade, and their wares, their fine mead, will flow fast to Gauntlgrym and from there through the other teleportation gates to the dwarf citadels of Adbar and Felbarr."

Braelin shook his head and gave a helpless chuckle. "How do you possibly know this miserable wilderness of Icewind Dale so well?"

Breezy, too, found herself amazed by Jarlaxle's depth of understanding of this remote place—a land she was sure he had rarely visited, if ever.

"I know it no better than any other land," Jarlaxle replied, eliciting another laugh from Braelin. "Who was most opposed? Bryn Shander and the three towns along Lac Dinneshere?"

"And the Reghedmen, from the rumbles I have been hearing," Braelin said. "More than any of the councilors of Ten-Towns, the Reghed tribes have gone so far as to hint at violence if the portal becomes operational."

"Unsurprising."

"Surprising to me that King Bruenor did not foresee this trouble."

"Bruenor knows his own heart, and thus, that his intentions are nothing but beneficent to Icewind Dale," Jarlaxle explained. "It is often hard for a good-hearted king to understand that those he helps may not see his actions as they are actually intended. There are many different reasons, particularly in a place as diversely populated and out of the way as Icewind Dale. Many have come here because it is the last refuge of those who cannot find acceptance anywhere else. And if everywhere else can come here, what have they left as their own?

"Except for the Reghedmen," Jarlaxle added. "They are here because they believe this land is a gift to them from their god-being."

"Regis is not Reghed, and he lived here for many years," Braelin reminded.

Jarlaxle smiled. "He ran to the farthest corner of the world he could find. Do you not know the story? He was likely the only halfling in all the dale at that time."

Braelin shrugged.

"For another day, then," Jarlaxle promised. "Suffice it to say that you would run as far as you could, too, if you learned that Artemis Entreri was hunting you."

Braelin's eyes went very wide, and Breezy could hear him sucking in his breath. "That must be a long story, then."

"Long and winding," Jarlaxle said.

"What of Bruenor? Why did he come here?"

"His clan fled the world when the shadow dragon Shimmergloom took Mithral Hall from them. I don't know why or how they came to this place—it was centuries ago, and many years before Drizzt was even born. Perhaps the dwarfs wandered aimlessly—"

"I like that," Braelin interrupted, clearly startling Jarlaxle.

"You like that they wandered aimlessly?" Jarlaxle asked.

"No, no," Braelin corrected. "I like that you don't know. Perhaps we should mark this day and celebrate it every year."

"There are many things that even I don't know," Jarlaxle replied.

"But very few you'd ever admit."

Jarlaxle shifted his eyepatch to his other eye and fixed the scout with a hard look, but Braelin just laughed, and Breezy had to bite her lip to keep her snort silent.

She truly liked Braelin, she was reminded. She knew, and he apparently knew, that he was one of the few people in the world who could speak like that to Jarlaxle.

"Tell all of Bregan D'aerthe now in the dale to stay low and avoid any contact with Bruenor and his companions," Jarlaxle instructed. "If the Reghedmen believe that there is any budding alliance between Gauntlgrym and the drow-controlled city of Luskan, they will be even more skeptical of King Bruenor's intended portal."

Breezy considered it for a moment, then nodded her agreement. Luskan was Icewind Dale's contact to the outer world, the closest city of any note. But the journey from there to here was treacherous and the caravans rare.

And many here, the barbarians most of all, probably wanted to keep it that way.

She wasn't sure what to make of Jarlaxle's explanations, but she knew there was something important nestled within them, as was usually the case with the mercenary leader. She thought back to her last ride on the back of a copper dragon, when Tazmikella had turned the high vantage point into a lesson, bidding Breezy to study the various kingdoms and tribal lands and species spread out wide below her. Understand the geography involved, the dragon told her, and the relationships between the various peoples of those lands would make more sense.

It was all about perspective—her own in looking down from on high, so very high, and the perspectives of the peoples living in those varied and often-competing lands.

Make sense of the world? she silently asked herself as much as reminded herself, for to Breezy Do'Urden, whose experiences were so very different from those of almost everyone she met (outside of her parents' tight circle), that had always been a challenge.

Breezy crouched when Braelin trotted back along the boulevard, rushing past her position, off on the new mission Jarlaxle had determined, no doubt. She looked back to Jarlaxle, happy to see that he had turned away from her, glancing back toward the largest, though still low and modest, structure situated at the end of the street. The building stood as the seat of power for the town of Bryn Shander and the entire council of Ten-Towns.

With a nod, Breezy turned to slip away.

"You could at least offer an opinion, daughter of Drizzt," came Jarlaxle's call before she had taken a single step.

Breezy completed her great sigh before she registered what Jarlaxle had called her. Her jaw clenched and she huffed, then spun about and walked out of the alley. Jarlaxle seemed quite pleased with himself, she noted, as he was grinning ear to ear.

"How many times will you try to eavesdrop, deluding yourself into believing that I don't know you're there?" Jarlaxle asked.

"I knew that you knew."

"Always know," Jarlaxle came back without hesitation.

Breezy just laughed.

"The town leaders aren't happy with grandda?" she asked.

"They have their reasons."

"Power? Do they feel threatened by the return of King Bruenor?"

"Perhaps, and particularly when King Bruenor can bring armies to his side with a simple call. But let us look deeper. There remain questions to which we still need answers."

"Us? We?"

"Are you willing to do some investigating for me?"

That piqued the young woman's curiosity, to be sure.

"I heard about your exchange with an old elf near Lac Dinneshere."

Breezy nodded, her expression puzzled as to how Uncle Jax could know about that. "Yes, Sylfae. I met her on the tundra one night when Uncle Wulfgar and I first set out on our yeti hunt."

"Sylfae has been here for centuries and keeps her senses outward, gathering information."

Breezy started to reply but paused and looked harder at the mercenary leader. She tried to remember if she had told Jarlaxle about it but was fairly certain that she had not. Still, with a moment's reflection, she realized that she shouldn't be surprised.

"Go to Sylfae," Jarlaxle bade. "See what she thinks of King Bruenor's plans regarding the magical gate."

"She said nothing of it when we met. Wulfgar and I camped—"

"That was when your caravan first entered the region. She wouldn't have known at that time. She would know now. Go and speak with her. Visit your friend."

"She's not really my friend."

"Go and visit your *friend*," Jarlaxle said again, and in a way that made it clear to Breezy that it was very important for Sylfae to think of her in that manner. "Don't inform her and don't ask her opinion."

"But . . ."

"You won't have to," Jarlaxle assured her.

"That's twenty miles, and Sylfae's home is outside the walls of Caer-Konig on the open tundra."

"Do you need an escort?" Jarlaxle asked with a wry grin.

"My parents—"

"You came to Bryn Shander with Regis," Jarlaxle interrupted.

"From the dwarf stronghold in the mountain of Kelvin's Cairn, yes. I grew bored with—"

Jarlaxle stopped her with an upraised hand. "You go to Caer-Konig and out to see your friend Sylfae. I will have Regis ride out to collect you. It is not so far off the trail that you would need to take to return to your parents at Kelvin's Cairn anyway, and it's probably easier to just follow the somewhat secured roads to Caer-Konig before crossing the open tundra back to Bruenor's caves in the lone mountain."

"Regis will tell my parents *what* when we get back to them?"

"Nothing unless asked. And why would they ask?"

Breezy hesitated, mulling over the offer.

Jarlaxle tossed her a small bag that jingled with coins. "It is a paying job," he said.

"I don't need your money," Breezy replied with a snort, and she lifted the bag to throw it back.

"No, I suppose not," Jarlaxle said right before she prepared to launch it. "You have your parents' good fortunes, and King Bruenor's treasures, after all."

Breezy's eyes widened with a flash of rage, and she even let out a little growl. Staring hard at Jarlaxle, she tucked the small bag into her pocket.

"The faster you get there, the more time you will have to listen to Sylfae's gossip." He reached into a pocket and pulled out a single gold piece, flicking it with his thumb, sending it spinning through the air to Breezy.

"Rent a horse," he told her.

Her moment of anger flew away. She considered her previous

snort, one almost of superiority—and superiority earned not by her, but by her parents and grandfather.

A reflexive snort touting all the trappings she hoped to get away from, trappings Jarlaxle had just mocked.

Her stare melted into a smile of appreciation.

3

UNEXPECTED ADVANTAGES

THE UNDERGROUND CHAMBER BENEATH THE WESTERN WALL OF THE MONAStery of the Yellow Rose was one of the most important training gyms in the structure. While a few glowworms wriggled about the high ceiling and stone wall, the large chamber was lit by many candelabras strategically placed about the hundred and forty-four posts set into the stone floor. These upright posts, all sectioned from the trunks of nearly identical trees, measured six inches in diameter but were of many different lengths, with some as short as a man, others as tall as an ogre. They weren't equally spaced about the floor, and not in a square of twelve by twelve. Rather, they seemed more a mob, set helter-skelter to the untrained eye, some as near to the next as a long step, others as far as a running jump.

To the monks who ventured in here to train, the tops of these posts served as the chamber's true floor. Once a monk ascended to the top of a post, they were to stay above the floor for the duration of their practice, without exception.

Master of Dragons Gregory Antoine found the chamber empty this morning, and so set about the long task of lighting the hundreds of candles set in their sconces. When he was done, he extinguished his own brand, leaving it and his robes on the stone floor near the room's single door. Wearing only a broad loincloth, his sculpted muscles already glistening with sweat, Gregory moved to one of the tallest posts, which towered more than four full feet higher than his head.

He brought his hands together before him in meditation and a silent prayer to Saint Sollars, then slowly slid down into a deep crouch, palms still together at his mid-chest. He breathed deeply, a great and gradual inhale, and held his breath there for just a moment, before blowing it out hard and swinging his arms out and up as his powerful legs uncoiled, launching him upward.

He caught the top of the post, fingers on either side, and held there for another breath. Then moving only his arms, no swing or jerk of his torso or kick of his legs, he rose, head coming above the post top, then chest, then waist, and there he curled his legs upward along either side of the post.

He bent his arms slowly before thrusting them straight to push off powerfully, lifting him up a few inches higher, where he got his feet onto the post top. There he froze, finding his center weight and his balance, his core tightening and holding that deeply bent pose. Slowly, his arms went out to the sides, steadying him more as his legs unwound, lifting him to stand upright atop the post, the crown of his head more than fifteen feet above the stone floor of the chamber.

He remained there, upright, standing very still, eyes closed, feeling the currents of air, picturing his every step. Time passed. He was in no hurry.

He considered his upcoming fight with this unusual young woman—he had a hard time accepting the fact that she was no more a girl. Gregory was only a few years older than she. He had known Briennelle Do'Urden since her earliest days at the monastery when she had been only four years old, and he, at that time, a bit more than twice her age. He tried to keep his concentration and resist a smile at those earliest memories, like the many times when Sister Brie had followed him and the other disciples about, a question coming forth from the curious child with every step. How he had teased her in those days!

But always lightheartedly.

He and many others of his age at the monastery had thought of Brie as their little ward, for she had come to begin her formal training in the Order of Saint Sollars younger than the usual age for entry, which ranged from seven years all the way to young adulthood.

From the beginning, Gregory had noted that there was something different about Sister Brie. Most of the younger acolytes here were either orphans or from very poor families, their caretakers using the monastery as a path to offer them a chance at a better life. Brother Gregory had met a few brethren of noble birth over the years, but almost without exception, they had washed out of their training, unable to deal with the hardships and discipline of the stoic Order.

Sister Brie was the exception. She was so full of life, so full of fire, so full of determination and talent.

And so very beautiful. He tried and failed to shake that thought away as soon as it came to him. He remembered one day in particular when Brie had returned to the monastery from one of her many long trips to the west. She had been gone for more than a year, nearly two, if he recalled correctly. He remembered when she walked back into the building as clearly as if it had been yesterday. She had left a girl and come back a woman, and the shock of seeing her in that new light had stolen his breath away.

No, he could not even begin to think of Brie as his ward now, as a child, and he certainly couldn't allow himself to feel the emotions that had slammed him upon her return.

For now, he would fight her, with so much on the line.

He focused on his breathing, timing the inhalations and exhalations to match in length. The concentration cleared his mind of distractions—up here on the posts, distractions led to disaster.

He breathed in, he breathed out, several times, then exploded into motion, leaping away to the right. He landed on a post six feet away and two feet lower, planting his right foot upon it and lowering into a deep, one-legged crouch. Up he came, spinning and kicking high with his left foot, and he held that kick, bending his knee and striking three times before swinging his leg down, using the momentum of it as it went behind him to twirl him about on the ball of his right foot, before leaping away to a pair of posts a bit higher than this one and just far enough apart for him to comfortably set each foot.

Into a crouch, he went, his hands coming together before him for a moment of salute and calm, taking in the scene about him, the shadows and flickers of the candles, surveying the possible routes before him.

He sprang off those posts into a backflip that put him up higher on a single post, his right foot touching down just long enough for him to spring away again.

And then again from the next, gaining momentum, gaining speed. He leaped and twisted, somersaulted forward and flipped backward, rushed through one post to the next or paused long enough to execute a strike or a kick or a strong-armed block from an imaginary foe.

This was not a set and practiced routine, but rather an instinctive and reflexive flurry of improvisation, taking every landing and redirecting it to fit the battle against multiple foes that was playing out in his thoughts.

It went on for a long while, until the Master of Dragons landed once more with both feet together on the initial post he had climbed, the tallest in the array. There he stood very still and tall, arms out wide before slowly bringing them in close, palms together before his chest.

The focus became his breathing once more, slow and steady, his mind emptying, the imaginary battle won. He became very aware. He heard the candles burning, felt the smooth wood of the post top beneath his bare feet, felt the lines of sweat weaving paths down his glistening frame.

He heard his breathing.

He heard someone else breathing, approaching from behind.

The sudden tap on his shoulder told him that the newcomer was trying to startle him. But he was not startled, not in the least. He had known.

He looked down from on high at her with a smile that did indeed become an honest look of true surprise, however, when he recognized Grandmaster of Flowers Savahn. Her hand was outstretched far below him, and he understood that she had tapped his shoulder by throwing a pinch of her ki, her life energy, up at him.

"You did not expect to see me, but you knew someone was here," she stated with a nod that seemed one of approval. Gregory dropped from the post to land easily beside her.

"I seek my center, always," Gregory replied. "Always now, at least, with so momentous a battle coming fast before me."

He was hunting for a hint here, but Grandmaster Savahn remained impassive, other than a slight tilt of her head to perhaps indicate that his words were interesting to her, at least.

"I have heard that Sister Brie has been dabbling along a different path, the Way of Shadow," he went on tentatively. "I know nothing of it, but it is likely a style seeking sneak attacks, or off-angle . . ."

Grandmaster Savahn's face seemed frozen.

"Her father is known for his ability to ghost step and strike from behind," Gregory said, and paused, and swallowed hard.

When he started to speak again, Savahn held up her hand to stop him.

"I had heard you were down here, and the word surprised me," she said. "The monastery has gone through a resurgence of recruits, of course, as we filled all the ranks in the wake of Grandmaster of Flowers Kane's transcendence. This room is little used now compared to the days of old. The newcomers favor strength and straightforward fighting styles. And in that manner of battle, you are perhaps the strongest of all."

"This room reveals my weakness to me," Gregory admitted. "And with an opponent such as . . ." He paused and held his own hand up, showing that he recognized that he was on the edge of propriety in mentioning anything about Superior Master Brie to Grandmaster of Flowers Savahn, who would, after all, be the primary arbiter of the upcoming battle, and would, among other things, be the one who designed the battlefield Gregory and Brie would fight upon.

"I feel that my speed and balance are the weakest parts of my repertoire," he said simply. "I wish to be fully rounded in skills, offensive and defensive, as I defend my rank as Master of Dragons."

Savahn walked past him into the array of posts, running her hand along the smooth curve of one. "When the Masters of the Winds and of the Seasons train here, strips of spikes are lain across the floor beneath the posts," she said, looking back at Gregory. "And they are tipped with a most fiery poison—oh, I have felt it more than once!"

"Grandmaster?"

"To slip is to suffer painful wounds, sometimes, though rarely, even fatal, I have heard," she went on. "Our focus is stronger when there is consequence, as it is for you in these days when you know that your rank and reputation are at stake."

Gregory sighed and shook his head ever so slightly.

"I will say nothing of Sister Brie, nor offer any advice to either of you at this time, of course," the Grandmaster went on. "As for her choosing a different path, rumors are often just that. Often but not always. For the tradition you named, the Way of Shadow, I know little and care less, and perhaps if ever I do care, I will take it up with Jarlaxle of Bregan D'aerthe."

She continued, "You know that if you are defeated and brought back to the rank of Superior Master, you will not have long to wait before you are given a try to return to your present rank?"

It took Gregory a moment to digest that last statement, as he was trying hard to unravel the remark about Jarlaxle of Bregan D'aerthe. Jarlaxle was no monk, surely, so what might that strange drow creature know of the Way of Shadow? But it occurred to Gregory in that moment of confusion that Drizzt Do'Urden had been no monk, so what would he have known of the Way of the Open Palm? Nothing, of course, and yet he did, as his martial training proved to be very much in parallel to the teachings of Grandmaster Kane.

He let it go and forced himself to focus on Savahn's last words. "And with a one-in-three chance of a rematch with Sister Brie," he replied, nodding.

"Perhaps," she replied. "It is possible that Master of Dragons Assante will try for Master of the North Wind before the end of the year, which would change your chances of such a rematch to one-in-two."

Gregory tried to hide his surprise but knew from Grandmaster Savahn's little grin that he wasn't doing a very good job of it. He had thought himself the most likely of the current three of his rank to try for the next rank, Master of the North Wind, of which there could be only one in the Order of Saint Sollars. Of his two current peers, Master of Dragons Grenadienne had suffered a terrible injury to one shoulder. She could still fight brilliantly, but not strongly enough to ascend against the likes of Jouvier, the current Master of the North Wind. And Master of Dragons Assante was growing older and slower, now well into his fifties. He had lost the rank of Master of the North Wind to Jouvier more than three years previous, and had lost badly. Assante had almost been killed in the fight, so it was rumored, and he had never sought a rematch. Among the monastery's traditions, such acceptance of defeat from an older monk like Assante would signal that he recognized that his time at the top echelons of the fighting masters, the Masters of the Four Winds, was at its end. Now, obviously, Assante had little chance of getting through those four wind ranks to the more elite titles among the Masters of the Seasons, where the physical body was less important and the mental training paramount. In fact, because more than two years had passed since Assante had lost his rank as Master of the North Wind, he was now susceptible to challenges from below, as from Sister Brie.

If Assante had been chosen for this fight, Brie would defeat him, Gregory believed. Master Assante wasn't improving. He spent more time in meditation than in physical exertion, more time serving as a clerk to the monastery than in physically training the lesser monks or himself.

It occurred to Gregory in that moment of clarity that Sister Brie had been truly unfortunate to draw him in her attempt to ascend, for Gregory was quite confident that she could defeat either Assante or Grenadienne much more easily than she could claim victory over him.

He stared hard at Grandmaster Savahn as that truth became clear to him, his jaw drooping open slightly.

The Grandmaster remained outwardly impassive.

But she knew, Gregory believed. Grandmaster Savahn knew that he was wondering if Sister Brie's opponent in this coming fight had really been randomly chosen.

The thought assaulted the young man. His Order was just that: *order*. The rules were rigidly set and fast, particularly those in regard to ascending the ranks. The entire purpose of this life was discipline!

When Grandmaster Kane had trained Drizzt Do'Urden at such high levels—training that only the four Masters of the Seasons could receive—there had been many rumblings of discontent and disbelief among the monks, the younger monks at least. Drizzt was not a monk, was not of the Order of Saint Sollars, and was . . . an udadrow, a drow hailing from the otherworldly, violent Underdark.

Even before that unusual event, when Grandmaster Kane had used his spiritual self to go into the body of Brother Afafrenfere and work through that man in the War of the Silver Marches, the whispers were almost always accompanied with a disapproving shake of a head.

It was true that these were extraordinary times at the Monastery of the Yellow Rose. A pair of copper dragons had befriended the monks, through the efforts of Jarlaxle of Bregan D'aerthe, and many new disciples had joined the Order at the monastery—perhaps in part because of the whispers regarding the copper dragons. The daughter of an udadrow had been allowed into the Order. Her parents were both great heroes of the western lands along the northern Sword Coast, true, and her grandfather, the dwarven king of Gauntlgrym.

But when did station and connections become such a factor in admission? Almost every monk here, from Grandmaster of Flowers Savahn to the youngest novitiates, had been born into poverty, with many arriving here simply because their families, if they even had families, could not afford to care for them. And Brie had been given so much more leeway than the other brothers and sisters. She had entered the Order at the age of four, yes, but in truth, in the more than a decade and a half since, she had been out of the monastery more often than in it. None of the others could make a claim anywhere near to that. Gregory himself had only been in the outside world a handful of times, and never for more than a two-week supply expedition to one of Damara's cities.

Brother Gregory vainly tried to sort through the muddle of

thoughts and contradictions that were spinning through his mind, tried to tell himself that the choice of him as Sister Brie's opponent had been a random thing.

But Grandmaster Savahn had hinted that Jarlaxle would have insight to Sister Brie's new course. She had given to Gregory, perhaps inadvertently, a valuable tip that might aid him in the fight.

When had Grandmaster Savahn ever done something inadvertently, particularly concerning the Order of Saint Sollars and the sacred rules that the monks at the monastery had ingrained in their hearts and minds, the rules that they lived every day?

4

PERSPECTIVE

Breezy rode into Caer-Konig late in the afternoon. She went right to the stables to drop off the horse, as had been prearranged—the grooms running the stables in each of the Ten-Towns had agreements for boarding and return. None of the stablers wanted the horses, which were few and prized in Icewind Dale, out on the open tundra, even for the short trip to Kelvin's Cairn.

Breezy left the town through its little-used northern gate as the sun was setting, then turned toward the bright colors of the western horizon and set out, keeping near the city wall. As twilight descended, the lights of the nearby clusters of houses twinkled on, candles in the windows—those facing the city, at least.

She sorted through the arrangement of the various huts easily enough, as she had been through this very area not long before, and started out fast for Sylfae's house.

She was a bit unsure of her final approach to the place. These people lived in a wild land and always had a weapon within reach. Even as she knocked on the door, she was expecting a growl as much as a polite greeting.

But no, the door swung wide, and wide, too, was the smile of Sylfae, the old elf who was perhaps the oldest resident of Ten-Towns and of Icewind Dale.

Breezy returned the warm look, but to her surprise, Sylfae's initial reaction did not hold up for long, nor did she step aside to invite Breezy in.

"Well met?" Breezy asked as much as said.

"I had thought so. Now I am not so sure."

"Have I done something . . ."

Sylfae's hard look and lack of a specific response was enough of an answer for Breezy to sort it out.

"Ah, my grandda, King Bruenor."

"You did not mention his intent over the course of our last visit," Sylfae replied.

"He's made no secret of the teleportation portal."

"He probably should have," Sylfae said. She closed her eyes for just a moment, then took a deep breath and did step aside. "Come in. I have some stew and bread, enough for the both of us."

Sylfae was already in the midst of her supper, Breezy noted when she stepped into the small and comfy home, meticulously maintained and decorated with woven rugs and wall hangings, and scrimshaw—lots of scrimshaw pieces.

Sylfae motioned to a chair, then hustled to the cookpot to put together a bowl for her visitor.

"The carvings are so lovely! Are any the work of my Uncle Regis?" Breezy asked, lingering at a hutch and its dozens of scrimshaw pieces before taking her seat.

"A couple of the oldest ones," Sylfae replied, and her tone seemed to be softening a bit, Breezy noted hopefully. "Regis's work now has become too rich for the likes of old Sylfae." She set the bowl and the board with bread down before the young woman, then grabbed a delicate glass from the shelf nearby and put it and the water pitcher within Breezy's reach.

"I'll get you some new sculptures!" Breezy promised.

Sylfae took her seat across from Breezy, staring warily.

"Uncle Regis likes me," Breezy explained.

"You seem likeable enough."

Breezy tore off a piece of bread and dipped it in the stew, then closed her eyes and groaned in pleasure when she tasted it. She opened her eyes hoping to see an appreciative host, but Sylfae hovered over her own bowl, eyes down.

Breezy tried to get a read. She considered all that she had learned . . . from Jarlaxle, most of all.

"They don't consult me on such things, you know," she said, and Sylfae did look up.

"Such things as the portal, I mean," Breezy went on. "They still think of me as a child."

"Were you full drow, you would be," Sylfae replied.

Breezy nodded and continued, "They didn't even want me to go on the yeti hunt with Wulfgar, and on the journey to the dale, were angered with me when I . . ." She paused there and heard Jarlaxle's voice in her head: *Listen more than you speak and do not feel the need to fill the moments of silence, which can be the most informative of all . . .*

It was probably not a good idea, she realized, to tell Sylfae how she had saved the mission to Icewind Dale before they had ever crossed the mountains, particularly if the old elf's attitude about the portal was indeed as sour as she was beginning to understand.

"Well, my parents and grandda are determined to protect me, and because of that do not include me in their *important* decisions."

The dramatic way she spoke that word brought a smile to Sylfae's face, a welcome bit of warmth, indeed.

"Yet they let you come out here alone."

Breezy laughed and shook her head. "Oh no, they don't know. I decided to come by on my return to Kelvin's Cairn and made the choice to stop and see you all on my own."

Sylfae nodded and seemed to appreciate the thoughtfulness—or perhaps it was the rebelliousness, Breezy thought.

"Well," Sylfae said, thumping her hands on the table. "In that case, I am glad you came, daughter of heroes!"

Breezy's smile disappeared in a heartbeat.

"And I am pleased—for you—that you obviously do not like that title."

Breezy just shook her head, collecting her thoughts and finding her emotional balance once more. Both went back to their food.

"Uncle Wulfgar and I killed a lot of yetis," Breezy said a short while later, thinking the tale might prove a good icebreaker before she got around to the portal.

"Every dead yeti is a good thing."

"So I have heard from everyone in the dale," Breezy said with a chuckle. She went on to recount her journey with Wulfgar, how he wouldn't let her get involved in the early fights, and how he didn't have a choice in the melee in the south, in the foothills of the Spine of the World, when the yetis set an ambush.

She told the tale dramatically, but truthfully, and tried not to brag, although she was very much aware that she had acquitted herself quite well in that battle.

Halfway through, Sylfae refilled the bowls, the old elf's eyes gleaming with every word spilling from Breezy's lips—no doubt remembering many of her own adventures in Icewind Dale.

"It's a fine tale, and remarkable for one your age," Sylfae said when Breezy was done. Her tone made Breezy think that, while impressed, Sylfae suspected quite a bit of exaggeration in the story of the fight with five yetis.

Breezy just smiled at that and let it go, for she hadn't exaggerated or embellished at all. Besides, she had only told the story to melt the rest of the ice and, yes, wanted to listen more than speak.

For now, it was Sylfae's turn to tell some tales of adventure, and oh, the old elf had many to spin! At first, Breezy listened out of simple politeness, looking for openings where she could bring the conversation to the gates and the feelings of the region's people, as Jarlaxle had instructed. After a while, though, Breezy put such ulterior motives out of her thoughts and just listened, amazed and truly entertained.

She had no idea if any of what Sylfae was relating was true or not, embellished or not, for these were tales from the days before Breezy's father was born, days when her grandda was still in Mithral Hall far to the east, before Bruenor had even known of Icewind Dale.

She figured, though, that if Sylfae was half the adventurer as she was storyteller, then most of what she was hearing was probably true.

The food was long gone and the sunset a distant thought by the time Sylfae finished, ending with a great sigh, her eyes full of wistful sparkles and moisture.

"What a wonderful journey you've known," Breezy said at length.

Sylfae smiled. It had been a long time since she had recounted those adventure-filled tales to anyone who hadn't heard them many times before, Breezy understood.

"More tea?" the old elf asked.

"You sit," Breezy said, rising. "You have won the storytelling challenge, to be sure, and so I'll prepare the tea!"

"You're a good girl," Sylfae said. "Your mother and father must be very proud of you."

"Protective, more so," Breezy replied. She tossed some peat and a bit of kindling into the bowl of the stove and snapped her fingers, casting a minor dweomer to produce a small flame that soon had the fuel burning. "But yes, I hope they are. I try to uphold their values."

"Good girl," Sylfae said again.

"I hope that I will be able to come and see you often in the future," Breezy told her without turning from the heating kettle. "The journey here from the southlands should be so much swifter and more convenient."

There came no immediate response, tipping Breezy off to the elf's feelings on the matter. Before her, the kettle was heating, the stove throwing warmth, but she sensed a sudden chill from behind.

"With the gate from King Bruenor's lands, you mean," Sylfae said. "The one connecting us to his lair of Gauntlgrym."

"You've heard much about the plans, I see."

"Everyone's heard." The elf's tone was stern, cold.

Breezy turned about and stared into Sylfae's eyes, studying her for a long while. "You are not happy with the news," she said.

"No one is."

Breezy feigned surprise, screwing up her face and even shaking her head a little bit. "Grandda will bring security and trade, and a fast way to the south for any who need it." She noted Sylfae's scoff with every word.

"Surely life would be—"

"Different," Sylfae interrupted. "The folk up here do not wish to be ruled and ask for no help."

"Ruled?"

"Fathered? Is that a better word?"

Breezy just stood there gawking, trying to digest it all. She realized after a few moments that, yes, *fathered* was indeed a better word for Sylfae to explain her perspective on the problem here. She thought about all the people she had met in Icewind Dale in the few days she had been up here, how they had eyed her when they met her, warmly enough but not without suspicion.

She thought of Jarlaxle's conversation with Braelin back in Bryn Shander.

She thought of her ride high in the sky with Tazmikella, and the dragon's advice to her about learning to study the perspectives of those in different lands, with different ways.

Why was there even a place called Ten-Towns, so removed from the civilized world?

Why did the Reghed clans live up here, existing every day on the very edge of catastrophe?

She went from gawking to nodding as she considered the view through Sylfae's eyes.

"I have heard you," she told Sylfae, who nodded in reply. "I'll take my leave now, back to Caer-Konig, and to Kelvin's Cairn tomorrow, where I've much to tell my grandda."

"You will do no such thing!"

"King Bruenor should know," Breezy protested.

"No, no, not that. You will not take your leave. The night has fallen in full and the wind will bite you—and oh, but you'll be a lucky girl to only have that biting you out here on the tundra in the season when hungry beasts are putting on their winter fat. I've extra bedrolls."

"I could not impose."

"Bah, but I do so enjoy your company, dear Briennelle Zaharina Do'Urden, and there's not many I'd say that of. You are my guest this night."

Breezy didn't argue, and was glad of the offer, for even after she tucked herself into the snug bedroll, the elf recounted great tales of adventure and battle in Icewind Dale and in lands distant. Breezy hung on every word until at last sleep overcame her.

She awakened soon after the dawn to find a lovely breakfast of eggs and bread waiting for her, along with a certain halfling she lovingly referred to as Uncle Rumblebelly, who had, of course, already eaten breakfast.

More than one, if the pile of empty plates sitting before him was to be believed.

Regis's curly brown hair was on full display, for his fabulous blue beret sat atop one of the knobs on the back of his chair. His weapon belts were looped over the other side, that beautiful rapier and three-bladed dirk in clear view on the waist belt, his clever hand-crossbow set in its holster on the sash he usually wore looped from right shoulder to left hip. He had his traveling cloak folded under him, an impromptu pillow hoisting him up high enough for him to comfortably access his food. Breezy couldn't help but smile at the sight of him, for despite the obvious carnage he had inflicted on his breakfast, not a spot or crumb or drip of egg showed on his always-clean fine clothes or nestled in the shadows of his meticulously trimmed brown beard.

That smile widened when the halfling patted his ample gut and stifled a burp.

Rumblebelly, Breezy thought, a name he had long ago earned, given to him by Bruenor.

"Your friend arrived some time ago," Sylfae explained. "Before the light of day."

"We are in a hurry," Regis explained. "The rains will come this night, and if we are not back to Kelvin's Cairn before them, the way will be too muddy for our ponies and may stay that way for some time. Your parents would not be pleased."

Breezy started to ask him how he even knew where to find her, as she was supposed to meet up with him at the stable in Caer-Konig.

But she held her tongue on that, considering her suspicions that Regis had been working ever more closely with Jarlaxle of late.

"Sit, eat," Regis said. "And let us be on our way." He looked to Sylfae. "And dear and gracious hostess, might I trouble you for a fourth plate?"

The old elf laughed in response and gathered another trio of eggs—then added two more when Regis put on a plaintive look.

"I thought we were in a hurry," Breezy noted, taking a seat at the small table.

"He will be finished before you," Sylfae assured her, tossing a wink the halfling's way. "That one's all mouth and belly."

"You flatter me, gracious lady," said Regis, and both laughed, while Breezy wondered if she was still in her bed and had somehow entered a dream that seemed too real.

By the time Sylfae took her own seat, Breezy was almost done with her breakfast and Regis was sitting back in his chair, an unlit pipe in his mouth. The conversation then was entirely small talk, with no mention of events or anything near the weighty conversation Breezy and Sylfae had engaged in the previous night.

Through it all, Breezy noted that Sylfae hardly stopped staring at Regis, giving the same awestricken look that she had seen among the younger monks at the Monastery of the Yellow Rose whenever her father had come to visit. That reminded her of Sylfae's collection, and she glanced that way.

"Our gracious host holds a keen appreciation for scrimshaw art," she told Regis.

"Aye, I was admiring her collection," the halfling replied.

"Are any of them your work? Sylfae thinks, perhaps, a couple of the older ones might be."

"I'm not sure, to be truthful," Regis answered. "Yes, a couple look like perhaps they could be, but that would have been from my earliest days, and back then I didn't sign them or use any original markings. But yes," he added, looking to Sylfae, "I do believe that the two you showed me were mine."

"I hope so, Master Regis," the old elf answered, and again Breezy was taken aback, this time by her tone, which was more one of a fawning child than of a seasoned and heroic adventurer. "I so love to believe that I have the works of Master Regis on my shelf."

Regis put down his pipe and fished into his belt pouch, bringing forth a small item wrapped in a thick cloth. He unveiled it slowly, taking great care and, obviously, great pride, revealing a lovely carving of a tundra yeti, its long and thick arms over its head in a menacing pose.

"And so you shall," Regis said, putting it on the table in front of Sylfae. "This one would seem appropriate, since you've been so hospitable to our newest yeti hunter."

Appropriate, Breezy thought. Too appropriate to be coincidental. Even if Jarlaxle was involved in Regis's unexpected arrival, how could he know of Sylfae's love of scrimshaw in the first place, let alone the "appropriateness" of this particular carving?

Because he was Jarlaxle, of course. Tuning back into the scene before her, Breezy thought the old elf was about to cry. Sylfae picked up the scrimshaw piece with great reverence, turning it over before her gleaming eyes.

"And now," Regis announced, clapping his hands together and hopping up from his chair, "we must be going. If we get caught by the storm, our road will be more miserable and dangerous by far. Farewell, gracious lady. It was lovely to make your acquaintance, and I am certain, or hopeful at least, that this will not be the last time we share a meal."

"This piece is priceless," Sylfae replied. "Surely worth far more than three breakfasts!"

"Four!" Regis corrected with a smile and a pat of his belly. "Four fat ones!"

"Worth more than a hundred," Sylfae said. "More than a thousand."

"Then expect many visits," the halfling said, pointing a finger. Smiling widely, Regis bowed and led the way to the door and out, where stood his pony and a fresh mount, another pony, for Breezy.

With kind words and hugs—the one Sylfae threw over Regis lasting many heartbeats—Breezy and her escort started off across the open tundra, making a direct line for the distant Kelvin's Cairn. The small mountain was only a few miles away, but their path crossed terrain so difficult that it was sure to take them most of the day.

"That was very kind of you," Breezy noted when they were away.

"You like Sylfae," said Regis.

"I do. I met her when Wulfgar and I first came out on our yeti hunt. She visited our little camp just to the east, and fed us. She knew my parents and my grandda."

"All of us, yes," said Regis. "Or knew of us, surely. There aren't many people in Ten-Towns, and it doesn't take much to get one noticed."

"She was one of the few who understood the goodness of my father in those early days," Breezy said, and Regis's snort surprised her. She looked over at him and noted then a ruby hanging on a chain about his neck. A magical ruby full of magical charm, one returned to him by Jarlaxle, and one which he could use to influence friends and enemies alike.

Breezy thought of Sylfae's surprisingly fawning looks toward Regis. She pulled her pony to a stop and stared hard at her companion.

"What?" Regis asked.

"Jarlaxle sent you. He didn't trust me."

"Of course he trusted you. Wasn't it Jarlaxle who asked you to come and speak with your friend?"

"The same Jarlaxle who sent *you* to use my friendship with her and my relationship with you to put that ruby to work on an unsuspecting target?"

"Jarlaxle was right," Regis replied. "You are very good at this."

"Is that supposed to make me feel better? Shouldn't you waggle your magical ruby before my eyes to convince me?"

"I would never do that."

"You just did."

"Not to a trusted ally."

"But to a gracious host."

Regis started to answer, but paused and shrugged. "This is important—more important than your grandfather understands. The whispers are not kind, and not innocuous."

"She was an ally to my father in the earliest days . . ."

"Hardly," Regis answered. "Every town had loud voices against Drizzt Do'Urden, and few were louder than Sylfae of Caer-Konig."

Breezy froze at that, blinking repeatedly, trying to sort it out. "She lied to me."

"Not really."

"She told me . . ."

"I know what she told you, and it's probably what she believes. Folks are very good at rewriting the past, particularly when it erases moments of shame upon them. Sylfae was no friend of your father in the beginning, I assure you, but she learned, as we all—well, as they all, for some of us understood the character of Drizzt right away—learned, the truth. She didn't really lie. She misremembered and did a bit of twisting, and it hardly matters, for your father certainly bears her no ill will."

Breezy sat silent and let that all sink in, wondering if it was yet another important lesson.

"What did she tell you last night?" Regis asked.

Breezy closed her eyes and took a deep breath, trying to convince herself that this was business, and that this was important. She wanted to be mad at Sylfae, but she had to consider that she had gone to the elf under false pretenses, however well intended. She carefully recounted Sylfae's words regarding the feelings on Bruenor's portal.

Regis nodded. "She didn't lie to you, then. She told me the same thing."

"Aren't elves good at avoiding the magic of your ruby?"

"What, this?" Regis snorted, then took a moment to light his pipe, before urging his pony forward. "I didn't need it with that one. She was apparently quite fond of me, and quite forthcoming regarding her feelings."

Breezy paused for a moment, staring at the brown-and-white pinto, which Regis had also named Rumblebelly. She giggled as she pondered if the pony, which was a summoned and magical mount, after all, also was common with the burping and farting.

"You doubt me?" Regis asked, apparently misconstruing the giggle as sarcasm.

Breezy cleared her throat and sniffed her amusement away. "You didn't use it on her?"

"Of course I did. But it wouldn't have mattered, I am sure."

Breezy clamped her jaw shut, trying to digest it all. She was finding the political intrigue quite confusing and frustrating.

But also . . . tantalizing.

"I have a lot to learn," she admitted after a long while of the lulling cadence of hooves clop-clopping in the muddy ground.

"That's the fun of it," Regis answered. He gave a helpless little laugh that turned Breezy's gaze upon him.

"I'm in my second lifetime," the halfling said, which was quite literally the truth. "And in this second chance at life, I was born with full consciousness and memory of my previous decades of adventure. As much as I thought I had some answers to it all after my stay in the afterworld and the magical forest of Iruladoon, I have come to recognize and accept the truth that I have a lot to learn, still, and too much for many lifetimes, I fear."

"Then we should all take heart, for everyone has a lot to learn, yes?"

"Of course." Regis paused and halted Rumblebelly and waited for Breezy to look back at him before continuing with a wink, "Except, perhaps, for Jarlaxle."

The two made good time for the rest of the morning, and though the sky was growing ominous with the coming storm, there was still adequate sunlight to keep the day tolerably warm. Regis pulled up suddenly and announced that he was famished, drawing an incredulous look from his companion who had recently watched him devour enough for a week.

The halfling started to dismount, but the horn of his saddle caught his fine overcoat, which he had unbuttoned both because of the sun and because of his too-full belly.

"Oops, oops, oops!" He giggled as he tried to undo it before the awkward angle could send him unceremoniously tumbling to the mud.

Breezy didn't hear him, nor did she move to help him. She sat transfixed, staring at the holster set across the halfling's chest, and at the white bone stock of a most magnificent hand-crossbow.

He hadn't been wearing that weapon at the breakfast table, of course, and Breezy hadn't seen him strap it on, nor even thought of it, as it had been concealed by his overcoat.

She knew that he possessed the weapon, of course, but hadn't seen it since . . .

"What?" Regis asked, drawing her stare, which he had obviously noticed. "The crossbow?" He finally managed to pull free of the saddle and drop to the ground. "Yes, it is a most wonderful little weapon, don't you think?"

As he finished, he drew it from the holster, its spring-set limbs opening wide.

"My own design," he said, holding it up for a better view. "Though with more than a little advice from Jarlaxle, of course. It can be quite a deadly little surprise when needed."

Deadly, yes. Breezy knew that all too well, and felt a tear coming to her eye. She tried to look away, but could not.

Regis hooked a thumb under his bandolier and moved it forward for a better view. "And with these bolts that the Bouldershoulders fashion for me, the surprise is multiplied many times over. The explo . . ."

He paused there and it took Breezy a few moments to even realize that the halfling was staring at her with clear concern. That broke the trance, and she managed to tear her eyes from the hand-crossbow—and tear her mind from the one time she had been forced to put a similar weapon to use.

"Would you like to try it?"

"No!" Breezy snapped, more sternly than she had intended, and she softened her voice when she repeated, "No."

"Well. Yes, you have Taulmaril, after all," Regis said and put the small crossbow away, closing his overcoat over it. "And even with the darts, I doubt this would seem little more than a toy when measured against that magnificent bow."

Breezy didn't answer, not then, and not through lunch. She spent the whole of their rest stop reminding herself of the challenge that she would face soon enough.

Sister Breezy Do'Urden, Master of Dragons.

Everything else, she told herself firmly, was noise.

Just noise.

5

READ THE GATHERING

"It's not the councilor o' Bryn Shander, me King," explained Stokely Silverstream, the leader of the Battlehammer contingent in Icewind Dale. A sturdy, broad-shouldered fellow with wide-set gray eyes, Stokely had led the Icewind Dale Battlehammers for decades and had ever been in the good graces of his friend, King Bruenor. "It's Markham Southwell."

"Markham? The sheriff?" Bruenor shook his head and moved for the main seat in the chamber that served as both the dining room and the audience hall inside the main entrance to the dwarf tunnels under Kelvin's Cairn. This main seat was Stokely's throne, except of course on those occasions when King Bruenor was in the dale.

"The same," Stokely replied.

"That one's been the sheriff for a long time," Bruenor remarked. "What's he now, in his eighth decade?"

"Gettin' close," Stokely replied. "I remember when he was born. One o' the few in Icewind Dale who were born here, eh?"

"Aye, not countin' the Reghedmen," Bruenor said. "I remember it, too, and his da who was sheriff afore him."

Bruenor was old, very old. Likely the oldest person in Icewind

Dale at that time, other than Sylfae or Jarlaxle, if he was still about. But with his honed muscles and fiery red hair and thick beard, he appeared no older than perhaps forty years, barely a teenager by dwarf counting. Like Regis, Catti-brie, and Wulfgar, he too had spent a century in the afterlife, in the magical forest of Iruladoon, held there by the goddess Mielikki during the tumult of the time known as the Sundering.

"Bryn Shander once answered me summons with more respect. Ye made it clear to them that this was important, eh?" he asked, turning to Drizzt and Catti-brie, who had delivered the invitation for the parley to Bryn Shander.

"We did," Catti-brie answered.

"And they send a sheriff?" Bruenor took his seat, though he was thinking at that moment that it might be a prudent reminder for him to turn Markham away, though he really didn't want to.

"Markham Southwell's still a good man, me King," said Stokely, as if reading his mind. "He's grown harder in his years, as've many in the dale, but he's keepin' to the law with a fair hand."

Bruenor nodded. He didn't know Markham Southwell well, but he'd never heard anything to make him think that the sheriff wouldn't be reasonable in his dealings with Clan Battlehammer.

The dwarf king considered his options here. It took him a while to tuck away his umbrage at the apparent disrespect, but perhaps there was a reason the sheriff had been sent to speak for Bryn Shander.

"Go get him," he told Stokely, who hustled out of the room and returned in just a few heartbeats with a tall human, his skin dark brown, his neatly-trimmed beard gone fully white and silver, and his head, as always, shaven to the skin. He was older and walked with a slightly noticeable limp, but his back remained straight, his broad and muscled shoulders squared. He was a veteran warrior, Bruenor knew. He would have easily surmised it even if he hadn't been so familiar with the man's background.

Bruenor motioned to the chair beside him, but Sheriff Markham walked up and remained standing just a couple of feet from the seated dwarf.

"Wasn't expectin' yerself," Bruenor said. "But ye're welcome here, o' course, and invited to a fine supper and a bed this night, when the rains're sure to begin."

Markham bowed deeply. "My thanks for your hospitality, King Bruenor, though I fear you might change your mind after I have delivered my message."

"Ye goin' to sit, or ye goin' to stand there?"

Markham didn't move. "I've come to ask a simple question."

"Ye can't be asking while sittin'?" Bruenor motioned to the chair again, this time rather insistently.

With a nod, Markham finally sat down. He locked gazes with Bruenor.

The king gestured with his hand. "So ask."

"It is true, King Bruenor?"

"Lots o' things're true, and lots o' things ain't."

"Your reason for coming to Icewind Dale," Markham somewhat clarified.

"Could be many reasons."

"The whispers say that you have come to Kelvin's Cairn bearing the pieces and the tools and the magic you will need to construct one of your teleportation gates, a doorway connecting this mountain with your kingdom of Gauntlgrym in the south."

"We made no secret of it."

"So it is true."

"We made no secret of it and I ain't denyin' it."

"We don't want it."

"I didn't ask ye." Bruenor tried hard to keep his voice even and calm.

"What you are intending will change Icewind Dale, and in ways that the towns do not want, and in ways that the Reghed clans most certainly do not want."

"Yerself's speakin' for all the towns, are ye? And the clan nomads? They gived ye that power as their representative, did they?"

"I am relaying the vote of the Council, a vote among the Ten-Towns that was not suspenseful and tense, King Bruenor, the outcome expected and overwhelming. And regarding the Reghedmen, I am merely offering advice."

"Sounds more like a threat."

"A prudent warning," Markham said. "Your portal is not wanted here."

"Not wanted by who? The councilors afraid o' losing all power?"

"By most," Markham answered without hesitation. "By almost everyone in the dale, to be honest. We don't want it. We don't need it. We reject it out of hand."

"Might be that it ain't yer own to reject, aye?"

The man didn't answer other than to offer a slight shrug, one accompanied by an expression clearly hinting that Bruenor wasn't thinking through the potential consequences of this monumental shift in the reality of Icewind Dale. A shrug and a pose that were very much a warning, and yes indeed, bordering on a threat.

"I am just the messenger, King Bruenor," Markham said after a long and uncomfortable silence. "We have an old saying here: *Read the gathering*. That gathering is easy to read in this particular instance."

"So now ye're to lecture me on old sayin's o' Icewind Dale?" Bruenor countered with a snort. "Ye know I been here longer than yer da's da's da's da—and then some—saw his first day, aye? And aye, as ye say, the gatherin's easy to read *at this time*. But who's to say twon't be a choice o' regret in the comin' days. What if an army o' orcs—"

"We could go around forever on possibilities. They do not matter. The people of the dale know the dale. They know the ways, they know the threats. And they do not want your magical portal here."

The two just stared at each other for a long while, until Markham bowed, begged his leave, and thanked Bruenor for offering the lodging through the storm. "If it still holds," he added.

"No one's to e'er say that King Bruenor's not good as a host and good on his word," replied the king of Gauntlgrym. Bruenor motioned to a guard by the door, a young fellow with just a bit of his beard in who, Bruenor noted, had watched the exchange with obvious interest and obvious disdain—though which side of the debate that scowl was attached to Bruenor could not be sure.

The young sentry escorted Sheriff Markham out of the room, barely getting the audience chamber door closed when an agitated Bruenor hopped out of his seat and began pacing about the chamber, muttering curses with every step.

WULFGAR AND BRAELIN JANQUAY HAD just entered the cave complex, chatting as they moved along swiftly. Rounding the last corner into the tunnel leading to the audience hall, they nearly ran into Sheriff Markham and the escorting Battlehammer guard.

The look on the sheriff's face told Wulfgar that the meeting hadn't gone so well, which didn't surprise him, given his present conversation with Braelin.

The sheriff nodded, the dwarf grunted, and the two pairs passed each other, but just then, Markham called out the barbarian's name, turning Wulfgar on his heel.

"Wulfgar, yes, of the Tribe of the Elk," the sheriff said. "Well met again. It has been far too long."

"And to you, good Sheriff . . . Markham, yes?" Wulfgar returned.

Markham nodded and smiled.

"You have spoken with King Bruenor?"

Sheriff Markham's smile turned upside down. "Your friend King Bruenor has been too long from Icewind Dale," he said. "I hope that is not true of those whose words he hears clearly. I hope that his friends, his advisors, remember the ways of this land." He paused and cocked his head in apparent consideration, then added, "And the whys."

He nodded goodbye to Wulfgar, cast a stern and suspicious glare at Braelin, and moved off with his escort.

"It did not go well," Braelin said, an observation strengthened as they neared the chamber door and heard shouting beyond.

Wulfgar sighed and moved to enter.

Braelin grabbed his arm. "You think we should?"

"It's Bruenor," Wulfgar said with a smile. "If he wasn't yelling and complaining, well, then I'd be worried."

He pushed through the door to see Bruenor and Stokely nose to nose by the main seat, with Drizzt and Catti-brie off to the side, shaking their heads and wearing plaintive expressions.

"I'm not disagreeing with ye, me King, but I'd be a lyin' son of a goblin if I told ye I was surprised," Stokely Silverstream declared.

"Because they're stupid," Bruenor muttered, shaking his head, and when Stokely harrumphed in reply, Bruenor snapped, "Aye?"

"Mayhaps," came Stokely's tentative reply.

"What? Ye don't think they're stupid?" Bruenor went on. "We're bringin' a fast trade route."

"And might be bringing an army," said Stokely.

"Aye, if one's needed and called."

"But they're not knowin' that part."

"I telled 'em!"

"Yerself telled 'em, and aye, and they have no small trust for King Bruenor Battlehammer, but . . ."

"But anyone who gets control of that gate could easily walk an army into these caves that could sweep the dale from the glacier to the sea," said Catti-brie.

"Meself controls the gate!" Bruenor roared. "And it'll be Battlehammer dwarfs after me and Battlehammer dwarfs after them, and Battle—"

"Battle," Catti-brie interrupted before he could finish the clan name. "Battle with Menzoberranzan, perhaps. We know they've added many Lolthian udadrow to replace those who emigrated, and we know they harbor no good feelings about yourself or your clan. They blame us all in no small part for the great heresy committed against their foul spider goddess."

"Bah!" Bruenor snorted.

"The drow of Menzoberranzan have already controlled Gauntlgrym once," Catti-brie reminded. "And not so long ago."

"And I'm fightin' against that!" Bruenor yelled back. "Connected through the portals to Citadels Adbar and Felbarr, we got power.

Connected, we got armies and allies and security. That'd be true up here in the dale, too!"

"Might that I'm wrong here, Da," Catti-brie said, "but I'm guessing that the folk up here don't even want that security. Not from you, not from anyone." She nodded her chin at Stokely.

"Aye," the dwarf confirmed. "Don't ye doubt, me King, that if ye called on us, the whole lot o' Icewind Dale Battlehammers'd be runnin' to answer, sword in hand."

"But?" Bruenor said.

"There's no conditions on that loyalty, me King."

"From these words, am I to understand that the sheriff came to deliver the demand that you not construct the portal?" Wulfgar interjected.

"Aye, because they're stupid!" Bruenor roared.

"He said that the vote in council wasn't close," Catti-brie added.

"Eight for nay, two for yea," Braelin said, surprising them all. "Only Bremen and Good Mead. Lonelywood was expected to vote in favor as well, but they changed their minds."

"There's gratitude to Regis, for ye," Bruenor grumbled.

"I asked some prominent halflings of the sleepy village about the surprising result," Braelin reported. "In the end, Regis was the reason they voted against your portal."

"Rumblebelly? Ye're saying that Rumblebelly went against me?"

"No, no, nothing like that," Braelin explained. "I doubt he's even been to Lonelywood on this trip as of yet. No, but what Councilor Nimsy of Lonelywood posited to me was a grim speculation of what might have happened to Regis those many decades ago if Pasha Pook of Calimport had been able to use a teleportation portal to get his assassins so easily and quickly to Icewind Dale. There are many such Regises in Icewind Dale, Councilor Nimsy insisted."

Bruenor mulled on that for a bit, then asked Braelin, "Where's Jarlaxle?"

"He has gone south back to Luskan, and out to the east, I believe."

"Would've been an easier trip for him if we had a gate to Gauntlgrym," Bruenor noted.

Braelin shrugged, but he knew that wasn't really true. Not for

Jarlaxle, at least, for the powerful wizard Ravel Xorlarrin had simply teleported Jarlaxle and a few others back to the Host Tower of the Arcane.

Bruenor looked to the room's lone remaining guard. "Tell Pwent and Athrogate to personally sit with the pillars and the essence o' the primordial," he ordered. "I'm goin' to the Climb to clear me thoughts."

"The storm is nigh," Drizzt said.

"I'll bring a tent," came the grumbling reply, and Bruenor stomped away.

Stokely fixed Drizzt and Catti-brie with a sad look, a shake of his head, and a helpless shrug.

"We'll get a big enough tent, then," Drizzt said to him and to his wife, then added to Wulfgar, "Breezy's still out?"

"She and Regis are ahead of the storm," Braelin assured them.

"Ye seem to know a lot," Bruenor interjected as he walked out of the room.

"That's my job," Braelin remarked quietly.

"I'll stay and wait for them and make sure all is well," Wulfgar promised.

"You don't want to go and sit in the rain on Bruenor's Climb?" Catti-brie asked him with a smile.

"No. If it was a snowstorm coming, you might convince me," Wulfgar replied with a wink.

"I'll join you," Braelin said, but Drizzt shook his head.

"Not there," he explained. "That's Bruenor's place, for him and for the Companions of the Hall, and he doesn't take well to visitors on his Climb."

Braelin bowed and said no more, and Drizzt and Catti-brie left the room to gather their tent and bedrolls.

"I'll be off as soon as the storm breaks," Braelin told Stokely and Wulfgar.

"Back to Bryn Shander?" asked Stokely.

Braelin considered it for a moment, then shook his head. "I'm not needed here anymore. Jarlaxle and Bregan D'aerthe have turned south for Luskan before the snows, and so shall I."

"A long and dangerous trek," Stokely said.

"Just the way we like it, yes?" came Braelin's answer, and as the dwarf sputtered over that, he bowed and took his leave. Stokely's heavy sigh was muffled by the closing door.

"The folk o' the dale, yer own people included, will never accept that gate," Stokely said to Wulfgar when they were alone. "If King Bruenor opens that magical door to Gauntlgrym, he best bring an army straight through to protect it, and leave 'em there until enough generations have passed for folk to forget all about it."

Wulfgar moved to speak—he wanted to argue.

But he knew Icewind Dale as well as any man alive, and he couldn't find any counters.

THE WIND HAD PICKED UP considerably and a light and cold rain was beginning to fall by the time Bruenor, Drizzt, and Catti-brie got out of the tunnels beneath Kelvin's Cairn.

"Double-pace it," Bruenor kept saying. "When them stones get icy, we'll have a bad time gettin' up the trail."

Drizzt silently mouthed along with the dwarf's every word, so predictable his chant had become. He smiled at his wife as he finished, for he had been mocking their friend for her sake more than anything. But she didn't return the grin, didn't even look at him, her head turned to look over her left shoulder, her gaze to the south.

Drizzt recognized the question on her face: Where was Breezy?

Through a narrow channel at the northern end of the valley beside Kelvin's Cairn, the trio came to a small tunnel, more of a channel whose tips touched or nearly touched up above them, and at its end, a small grotto.

The wind whistled through the varied holes in the ceiling of the small cave, and there was still enough daylight for them to make out a small smithy carved into the stone of the cave's back wall. A flash of lightning shot the sky above, revealing the forge clearly, as well as the freestanding anvil before it.

Bruenor walked over and reverently rubbed his hand across that anvil, feeling the iron and the veins of mithral he had put into it.

For this was Bruenor's grotto, built with great care and love. It had become more a shrine to the king of the Battlehammers now than a working forge. Here, Bruenor had carved Aegis-fang, his greatest work, for the barbarian boy he had captured on the field of battle and who had become an adopted son to him. A son who was now a dear friend and a Companion of the Hall.

"I thought we were in a hurry," Drizzt remarked.

Bruenor didn't look over at his friends now, revealing to Drizzt just how angry and hurt his dwarf friend was at being rebuffed so unexpectedly for a portal that was to be another crowning achievement, a magical gate that would tie Kelvin's Cairn and the Battlehammer dwarfs up here to Gauntlgrym, the hub of the magical gates that also connected to Mithral Hall and to the dwarf citadels of Adbar and Felbarr.

This portal would complete the joining of the Delzoun dwarfs in a manner unprecedented, in an alliance as strong as the stones they mined.

"Come on, then," the dwarf muttered after a bit and led them back out of the grotto and out of the valley on its northeastern end, coming to a high arm of the mountain, and atop it a small plateau ringed by a parapet of stones that Bruenor had used for centuries as his private place of reflection. The rain was coming down heavier then, the wind blowing harder, the temperature dropping. The three had to pick their way carefully among the stairs, which were just a pattern of stones of various sizes climbing up and around the small pinnacle.

They came to the plateau, which normally sported a grand view of the candles and hearths of Lonelywood and Easthaven, and even those running lights of the boats out on the large lake called Maer Dualdon. But not this night, the wind turning the rain into sheets of nearly opaque gray, blurring and distorting any distant fires.

Drizzt and Catti-brie immediately set up their small tent on the western edge of the platform, but Bruenor stubbornly stayed out in the wind and cold rain, standing at the eastern edge, staring out across the storm, his orange hair and beard dripping.

"Was I wrong in thinkin' they'd be trustin' Clan Battlehammer?" the dwarf asked after a while. "We been friends o' Ten-Towns for centuries, and friends, too, o' the Reghedmen."

"It's not about that, Da," Catti-brie called back from the open flap of the tent. "Ye know it's not about that."

"Thought I knowed," Bruenor grumbled. "Ye serve and ye do what's right by 'em, and their gratitude fades."

"You haven't been up in Icewind Dale for a long stay in generations, by human standards," came another voice, and Bruenor turned, and Drizzt and Catti-brie poked their heads out of the tent to see a familiar figure coming onto the platform.

"My Brie!" Catti-brie said with great relief.

"How many now living here have ever spoken with you, Grandda?"

Bruenor stood in the pouring rain, dripping and seething, but he simply couldn't aim any of that frustration at Breezy. "Girl, ye're not knowing the dale," he said calmly.

Breezy stood perfectly still and took a deep breath. She was gathering her courage, the other three understood.

"Grandda, if you are truly surprised by the reaction to the portal, then it might be that I understand the folk up here better than you do," she boldly stated, drawing a look of shock from all three.

"Bah!" Bruenor snorted. "Icewind Dale ain't changed a lick since I lived here, nor have the folk!"

"But maybe you have," Breezy said. "As would anyone who's lived outside of here—by choice—for many years. Because few to none living here would choose another place as home."

"Brie, hush now and come in out of the rain," Catti-brie bade her.

"And you, too," Drizzt added to Bruenor, opening the tent flap a bit wider. "It will chill your bones."

Neither the dwarf nor the young woman moved, nor looked away from each other.

"Ye comin' by this on yer own, are ye?" Bruenor asked.

Breezy shrugged. "Been listening more than talking," she said. "As you taught me. Hearing the voices."

"And what voices might them be?"

"Just voices," Breezy said, moving for the tent. "And one elf who's lived here longer than you, and was here before you."

That drew a surprised look from all three, Breezy noted. "She lives outside of Caer-Konig, out on the open tundra, and she knows the folk of Ten-Towns so well, and the Reghedmen, too."

Bruenor began to chuckle. "So ye say. And what's this wise old elf's name?"

"She calls herself Sylfae."

Bruenor's snort was accentuated by the rumble of thunder. Breezy heard the chuckles of Drizzt and Catti-brie.

"She has been here for centuries," she protested against the three. "She knew when you first came here from Mithral Hall, Grandda, and remembered you, Ma, from your earliest days. And she was one of the few who accepted Da from the start!"

"She told ye that, did she?" Bruenor asked, standing stubbornly in the storm, hands on hips. Breezy, too, stopped her move for the shelter and brushed her hair from her face, clearly determined to show that she could match Bruenor in stubbornness.

"Aye, when I first met her, camping out near to her house with Wulfgar in our yeti hunt. She said so many others wouldn't give Da a chance, but she knew early on that he wasn't of the Lolthian ilk."

"Interestin'," Bruenor said with a snort.

"Regis has told me differently," Breezy admitted. "But even if that is the case, she's no enemy to you—to any of you—now. I believe her opinion."

"Do ye? Opinions? Her opinions, ye say? So tell me, girl, what opinions might that old elf have? What ideas about me gate? She's knowing me intentions, is she? Like she knowed yer da's intentions when he come to the dale?"

"The construction of the portal is common knowledge through-out Ten-Towns and all of Icewind Dale," Breezy answered. "Sylfae knows about it, and she doesn't want it, and truth be told, Grandda, I am hearing many voices, but very few who do want it. All about Bryn Shander and Caer-Konig, the folk are grumbling. Regis is in the caves below taking another supper. You should speak with him if you want to hear the same as I am now telling you. Few folk accept your choice, fewer still want it, and the many who do not are very forcefully against it." She pushed her wet hair out of her face and started once more for the tent flap.

"None but me own dwarfs, then," Bruenor grumbled, also heading that way.

"Aye, and not all o' them, neither," said yet another voice, that of a young dwarf lass coming up onto the Climb.

That brought shocked expressions from Bruenor, Drizzt, and Catti-brie, Breezy noted, and she understood, for this was King Bruenor's private place and every dwarf in the dale knew that he wasn't fond of anyone beyond his closest circle coming here.

"I'm not knowin' what ye're sayin', so just be sayin' it!" the obviously angry King Bruenor replied to the bold dwarf. "And I'm not even for knowin' yer name."

"Holiday," she replied. "Me name's Holiday Leathergirdle Battlehammer, o' the Bremen Leathergirdles. Well met again, me King, though I'm not expectin' that ye'd be rememberin' meself, for I was but a young lass when we last, and only, met."

"Ye're still a young lass," Bruenor replied. "But one with the rocks of a Gutbuster, not to doubt. Get in the tent. We're all wet and cold enough."

Drizzt tossed Bruenor a towel when he came into the small shelter, one crowded with just the four of them sitting, and crowded more so when Holiday came in, Catti-brie closing the flap and tying it off behind her.

"Since ye're a Battlehammer, I'm sure that ye know I'm not too fond o' folks on Bruenor's Climb when I'm up here," Bruenor said to Holiday. "And even when I'm not!"

"By the many in this tent, I'd be thinkin' it's a party, me King."

Bruenor tried not to laugh, but he couldn't help himself. "Cheeky lass, ain't ye?"

"Me King, I'm using all me respect and tact . . ."

"Ye're befuddling yer king's sensibilities, lass Holiday," Bruenor assured her.

The young clansdwarf—she couldn't have been more than twenty-five years—took a deep breath to steady herself.

"I thinked it important to come and speak with yerself."

"And ye talked to Stokely?" Bruenor asked.

"Soon before ye got into Bryn Shander, once we heared the reason for yer visit."

"And he telled ye to come up here to pester me?"

"He telled me not to talk with ye, and likely wouldn't've let me if I tried to find ye in the caves."

"And so ye come up here anyway?" Bruenor asked with a snort.

"Aye."

"Cheeky lass," Breezy said in a Bruenor imitation.

Bruenor didn't share the mirth and glared at her.

"I'm here bein' asked to speak for many o' the dale's Battlehammers," Holiday explained. "Loyal servants to our King Bruenor o' Gauntlgrym, to Queens Fist an' Fury o' Gauntlgrym, and to Queen Dagnabbet o' Mithral Hall. But mostly, o' course, to King Bruenor Battlehammer, who once ruled in these very mines, who journeyed to Mithral Hall and took it back from Shimmergloom the shadow dragon, who brought together the Delzoun dwarfs o' the Silver Marches to glorious and needed victory over Many-Arrows, who sought and found Gauntlgrym and took it back from them durned drow . . ."

Holiday chortled on that and sucked in her breath, glancing across the small tent to Princess Catti-brie Battlehammer Do'Urden and her husband, the hero Drizzt.

To Holiday's relief (and a bit of confusion), the "durned drow" over there was grinning at her.

"Much as I'm liking hearing of me greatness, I'm a bit busy bein' king and all," Bruenor deadpanned.

"You're always liking that," Breezy said.

"Wouldn't think ye'd've been climbing the mountain to just blabber about meself, and suren not to enjoy the cold rain," Bruenor continued, stifling a chuckle and taking any remaining edge off his voice. "So speak."

"I'm talkin' to me King," Holiday quietly replied with clearly sincere and deep respect. "I'm not knowin' King Bruenor well enough to call him me friend, and that's to me own loss . . ."

"Ye dwarfs up here in the dale are me family," Bruenor said calmly. "Don't ye e'er be doubtin' that."

Holiday nodded.

"So speak it plain," Bruenor demanded.

"Many of the boys're thinkin' that ye might not want to be puttin' yer portal up here, me King," the lass stated.

Bruenor's eyes went wide. "Many o' what boys?"

"Us Battlehammers. We're thinkin'—"

"That'd be yer first mistake!" Bruenor growled. He looked to Drizzt and Catti-brie and shook his head, spraying water everywhere. "By Moradin's hairy arse, y'ever heared such impudence?"

Catti-brie smiled and nodded. "Heard you ask that exact question many times when I was even younger than Brie and Holiday."

"Meant it then, too," Bruenor groused. He stared hard at Holiday. "I'm yer king," he reminded.

"Aye."

"Bein' such, if I say I'm puttin' in the portal to Gauntlgrym, ye're bound to accept it and guard it and do as ye're told."

"I been told that King Bruenor's more open to hearin' the concerns of the Battlehammers."

"I am."

"And I'm tellin' ye true. Some o' the dwarfs up here in Icewind Dale—nay, I say, not a one of 'em want yer gate here, and not just because o' the anger o' those around us. We're here because here's where we choose to be. If asked, would King Bruenor deny any of us travel back to Gauntlgrym to live there, or to the Silver Marches, even?"

"Course not."

"Ye hear any askin'?"

"Blunt as a smith's flattener, ain't ye?"

"Aye. Blunt and with a point."

"Well, ye said what ye said, and I heared ye," Bruenor replied.

Holiday nodded. "Then I'll be away and bother ye no more, me King."

Bruenor shook his head. "Ye stay and be warm. We got the room and we got the food."

The others in the tent nodded their agreement.

"But it'll cost ye," Bruenor added. "One with yer sparks had some fights and adventures, even at yer young age, I'm bettin', and them are tales ye're tellin'."

Holiday's smile took in her ears.

"Sank a boat on Maer Dualdon," she said.

"Good fight?"

"No fight. More of an accident."

"Bwahaha, do tell, girl. Do tell."

And she did, while Drizzt put together a meal for them all and Catti-brie used some interesting spell combinations to create a fire that warmed but did not burn, drying them all, warming their bones, and heating the meal perfectly.

The rain and the wind made for a noisy night, but four of the five slept quite soundly, the fifth being Bruenor, who was indeed hearing the echoes of the words of Breezy and Holiday.

The storm broke before the dawn, and the troupe set off for the main dwarven complex.

Breezy and Holiday remained far back of the others, chatting lightly and merrily, both relieved that they had had their say, and had found the courage to say it straight.

"Ye think King Bruenor heared us?" Holiday quietly asked as they neared the cavern compound.

"He heard, they all heard," Breezy replied. "But they heard through the ears of cynical olders."

"Ain't that old."

"Ma's a Thirteenther, Da's a Twelfther, and Grandda might even be a Tenther, as I'm not knowing what year he was born in. They're folk of different centuries and different eras."

"Not so different," Holiday replied. "Bettin' that Icewind Dale looked the same even back then."

"Then think of them as folk with many years of fighting and disappointment. They get stubborn, and probably gave our words all the weight they think the words of children deserve."

"Aye, maybe they're all like that," Holiday said with a sigh.

"Not all," said Breezy, and she was thinking of Uncle Jax.

The two left the others in the compound and went their own way, swapping more tales of their adventures. They spent the rest of the day together, long into the night, with Holiday introducing Breezy to a few other young friends.

It was a good day.

6

HOLIDAY'S EYES

"Cheeky girl," Bruenor grumbled late the following morning, when he and the Companions of the Hall were sitting with Stokely and a few of the elders of the Icewind Dale Battlehammers. "And where's she off to now?"

"Just to Lonelywood," Catti-brie answered. "Breezy is meeting some of Holiday's friends from the towns about Maer Dualdon."

"They'll get in trouble, the lot o' them," said Bruenor.

"Holiday's got a mouth on her, aye," Stokely Silverstream chimed in.

"But . . ." Bruenor prompted.

Stokely just shrugged.

"Ye're thinkin' that she told me the truth."

Another shrug and a little nod.

"It would seem that Sylfae, however she might have disguised her initial feelings about me, was also speaking truly to Breezy on other matters," Drizzt chimed in.

"Few in the dale would admit the feelings they held for Drizzt Do'Urden back then," Wulfgar replied. "Or perhaps they see their own pasts in a manner more flattering to the truth they know now."

"Either way, it hardly matters," Drizzt said. "All that matters is the surprising vigor of the resistance to the portal."

"It be real," Stokely said grimly.

"Ye ain't speaked yer own true feelin's on it, have ye?" asked Bruenor.

"Ye're me King. I do as ye tell me."

"Ain't what I'm askin'."

Stokely took a deep breath. "I wish ye'd sent word and heared the answers afore ye came," he admitted.

"Good dwarfs died bringin' the goods up here," Bruenor replied with a bit of a snarl.

"Ye're me King. I do as ye tell me."

"All the Battlehammers up here feelin' that way?"

Without hesitation, Stokely nodded. "Aye, when it comes down to it, aye. Ye can make 'em agree, but ye can't make 'em like it."

"Bigger trouble from outside the clan than inside," said Athrogate, who sat with Pwent at the far end of the huge dining table. "Hearin' grumblin's o' war, or raidin' parties at least, to tear the gates down."

"Then we bury the portal chamber deep," said Regis. "Put it in the lowest tunnel that has no path to the Underdark. Hidden away."

"Aye," Athrogate cheered. "We put it deep, below their feet. They'd not find it, so they won't mind it."

"Rather just punch 'em in the face and send 'em home," Pwent mumbled through a huge bite of his food.

Bruenor looked to Stokely, who sat very still. "It'd give ye security," Bruenor reminded him. "Put armies at yer call in short order."

Stokely didn't seem convinced.

"Ye goin' to still feel like that if a clan o' giants falls over Ten-Towns?" Bruenor asked.

"We're knowin' the life. We're knowin' the danger," said Stokely. "Might be why most of us stayed instead o' goin' to the south when ye gived us the choice."

Bruenor turned his gaze to Drizzt, and Drizzt obviously understood the look and returned a slight nod.

"Ye go fetch yer troublemakin' daughter tomorrow, elf," the dwarf king told his dear friend. "We leave in the mornin' after and the gate's comin' with us."

"Me king?" Stokely asked with a gasp, one echoed by Pwent and Athrogate and the other four dwarfs in the room.

"I ain't for puttin' this on ye, Stokely Silverstream," Bruenor explained. "Yerself and yer boys've been more than loyal. I seen all the good the gate might bring—includin' bringin' meself up here more often, and not as a king to ye, but just as a friend."

"There's a tower full of wizards who could take you up here whenever you desire," Catti-brie reminded her da. "And a host of Harpells as well."

Bruenor nodded.

"You had visions of a tighter family, a more connected circle of friends and allies," Drizzt said to Bruenor. "A tamer world, from Gauntlgrym to the Silver Marches, to Longsaddle to Luskan to Icewind Dale. I understand the thought, but . . ."

"But?" Bruenor echoed when Drizzt let it hang there.

"Isn't part of the reason you like coming up here because it's not tamed?" Catti-brie answered for Drizzt.

"How many times have you threatened to leave the throne of Gauntlgrym to Fist and Fury and run off on adventures?" Regis added.

A barrage of agreeing statements came at him, and Bruenor just threw his hands up in defeat.

"We're goin' home and the gate's comin' with us!" he roared to silence them all. Then, to Stokely and in a quieter voice, he added, "But I'll be back more often than of late, don't ye doubt. And it might be just to hunt some durned yetis."

"Ye're always welcome, me King," Stokely said, and for the first time since Bruenor's arrival, Stokely Silverstream was smiling to take in his ears.

A DOZEN MISSILES FLEW AT her, but Breezy ducked and dodged, twisted and dove aside, avoiding every one.

"Not possible!" cried Belter, a dwarf of twenty-four winters.

"How can it no be possible when ye just seened it?" Holiday asked, howling with laughter. She had taken Breezy out to Lonelywood on the banks of Maer Dualdon. What had fallen as cold rain just a few miles away had landed as a heavy and wet snow here in the small forest surrounding the community, which was made up mostly of halflings.

Holiday had already witnessed Breezy's uncanny ability to avoid snowballs, as they had engaged in one-sided battles all through the wood before meeting up with Holiday's friends from Bremen, Easthaven, and Lonelywood, the three towns situated on this particular lake.

Shaking her head, Holiday turned to Numtummy Applecheeks, a halfling of thirty winters, the oldest of the group of eight that had gathered for the snowball fight on the northern edge of Lonelywood.

Numtummy motioned for the dwarf to stay silent, while fitting a perfectly shaped snowball into the basket of her sling.

Across the way, Breezy was in the act of not only dodging, but catching a pair of snowy missiles, and with the added flair of a standing back somersault, just for effect. With grand accuracy, she redirected those snowballs at the two dwarfs who had thrown them, painting the orange beard of the first fellow white and giving the young dwarf woman an eyepatch to make Uncle Jarlaxle proud.

A snowball zipped past Holiday as Numtummy called out, "Hey, ye durned elf!"

Breezy turned and dodged—or tried to, but a speedy one coming from the sling caught her by surprise, tipped off the edge of her quickly-lifted hand, and popped her in the ear with a resounding thud as she turned her head aside.

Holiday's half dozen friends, three dwarfs, two halflings, and an elf who was almost exactly Breezy's age, all cheered at a throw that finally struck the elusive girl.

Breezy laughed, then yelped when all seven of her new friends let fly a coordinated barrage. She dodged or deflected all but two.

"Best I ever seen," Numtummy congratulated, walking over.

"Ye know who her ma and da be, aye?" said Holiday.

Breezy strained to smile.

"Don't care," said Numtummy. "I care what she can do, and indeed, I find myself impressed."

"Brilliant, I agree," Holiday congratulated, nodding in accord with her halfling friend.

"Hardly. They got me," Breezy countered, wiping the snow out of her ear.

"Aye, but ye had no chance and held them off longer than any I've e'er seen," said Holiday. "And Numtummy cheated. Not supposed to use a sling, what? And what's next, a bow?"

"Hard to throw a snowball with a bow," Numtummy replied.

"Bah, she's a dancer," Belter declared and spat.

"A great one, eh?" Numtummy said.

Belter snorted. "Won't matter."

"Matters if ye can'no hit her," said Holiday.

"Matters if ye can'no hit her and she can hit ye hard enough to stop ye," Belter corrected. "Seen it all the time. Dancers hit ye a lot afore ye finally hit 'em back, sure, but when ye hit 'em back, fight's over."

"Am I hearing a challenge?" asked the halfling named Melkin. He smiled widely. "Pond's only a bit iced over."

"Thumping!" said Numtummy. "Breezy and Belter."

"Nah, thumpin's not fair when one's a dancer and one's a slugger," said Holiday. "Ye're takin' away one's advantage and playin' to th'other's."

"What's thumping?" Breezy asked.

"You trade hits until one's done with it," Bowser explained, still combing snow out of his orange beard. "Punches, but not in the head or the groin. All else is a target."

"And the loser's strippin' down and jumpin' into the pond," Belter said with a laugh. "And oh, but that's goin' to hurt!"

"Yes, and do not accept a challenge by Belter," said Avilon the elf. "Fancies himself joining Pwent's Gutbusters in Gauntlgrym. And he's got the thick skin and thicker skull to maybe make the cut!"

"While I'm in no hurry to see that hairy little runt in his skimpies, he could use a cold bath," Breezy said.

"No worries," said Belter. "Y'ain't winnin' and I ain't wearin' any!"

"Even worse, then," Breezy muttered.

"Ye sure, girl?" asked Holiday.

"Don't do it," Avilon said.

Breezy heard the warning, and knowing the truth of Thibbledorf Pwent and his Gutbusters, understood the sentiment. Punching Pwent was like punching a stone wall, except that the wall would complain more. But she was being sorely underestimated here, she knew, and she was having fun, so much fun.

She wanted to fit in.

"Here? Or near the pond?"

"Girl . . ." Holiday said.

"I understand," Breezy replied. "I don't want to see him naked any more than you do."

The others howled in laughter, Belter most of all.

"Start a fire by the pond, then," Holiday told Avilon. "And get some warm blankets ready."

The storm had fully passed by the time the troupe got to the pond and set up a small camp, the brisk winds of Icewind Dale pushing the clouds away, with stars already beginning to twinkle above. Avilon proved quite adept with a flint and steel and got a fire blazing in short order.

"All right, then," Holiday said and led Breezy and Belter to the edge of the pond, facing each other.

"Not in the head," she said to Breezy.

"And not in me nuts, ye durned drow," Belter added.

"Who swings firs—" Breezy started to ask, but Belter slammed her in the gut hard.

And oh, but it hurt! The dwarf packed a wallop, indeed. She coughed a few times and doubled over, silently cursing for getting caught by surprise.

"Shortest first," Holiday explained.

"Couldn't have told me that earlier, eh?" Breezy wheezed out.

"So, ye done? Take a bath and save yerself some pain."

Breezy answered with a closed fist, middle knuckle protruding just a bit, in a short jab that caught the dwarf just inside his right shoulder. He gave a little grunt and fell back a step, seeming genuinely surprised at the power his lithe opponent had delivered.

He didn't know, though, that Breezy was a trained monk, a Superior Master no less, and one who had learned to strike with deceptive power, and against vulnerable places.

"Ha! That the best ye can do?" Belter boasted.

He was bluffing, Breezy knew. She had hit him solidly in exactly the right place.

"Well, now ye're done," said the dwarf, and he dropped his right shoulder back and stepped his left foot forward, as if to come in with a heavy right cross. He started to stride at her, but stopped suddenly, a curious expression on his face as he stared at his right shoulder, his arm still hanging at his side.

"Any good with your left?" Breezy flippantly asked.

"What?" Melkin exclaimed and the others gawked.

"Bah!" Belkin roared and he hopped back to reposition and came in with a heavy left, again at Breezy's gut.

She was ready for it this time, and she tightened her stomach muscles and rolled her hips back expertly to absorb the blow.

Even as Belter squared himself, she hit him on the left shoulder, a mirror image of the strike to the right. She knew she had to be quick here, as she didn't want to keep trading blows with the strong dwarf, understanding that the numbness in his arms wouldn't last long.

Belter looked at his drooping left arm, then over at his right and back to his left.

"No head-butting, I hope," Breezy remarked.

"Punches only," said Holiday.

"Well?" Breezy asked her opponent.

"But . . . but . . . ye're cheatin'!"

"If he's not swinging," Breezy prompted.

"Forfeits this turn," said Holiday.

"Wait a durned heartbeat!"

"Nope!" Holiday declared, and when Belter started to protest, Breezy strode forward with her right foot, putting it almost beside

Belter's left, her shoulders turning powerfully, her right arm stabbing ahead, open palm, striking Belter right in the center of his chest and sending him staggering backward.

"Can ye lift one o' yer durned arms yet?" asked Holiday, who seemed to be truly enjoying this unexpected turn.

"Ye're a wizard! Ye cast a spell on me!" Belter howled, then grunted when Breezy's open palm slammed home again.

"Do it now," Holiday told the dwarf. "Hit her!"

"I can'no!" Belter yelled.

Breezy grinned and strode forward, but Holiday grabbed her by the arm and held her back. "Fight's over, I say."

Belter sputtered while the others cheered and laughed.

"Wait, wait," he said. "I can hit her now." He struggled a bit, but managed to lift his right arm.

"Too late," said Holiday. "Ye lost."

Belter started to protest again, but just snorted and shook his head. He had no strength in his arms, obviously, as he waggled them about. "How'd ye do it, girl?" he asked.

"I'll show you," she promised. "But once I do, I won't fight you again. You hit too hard."

The dwarf smiled and puffed up at the compliment, and Breezy was glad that she had given him back some of his pride here.

She held out her hand and Belter clasped her by the wrist, nodding.

"Melting some syrup on the apples," Numtummy called from the fire, and the others hustled about for the treats—except for Belter, who moved off behind a pine tree.

The first apple was for the victor. Breezy took the skewer and lifted the treat carefully to her mouth, just barely tasting it, then moving it back to cool a bit more.

Then came Belter, running, flying past, and curling up tight, and Breezy thought he looked more like a hairball Guen might cough up than a living dwarf in the fleeting moment before he slammed down and through the thin ice on the pond, disappearing only briefly before popping back up with a great shivering gasp.

Holiday met him at the small pond's edge with a heavy blanket.

"Well?" Avilon asked.

"Refreshing!" the dwarf bellowed, and the others echoed and began stripping down to their skimpies or to nothing at all. One by one, they splashed into the cold water. And one by one, they came back out, disappearing under a heavy blanket and plopping back down at the edge of Avilon's blazing fire.

Breezy's teeth were chattering when she got back, the last one, to the edge of the warmth, only to find Belter eating the syrupy apple Numtummy had given to her. "Hey, that one was mine," she protested.

"Ah, shut up, ye durned cheatin' drow," the dwarf replied with a laugh. He threw a huge wink her way a moment later, though, and reached forward to get a second skewered treat, which he presented to Breezy with a respectful bow.

Numtummy had come with full packs of food and had many more treats cooking long before the apples were consumed. To Breezy's surprise, the group didn't head back into Lonelywood after eating, but just dressed when they were dry and camped right there by the fire, in the snow.

Breezy lay back against a log, pulling the thick blanket tight about her, staring up at the clouds rushing past and the stars peeking out about them. She lost herself in that view and felt as her father had described to her on his many trips to the little plateau called Bruenor's Climb, felt as if she had floated up among the stars, or as if they had come down to meet her where she lay, inviting her imagination to think of things beyond her ken.

"I wonder what Grandda decided," Breezy said quietly to Holiday a long while later, when she noticed that her new friend was not snoring like the other three dwarfs, and not curled in sleep like the two halflings, nor lost in reverie like Avilon the elf.

"Old and grumpy," Holiday whispered back. "The world's changed and Bruenor an' th'others don't know it, and don't much like it."

Breezy chuckled. "I'm not so sure the world's changed," she said.

"Then it's just them. Old and grumpy."

"Not so old," Breezy whispered. She turned back to the stars, trying to make sense of it all. "Not so old," she whispered again a short time later, when she knew from Holiday's rhythmic breathing that the dwarf had fallen asleep.

No, it wasn't that the world had changed or that Bruenor was old and grumpy, she decided.

She let her thoughts fly free, up to the stars, and tried to think about this as if it were her choice and not Bruenor's.

He was disappointed.

Yes.

The world hadn't changed, but Bruenor wanted to change it—here, at least. He wanted to make it safer, to make it better.

And now he could not. They wouldn't let him. They didn't want him to.

Breezy nodded and the stars seemed to twinkle in response.

Familiar stars, she thought, and they and the chilly breeze sent her thoughts cascading back across time and space nearly a decade before upon the field behind the Monastery of the Yellow Rose. She had tricked Gregory into sneaking out of a lesson with her, telling him that she had discovered something quite important that would give them a huge advantage in their training practices.

She had led him to a lower area of the field, to the edge of a bowl waist-deep with wet leaves, some still icy from the cold of night.

"You see?" ten-year-old Brie asked the teenager, pointing out from the bank.

Gregory shook his head and looked at her curiously, but she pointed more insistently and said, "There!"

How trusting he had been! He followed her point, even leaning over to peer more closely at the indicated spot.

Breezy hit him in the butt with a circle kick that launched him out into the leaves, and before he could find his footing, she leaped upon him and set him back down deep into the pile.

She remembered his great strength, even back then, when he stood right up under her and tossed her from him farther into the bowl and deeper into the pile.

At first, she thought he was mad, particularly when she managed to get her head out of the mess to see him charging her way.

But no, in that moment of playful abandon, she had at last freed Gregory from his incessant, up-buttoned dedication.

She had given him a moment of childhood, of play, of joy without fear of consequence, and they had wrestled and dodged, crawled through and ducked under that filthy, soaking pile of autumnal detritus, laughing.

Just laughing and wrestling and chasing and playing.

They got caught out there by one of the masters, of course, and took a great scolding, during which Gregory had scowled at Breezy repeatedly.

But he was just embarrassed, she knew then even at her tender age, and he wasn't really mad at her, or if he was, it wouldn't last.

That had been a good morning, and now a fond memory.

This had been a good day, so similar.

Now, under the twinkling stars, the memories coalesced, joyful signposts on the road of Breezy Do'Urden's life, and she lay there for a long while simply basking in the wonder of it all. It was a good night.

7

TRYING TO FOCUS

Breezy sat at the back edge of her rolling wagon, staring at the distant trees she knew to be the forest of Lonelywood. She had truly enjoyed her time with Holiday and the others, and while she resisted the urge to jump off the wagon and go running back to join their little gang, she did promise herself to look in on them whenever she happened to be in Icewind Dale, and even to make special trips up here to visit, if the opportunity ever came up.

The time with them had been so frolicky, so fun, so . . . *normal.*

With them, other than in the introductions, she wasn't the daughter of anyone. She was just Breezy, just one of them lying out under the stars by the campfire. She felt as her parents must have felt in the early days of the Companions of the Hall, and it was glorious and free, indeed!

And now she was leaving, heading south back to Luskan in the wagons of Bruenor's caravan. From there, either through a Teleport spell or on the back of a dragon, or a combination of both, she would travel to the Monastery of the Yellow Rose for the final preparations for her battle with Master of Dragons Gregory.

She worried what new duties might befall her when she won that fight and assumed the rank among the officers of Saint Sollars. After her victory, she would become one of the dozen highest-ranking monks in the Order, after all, and she would likely spend much of her time guiding and instructing the newer acolytes in the monastery.

Perhaps that would be fun.

But it also would be safe.

Too safe?

Her grandda Bruenor often complained about the boredom of the throne, and he sometimes created reasons to get out of Gauntlgrym and on the road of adventure.

"The road of life and living," Breezy whispered.

She lingered at the back of the wagon all through the first day out of Bryn Shander, until the trees of Lonelywood were out of sight and Kelvin's Cairn was no more than a bump on the northern horizon. She knew she had to tear her eyes and, more importantly, her thoughts away, and focus instead on that which lay before her. She had a lot of work to do. She was behind in her training and the fight was coming up fast. She turned her thoughts to that and forced them to stay there.

She pictured her opponent, a not-unpleasant image. She had seen Gregory quite regularly over the last few years, had trained with him on many occasions, and had spent many hours beside him in their duties as scribes, for his standing desk was right beside hers. She could almost smell him now in just thinking about him, and that, too, was not an unpleasant sensation. She could imagine the muscles in his thick arms, tightening with every movement, whether in holding a quill or in his exercise and fighting routines. She loved sparring with him, the feel of his chiseled body as he tossed her aside or when she flipped him over her shoulder and then fell upon him to pin him.

He'd smile sincerely at her whenever she managed to execute a move correctly. He was truly happy for her successes. Yes, Gregory was a good man, Breezy thought, and so undeniably attractive.

She grinned at that thought, wondering what his pretty face would look like when she was done with him in the challenge.

Not too bad, she hoped, for she quite liked Gregory, and mostly quite liked teasing him in ways that made him uncomfortable. Incredibly dedicated to his studies, physical and mental, Gregory was an easy target for Breezy's pranks in the library. She would scribble little notes on a ruined parchment, tear them off, ball them up, then toss them against Gregory's face while he so studiously went about his calligraphy.

The notes were silly, mostly, with jokes about the stern master overseeing the work, or suggestions that they sneak out and go play in the back field, and now, as Breezy had passed through her teenage years, they had become often suggestive in other ways.

She smiled again, wider, for she could always get Master Gregory to fiercely blush—so fiercely that he had been scolded on more than one occasion by whichever higher-ranking monk was leading a particular lesson.

It had been all in good fun, and though Gregory would sometimes leave the room fuming, Breezy could always coax him back to his typical good nature.

She truly liked him, even despite his strict adherence to the rules. And she admired the fact that although he was only a few years older than she, Gregory was already established as a Master of Dragons.

He wouldn't have been her choice in this fight if she had been given her pick of the three who held the rank she now desired, and not because he was likely the most formidable of the trio. No, Breezy would have liked to train beside Gregory at this new level, sparring with him, joking with him, trying to get him to loosen up and smile more.

Breezy shrugged the notion away. Perhaps Master Gregory would win a challenge against one of the other two Masters of Dragons and ascend again to the coveted rank beside her after she had defeated him.

She shrugged that notion away, as well. The victory was not at hand, she pointedly reminded herself. "Don't underestimate Gregory," she whispered under her breath.

She had to find an effective way to incorporate her new insights about the nature and utility of shadows, about fast and secret movement into her preparations for the challenge. With her ability to step seamlessly from shadow to shadow, as she had done with the yeti, she was confident that she would get a few open strikes against the larger and stronger Gregory. Larger and stronger, indeed, she thought, so she had to make every unchallenged attack count.

Two days later, the wagons entered the pass through the mountains, leaving Icewind Dale behind.

Still, Breezy spent most of her time in the back of the wagon, but now she was standing, practicing her pivoting strikes, up high, down low, and rapid combinations that would force a surprised and quickly turning opponent off their balance.

More than once, she leaped a sidelong somersault over the wagon rails, landing lightly on the ground beside the cart and immediately sprinting off one way or the other.

Speed, quickness, sure and solid strikes, and using the Way of Shadow to gain opportunistic attacks would win the day, she believed. She certainly didn't want to get into a slugging match with the likes of Master Gregory, who outweighed her by seven stones at least and had a palm so large that it would cover her whole face.

But he'd never hit her solidly, she decided, and she'd be moving too fast for any grappling, where again, the sheer weight and strength of the man could prove to be too much for her. She thought of her father, and the stories he had told her of his days training Wulfgar.

Breezy intended to similarly teach Master Gregory.

He had heard the whispers of the copper dragon landing before the monastery's main door, but Master Gregory was surprised to learn that the rider of that dragon was none other than Jarlaxle of Bregan D'aerthe, and more surprised still when another monk caught up to him and told him that Jarlaxle had asked to speak with him. Gregory's fight with Sister Brie was still a few months away. What might Jarlaxle, considered an uncle by his upcoming opponent, have to say to him now?

His thoughts went to his unexpected encounter and discussion with Grandmaster Savahn in the training arena. She had mentioned Jarlaxle, quite cleverly he thought, and she had injected an unexpected and not-so-subtle bit of hinting that Gregory might be well served to speak with the man about the mysteries of shadows.

And here Jarlaxle was, thousands of miles from Luskan.

The notion bothered Gregory more than it excited him. Of course, he wanted to defend his rank and defeat Sister Brie, but he felt again the nagging suspicion that rules had been bent in the selection of which of the three Masters of Dragons would answer Sister Brie's challenge. And the hints that Grandmaster Savahn had dropped regarding Jarlaxle gnawed at him.

He detoured from his trek to meet Jarlaxle in an outer hall, instead turning down a corridor to a reserved wing of the monastery and its Titled Meditation Hall, where he hoped he might find a helpful voice. He removed his shoes, placed them on a rack, and went through the large oaken door as quietly as he could, entering a circular room of steamy braziers, its earthen floor set with white stones arranged in spiraling patterns.

A dozen alcoves had been cut along the curving wall, three for the Masters of Dragons, four for the Masters of the Winds, four more to accommodate the Masters of the Seasons, and one, of course, for the Grandmaster of Flowers. These were the titled monks, the brothers and sisters who had attained their ranks through combat and had to defend them similarly.

Gregory breathed a sigh of relief to discover that only one of the alcoves was occupied, and by Master of Spring Perrywinkle Shin, the oldest person at the monastery and a man of unassailable character.

Silently, Gregory drifted across the floor to stand before the seated Master of Spring, who had his legs folded up beneath him on the bench, hands on his thighs, eyes closed, breathing perfectly steady, his chest rising and falling for equal lengths of time.

Gregory folded his hands before him and lowered his gaze, patiently and silently waiting.

"Yes, Master Gregory?" Perrywinkle Shin asked almost immediately.

Gregory was sure that the old man had not opened his eyes. "Master Perrywinkle," he stammered. "I did not want to disturb you."

"Of course you did or you would not be standing there. But I appreciate that you did not interrupt."

"Apparently I did."

A big smile that was more gum than teeth came back at him, and those few teeth remaining in Perrywinkle Shin's mouth were crooked and yellow, indeed. "What do you want, brother?"

"Perhaps you have heard of the arrival of the drow, Jarlaxle."

"He is here?"

Perrywinkle Shin's inquiry seemed sincere, Gregory thought.

"Well, that is likely good news for you then, I would say," Perrywinkle Shin went on.

"For me? Master, I . . ." Gregory wasn't even sure how to reply to that.

"Jarlaxle has extensive understanding of the properties of shadows, no doubt, if not precisely the Way of Shadow, and he has likely been watching, perhaps even training with, Sister Brie. You would be wise to find him before he departs."

"I am troubled by that, Master," Gregory blurted. "It feels as if I am seeking unfair . . ."

"Unfair?" Perrywinkle's laugh sounded more like a cough. "Master Gregory, do you doubt that Sister Brie is hard at work battling her father, who was trained by Grandmaster Kane himself? Or studying with her mother, formidable in both divine and arcane magic? Or with the other heroes she calls her family, likely Jarlaxle included? What do you think unfair?"

"I understand what I am to do in my own training, but this seems as if I am seeking secrets specific to my scheduled opponent."

"Learning?"

"Spying," Gregory corrected.

Another wheezy laugh came back at him. "Dear, dear Gregory. Always proper and within the rails of the rules."

"Of course," Gregory replied, but he was off balance by the tone, which was more sarcastic than complimentary.

"Why are you here in the Order of Saint Sollars the Twice Martyred, Master Gregory? Why have you spent your entire time for these last two decades inside these walls following strict regimens and sometimes mind-numbingly boring routines? Why have you put your body and your mind through such hardships?"

Gregory replied with a blank stare.

"Is it just for the rank?" Perrywinkle Shin asked. "For glory?"

"No, no!" Gregory immediately denied. "Of course not, Master!" He launched into the precepts of Saint Sollars, the notion of the monks as noble and righteous guardians of the peoples around them, and the value of dedication—the very speech a novitiate would hear when first they walked through the great doorway of the Monastery of the Yellow Rose. It wasn't a rote recital, though, for Gregory believed in those precepts and qualities and duties with all his heart, and every syllable now was filled with heartfelt passion.

"You are here to learn," Perrywinkle Shin said calmly and definitively when Gregory was done with his many recitations. "To learn about life, about the world, and to learn, mostly, about yourself. These are the challenges we place before you, and that you will place before those who come after you. *Who* is Gregory Antoine? *Why* is Gregory Antoine? Don't you see?"

He thought it over for a few heartbeats then nodded in reply.

"Jarlaxle is here, and he most likely possesses knowledge of the challenge now placed before you in the journey of your life. Go and learn, young Master of Dragons!"

Gregory hesitated. "But . . ." He sighed.

"But what? Just say it."

Gregory mulled it over for a bit. "I feel as if I am going out of my own tradition of training and into the tradition of Sister Brie. It feels as if I seek advantage away from merely perfecting my own craft."

"Drizzt Do'Urden is trained in the Way of the Open Palm, trained by Grandmaster Kane himself. That is your chosen tradition, of course?" Perrywinkle Shin asked.

Gregory nodded.

"Isn't Sister Brie then entering your tradition when she spars with him, since she has abandoned the Way of the Open Palm for the Way of Shadow?"

Gregory stared at the old man blankly.

"You are here to learn to overcome challenges," Perrywinkle Shin said. "Go and learn, young master."

Gregory nodded and backed away, bowing with every step. So flustered was he that he forgot his shoes when he left the chamber and padded barefoot along the cold stone floors of the great structure. What the Master of Spring had told him made sense to him, but still, he could not shake away the nagging feeling that there were forces at work here beyond a typical fight for a rank within the Order of Saint Sollars.

But what would be typical about it, after all, he decided? For surely Sister Brie was anything but typical among the Order. She was so brash, so full of fire, so willing to cross the line of impudence.

She was so beyond his experiences, so mysterious.

She was so frustrating.

And so alluring.

THE FEW WITNESSING THE DISPLAY just grinned and shook their heads, awestruck by the sheer martial competence of the combatants. Of particular surprise to them all was Breezy, her hands and feet moving with precision and blurring speed.

Even Catti-brie, who had watched Breezy many times at her practice over the last year was surprised at how far her daughter had come.

"I cannot even follow their movements," Regis said with a snort and a headshake. "Has either of them even landed a blow?"

"Drizzt is defending," Bruenor explained. "Don't know that he's thrown many with any intention o' gettin' through to the girl's body."

Even as he spoke it, Drizzt blocked a left-right strike combination from Breezy, ducked a spinning circle kick, dropped straight to the ground, then popped right back up, jabbing a left hand into the inside of Breezy's thigh.

Breezy gasped and stumbled back.

"I might be wrong," said Bruenor.

"The kick was foolish, desperate almost," Wulfgar remarked. "Drizzt is too skilled and too fast for her."

Breezy went right back in with a heavy barrage, grunting with every strike, her teeth clenched. The sound of Drizzt's blocks came louder then, reflecting the added weight Breezy was putting into each punch and each kick. She had to be getting tired—this exchange of pure fury had been going on for a long while now—but she just growled and grunted louder, bearing in, leaning forward.

"He's goin' to drop her," Bruenor said.

"He'd better not," Catti-brie muttered.

Breezy came with a sweeping left hook, but Drizzt's right arm was up and out to block.

Her right hook followed before she had finished the left, and as he threw his left arm out wide to stop that, Drizzt gasped in exasperation and said, "No!"

The onlookers understood, for the young woman had left herself wide open, both of her arms extended out to the side, with both of Drizzt's hands inside them, leaving an easy path for a jab or two, or a half dozen for the lightning-fast Drizzt, to her face.

But he didn't hit her, clearly meaning to pause and explain her error, for he didn't understand that Breezy knew he would become the teacher here, yet again, instead of a true sparring partner. He hadn't even begun to bring his arms in close defensively when Breezy rushed forward and snapped her head out before her.

Her forehead collided with Drizzt's face, sending him staggering backward.

Bruenor laughed, Catti-brie gasped, Wulfgar groaned, and Regis blurted, "Sneaky!" He meant it as a compliment, but a quick look around at the others told him that he was the only one taking that point of view. Catti-brie, in particular, wore an angry expression.

Drizzt stepped back from his daughter as she moved away from him. He stared at her with an expression of pure shock, brought a hand to his nose, and took it away bloody.

"I don't want to fight you anymore," Breezy said.

"You know that I could have—" Drizzt started to say, but Breezy cut him short.

"This sparring does me no good at all. You block my every strike, duck or dodge my every kick. I cannot hit you!"

"It's a lesson, not a fight," Drizzt replied.

"What lesson and what value to me? I am fighting Master of Dragons Gregory Antoine, not some annoying quickling."

"His blocks will be the same . . ."

"He won't get half of them up in time," Breezy said. "I would have struck him a dozen times in our last exchange!"

The two stared at each other for a very long while, until Drizzt showed Breezy the blood on his hand. "Perhaps we shouldn't spar for a few days," he said, and his tone made it pretty obvious to everyone that if they did, Breezy might get a different lesson than she was asking for.

"I'm sorry," she said, lowering her gaze.

Drizzt moved toward her and quietly responded, "You grow by fighting those more skilled. My blocks pushed you to try new tactics and angles, though I wish you had deferred on that last one."

"At least I got one through."

Drizzt understood that she knew he would have knocked her flat before she had ever begun the head butt if this were a true match, but it didn't need to be said.

"I should train with him," Breezy said, pointing over at Wulfgar. "He's more like Master Gregory than you are."

"I doubt your Master Gregory would last long in a fight with Wulfgar," Drizzt said.

"But Gregory is as fast as him, I expect, so at least I might slip some of my strikes through."

"What do you think, Wulfgar?" Drizzt called.

The big man shrugged in confusion, for he and the other onlookers had not heard the last part of the conversation.

"My daughter would prefer to spar with you," Drizzt explained.

"Yeah, and not with the hammer," Bruenor warned, casting a glare over his adopted son. "Don't ye be hurtin' me little girl!"

"You want me to trade punches with a monk?" Wulfgar asked incredulously.

"Unless you're afraid," Breezy said.

"That's not it, girl," Wulfgar replied.

"Ah, so again you show that you do not think much of my skills. That you—that you both—still think of me as a child."

Wulfgar laughed and looked at Catti-brie.

"Just pull your punches," Catti-brie told him.

"And my kicks?"

"Ye try to kick that little badger and she's goin' to put yer man-dangles into yer throat," said Bruenor, drawing a hearty "Bwahaha!" from Pwent and Athrogate.

Wulfgar sighed and shrugged.

"You need a rest?" he asked Breezy.

"Not for you," she taunted. She turned to the others and said, "Go away," waving her hands at them as if shooing away some birds.

"You need a priest nearby, just in case," Catti-brie said.

"Then stay nearby, but out of sight. I'll carry him to you when I'm done with him," Breezy replied, drawing a chorus of "oo" from the three dwarfs and Regis.

After a look of recognition toward Breezy—and the young monk was glad to see that he understood—Drizzt nodded for Catti-brie to follow him and led her and the others away.

"I'm picking the battlefield," Breezy told Wulfgar. "We're not standing toe to toe as I was with my da."

"Then let me pick it," he said.

Breezy sighed. "I know what I will be up against at the monastery, and the battle arena will be designed to satisfy my style and that of my opponent. I know Master Gregory. My chance will be in movement, and movement over uneven ground and—"

Wulfgar's chuckle stopped her. "Find your place," he told her.

A short while later, twilight falling along the pass through the mountains, Breezy and Wulfgar rejoined the caravan, the big man carrying a multitude of small bruises which included a black eye, and the young woman holding her right arm and shoulder low and working her jaw tentatively side to side.

"She's fast," Wulfgar said to Drizzt and Catti-brie as he walked past them.

"What did you do?" Catti-brie asked, looking to her daughter with concern.

"I only managed to hit her once," Wulfgar explained. "I thought she'd duck, but she tried to block." He shrugged. "I pushed right through it."

Catti-brie looked to Drizzt, who only shook his head and chuckled. "Master Gregory is nowhere near as strong as Wulfgar, I am sure," he said.

"I still think she should be a wizard," Catti-brie muttered and moved to her daughter, a spell of healing already beginning.

To her surprise, however, Breezy refused her mother's divine magic. "I am a monk, a Superior Master in the Order of Saint Sollars," she flatly declared. "We are trained in self-healing. I learn from my wounds as much as I learned in giving Wulfgar his wounds."

"And in flattening your father's nose?" Catti-brie sarcastically replied.

"That, too. More than you can understand."

"YOU ARE NOT WRONG," JARLAXLE said. "She moves with grace rarely seen. I think she gets it from her grandfather."

"And some of her movements are not . . ." Master Gregory hesitated, searching for the word.

"Physical?" Jarlaxle asked with a smile.

"Perhaps, but I cannot decide if the Way of Shadow is physical or magical. Or neither."

Jarlaxle nodded. "I go with neither and both," he said. "I found my dealings with the Shadovar all but inconceivable at times. And a shadow dragon who once worked for me had me truly flustered on many occasions."

Jarlaxle paused, giving Master Gregory a moment to digest that statement. When Gregory's face registered that all-too-expected "what did you just say?" expression that Jarlaxle knew all too well, he added, "I don't know if your Way of Shadow is the same, but . . ."

"It is not my Way," Master Gregory insisted quickly and curtly, as if he was anxious to move the conversation along this path instead of toward the many questions the mention of the shadow dragon had sent spinning through his thoughts. "Nor is it the predominant path of any here in the Monastery of the Yellow Rose or under the guidance of Saint Sollars the Twice Martyred, other than Sister Brie."

"Of course," Jarlaxle replied, and sipped his wine. He sat with Gregory in the room Grandmaster of Flowers Savahn had afforded him at the monastery, a small and rather sparse affair by his standards, but one that nevertheless served his purposes on occasions when he was visiting. The hearth was fine, the chairs and bed comfortable enough. "Master Breezy's new and almost unique path, then."

"For now, perhaps. Who knows with Sister Brie?"

"Yes, she does seem a bit scattered at times," Jarlaxle admitted with a chuckle, but he grew more serious immediately after that. "You think it a weakness, a lack of discipline."

"I . . ." Master Gregory stuttered, shaking his head.

"If you do believe that, then," Jarlaxle corrected, "throw your confidence from your thoughts. Breezy has many interests—and brings them all to bear when necessary."

"I am aware of her training in the priesthood and with the wizards of Longsaddle. None of that will be allowed in our match, of course."

"None of the spells, but do not discount the value of knowledge. Learning to heal wounds is not so different than learning how to create them, you see?"

That clearly gave Gregory pause, and it took him a few heartbeats to bring the conversation back on track. "I am merely interested in the hidden nature of shadows, in this concept that a shadow isn't simply the result of an object blocking a source of light."

"I am, of course, as curious as you on this," Jarlaxle admitted. "And almost as clueless! It seems to me that those who find this path, this tradition or Way, as you call it, find substance in shadows, almost as if they learn to separate the shadowy places from those lit, and from what I can discern, the deeper the shadow, the greater the substance to be found."

"And the greater the invitation for travel," said Gregory.

"Not unlike a wizard's ability to travel in a space outside the plane we traverse to arrive in a spot removed without walking there," said Jarlaxle. "A blink." He snapped his fingers. "And they are there."

"Would the shadow have to be large enough to hold the traveler, then, or is even a darkened sliver enough to accept an entire body in such a mystical step?"

"I think it would have to be, yes," Jarlaxle replied. "From everything I have seen, the stepper—Breezy—emerges from a shadow, and in the same posture from when she started the step, almost as if creating a short tunnel between where she was and where she so suddenly is. It's quite remarkable to witness. Truly akin to a magical spell but one created by some deeper level of understanding and not an incantation. Like when the greater monks use the vibrations of a palm to disrupt the life force of another, sometimes mortally, or when Grandmaster Kane enacted Transcendence and became one with all.

"Now any of that would be allowed in your fight, wouldn't it?" Jarlaxle continued. "In line with that, Sister Breezy's ability to use shadows to her advantage is not a wizard's trick, nor a priest's divine magic. It is, is it not, the very core of the Way of Shadow?"

Master Gregory sat and stared, digesting it all, relating everything to the preparations he must make in anticipating and countering his upcoming opponent.

Jarlaxle lifted the bottle of wine and offered a refill to Gregory, who put a hand over his glass and shook his head. Jarlaxle filled his own glass, though, for the third time. They had already finished the supper they had shared, and indeed the night was growing long.

"I don't know if I should be telling you all of these things," Jarlaxle said. "Though I suppose it does not matter. Breezy will do what she will do, and you won't be able to stop it, after all."

"And you believe she will defeat me and become the next Master of Dragons."

"I make no such prediction," Jarlaxle replied. "I know not all that much about your Way of the Open Palm, except to be wise enough to remember the lessons Grandmaster of Flowers Kane once taught me, quite painfully. You know that tale?"

"You were in Vaasa, then, many decades ago?" Gregory asked with a nod.

"I was with the king of Vaasa, Artemis Entreri," Jarlaxle said, perking up. "Oh, it is a grand story!"

Gregory held up his hands, inviting the story, and when Jarlaxle moved back toward his glass with the bottle, the Master of Dragons didn't block with his hand.

Jarlaxle launched into the tale of traveling this region, the Bloodstone Lands, with his friend Artemis Entreri, of their many adventures in the region, of meeting the copper dragon sisters Ilnezhara and Tazmikella—and of their battle, their . . . misunderstanding with King Gareth Dragonsbane and his merry band of heroes, including the great Grandmaster of Flowers Kane.

Gregory listened as intently as he could—it was a fine and long tale of adventure, of drama, and of more than a bit of humor—but his thoughts kept going back to their earlier exchanges, when Jarlaxle had given him many clues about what he might expect from his upcoming opponent and her shadowy games.

Their battlefield for the fight would not be an empty arena, after all, but a room of substance, with various levels and ascents, training posts and uneven barriers. Sister Brie would come at him from unexpected angles, he now understood, appearing from the gloom off to the side or behind him, teleporting, or dimension stepping, or misty stepping, or whatever else one might call such a step that transversed the planes.

And, if he had heard Jarlaxle correctly that shadow itself was substance and not just a lack of light, Sister Brie might have with her an additional weapon in her sudden ambushes.

Jarlaxle rolled along in his tale, but Gregory's gaze went to a torch in a high sconce on the wall and, more importantly, to the shadows all around it, the relative depths and sizes of them.

As much as anything else, the Way of Shadow was a manner of movement, a way of understanding time and space through a different prism.

I must anticipate the movements, he thought.

She would emerge from the chosen shadow as if distance did not exist within the mystical movement. Thus, she would emerge as she had entered.

The countering move would be determined by his last vision of her posture.

Gregory shook his head. It was a lot to digest.

PART TWO
THE DISTRACTED MIND
SPRING, DALERECKONING 1509

As soon as I had finished my first sparring contest with Wulfgar, I understood that I hadn't been training as much or as focused as Grandmaster Savahn would have liked on this diversion to Icewind Dale. Every day before and every day after that match, I should have been toe to toe with the huge warrior, tightening the precision of my strikes, practicing more dodging, ducking, and retreating than trying to block the enormous weight of his blows.

I learned that the hard way.

I should have been toughening my skin and better reacting to any strikes with a proper retreat or a diving roll to absorb the blow.

I knew it before my mother had even healed my wounds, injuries too extensive for my ki to overcome, and those from only a few blocks and one landed punch! I heard the Grandmaster's voice in my head (so much like my father's) telling me that I should have gone right back to Wulfgar and begged him to fight me every day, twice a day, three times a day, all the way back to Luskan.

But no, I decided. I wasn't going to fight their way. I

wasn't going to go toe to toe with Master Gregory. In that fight with Wulfgar, what I learned most painfully was that a single hit had nearly broken me.

Or more likely, I had already understood that probability, and Wulfgar's punch had forced me to admit it to myself. Perhaps it was this understanding that had led me away from the Open Palm tradition, and thus I had found a way, a path, a Way, to minimize this disadvantage of size. For I had found the secrets of the Way of Shadow, and oh, what a surprise that would be to them all, I was sure, as it had been such a surprise to the yeti when I shot from the front, then stepped into the cave from which it had charged and shot it again from behind.

Despite the weaknesses revealed to me against Wulfgar, I left the sparring fight with more confidence, though I realized that I hadn't been learning more about the Way of Shadow, either. And thus, I resolved to correct this in the short time left to me before my duel with Master Gregory.

My thoughts, however, remained in Icewind Dale, in the many revelations that had nothing to do with fighting or with shadows, for I felt as if I had learned more on that journey to the isolated and brutal tundra than I had in many months of training at the monastery—or anywhere else, for that matter. Yes, I had learned lessons that would not be found within the walls of a monastery in distant Damara, or in the library in Longsaddle, or in the caverns of Gauntlgrym.

My grandda Bruenor along with Ma and Da were all surprised to find such strong resistance to the placement of a magical teleportation gate connecting Gauntlgrym to the complex under Kelvin's Cairn.

"They're not understandin'!" Bruenor roared often on that journey home.

But they were understanding. He wasn't.

"The security!" he bellowed incessantly.

Grandda didn't understand. They didn't want his security or his magical portal. It wasn't just the fear that some enemy might get control of the gate, I now understand. But Bruenor never did (nor did my parents, I expect), it was simply that they didn't even want the security of having a dwarf army at their call.

They did not want it. Even the dwarfs living in Icewind Dale did not want it. Nor did they want the connection to the more "civilized" world, and for many different reasons. Sometimes it was rooted in a matter of pride among those folks of the dale to not ask for handouts and assistance. Just being in that forlorn and dangerous land was a personal challenge that gave their lives meaning! Beyond that, oftentimes such suspicions as to the true selfish intentions of any would-be savior are rooted in the character of the intended beneficiary. And the gods know that Ten-Towns brims with wanderers of ill intent. More people immigrate to the dale than are born there each and every year, and they come to that isolated land not because they crave the feel of icy wind cracking their skin, or the ever-present yetis and goblinkin lurking outside their windows, or the near-constant growls of their bellies when food is scarce.

The truth is that most of the people living in Icewind Dale prefer older and simpler ways—and their absolute freedom to live as they choose, where they choose, even with the extreme risks accompanying such decisions. With very few exceptions, they want nothing to do with the civilized world, and even with those exceptions, only to trade and be done with those merchants bringing goods. They want the journey from the lands south of the Spine of the World to be dangerous and difficult and rarely undertaken.

That is my lesson, one that started on the back of Tazmikella those tendays ago, flying high across the Bloodstone Lands, the Silver Marches, and the northern Sword Coast to Luskan.

That lesson was perspective.

Whether because of culture or geography, need or tradition, religion or upbringing, people see the world differently. While they might want many of the same things out of their lives, they see different paths to getting them.

Some want to be part of a community and some want to be left alone.

Some want to explore other ways and cultures and others want nothing to do with that.

Some want comfort and security and some want complete independence.

Some want a voice in their governance and others want a benign king.

This is the wide world in all its confusing and dangerous and glorious and miserable reality.

Perspective. Everyone has their own, and many are too self-centered, too quick to judge without really seeing the other side of any decision or issue.

Grandda, Ma and Da, even Regis and Wulfgar to a lesser extent, were surprised by the rejection of Bruenor's designs because the benefits of the gate seemed so obvious to them. How could anyone object to that?

But the people of the dale, tribesmen, hermits, and townsfolk alike, did indeed object. And not out of fear or because they didn't understand.

The people of Icewind Dale rejected the taming of their land.

Their land.

Their ways.

Their risks.

Their freedom.

Everyone was surprised . . . except for Jarlaxle.

I vow to never forget this lesson. I have so much to do before my battle with Master Gregory, but the journey to Icewind Dale was very much worth the time.

I have learned to fight while facing the highest stakes.

Sadly, but necessarily, I have learned to kill . . . another person. The agony of it. How it sacrificed of a piece of my own soul—a sacrifice, I fear, that I had to accept for the greater good.

And I have learned most of all that the perspective of a potential friend is of great benefit to a relationship or alliance, and the perspective of a potential enemy is critical to knowing whether a fight is needed—and, if so, critical to victory.

I came south from Icewind Dale with my eyes wide open.

—Breezy Do'Urden

8

THE EMBRACE OF NIGHT

Jarlaxle leaned back in the chair set before the pedestal that held the crystal ball. Within the ball, mist swirled and roiled, occasionally dotted by what looked like eyes—drow eyes, the eyes of his dearest friend who had been killed in the battle of Menzoberranzan.

Kimmuriel's eyes.

"It was a deck, though?" Jarlaxle asked. "You and your hive mind are certain of that?"

A Deck of Many Things, he heard in his mind. *We believe that to be true.*

"Donjon. The card of Donjon."

He felt Kimmuriel's agreement with that assessment. Jarlaxle could hardly believe what he was hearing, though he knew that he'd be foolish to doubt the spirit of Kimmuriel. When his physical life had ended, Kimmuriel's spirit had gone to the oneness of the strange and otherworldly illithid hive mind. His consciousness was there with the mind flayers, the illithids, and that great shared consciousness carried the secrets of the multiverse: the actions, the thoughts, the magic of all that was.

The ghost of Kimmuriel couldn't find everything, for the pool was too vast, of course, nor was this specter readily available to Jarlaxle—Kimmuriel's path now had unlimited trails to walk, unlimited knowledge to gain. But when Kimmuriel was here in this crystal ball with answers, Jarlaxle knew to trust them.

But a Deck of Many Things? That had shocked even Jarlaxle, for such card decks, whether of ivory or vellum, were artifacts of legend, and thankfully extremely rare. Such decks were the tempters of fate, for drawing a card carried unavoidable consequence that could bring vast treasures or power, or unavoidable doom.

The fate card Kimmuriel had mentioned, Donjon, was one of imprisonment, and from a cell that would not likely ever be discovered, let alone opened.

"Then Yvonnel is still alive," said Jarlaxle.

I am not sure what that means any longer. The creature you know as Yvonnel Baenre, daughter of Archmage Gromph and Minolen Fey-Branche, remains intact. She has not been scattered to the everythingness of the multiverse.

"And she is no prisoner to Lolth," Jarlaxle said and breathed a sigh of relief. Not that the reported fate wrought by *Donjon* was any better, he realized, if his understanding of the damning card was correct. Sos'Umptu Baenre, acting as the Avatar of Lady Lolth, had thrown Yvonnel into an extradimensional prison . . . somewhere. Somewhere, anywhere, with an infinite number of possibilities.

One could not search an infinite number of possibilities!

"Keep looking," he told Kimmuriel. "I cannot abandon her."

Again, he felt the agreement of his old lieutenant.

"Be well," Jarlaxle said. "I am pleased to know that you are where you belong, amid the great synapses of the hive mind." He reached for the cloth to cover the crystal ball.

There is one other thing, Jarlaxle heard in his mind, and he pulled back the cloth.

In the casting of my consciousness about the planes, more specifically, about Faerûn, I stumbled upon another person whom you and I thought lost. A troubled soul, once an agent of the archlich Szass Tam . . .

ALL EYES WERE UPON HER when she stepped out of a gilded carriage onto the wide brick walkway winding toward Ghaliver Longstocking's mansion. She was the height of fashion in the prospering town of Westbridge, with her exquisite taste in gowns and jewelry and shoes, and clearly all the coin in the world to commission the very best. She was tall, she was shapely (and knew how to accent every curve with her revealing outfits), and she was undeniably beautiful, with her thick red-and-black hair, her startlingly blue eyes, and her perfectly symmetrical features.

She always wore her hair back on the right side, showing off her eight diamonds, one black, set in her right ear.

Yes, Dahlia, known in Westbridge as Delilah Dorcrae, felt the eyes of the commonfolk upon her through every slow step up the path to the great doors of Westbridge's most famous and wealthy person. And she loved every moment of it. They called her Etriel Ath Tel'Daoine, the Lady of the Stars, which played right into her appearances among the townspeople, her visitations occurring only after the sun had set.

The whispers became cheers for those gathered at the iron fence, and those cheers inspired whispers among the guards on the porch of the mansion, one of whom moved to the door and called something into the foyer.

Dahlia wasn't surprised to find Ghaliver himself rushing out to take her hand and help her ascend the ten wide stairs to the porch. She quite liked the charming little fellow who had been the Westbridge burgomeister for many years before his retirement a decade ago. He was still the town's most influential citizen—it was he who had brokered the newest revisions with the prominent Caldwell family for their timber rights in the nearby forest.

Dahlia had played a major role in those negotiations, having stolen the heart of young Gershwin Caldwell of Baldur's Gate.

Oh yes, young Gershwin was quite taken with her. Every encounter, she could hear his moans of anticipation even before her fangs entered his pretty neck.

He wouldn't be here for this party, she knew, and she was glad, for Brevindon Margaster, her other current lover and benefactor, would be—and indeed already was, coming down the hallway to rush to her side even as Ghaliver accompanied her over the threshold of the wide oaken doors.

Dahlia tried not to wince at the smell of the man, or at blue bags beneath his sunken eyes, or at the drink he had spilled on his silk shirt and pants. Brevindon was twice the age of Gershwin and nowhere near as attractive as Dahlia's younger lover, or even remotely as handsome as he himself had been only a decade or so before. For Brevindon was, more than a bit, a broken man, having never recovered from his time under the influence of a vile demon, nor from his role in a war that had caused so much suffering.

Nor, Dahlia knew, from his time serving as a patsy for Jarlaxle up in the town of Luskan since the drow mercenary had taken full control of the place.

Yes, he was a man racked with turmoil, guilt, and the anger of so many injustices heaped upon him.

Dahlia certainly understood that.

It wasn't pity that had attracted her to him, though. Certainly not! To Dahlia, who fancied herself as the ultimate survivor, Brevindon's depression was weakness, and she, who had been groomed under the whips of an archlich, had no sympathy for such a failing as that. Still, Dahlia had taken great pleasure in seducing this one, even more than with the pretty Gershwin, both because Brevindon was wealthier than Gershwin, and also because engaging this one was dangerous to her, very much so.

Brevindon had once known of her, of Dahlia at least, and had worked for a long time with the ever-dangerous Jarlaxle and his Bregan D'aerthe, establishing Ship Margaster in Luskan after the Demon War of the northern Sword Coast. Spared for his efforts on the side of Lord Neverember and a group of demon-infused corrupt lords, Brevindon had become a tool of Jarlaxle, serving as Luskan's high captain for several years, acting as a proxy voice for the wily drow. Brevindon's subsequent fall had been as fast as his climb to that position, though, as the haunted man had fallen deep into depression and intoxicants.

He had returned to Waterdeep on Jarlaxle's orders, and had been cut off from Bregan D'aerthe and any influence in Jarlaxle's Luskan, so he claimed to any who would listen to his tale of woe. He still had access to quite a bit of the wealth of the resurgent Margaster family, though. This prompted Dahlia to ignore the embarrassment of his public drunken fits, and even the unpleasant sting of alcohol when she drank his blood.

She entered the grand ballroom on his arm and watched the fool bow and take in all the admiring stares—stares that were for her, Dahlia knew, most assuredly not for him.

She took in another stare, too, of a twisted man with one dead arm hanging limply behind his back.

Effron tipped his glass and his chin to her, then gave a helpless grin and shake of his head when he turned his gaze to the man on her arm.

Dahlia chuckled at that. Effron knew that her relationships with Brevindon and Gershwin were purely transactional—from her point of view, at least.

They, however, were both helplessly in love with her.

Truly helplessly, because she had told them they were, and her words to them came as if they were commands from their gods.

She had always been a charming creature when she had put her mind to it, but her previous dalliances in seduction had been child's play compared to the charming powers she now possessed as a true vampire.

She chatted and laughed and danced her way through the ball, then left with Brevindon in her gilded coach, taking along a young woman he had brought with him from Waterdeep.

A delicious young woman.

Effron couldn't help but silently congratulate his mother. Her accomplishments in Westbridge these last few years had been simply amazing. He was reminded of this when his coach rode up to the fantastic mansion she was building on a bare and rocky hill a few miles outside of town, one that wasn't visible from Westbridge or from any of the main roads.

Scaffolding dressed the building like the robes of a modest monk. There were only a few workers out at this time though, finishing the siding on one of the wings, and Effron understood why.

It was daylight. The bulk of Dahlia's workers, and the ones she didn't have to pay, came out at night.

Most of them, at least, for those now hammering about the mansion were not undead servants. And that truth, Effron knew, had been the real beauty of Dahlia's work in Westbridge. Somehow, she had controlled her bloodlust enough to become a major player in the secluded town's high society. Some of them—certainly the worldly Ghaliver Longstocking—knew of or at least suspected her true nature. But they didn't care, because Dahlia had made the benefits of her friendship outweigh the potential downfalls.

Truly, she had struck a perfect balancing act.

Even as his coach rolled up before the carriage house, Dahlia's coach rolled out, and out of the house came a disheveled, surely hungover Brevindon Margaster, stumbling down the stairs and into the vehicle.

The twisted warlock didn't exit his coach to speak with the man. He just watched, noting how pale Brevindon seemed.

His mother had sated her thirst last night, he realized. But carefully, never enough to kill him or to make the man into an undead vampire spawn. Gershwin Caldwell would probably visit soon enough.

It wasn't until Dahlia's coach was long away and he was at the mansion door that Effron realized the young lady who had accompanied Brevindon to Ghaliver Longstocking's ball wasn't with the Waterdhavian noble this morning.

He swallowed hard and rapped the demon-faced knocker.

A gray-haired butler escorted him in and led him to a waiting room, offering him drinks or breakfast, which he declined.

When left alone, Effron began to walk about the bottom floor of the place, noting the few windows and heavy curtains, all closed. It was more than that, he realized when he walked to one window. The curtains could not be drawn. They were a single piece of heavy cloth, damask or silk.

The windows were only there to give an appearance of normalcy to anyone who happened to view the place from outside.

There wasn't a detail Dahlia had missed.

A long while passed before the lady of the house came to greet Effron—probably waiting until the sun had risen enough to not shine directly into any of the curtained windows, he thought. She wore a nightgown and fashionable housecoat and a pair of furry slippers. Notably, Dahlia didn't come down the grand staircase, but rather, came up from somewhere below, though Effron had noted no stairways or trapdoors to even hint at a substructure.

"I am surprised to see you," she said, indicating a nearby divan for Effron and taking her own seat in a magnificent cushioned chair. "Do you come with news?"

"I just thought I would see the house that mother built."

The vampire laughed. "You've known of its construction for years, of course, yet never once bothered to even speak to me of it. The only time I have seen you is at Leatherstocking's events, or those very few happenstance crossings we have in Westbridge."

"I have my studies and my work."

"You have your mother barely an hour's walk . . ."

"I rescued my mother," Effron reminded her rather curtly. "Or have you forgotten that already?"

"Yes, you aided me in my problems with Bedorijay."

"I saved you from Bedorijay."

"I wouldn't have needed saving if I hadn't been distracted by you in the first place."

"You enjoyed your life as a slave to a vampire, then?" Effron came back at her. "He would never have given you what you wanted. My magic compelled him to let you taste of his blood. My powers granted you your rise to this station."

"My rise to become a *vampire,* that is all," Dahlia retorted.

"That is what you wanted."

"This," Dahlia said, pointing to the floor of the mansion, indicating all the trappings and luxury and power about them. "*This* is what

I've wanted since my childhood in Thay, and I created it for myself. One powerful friend at a time."

"Am I not your friend, mother?"

Dahlia laughed at that. "You have given me small favors only since that day with Bedorijay because, in your mind, your actions there made us even and ended any responsibility you might feel toward me. You have mentioned so yourself, more than once."

"You threw me off a cliff on the day I was born." To further his point, Effron shook back and forth, letting his dead arm swing out widely.

"It always comes back to that."

"Of course!" Effron took a raspy breath and calmed down, smiling to deflect the attention his loud response had put on him and Dahlia. "And I have even done you small favors, as you mention."

"But that is all. You never come to the house I have built. You have never invited me to be a guest in your tower."

"You will never be invited into my tower, mother," he replied, then whispered in her ear, "You are a vampire."

"And you are my son."

"Yes, I am your son, a mighty warlock who can more than defend against you should you attack me when I am awake."

"I would never," Dahlia said through gritted fangs.

"That is a promise we both know you can never make."

"You are wrong."

"Fine, I accept that you believe differently, so let me rephrase. That is a promise I know you may not be able to keep. Do I really understand the compulsions that drive you better than you?"

"You take great pleasure in wounding me."

"I take no pleasure in any of this, and little pleasure in anything else. To be truthful, I don't know why I saved you from Bedorijay— perhaps I figured that it would be better the monster I know."

Dahlia hadn't the fluid to shed tears, but her crestfallen expression obviously caught Effron and interrupted his stream of invective. He winced and swallowed hard.

"I apologize," he said. He moved as if to put his good hand on her shoulder, but instead gave a slight bow. "That was unfair, and certainly so in light of what you have made of yourself. The people here love you and are glad of you, even the ones who suspect your true nature, and that is something a beast like Bedorijay could never have accomplished. You have handled yourself with grace and dignity beyond anything I would have expected, given the many tribulations that befell you even before you were victimized into this peculiar state of existence."

"I am not a victim," Dahlia stated with confidence.

"No, you certainly are not."

"And I am not a monster."

Effron bowed again.

"I am pleased by you," Dahlia said. "By your decision to change your surname back to reflect me instead of your ghastly father. Every time I heard the name Effron Alegni, it brought bile to my throat, for Herzgo Alegni is a man I do not wish to remember. Syn'dalay suits you better, I think."

"Syn'dalay is a surname for which I should be proud?" he asked sarcastically.

"Why not? Did we not just speak of—"

"Do you really need to ask me? Do you not understand the truth of Dahlia—"

"I survive," Dahlia interrupted sharply. "That has been the story of my entire life. Look me in the eye, Effron, and tell me that you have not killed your enemies, and horribly?"

"You think it the same?"

"It is exactly the same. Do not lecture me. From the time I was less than half your age now, I had to fight back or die, or worse. I survived Szass Tam. I survived Selora and Valindra Shadowmantle. I survived Herzgo Alegni! Survived and thrived. Please do not come into this, my home, and pretend to be an adjudicator of the paladin gods, Torm and Tyr!"

"Where is she?" Effron asked, and Dahlia furrowed her brow. "The young woman who accompanied Brevindon Margaster to the ball," he clarified.

"An urchin," said Dahlia. "A concubine debasing herself for nibbles of food."

"And where is she?"

"She decided to remain here."

"Decided?" he echoed dryly.

"She was a refugee to Waterdeep from parts unknown, with no family and no friends. She will not be missed."

Effron scoffed. Truly, he wanted to scream in rage.

"Her kind do not live well in Waterdeep, and do not live long," Dahlia said. "They are playthings for rakish lords and ladies, dependent upon intoxicants, murdered if they become with child, or they will die in a gutter by the docks anyway, and usually violently."

"And that gives you permission?"

"I did not ask for permission! And I did express my gratitude to Lord Brevindon for bringing her to me," she added with what Effron viewed as a truly repulsive shrug.

Effron put his good hand over his face and blew a long and resigned sigh.

"She is not dead," Dahlia said.

Not yet, Effron thought, but did not say. No doubt, the poor victim was feasting on fine food and drinking the finest wine—lots of it to make her blood all the sweeter for Dahlia. He got up, gave a slight bow, and turned for the exit.

"Was there anything else?"

"No, mother, I simply wanted to see your progress here on your palace, and I do admit that it is impressive."

"Manse Dorcrae," she said.

Effron cast a puzzled gaze.

"The house," Dahlia explained. "I have named it Manse Dorcrae. Appearances, my son. In the societies of Faerûn, appearance is everything."

Effron sighed and shook his head.

"When will I see you again?" Dahlia asked.

"I do not know."

"Perhaps I will come and visit you at your tower."

That had Effron's hair on the back of his neck standing up. Something about the timbre of Dahlia's voice had plucked at his sensibilities. He turned back and looked at her, so sure of herself and so deep and comfortable in her fine clothing on her plush chair. His eyes scanned the room, the fine artwork, the sculptures and expensive bric-a-brac.

He could easily visualize the bodies his mother had left in her wake for this climb to comfort and societal respect.

The many bodies.

"You are not invited," he pointedly and bluntly reiterated.

One simply did not invite a vampire into their home, not even if that vampire happened to be one's own mother.

9

MASTER OF DRAGONS

opponent, a few years her senior, but truly a peer. Yes, she sincerely liked Master Gregory. He was kind and undeniably handsome, humble and generous with his time whenever any younger brothers or sisters asked him for advice.

She liked his dedication and his decency.

When she defeated him, he would return to the rank of Superior Master. Surely the leaders would allow him to challenge for ascension within a year, and Breezy hoped that he would regain his rank as a Master of Dragons quickly. She and Gregory could then train together and push each other to prepare for battle with Jouvier, the Master of the North Wind, and so on through the nine ranks above Master of Dragons, where for each there could be only one. How many times would Gregory challenge her over the coming years, trying to leapfrog her? she wondered.

And yes, she believed, it would always be Gregory challenging her, for she would ever hold the rank right above him.

She fantasized a bit about him being her Savahn, her Master of Spring, second in command and most trusted advisor, when she defeated Savahn to become the next Grandmaster of Flowers.

With a snort, Breezy threw those notions aside and tried to focus on the present. She had only been back in the Monastery of the Yellow Rose for two tendays, but already she felt caged. The weather outside was turning, a beautiful spring growing in the forests scattered along the Galena Mountains and far below the monastery in the great forest known as the Earthwood. How she wanted to be outside experiencing the rebirth of the region!

But the goal held clear to her, the challenge fast approaching.

She took another deep breath, blocking out the birdsong she had heard that morning, and the aromas of spring drifting on the southern breeze, and the puffy white clouds rushing overhead, calling to her imagination, to her memory of riding on the back of a dragon.

She launched off a pair of posts into a backflip, planting her feet on those behind the ones where she had been standing. Instead of fighting for her balance, she just measured the extent of it. Where was her lean? Had she landed short, or thrown herself too far back?

Those were easier questions to answer. She clarified the balance of her posture and sprang away again, a leap to another post at her left, landing on one foot, then back to the right, planting both feet and spinning away in another backward somersault, pausing briefly before flipping forward once more. From there, she landed in a run, hopping and springing along the length of the posts, then throwing herself down to the right, hooking her hand about the next post in line and using it to swing herself around and down. She let go and let her momentum carry her to the post from which she had jumped, catching it halfway down, spinning around the back side of it, then launching out and away to the chamber floor.

She landed with her legs angled, falling into a roll, a second roll, then a leap, a spin, and a kick into the imagined face of her opponent.

Breezy set back down with a satisfied nod, and a quiet salute to Uncle Jax and his band for training her in this acrobatic movement they had named cavern jumping.

This skill would serve her well for all her life, she believed. In cities, in forests, along the sides of mountains, and yes, in Underdark caverns, few enemies would keep up with her.

It would help her in her fight, as well, though she wasn't sure how much. Certainly, if she found the need to run away and gain some distance from powerful Master Gregory, this would be the way.

But the true advantage lay in a different manner of movement.

She went to her towel and wiped the sweat from her eyes, then continued honing her new skill, the Way of Shadow.

She rushed forward and was gone in an eyeblink, coming out from a patch of darkness halfway across the room, heading the opposite way, right back to where she had shadow stepped. She went through a series of strikes, full weight.

She would only truly surprise the intelligent and skilled Master Gregory through shadow step once.

Once had to be enough.

MASTER GREGORY WASN'T SURPRISED WHEN he entered the combat chamber and found an unevenly lit room, with torches spaced at irregular intervals in sconces along the walls, their dancing flames casting uneven shadows across the busy layout of the large room. He knew that the Chamber of Mastery would be adapted to the particular combatants, balancing the field to evenly display the fighting monks' strengths and weaknesses. The room was often lit with magical light that wrapped about every post, permeated every corner, and filled every space. But of course it was lit by torches now, since Sister Brie had sacrificed so much to train in a new tradition, and one that depended on an abundance of shaded areas.

The room wasn't often used, for ascension challenges among the highest dozen monks of the Order were not common occurrences, sometimes taking place years apart. There had been more battles since the loss of Grandmaster Kane, though. Kane had gone to the very highest levels of achievement, had become a thing of legend, but his last score of years had been spent looking inward as much as outward, and when he had searched beyond the walls of the monastery, it had either been on solo journeys of physical transcendence into the *everywhere,* or to intervene in desperate situations about the lands, most notably the War of the Silver Marches.

For all that he had done for the monastery and the Order of Saint

Sollars, Grandmaster Kane's caretaking of the Order's other monks had been lacking in his last decades.

Thus, when Savahn had become Grandmaster of Flowers, her first order of business had been reaching out across the breadth of the lands, and she had recruited more than a hundred monks, many of them children, but with more than a few accomplished fighters and seasoned warriors looking to better their craft. The last five years had seen more jostling among the top twelve ranks than in memory, mostly to fill vacant spots instead of simply to replace other monks.

The top masters had been given much experience in creating battlefields for this chamber, and they had put it to fine use now, Gregory thought. To his left as he entered stood an array of a hundred upright posts, filling the entire southwestern quadrant of the square room. To his right was a wide circle of open floor sunk three steps down from the main floor. That combat arena was always there—they hadn't cut into the floor just for this challenge, of course—but sometimes, as when Gregory had challenged and won his current rank, they had constructed a higher wall around the perimeter of the circle, forcing a ten-foot fall into the arena should either combatant choose to take such a route.

Not now, though. Now it was open and easily accessible, likely to take away some of Sister Brie's obviously superior movement skill and thus offset somewhat the advantage she would have among the upright posts.

Her expected advantage, Gregory thought, considering his many practice sessions on posts similar to these.

In the northwestern quadrant, just beyond the posts, the floor had been covered with platforms of various levels, climbing up like some giant, misplaced stairway, with steps scattered all about, rising to a height of fifteen feet, he estimated, because the highest platform was certainly more than halfway to the twenty-five-foot ceiling.

Filling in the last quadrant, past the circular arena and to Gregory's right of the platforms, was a jumble of boulders and constructed pillars, half of which were circular columns, and half of which seemed quite like natural stalagmites one might find in caves.

Master Gregory paused and did a second, slower scan of the

chamber, focusing on the changing shadows cast by the torchlight. The Chamber of Mastery was on the top floor of the monastery, and its roof could actually be removed fairly easily if the masters decided a combat should be in rain or snow, or under a brilliant sun or the dark of night. Because of that, the roof here was not thick, and it was not as tightly tied down as it was along the rest of the huge structure.

Gregory listened as he watched, nodding as he considered that this particular chamber was often laughingly referred to as the Owlbear Haunt due to the sounds of hoo-hooing from the many wind drafts along the ceiling. The day outside was quite windy, as was usually the case up high in the Galena Mountains, and so the torches even inside the room and the shadows they cast elongated and shifted irregularly.

Gregory played out his expected dance with Sister Brie, thinking on where she would most like to take him. He warned himself not to get too set on his imaginings, for the younger woman was anything but predictable.

She wouldn't want to fight him toe to toe, he was fairly sure, and so it was unlikely he would be able to corner her in the flat and empty circular arena.

The posts and the pillars would be her ideal playing field, he realized, which meant that the quadrant with the platforms of varying heights wouldn't see much play. He kept his gaze on that quadrant as he crossed the room to the waiting masters, visualizing paths Sister Brie might choose if, as he hoped, she found her advantage on the upright posts was not as great as she had believed.

Sister Brie would avoid the arena area in crossing the room, likely, and might ascend the platforms, but as they were fairly wide and flat and well lit, she wouldn't want to remain up there for long, he figured.

"Movement," he mouthed. Movement was her game.

As he neared the masters, Gregory looked back over his left shoulder to the hundred upright posts. Some were as low as six feet, he estimated, with others nearer to ten, but most were in the middle range. He and Sister Brie could have a long and drawn-out fight just among those.

He was glad again that he had trained so extensively on the posts.

But he still wondered if he could really match the wily and agile Brie up there.

He shook the thought away immediately, focusing solely on the task at hand. He studied the terrain and took note of the true size of the room: perhaps ten thousand square feet, thirty strides wall-to-wall.

Most of all, he looked to the shadows dancing about the chamber. Which were deepest?

Which were fleeting in the flickers of the torches and which were most enduring?

He considered his studies, his training, and most of all, he tried to put that which he had learned about the Way of Shadow into the context of this particular battlefield.

He couldn't see the shadows exactly as Sister Brie would, he understood, but he hoped he had enough hints about the substance of those dancing pools of darkness to predict her anticipated routes.

If not, she would gain a great advantage, and he would be again a Superior Master, no more a Master of Dragons.

Breezy walked the monastery corridors behind Master of Autumn Calvin Bohannin, the fourth-ranking monk in the Order. In reality, the young woman walked those corridors alone, buried within the swirl of her own thoughts. Her parents had arrived two days earlier, but she had spent very little time with them. They wouldn't be watching the fight. No one would watch it besides the Grandmaster of Flowers and the four Masters of the Seasons, who would determine the winner in the event that neither she nor Gregory were knocked out or worse.

But this fight wasn't going to come down to the decisions of the masters, Breezy knew. As long as she could wear Gregory down enough before springing her big surprise on him, he would be defeated clearly and fully, with no interpretation needed.

She looked both ways along the torchlit corridor, slowing to allow Master Calvin, who seemed to be taking little if any note of her, to get far enough ahead. Then she found a patch of shadow farther along and called to it, stepping from her position nearly twenty feet away and coming back fully into the corridor, fully back into the Material Plane, only a few strides behind Master Calvin, who clearly heard the whipping of her loose sleeves as she launched a flurry of practiced strikes.

Grinning, she met Master Calvin's doubting look. She understood his apparent skepticism, for her defenses had been down throughout her attack routine, and if she did that in a brawl with Master Gregory, he would break her nose and blacken both her eyes in short order.

Master Calvin didn't realize that she'd likewise appear behind Gregory, of course, and so she returned his open skepticism with a more pronounced smile of confidence.

With a sigh of obvious impatience, the man turned and led her on, and now Breezy kept up with him, though she again fell deep into her own thoughts.

It occurred to her then that throwing a few punches took more out of her than the shadow step. The multidimensional, interdimensional movement was becoming almost second nature to her, accomplished with a figurative snap of her fingers.

She played the fight in her head a hundred times during that walk. She wasn't sure what the room would look like—the masters would put in some training posts, likely, and other obstacles like platforms and perhaps even boulders. She knew that the monks hadn't removed the roof of the Chamber of Mastery, so she expected the room to be torchlit, creating so many beautiful shadows for her to dance through, allowing her to hit and step away again before Master Gregory could respond.

She had to hope that it was torchlit, she suddenly realized.

She shook that fear away.

"Wear him down," she whispered under her breath many times. Body blows would take his strength. She needed speed and surprise, and mostly, she needed to exercise patience.

Gregory was not unlike Wulfgar. One blow, however well delivered, wasn't going to bring him down, but coming out of a shadow step with a perfect blitz of practiced strikes, timed correctly against a man she had already worn down, certainly would.

Master Calvin led her along the winding corridors and up the various stairways to the last corridor ending in the doors of the battlefield. Breezy noted the gathering in the anteroom before those doors. Two of the four Masters of the Winds sat on stones, legs crossed, hands on knees, and eyes closed in meditation, while the other two stood in quiet conversation, each nodding and bowing in deference to Master Calvin.

At the other side of the chamber, past the ironwood doors leading into the battle chamber, a trio of clerics milled and fumbled about a table covered in scrolls. Breezy recognized the oldest as Canon Josupp of Sudrav, a small mining community down the mountains to the east. He was here with spells of healing, she knew, and probably with scrolls of restoration and even revivification. Yes, these rare contests among the monks had sometimes ended in the death, or near death, of one of the combatants.

Breezy snorted a bit at the bald man's fumbling. Canon Josupp was not one she'd want to rely on to bring her back from a grievous wound, or to snatch her back from her slide into the darkness of the grave, surely.

They could have just asked my mother, she thought but did not say. For obviously Catti-brie was far more practiced and powerful in the healing arts than these three.

Indeed, far more practiced than most of the priests in all the Realms!

She was a Chosen of Mielikki, a woman who had come through death itself, a warrior, a wizard, a priestess of the highest order. She had fought more battles than most of the monks in the monastery combined, Breezy believed, and what a wonderful thing . . .

Breezy shook her head so forcefully that her lips smacked together. She threw out thoughts of her mother.

"Fool," she quietly scolded herself. "The fight is here, right here, before you."

She took a steadying breath, regained her focus, and reminded herself not to hold back when she got her opening with Gregory. If she crippled him or killed him, the monks and Canon Jessup would do their best, and if that failed, she could certainly press upon her mother to help the poor man back from the nether realm.

She was wearing that confident little smirk when she entered the Chamber of Mastery, her eyes scanning similarly to her opponent's when he had first entered the chamber.

Unlike Gregory, though, Breezy didn't have to look for the shadows. She heard them calling to her.

Grandmaster Savahn had promised a fight that would allow her and Gregory to showcase their varying traditions, and Breezy was quite pleased at the scene before her.

Grandmaster Savahn had delivered on that promise.

Master Calvin brought her to Savahn, who stood with the other three Masters of the Seasons, with Gregory standing a little off to the side. Calvin bid her farewell immediately, nodded to Gregory, and moved away as the third of a line of four. Aged Perrywinkle Shin, the Master of Spring, second only to Grandmaster Savahn, led the group, followed immediately by Master of Summer Yterralde, an ageless woman with brilliant red hair and shining, penetrating, knowing eyes that always made Breezy feel naked before her. Yterralde understood a lot more about everything than she was ever letting on, Breezy believed, and was rumored to be as formidable in her fighting as she was with her wit. Calvin Bohannin walked behind her—would he soon challenge Yterralde, Breezy wondered?

Yterralde would defeat him, Breezy suddenly thought, though she had no idea of what she might be basing such an assumption upon.

Behind Master Calvin came Master of Winter Varick, a very tall man with short blond hair and blue eyes so light of hue that they often appeared silvery gray. He seemed lanky at first glance in his loose-fitting robe, but Breezy had seen him once emerging from the nearby lake without that garment. He was more sinewy than lanky, his shoulders, arms, and torso chiseled from long hours of training. Master Calvin might do well to look over his shoulder more than ahead in consideration of his next fight.

Lost in those observations, Breezy only realized that she had missed Grandmaster Savahn's greeting and short speech when Savahn sharply asked if there were any questions.

Master Gregory declined and bowed, and Breezy did, too, though only because she didn't want to tip Savahn off to her wandering thoughts. She could only hope that she hadn't missed any new rules regarding the fight.

She watched the Grandmaster move to the southern, open area of the room, noting that the four Masters of the Seasons were now sitting upon a ledge some dozen feet up from the floor just above the doors. Savahn broke into a sudden run as she neared that wall, leaping up, catching a foothold on some unseen jag, and leaping again to come upon the ledge and take her place at the center of the five.

Her sudden and graceful movements surprised Breezy, and if that was the only way up to the viewing platform, she had to wonder how old Perrywinkle Shin had possibly climbed up to it. As if reading her mind, Perrywinkle smiled at her, gave a little wink, then rose and whistled, quite suddenly and sharply.

It took her a moment to realize that whistle as the start of the fight, and had barely turned her head to consider Master Gregory by the time she saw him coming fast and high in a flying leap, his arm cocked to end the fight before she was even ready to begin it.

Breezy stopped thinking and just let her warrior instincts take over, her body twisting and ducking before her mind had even caught up to Gregory's sudden attack. His punch stung her though it just glanced the side of her face, opening a cut on her cheek, and she was twisting away as his weight came down upon her, bearing them both to the floor.

Gregory tried to grapple her—with his huge advantage of strength and size, a fight on the ground offered her almost no chance at victory—but the agile Breezy tucked her left shoulder as she came around and down just enough to throw herself into a roll with sufficient momentum to break Gregory's attempted grasp.

She came up and ran off for the nearest pillar, leaped to it, then from it to another, then from that in a somersault to land atop a large stone near the middle of the room. She sprang away again to one of the stair platforms some five feet above the main floor.

Gregory came in fast pursuit, jumping to the lowest platform, then to the next, which took him near to the side wall. He copied Breezy, though not as gracefully or as speedily, by leaping up against that wall, planting his feet at the proper angle, and springing up and back from there, going into a roll across and over a platform higher than Breezy's, then spinning down to plant his feet right beside her.

She hit him twice before he fully landed, a pair of body blows just under his ribs.

They were toe to toe then, fists flying, kicks sweeping in left and right.

He wasn't as fast as Drizzt, of course, and not even as fast as Wulfgar, and Breezy managed to block or deflect each blow while countering successfully several times. She couldn't put much behind her strikes, wary of Gregory's sheer power, but she landed a few solidly, including an uppercut that bloodied the man's nose as he lurched forward and tried to bear in on her.

Perhaps she had been wrong, she thought. Perhaps she could simply defeat Gregory in a straight-up striking fest.

That hope flew away along with her breath when she got her left arm up to block a hooking right from Gregory, only to learn, too late, that he was fully committed here, to the point of lurching off to her right as his arm came across. In that move, up came his knee, so cleverly, slamming Breezy in the side.

She gasped at the sheer weight of it and fell back, and Gregory was there, wailing away.

She blocked, she blocked, she blocked, over and over again, trying to set her feet, feeling the edge of the platform with her heels.

Gregory came with a roundhouse right hook that would have torn her head off had it connected, she realized, and she could only breathe a sigh of relief as it snapped harmlessly high above as she fell into a deep crouch. The man rushed forward, but Breezy sprang upward into a backflip as Gregory pitched headlong from the platform before her. He landed well, though, as Breezy fortunately anticipated. For the man rolled forward and came up to his feet swinging, and if she had taken his fall as a chance to gain some opportunity strikes, she would have surely suffered several of those heavy hits.

But Breezy was off and running, and leaping, right back to the five-foot platform, then to the higher one that Gregory had rolled across, then back the other way, coming to the highest platform more than a dozen feet above the floor.

She was surprised to find Gregory in close pursuit—how could he have reacted to her so quickly?

She hit him hard as he came up onto that highest platform beside her, a wicked left hook that snapped his head to the side.

He shook it off, parried her following right jab with an in-swinging left arm, then struck her with a sudden and jolting jab in the ribs with that left hand.

Breezy briefly looked to the flickering torches as she broke back from the clench, wondering if she should shadow step away.

Not yet, she decided, and went right back at Gregory with fury, trying to keep him on his heels, landing body blows as he kept his hands up to protect his face. He was calculating that his thick and muscled torso could handle all that his opponent, barely half his weight, could deliver before she tired, Breezy understood, and she knew, too, that his calculations would prove correct if this had really been her play.

This was just the setup. She traded blows with Gregory for a long while, both of their arms showing welts and bruises from the constant blocking. After landing a pair of solid left-right combinations to his body, Breezy was pretty sure she had cracked a rib or two, and for a moment she considered that maybe she could finish it and win here.

For a fleeting moment, that proved, until Gregory's down-chopping right hook got through her attempted block, slamming her shoulder with such force that it drove her down to one knee. She sprang back up right away, eating a left jab that rattled her teeth.

Instead of countering, she just kept going upward, and then away, off the ledge, backflipping out from the platform to come atop the pillar behind her in a controlled crouch. From there, she launched back the other way to the original platform she had climbed.

Dropping down in pursuit, Gregory was not nearly as agile or clean on his landing, giving Breezy the chance to hit him with a flying kick that threw him backward and to the ground.

He rolled, absorbing the blow, and came right back at her.

But now she had space to move.

She leaped from the platform and ran to the nearest torch along the northern wall, tearing it from its sconce and throwing it into the far corner, under the next-nearest torch.

Gregory slowed in confusion; the masters let out a collective gasp of surprise.

Breezy just smiled and went the other way, leaping back up to the lowest platform, then to the eight-footer in a roll that brought her to another torch, which got similar treatment.

She jumped from on high, sprang from her angled landing against the side of a column, hit the floor in a straight run, crossing to the south and the circular arena. With Gregory close behind, she reached into a shadow there and mystically stepped, again giving her space.

Another torch flew away, and then another, and Breezy noted the perfect location where she might finally end this challenge.

She sped for the upright posts, leaped up to catch the nearest, pulled herself atop it gracefully, then moved fast along the array, taking its measure.

Master Gregory came in with unexpected ease, setting himself squarely and in perfect balance on a pair of posts.

Breezy shifted along to her right, toward the middle of the room. Gregory paralleled her step for step, and the varying heights of the posts seemed to bother him no more than they bothered Breezy.

She thought that interesting, surprising, and admirable.

Gregory had trained hard for this challenge.

She almost felt bad about how she would finish him, so painfully, up here. She noted the deepest shadow, in the very corner, and the poles nearest its transition to torchlight, and she knew where she had to position her opponent.

But first, she had to use her superior agility and speed to wear Master Gregory down just a bit more.

Perhaps she wouldn't even need the shadow step, she mused, hopping a line from post top to post top, bringing her in at Gregory's left flank. She wanted his weight shifting to the edge and his devastating left hook coming in from beyond the post array.

She rushed in hard, dropping low on the ball of her lead foot and spinning about to sweep with her right leg.

Gregory hopped it, landing easily and countering with a barrage of heavy strikes as Breezy came up straight. She worked her hands wildly, deflecting, re-aiming, and blocking, partially at least.

Miffed that she had taken the worst of the initial exchange, Breezy sprang straight up into a backflip, coming over and around up high enough to snap a kick out at Gregory.

He slammed her calf with a vertical sweep of his left arm, though, and Breezy landed on one foot, overbalancing, and had to desperately fend Gregory's riposte while getting her second foot back securely atop the perch.

Breezy scolded herself. Her move had been desperate—and stupid.

Now she worked with patience and used her speed, trading punches while marking carefully the third post in a line to her left, the three behind her position, and the three behind those.

Finally, she gained an edge, moving all about those nine in coordination with the flow of the battle. She flipped up to the highest, the one in the middle of the nine-square, spinning back down gracefully, feigning a kick more than attempting one.

Gregory tried to keep up but could not, and Breezy was hitting him three times for every blow he got in.

Still, the odds favored him, she came to believe when a sweeping right hook flashed before her face.

If that had landed . . .

She kept her patience, though, and kept to her original plan, taking the openings for body blows, then bouncing and hopping away. She struck and fell back, when Gregory's open hand came in for her torso. She continued falling back, spinning around, darting in toward the center of the post array, then coming right in to attack again.

She was the crow chasing the larger hawk from its nest, clawing and flying away. Indeed, this battle atop the array of posts almost felt aerial!

After a long while, the two came back to their original positions atop the array. Breezy called upon every bit of her energy, working furiously with her hands, not trying to finish the fight, but to keep Gregory's hands up high.

Then she changed, suddenly, dropping her right shoulder and feigning a right jab toward Gregory's ribs.

She pulled that hand back in and spun, expecting Gregory to take the opening and sweep that left hook at her. She went up on the ball of her left foot as she did and threw herself around for a circle kick that would send the man flying from the array.

But he didn't take the bait, she realized as she came rotating about.

Only her great balance and agility saved her there, for she desperately pulled that kick short, avoiding Gregory's trap, and went around another tight circuit to square up to her opponent.

She saw something then—not consciously, but in her deep instincts. Her move should have ended there, as she'd recalibrated her exchange with Gregory, but it didn't. Up on the ball of her left foot again, she spun a second circle kick, this time leaping and leaning back just a bit to angle the flying right foot for Gregory's head.

She knew he'd block, so she pulled that kick, too, up short, but spun a second circuit while still in the air and came around with the same foot yet again just as Gregory was moving forward to fall over her.

Her heel caught him on the jaw—she heard the crack of bone—and the man's eyes were wide indeed when he fell off the side of the array.

Breezy had no time to celebrate her double-spin circle kick, had no time to relish in the wide eyes of the clearly impressed masters overlooking the battlefield, for she had landed awkwardly atop one post on her left leg, her right foot fishing for a secure perch.

But she was too far out past the array and could not pull back in.

So she didn't try, instead spinning off over the fallen Gregory, who was already climbing to his feet. She tucked and double-knee-dropped the man, thinking to finish him. She heard him grunt and almost buckle beneath her.

Almost.

But no, the man became almost immovable, as if he had become stone.

Breezy couldn't believe his strength as he returned with a roar, throwing her straight up into the air, spinning wildly.

She frantically caught the top of the pole on her descent and swung herself farther into the array just out of Gregory's reach. She moved like a monkey, post to post, until she gathered enough balance to catch a pole, let her momentum swing her past it, and flip back up to stand atop it, then atop the one next to it, facing the other way.

To her surprise yet again, Gregory was already back up there, blood streaming from his mouth, but with his eyes full of fire.

He came at her fast.

She moved left, then leaped and sprinted right, fading deeper into the array and moving toward the shadowy corner.

She cut short when Gregory moved to intercept and sprinted away toward the northern edge of the array, turning fast to face Gregory, merely four posts from him.

He stood right where she needed him to be.

Breezy charged and leaped, rushing in and down at the man.

She called to the shadow and was gone in a blink, coming out the other way *behind* Gregory, ready to execute her practiced kill shots.

She didn't surprise him.

She didn't know how he knew.

All she knew was the flying elbow that met her face when she burst out of the corner shadow.

All she knew was the stunning blow, the crunch of her nose and her facial bones.

All she knew was the taste of her blood.

All she knew was the sensation of falling.

Falling . . .

She swept her left arm about a post. She changed her angle to turn her momentum into a spin, lifting her legs in a last desperate attempt to sweep the man from the posts.

But Gregory had already jumped away, dropping right behind her, driving his elbow hard upon Breezy's collarbone and destroying her grip on the posts.

She hit the floor hard and awkwardly.

Somehow, she got back to her feet, turning to face Gregory.

His right jab came flying in at her.

She couldn't lift her left arm to block.

A second jab snapped in, a third.

Breezy hit the floor.

Gregory crashed down upon her, grabbing under her right arm and yanking it upward, rolling her a bit to her left and sending waves of agony coursing through her. His left forearm stamped down on the back of her neck as she tried to lift her head, slamming her into the floor.

She didn't feel it.

She didn't feel anything—until she awakened in her room the next day.

10

HUMBLED

The first sensation she felt was a throbbing pain across her face and encircling her eyes. It led her back to consciousness and brought back her very last memory: coming out of the shadow step and running face-first into Gregory's flying elbow.

The suddenness. The shock.

Breezy didn't open her eyes, trying to settle into the painful reality before attempting any movement about her face.

That was her plan, at least, but her eyes popped open when the realization hit her that she had obviously lost the fight.

She was not a Master of Dragons.

The physical pain became a secondary thought as she tried to come to terms with that reality.

She had lost.

For the first time in her life, she had failed. She had never thought that possible. She was the daughter of Drizzt and Catti-brie, blessed with her father's speed and agility and her mother's understanding of magic. She had everything, every advantage. She had trained in fighting with Drizzt and Wulfgar. She was schooled in the arts of legerdemain from Regis and Donnola Topolino. She learned politesse from Jarlaxle, studied magic at the Ivy Mansion, and was toughened in Gauntlgrym beside the likes of Bruenor, Pwent, and Athrogate.

How could she lose?

She felt moisture in her eyes, and it was not from physical pain (though surely there was enough of that to justify some tears).

How could she lose?

Embarrassment shifted to anger. At herself, at Gregory, at Grandmaster Savahn—had they properly and honestly prepared the battlefield to account for Breezy's shift to the tradition of the Way of Shadow? Perhaps not, she thought, for she knew that Savahn had frowned upon the change in her studies.

Something had gone wrong. Terribly wrong.

How could she lose?

"She's awake," came a familiar voice, her father's voice.

"How are you feeling, my love?" her mother asked, coming over and hovering above her.

Breezy felt her face flushing as her embarrassment resurfaced. She wanted to cry, to scream, to lash out.

"What are you doing here?" Breezy snapped, because anger was the easiest of those emotions to deal with at that terrible moment.

Catti-brie fell back, her face a mask of surprise. Breezy pushed herself up to her elbows to cast a stern look at her parents.

"Why?" she demanded.

"We've been here for several days," Catti-brie replied. "We spoke before your match with Master Gregory. Surely you remember . . ."

"Why?" she asked again. "Why would you come here?"

Breezy was focused on her father, on the curious stare he was giving her. She feared he was about to reply with some snitty remark about coming to celebrate her victory.

"Because we love you," he said instead, and Breezy felt a bit embarrassed again, this time about assigning her irrational fears to her father's voice. When had he ever judged her poorly, after all? "We always hope to support you."

"Support me? I'm not a child!"

"Then do not act like one," Catti-brie said.

Breezy narrowed her eyes. "Then don't treat me like one," she retorted. "Have you met the parents of Master of Dragons Gregory?"

That brought curious looks from both. "Are they here?" asked Catti-brie.

"Of course they're not here!" Breezy yelled, and the effort physically pained her. She pressed on, "Why would they be here? Why are *you* here?" She wanted to hurt them, because she had to hurt something to take away her own misery.

Still, she felt bad about it the moment her ma turned to her da, their expressions showing that she had indeed succeeded.

She felt the tears welling up, and not just from the dull aches in her every joint, and the not-so-dull ache in her face. "I failed," she whispered.

"Hardly," said Catti-brie.

"You saved the primordial essence in the journey to Icewind Dale," Drizzt reminded her. "You have accomplished more for the good of the world than almost anyone in this monastery."

Breezy snorted dismissively, leaned her head forward, chin on chest, and tried to breathe her emotions away. Catti-brie moved as if to hug her, but Breezy held her hand up to keep her mother back.

"That was your first try in such an arena," Drizzt went on. "It wasn't Master Gregory's. You will be better prepared next time. You must wait two seasons, I believe."

"It might not even be against Master Gregory next time, from what I have heard," said Catti-brie. "And the whispers say that he was the most formidable of the three current Masters of Dragons."

Breezy closed her eyes. She wanted to scream again. They were being parents, which meant that she was being seen as a child. She certainly didn't need this type of applause, as she knew what might be next in her journey better than they, and she knew what, if anything, she might try to do to change the outcome.

They kept rambling.

Breezy kept her eyes closed, ignoring the chatter, until she heard

Drizzt say, "Perhaps you can show me the evolution of the fight with Master Gregory, and together we can . . ."

Breezy's head came up, her eyes opening into a pure glare. "That is what you need, isn't it?" she asked.

Drizzt wore a puzzled expression.

"You need me to win," Breezy explained.

Drizzt's mouth dropped open as he was obviously trying to formulate some response.

"How does it look, how does it reflect on the great and mighty Drizzt Do'Urden if his daughter is beaten in single combat?" Breezy asked with dripping sarcasm. "How could this girl, with every advantage in the world, with the great Drizzt and the great Catti-brie as her parents, lose such a fight? How could she lose at all?"

"Brie," Drizzt replied.

"No one is saying—" Catti-brie started, but Breezy cut her short.

"I can only imagine the horror on Grandda Bruenor's face when you return with the grim news."

She fixed them with a stare.

"You don't belong here," she said coldly. "Not now."

Her parents exchanged looks once more, both ending with a shrug.

"At least let me heal you more fully before I go," Catti-brie said, coming forward.

"No!"

Catti-brie stopped abruptly.

"No," Breezy said in a more conciliatory tone. "I am a Superior Master in the Monastery of the Yellow Rose. I can take care of myself, if I choose, for let every ache remind me."

"When you battled Wulfgar . . ." Catti-brie reminded, for Breezy had refused her help initially then, too, only to change her mind.

"I have more time now," Breezy countered. "There are no sparring matches, no training demanded of me in any near term."

She shared a determined look with her mother, then accepted the hug when Catti-brie came forward. Drizzt came in next and had barely let her go when Breezy said, "Now get out of here. Go back to the west where you belong."

"Are you remaining here for now?" Drizzt asked.

"I don't know."

"Come home, at least for a while," Drizzt told her.

Breezy shook her head and waved them away, and as soon as they closed the door behind them, she fell back into her bed and let herself cry, and felt the embarrassment.

And channeled it all into anger.

"It is my understanding that you have come to tell me that you are leaving us," Grandmaster Savahn said to Catti-brie and Drizzt when they were led into her chamber by Master Perrywinkle Shin.

"We are," Catti-brie answered. "We have much work to catch up on in the west. We haven't been home for more than a single tenday in these last few months!"

Savahn smiled. "Well, you know that you are both always welcome here at the Monastery of the Yellow Rose. Always our door is open to you both. The friendship runs deep, and I am sorry that the outcome of your daughter's challenge against Master Gregory did not turn out as you would have liked. He is a fierce one, truly accomplished, truly dedicated, and truly formidable."

"It is a lesson, not a defeat," said Drizzt. "She lives to fight again."

"I hope she takes that lesson back with her to the west."

"Brie . . . Master Brie, is staying here," Catti-brie explained. "I know this loss has stung her badly—she should have better prepared—"

"She is leaving," Savahn interrupted.

"She told us that she wouldn't be returning with us," said Catti-brie.

"Perhaps not, but she is leaving the monastery."

Catti-brie cast a puzzled look at her husband, who could only shrug. "Do you believe that Breezy would be better served in training away from here?" Drizzt asked Savahn. "She can challenge again after the next full season has passed, correct?"

Savahn shook her head.

"Brie will not fight Master Gregory again," Perrywinkle Shin explained.

It was not lost on Drizzt and Catti-brie that he had left off Brie's title.

"Another of the Masters of Dragons, then," said Drizzt.

"She will not fight for the rank," Savahn flatly stated. "Like your-selves, Brie is welcome to come and visit us any time, and I hope she will, for I truly care for the young woman. So full of life and love and energy. She is a pleasure, indeed. But her time here, I am afraid, is ended."

"She quit?" Drizzt and Catti-brie blurted together. Both began talking at once, an indecipherable jumble that was gradually stilled by Grandmaster Savahn's shaking head.

"Brie . . . Breezy, has earned the right to call herself a Superior Master," Perrywinkle Shin explained. "But she is no longer listed among our ranks, not as a member of the Order of Saint Sollars the Twice Martyred, of course, as she never really was, but neither of the Order of the monks of the Monastery of the Yellow Rose."

"She did not quit," Savahn admitted. "I expelled her."

"Why?" came Catti-brie's question, anger evident.

"She climbed your ranks as fast as any," Drizzt argued.

"And she has reached her zenith," said Savahn. The Grandmaster took her seat behind her desk and motioned to a pair of chairs, which Drizzt gathered and put opposite the Grandmaster, he and Catti-brie quickly sitting.

"This decision was not easy for me," Savahn explained. "You know I love your dear little Brie, for she and both of you are as my family."

"You did what was best for the Order," Drizzt said, his tone mak-ing it clear that he was obviously unconvinced.

"Partly, yes."

"Because she changed her path to the Way of Shadow?" Catti-brie asked.

"Not that, exactly, but it is a fine example of my grounds for dis-missal." Savahn took a deep breath. "Trust me, I beg. I have done this for the good of Brie, of dear Breezy, most of all. She is no monk." She held up her hand to stop Drizzt's forthcoming protest. "Despite her quick advancement to this point. Look into your own heart, Drizzt Do'Urden. You know this to be true. Life here at the Monastery of the Yellow Rose is one of full dedication, one of giving all that you can to the teachings and the techniques. It is not simply a matter of fighting, but entirely a way of life."

"Yet you use physical battles to determine your highest ranks," Catti-brie muttered crossly.

"The physical battles are an extension of discipline," Savahn answered anyway.

"Has Brie been a discipline problem?"

"A problem? For us? No. Never. For herself? Yes, absolutely."

"Because she switched her path at an inopportune moment?"

"Because she cannot hold her attention to any tradition for any true length of time," Savahn immediately retorted. "I mean this as no insult, only as the truth. Brie finds focus as deeply—more deeply—than anyone I have ever known, but only until the wind blows a leaf in front of her eyes. She is scattered like those leaves. Her eyes, her heart, her thoughts, flitter on the gale and spin to new and wondrous places as they will. Every level of ascension here among the masters gets more demanding of full—full—dedication to the teachings, to the fighting movements, to the song of ki.

"Your daughter is not possessed of this personality or mentality. She wants to learn about everything all at once, then one thing—whether or not it is in her immediate interests—distracts her with the intensity of a hunting predator. Then another when she has eaten her fill, or simply lost interest in the previous course. Is she a fighting monk? Is she a swordswoman? Is she a budding priestess of this god or that goddess or is she a wizard acolyte? I have seen her playing with cantrips, using Prestidigitation to create little lights about the book when she is reading at night."

"That sounds useful," Catti-brie said.

"Until the lights start dancing to her motions of conducting them, as if they were her playthings or orchestra. And then, of course, the reading has stopped, unexpectedly, and so she must begin anew."

Drizzt rubbed his face and shook his head. There really wasn't much of an argument to be made against Savahn's description of his little girl.

"Brie—" Savahn began.

"Breezy," Drizzt corrected, and when both Catti-brie and Savahn looked at him in surprise, he merely shrugged and said, "It better fits."

"I hope you will not take this as criticism of Breezy," Savahn said. "She is as intelligent and talented as anyone I have ever known, and with a lust for life that I truly envy. But that is not what we do here. We hunch over books day after day. We train and train and train some more. Before you argue, or try to convince me otherwise regarding my decision, is that really how you see your dear Breezy spending her tendays, her months, her years, her life?"

A long pause ensued.

"Does she know?" Catti-brie asked.

"No."

"We will go and tell her, and collect her for the spell of recall that will take us all back to the west."

"No, I respectfully demand. This is my decision, and I should be the one to take it to Breez . . . to Superior Master Brie. I will give her a little more time to come to terms with her defeat before informing her of my decision. And that, I am afraid, is a final decision and one that I expect you to honor."

"So, we should wait?" Drizzt asked, and Savahn shook her head.

"No, you should go straightaway. The monastery will arrange for her transport back to Gauntlgrym, or Longsaddle, or wherever . . ."

"Longsaddle," Catti-brie decided, looking to Drizzt for confirmation. "She'll need time to come to terms—"

"Or wherever *she* chooses," Savahn said in a voice that brooked no argument. "Wherever she chooses," she insisted again when the surprised couple turned back to her.

Drizzt laughed, quite sincerely, and broke the tension. "Of course. It is indeed Breezy's choice to make. But I tell you, Grandmaster of Flowers, this is so hard."

"I wish you well," Savahn said, and both knew that she meant it.

BREEZY FELT MUCH BETTER WHEN she woke up the next morning. She had spent a long while in meditation before retiring for the day, and had used her monastic self-healing techniques and had even cast upon herself a pair of minor clerical spells of healing. Minor spells, indeed, for Breezy was much more accomplished in the arcane magic of wizards than in the divine magic of clerics. She vastly preferred the mage manner of study than the clerical teachings, and indeed didn't much care about Mielikki or any other goddess at this time. On those occasions when she had studied in Longsaddle, she hadn't spent much time or effort in Catti-brie's divine ceremonies or studies, either.

But she had learned a couple of minor spells of healing magic, at least, and they helped.

She got up and moved to prepare for the day, going first to her dresser to brush her light auburn hair back enough to keep it from falling in front of her eyes. It was getting lighter now, with as much white as red, and long, hanging to her shoulders. Breezy smiled when she noted that the natural highlights sparkled quite vibrantly with hints of violet.

Her left eye remained swollen and nearly closed. Just seeing it, she couldn't help but relive that shocking moment coming out of the shadow step right into Gregory's flying elbow.

She laughed at herself.

She had failed, but that was behind her, she decided. She'd know better next time.

She finished with her hair quickly, rubbed her hands briskly over her face, which hurt with every stroke, and grabbed up her tan trousers and shirt, throwing them on. She stormed out of her room.

No breakfast, she decided.

No morning meditation, she decided.

She moved determinedly along the corridors straight for the chambers of the Grandmaster of Flowers.

She would apologize to Grandmaster Savahn. She would ask for guidance—perhaps she should return to the monastery's predominant tradition, the Way of the Open Palm.

That notion stung her and slowed her steps. Shadows called to her.

But she had failed and had to correct that.

She wouldn't, she couldn't, fail again.

She didn't want to see that look of disappointment on the faces of her parents again.

Or had she imagined that look?

With a huff of anger, Breezy picked up her pace again. To her surprise, she was allowed right into the Grandmaster's audience hall, passing by the departing Master Perrywinkle, who shut the door behind him, leaving her alone with Savahn.

"You are moving quite well," Savahn said, motioning for Breezy to sit across from her. "I am pleased."

"I feel much improved and ready to continue my training," Breezy answered. "I wished to speak with you first—thank you for honoring me in allowing this audience."

"I've known you since you were a toddler, and care for you as if you were my own daughter. You need not be formal with me this day."

Breezy was quite relieved by that, but only for a moment. Then she found herself a bit confused, for never had Grandmaster Savahn spoken to her quite like that.

"I find myself at a crossroads," Breezy went on after collecting her thoughts a bit.

"You are indeed, and more than you understand."

Breezy nodded, then screwed up her puffy face as the weight of Savahn's reply fell over her. "I . . . I came for advice as I continue my journey here at the monastery."

Savahn raised her hand to interrupt. She cleared her throat and started deliberately, "Sister Brie . . . Breezy . . ."

A pause and a sigh.

"There is no easy way to say this. Your time at the Monastery of the Yellow Rose is ended."

Breezy fell back in her chair, eyes wide—or as wide as the swollen left eye would allow.

"You're throwing me out because I lost the challenge? Others have—"

"This is not your journey," Savahn interrupted. "Sister Brie . . . Breezy, dear young woman, I want you to look honestly within yourself now. Honestly. Listen to your heart and not your wounded pride. You are not of Saint Sollars the Twice Martyred and never will be."

"You knew that when I began my training! The agreement was made . . ."

"I did, and there are others here who are of similar agnosticism. Not being a follower of Saint Sollars is not in and of itself disqualifying from joining the Monastery of the Yellow Rose."

"But you just said . . ."

"Speak less and listen more and you will know exactly what I have to say, and the reasons for which I say it," Savahn demanded.

Breezy huffed and crossed her arms over her chest, but shut her mouth.

"If you were dedicated to Saint Sollars the Twice Martyred, you would wish to remain here."

Breezy started to interrupt, but Savahn was having none of it and stabbed her finger into the air to silence her.

"In that event, you would be content," the Grandmaster explained. "Without that fealty and faith to the holy Order we serve, you cannot be content here with your present station, and your present station is where you will remain." Savahn stood up and walked around the desk, settling on the edge of it right before the young woman.

"You will never ascend to where you want to be in this Order," Savahn said bluntly. "You are a Superior Master and that is no small thing. Not one in a hundred people could ever reach such a height as that. But this rank is not acceptable to you, and the height, the rank that would satisfy the fiery Breezy Do'Urden will not ever be attainable to you, I fear." She paused and allowed Breezy to interject.

"I could defeat either of the other two Masters of Dragons," she declared. "And I would not make the same mistakes in a rematch with Master Gregory. I could become one of the three this very year."

"Perhaps, and perhaps you would in time even find your way among the Masters of the Winds. Perhaps, but certainly no further."

The surety in her voice shocked Breezy to the point of taking her voice away. She sat there staring blankly at the Grandmaster and slowly shaking her head.

"Sister Brie, think hard and with all seriousness, I beg," the

Grandmaster began deliberately. "You are surrounded by heroes, by kings and queens, lords and ladies, and champions. The greatest heroes of the north, a collection of mighty mages in the Host Tower of the Arcane and in Longsaddle. Dwarf legends and warriors without peer."

"You tell me nothing I haven't been reminded of every day of my life."

Savahn shook her head and waved her hand vigorously, signaling to Breezy that she wasn't going down that all-too-well-worn path. "Who is the most formidable of them all, of all these great champions and heroes?"

Breezy stared at her blankly, her expression correctly reflecting the confusion of such a seemingly ridiculous question.

"Look at it this way, then," Savahn said. "Who among that group—pretend they are not your relatives and dear friends, nay! I ask of you to wear the mantle of a stranger coming into the north for a moment. Who among that group of heroes and champions and warriors and mages would most concern you if you knew they had decided that you were a sworn and mortal enemy?"

Breezy considered it for just a moment before blurting, "Uncle Jax."

"Jarlaxle?"

Breezy nodded.

"You are close to Jarlaxle, yes?"

"Uncle Jax? Of course."

"You like him? You respect him?"

Breezy stared, uncertain of Savahn's path here, but then nodded.

"Jarlaxle, your Uncle Jax, he has taught you much, I believe. He introduced you to the art of cave jumping, which we call freerunning."

"Cavern jumping, yes."

"Is he the best freerunner you know?"

"He's very good."

"The best?" Savahn reiterated.

Breezy shrugged. "No. My grandda Zaknafein is without equal, I am told, and my father is likely close in skill to Zaknafein now, after incorporating his training with Kane."

Savahn scowled, which confused Breezy for a few heartbeats.

"Grandmaster of Flowers Kane," Breezy quickly corrected. "My da can . . ."

"And tell me, is Jarlaxle the best swordsman you know?"

"He is very skilled with the—"

"The best? Better than Artemis Entreri?"

"I don't think so."

"Than your da?"

"No. By all that I have heard, my da is the finest swordsman in the north and beyond." She wanted to elaborate, but Savahn cut her short again.

"Jarlaxle dabbles in magic, of course. Is he the most powerful of mages? More powerful than your ma?"

"No," Breezy answered. "And no, even then. Gromph Baenre is the most powerful mage at the Host Tower of the Arcane, and in the entire north, I am told. His peers number very few. Elminster himself?"

"Is Jarlaxle the best thief? The best in all the fine skills of legerdemain?"

"Uncle Regis and Donnola Topolino are . . ."

"The best assassin?"

"Entre—"

"Entreri," Savahn flatly stated. "If an enemy needed to be quietly removed, Artemis Entreri would be the person for the task, yes?"

Breezy had to nod her agreement with that.

"Of all of your acquaintances, who is the most formidable, Sister Brie?" Savahn asked again.

"Uncle Jax," she answered, finally catching on, and Savahn shrugged.

"For all of his talents, all of his skills, and all of his considerable powers, Jarlaxle could never be the best here at the Monastery of the Yellow Rose. I doubt he would become a Superior Master, let alone train for the higher ranks."

"You underestimate—"

"I do not, and I defy you to ask Jarlaxle himself. He will tell you. He knows. For all his powers and talents, Jarlaxle would seek out every one of the many monastic traditions. He would grow bored with Open Palm, seeing the Shadows, as you have. He would explore the Long Death, the Way of the Kensei, the Four Elements—all of them. He would revel in their differences and flitter about them as if exploring a dining room filled with the sweetest desserts."

"Is that a bad thing?"

"No," Savahn answered emphatically. "But in terms of the Order of Saint Sollars and the climb through the ranks, it is certainly a limiting thing. And it is a trait that you and Jarlaxle share. Look into your heart. If I am correct in my assessment, would remaining here for years and years satisfy you?"

"You aren't correct."

"But I am, and I have no doubt of that. The progression of a monk slows greatly once they have moved into the challenge ranks, as you have now. To even qualify to challenge the Master of the North Wind, the ninth-ranked monk of the monastery, often takes several years as a Master of Dragons, and each successive rank requires even more years than that of training. Do you think it an accident that all the Masters of the Seasons and myself are thirty years your senior and more?

"The journey of a monk is a long and straight climb up the side of a towering mountain, but you, dear girl, take a meandering course. It is your way. You cannot walk a straight trail when the hoof marks of a deer would lead you astray, or a squirrel's chattering would invite you on a grand chase to catch the creature. This is not your journey, and the eyes-down, straight-line dedication of a monk will never be the path for Breezy, and it would madden you as surely as it would Jarlaxle!

"Some of the brothers and sisters here live for that discipline, for that prescribed and well-marked path up the mountainside. It brings them comfort and purpose and a profound sense of the highest achievement. But that's not you. No, no. Breezy will scout every trail, will know every ravine, will meet every animal, will learn the patterns of the seasons and relish every flower that blooms and catch every snowflake she can upon her tongue. Am I wrong here, Breezy? Answer honestly for the sake of your own life, because that is what is at stake here in the Monastery of the Yellow Rose. This is not a challenge of one battle after the next, nay! It is the journey of a lifetime and nothing less! To continue here, to ascend the ranks, means that *this*, this place, whichever tradition you choose forevermore, becomes the walk of your life. All of your life, to the exclusion of these side avenues. Forsake your studies of arcana, your dabbling in the manner of the divine magics, your sword fighting, your adventuring. Nay, none of that can remain. You become chained to the tradition, to the discipline, from this point forward. Is that really appealing to Sister Brie, to Breezy?"

The young woman stared blankly at Savahn.

"That is not who you are, Breezy. You are curious to the point of distraction."

Breezy felt the tears welling in her eyes—it wasn't so much that she was disagreeing with Savahn here. Quite the opposite! It was just the embarrassment of losing, the sting of failing yet again.

"I can be . . ." she started to reply, barely able to get the words out. "I would win my next fight, against any of the three. I know it."

Savahn looked down at her sternly.

"I . . . I . . . I can find focus when I need it."

"For years without fail? Our traditions are called Ways because they are indeed a way of life, all-encompassing."

"I . . ." Breezy lowered her gaze and exhaled.

"Your time here is done," Savahn insisted. "I am too fond of you to give you any chance at living what for you would be a lie. This is not about failure, dear, dear Breezy, but about philosophy." She ended with a soft smile that was both warm and sympathetic.

"My father could defeat anyone here in single combat," Breezy said.

"I don't doubt that."

"One day, I will be able to do the same," she vowed.

"I don't doubt that, either. But ascending the ranks of our Order is about a lot more than being able to fight."

"Yet that is how you choose the highest ranks of your Order!" she snapped, and it sounded quite clearly as an accusation.

Savahn just stared at her and sighed, and Breezy knew that her claim was beside the point.

"Go and collect your belongings that you wish to take with you," Savahn ordered. "Say your farewells if you desire, take your morning meal, and return to your room. I ask that you spend the day hearing again these words we have exchanged and honestly listening to that which is in your heart. My decision is final. Your time here is ended, for your own sake. I hope that you will be able to step far enough aside your pride to accept that now, as I know you will soon enough when these drab and dark halls are in your past and you are chasing squirrels freely among whatever next mountain—and there will be many!—you choose to climb."

Savahn stood up, then bent over and kissed Breezy on the cheek, then whispered some words of comfort, some platitudes, an invitation to visit.

"You will leave for Sudrav in the morning, and there catch on with a caravan that will take you to the Sea of Fallen Stars and a waiting ship. Your journey back to the Sword Coast is all arranged."

Breezy was too full of tumult and turmoil to pay attention. She was hardly even aware when Savahn went back around her desk and sat in her great chair, and Breezy jumped as if snapped out of a light sleep when Savahn said, rather loudly, "Take your time."

Embarrassed and full of anger, Breezy hopped up and gave a curt bow, turning and moving away before she even fully straightened.

She didn't go and get her breakfast but ran swiftly and directly back to her room. She stopped and gasped when she entered, for there on her bed lay the scimitar Icingdeath, the belt containing Taulmaril, its accompanying quiver of endless arrows, and the pendant holding the scrimshaw statue to summon the unicorn Andahar.

And a folded parchment, a note from her parents, she knew, and a long, long while would pass before she even gathered up the courage to approach it.

11

REDIRECTION

"She lost, badly," Tazmikella reported. The copper dragon was in her human form, appearing now as a handsome though plain-looking woman dressed in simple garb.

"She came out of a shadow to find an elbow waiting for her," her sister Ilnezhara added. Dressed in the clothing of a Waterdhavian noble, Ilnezhara assumed a very different aspect when out of her dragon form. Her hair was thick and long and vibrant, a mane of copper red, her stature imposing, dangerous, and undeniably sexy.

"Waiting perfectly," Tazmikella put in. "Almost as if this handsome Gregory creature knew exactly how the shadow step worked."

"He was well trained, obviously, sister," said Ilnezhara.

"Obviously," Tazmikella agreed, and both sisters settled their gazes upon the flamboyant mercenary leaning against the tree in the shadows of the small forest beyond the fields surrounding the Monastery of the Yellow Rose.

"You flatter me, I suppose," Jarlaxle dryly answered those looks. "Though I would prefer that any further such conversations are spoken only in the tongue of dragons."

The sisters giggled.

"He is concerned, dear sister," said Tazmikella.

"He should be."

"This was the preferred outcome, and not just for me," Jarlaxle assured them.

"But not for Drizzt Do'Urden and Catti-brie," Ilnezhara said. "Their mood when they departed this morning was dark. I could see that even from on high, circling the monastery."

"Dragons have such amazing sight," Jarlaxle remarked. "Apparently they can see emotions from a mile high."

Ilnezhara laughed at him.

"Oh, he knows," Tazmikella said. "He knew before it happened what the outcome would be. But he believes this is what is best, for that adorable little Breezy and for the monastery."

"And for Jarlaxle, of course."

"Ah, you wound me, Ilnezhara," Jarlaxle said.

"Not as much as Drizzt will," the dragon replied.

Jarlaxle shrugged and cast his gaze across the field to the dark walls of the great monastery. He wanted to remain outwardly confident, for he certainly wasn't going to give in to the chiding of the dragon sisters. If they saw his doubts, the two would play on them and heckle him forevermore.

And if this grand subterfuge with such unexpected and unlikely partners ended badly, these two would never, ever let him live it down.

"Does the girl know yet?" he asked, aiming the question at Ilnezhara, who had just come from the monastery.

"Likely. She was in with Grandmaster Savahn, if the whispers are to be believed. Or perhaps she spoke with her parents before they departed."

"She would have left with them, were that the case, would she not?" Tazmikella said.

"Probably not," Jarlaxle answered with a shake of his head, though his gaze never left the monastery's dark walls. He understood Breezy enough to realize that her failure would be multiplied in her own heart whenever she looked upon her champion father, as great a warrior as Menzoberranzan had ever produced, to say nothing of his exploits with Grandmaster of Flowers Kane, and her accomplished mother, who was, after all, the Chosen of a goddess.

It pained him to think of the emotional turmoil he was sure Breezy was feeling in this hour, to say nothing of the physical battering she had taken. The wounds to her body would heal, if they had not already, of course, but the other pain was one, he knew, that would follow her out of the monastery. Breezy had been forced to face her true image in the mirror, and it was not likely what she had expected.

He didn't like being the one to craft the mirror, but he remained very confident that it was a reflection young Breezy needed to see.

That pain would endure, and it was something that Jarlaxle felt compelled to channel into something powerful.

"Your plans for Breezy," Ilnezhara remarked. "Are you aware of the battle she found when King Bruenor's caravan was traveling through the pass to Icewind Dale?"

"Her training battles with her father and Wulfgar?"

"No, the real one, on the way to the dale and not the return."

Jarlaxle arched the eyebrow over his one uncovered eye and regarded the dragon curiously. "Now how would Ilnezhara know of such things?"

"We are dragons, Jarlaxle," Tazmikella said, as if that explained everything. "We travel great distances in a short time."

"And we know how to coax gossip from humans and halflings, dwarfs and elves."

And from drow, no doubt, Jarlaxle thought but did not say, and he made a mental note to have a word with Braelin Janquay, who had flown with Ilnezhara only days before.

"Yes, I have heard of Breezy's encounter rescuing the primordial essence from raiders on the road," he answered.

"Then you know that this latest trauma is not the first," Ilnezhara said. "I understand your designs for the girl—do you believe that she is ready for them?"

"Why, my dear Ilnezhara, I didn't know you cared so much for her."

"I speak for my sister," the dragon replied. "Taz is quite fond of Drizzt."

"You call her a girl, but she is a woman, grown and proud and extremely capable—more so than she even understands."

"But you will make her understand," said Tazmikella.

"I will have a lot of help, yes?"

The dragon sisters shared a smile.

"A lot of help and, should you anger Drizzt, perhaps you will need a quick escort far, far away," Tazmikella added.

Jarlaxle shook his head as if dismissing it all. Privately, though, he was doing no such thing. He knew about the battle in the pass and had heard whispers of how troubled Breezy had been. He knew he had to be careful here.

She sat on her bed staring at the belt, the quiver, the pendant, and the scimitar.

A belt that held a magical bow that was likely unequaled throughout the lands.

A quiver that would never run out of enchanted arrows.

A pendant that summoned a magical unicorn able to outrun and outlast the best of horses or any other mounts available to almost everyone in Faerûn.

A scimitar that had saved her grandda Bruenor from a keg of exploding fire, that had banished a balor, that had helped her father survive the frozen north for many years after he had taken it from the lair of a dragon he and Uncle Wulfgar had slain.

All of that sitting here, in her room, waiting to assist her.

She was looking at the naked truth, the undeniable privilege of her entire existence, she realized.

She thought of the brothers and sisters she had met here at the monastery. She thought of the stories, the circumstances, that had brought most of them to this place as a sanctuary of last resort.

Breezy swallowed hard in the face of that reminder—she had not done it on purpose, but she couldn't deny the truth to herself on this disorienting and disconcerting spring day: As much as she had tried to pretend otherwise even to herself, in her deepest heart she had thought herself better than them, than any of them.

Where had she gotten that attitude? she wondered. For she knew that her parents and grandfathers would not approve, and it was certainly not their way, nor the way of most of the other important people in her life.

"None of them," she whispered as the daylight waned, though she quickly corrected herself by adding, "Well, Gromph."

That brought a much-needed smile to her face, for the former Archmage of Menzoberranzan, now the Archmage of the Host Tower of the Arcane in Luskan, certainly thought himself superior to any and all, and he didn't try to hide it. Her little joke served as a very temporary reprieve, as it didn't diminish the painful truth she had learned this day. Among her peers at the monastery, she was the most battle-seasoned, certainly, and by a lot. She had killed monsters, she had killed a person. To believe that her heroics had saved Gauntlgrym, as her parents had reminded her in their last exchange, was not some outrageous exaggeration at all.

But these other brothers and sisters, almost—nay, likely—without exception, had faced trials of simple survival as children that she could not imagine. Had she ever felt the pangs of profound hunger in her belly when she was trying to fall asleep? Had she suffered the loss of a mother, a father, even both, like so many here, and at a young age of great vulnerability?

And yet, Breezy, deep in her heart and mind, had thought herself superior. As much as she had continually complained about the benefits constantly surrounding the granddaughter of a dwarven king, the daughter of a renowned champion and hero and a Chosen of Mielikki, as much as she had tried to distance herself from all of that, deep inside loomed a place, clearly, where she had internalized those benefits as earned, simply because of her own superiority.

What a lie!

She rubbed away her tears, but could not rub her face hard enough to straighten the swirling emotions.

She had to leave in the morning. Her time here was done.

No, she decided, it was *almost* done.

Breezy jumped up from the bed and moved for her overclothes, then laughed, changed her mind, and went out of her small room wearing nothing but the simple shift in which she slept.

She knocked softly on the nondescript wooden door, one just like her own, for rank mattered little in the living conditions at the monastery for all but the very highest levels. She heard a bit of a commotion within the room, someone fumbling about, saw a tiny light appear around the edges of the door and its bottom seam, then heard the wood creak in before seeing the backlit form of Master Gregory.

"Sister Brie?" he asked incredulously.

She watched his eyes shift down—even in the dim light of the single candle burning in his room, she knew that her slight nightgown was covering very little.

"Sister Brie," he said again, barely gasping out the words.

Breezy went up on her tiptoes, wrapped her arms about Gregory's muscular shoulders and neck, then whispered, "Don't tell Savahn," and kissed him deeply and passionately, and held for a long while against his half-hearted pushback.

She set down and bulled forward, backing him up and closing the door behind them with her foot, never letting go.

He grabbed her forearms to pull them away, but she went up again and kissed him.

She felt his resistance falling away. She felt his passion growing.

She pushed him back to his cot, which tripped him into a sit. She fell over him, kissing him over and over again, and he whimpered just a bit.

She pulled back just an inch from his face, locking stares with him.

"We cannot do this," he said, for of course such amorous exchanges were greatly frowned upon by the leaders of the monastery.

Breezy had no doubt here regarding the man's lack of conviction.

"Do you want me to leave?" she whispered teasingly.

He grabbed her hard by her thick hair, pulled her lips to his, then pulled her atop him as he lay back on the bed.

He fumbled about.

She fumbled about.

They didn't know what they were doing, but somehow, they figured it out.

The candle was burning very low when Breezy woke up in Gregory's strong arms. She slipped out of the bed quietly and slowly, then searched about in the near darkness to find her shift and managed to pull it on, though from the feel of the stitching, she realized that it was inside out, which made her giggle.

She felt light and full of life!

She understood that she had just explored one of those metaphorical valleys along the mountainside that Savahn had described to her, and this was a beautiful valley indeed, and one she intended to visit again quite often in the years to come—and she giggled again at the thought.

She cut that short, realizing she had awakened Gregory.

"Shhh," she whispered, and he groggily pulled himself up on one elbow. "Don't tell Savahn."

"What have you done?" he asked, and he looked all around for some reason, as if he expected some stern master scowling at him.

"What have *I* done?" she echoed with a little snort.

"What have we done?" he corrected, obviously alarmed. But it didn't last. He shook his head, and even in the dim light Breezy could see his anger.

"I offered to leave," she said into that scowl. "You didn't want me to leave."

"I . . ."

Suddenly, Breezy was the one scowling.

Gregory shook his head. "I don't want you to leave now!" he said, loudly, and he caught himself quickly and Breezy giggled, shushing him between and through her laughs.

Gregory certainly didn't think this situation funny at all, and his frenetic movements and clear panic only made it even more humorous to Breezy.

"What will happen if we must fight again?" he stammered. "How could I . . . how could you?" He stopped abruptly and stared at her hard.

"There will be no rematch," Breezy assured him. "I am expelled. I am out of the Order of Saint Sollars. I am out of the monastery. I came to say farewell."

Gregory gasped so hard that Breezy imagined that he might have swallowed his tongue.

"You cannot," he whispered.

"It is not my choice. I have been dismissed, without recourse."

"And you came here for this?"

"You have been very important to me these years," she replied, sincerely. "I wanted to say farewell in a way that I would never forget. And I will never forget this night, Gregory, nor, I hope, will you."

"The Grandmaster of Flowers must reconsider," he started to argue, but Breezy ended that debate.

"This place is not for me. Savahn is doing me a favor in showing me out to the wider world. I am not like you. Your path here is all but assured, with your single-mindedness and dedication to your studies."

"How can I possibly maintain that discipline now after this . . . experience?" he asked. "How can I maintain the focus to leap about high posts on the edge of disaster when the image of you and your beauty flashes through my thoughts? How can I do that knowing the joy? Needing the joy?"

Breezy flashed a wicked smile. "I am confident that you will find a way to exorcize your demons."

Even in the dim light, she could see that Gregory was blushing fiercely.

"You're welcome," Breezy said with a crooked little smile, and surprisingly, she found in her thoughts a picture of Jarlaxle's grin if he ever learned of her antics this night. She gave Gregory a mischievous little wink, then went and quietly opened the door.

"Brie, don't leave," he pleaded.

Breezy didn't look back, but said, "On the day you are named Grandmaster of Flowers—and I have no doubt that day will come—I will be here as witness, with respect and happiness for Grandmaster Gregory."

Breezy entered the dark hallway and closed the door. She truly believed her parting promise. Gregory had all the makings of a Grandmaster, all the traits, all the dedication, all the strength and graceful movements.

She knew he could get there, but Breezy knew, too, without doubt, that if she ever did fight Gregory again, she would destroy him.

He would hesitate.

She would not.

The eastern sky was beginning to brighten when she returned to her room. She sat there on her bed, staring at the belt, the quiver, the pendant, the scimitar.

Staring at the reality of her life.

Her fight, her failure, had upended that course indeed, but she felt a part of herself, deep inside, that was beginning to think that her defeat was not such a bad thing.

Her pride wouldn't let her fully hear that voice just yet, and her anger wanted her to just leave these magical items behind and rush out of this monastery forevermore—or at least until she had to fulfill her promise to Grandmaster of Flowers Gregory, should that ceremony ever come to pass.

The room brightened, the image of the four items coming clearer.

Breezy nodded—at them!—overruling her stubbornness. She rushed to clean up and get dressed, donning the clothes she had worn on her return to the monastery from Icewind Dale. She pulled her tan clothing of the Order of Saint Sollars—her breeches, shirt, robe, and cloak—from their neat piles in her small closet and threw them in a jumble on the floor.

She was out of the building at first light and summoned the unicorn Andahar on the porch.

She climbed up and smiled wickedly, wishing that she could command this wonderful magical steed to leave some road apples right before the door.

At her urging, Andahar leaped away.

Breezy didn't look back, nor did she turn east toward the trail to Sudrav, as Grandmaster Savahn had instructed.

She went west.

She'd find her own way.

GRANDMASTER SAVAHN CERTAINLY UNDERSTOOD AND sympathized with the emotional torment troubling the young man standing before her and Master Perrywinkle Shin, but she had to work very hard to suppress her amusement as the ridiculously repentant Master Gregory told them of his midnight adventure with Breezy.

More than once, Savahn shook her head and sighed, and realized that she shouldn't be surprised by Breezy's seduction of this man. It fit so well with the impetuous and adventurous young woman.

She looked to Perrywinkle, whose visage remained mostly stern, though whether that was an accurate reflection or not, she could not be sure.

"I should not have done it," Gregory said.

"Do you regret it?" Master Perrywinkle pressed.

"Ye . . ." Gregory hesitated, nodded, shook his head, and sighed heavily.

"Well, that's encouraging," Perrywinkle muttered.

"I will accept your judgment, of course," Gregory insisted. "I know that Breezy . . . Sister Brie, has left, and I will go, too, if that—"

"Is it our judgment you seek or your own?" asked Savahn.

Gregory didn't seem to understand, Savahn noted. He shuffled uneasily from foot to foot, seeming off balance both physically and emotionally. "I accept whatever punishment you think fair, of course, Grandmaster."

"Why should you be punished?" Savahn asked.

"What we did," Gregory stammered. "In the dark of night. The Order of Saint Sollars is about discipline and dedication. There was no discipline there, just a pursuit of—"

"Just a lesson, one of life," Savahn said. "But very well. As punishment, I sentence you to go and meditate, for the whole of this day. You are overwhelmed after so unexpected and powerful an encounter, and that so soon after so difficult a defense of your rank."

Gregory didn't move, other than to chew his lip.

"Go, young fool, before Grandmaster Savahn changes her mind and offers a more substantial punishment for your . . . transgressions," said Perrywinkle Shin. "You remain a Master of Dragons, and lo, there are no superior masters worthy of challenging. Look ahead!"

"I do not know if I can," Gregory admitted. "I cannot look anywhere without the vision of Breez . . . Sister Brie."

"Breezy," Perrywinkle insisted. "Just Breezy. She is no more of this Order."

"I am haunted by her," said Gregory. "By the image of . . . by the feeling of . . . I did not expect such intensity, such j—"

He bit the word off—the word "joy," Savahn realized, and she clenched her jaw so that she would not laugh.

Gregory took a huge breath and seemed as if he might fall over, so thoroughly flustered was he.

"Go and find your center," said Perrywinkle Shin.

"But my discipline . . ."

"Will return to you," Savahn insisted, and she forced a bit of stern disapproval to seep into her tone.

Gregory bowed several times before he finally reached and fled through the door.

"That girl, she is quite a marvel," said Perrywinkle Shin. "I wonder if Drizzt and Catti-brie truly understand that they have given birth to a succubus!"

"Why would you say such a thing?"

"Why do you think she went to him last night?"

"I know not, nor do you," said Savahn. "But I do know that she is a young woman, full of life and full of adventure."

"An adventure that leaves our young Master of Dragons haunted."

"Pleasantly so."

Perrywinkle Shin scoffed openly at that.

"You're jealous of him," Savahn accused, laughing. "Admit it, old Master Perrywinkle. How you wish you were decades younger and a woman as beautiful and formidable and full of spirit and health as Breezy Do'Urden came to you in the night!"

"Grandmaster!"

"What?"

"Surely you cannot approve of this licentious behavior!"

Savahn shrugged. "Our dear Breezy is not so little anymore. She is a grown woman, and Master Gregory is nearly halfway through his twenties. Is not joy a part of life, my dear Perrywinkle? Our stoic and stolid Master Gregory could use a bit of joy in his existence, I think. He is troubled now, but he will oft recall last night, I dare say, and will do so with a smile."

"And his tension? And his distraction? And his . . ."

"Guilt?" Savahn asked. "That will pass, of course, and we will offer no judgment beyond what has already been levied. For his . . . tension? I am sure he will sort it out." She was laughing then, and shaking her head.

"And what of Sister Brie?" Perrywinkle Shin shook his head, but very differently than the lighthearted manner of Savahn, and growled. "What of Breezy Do'Urden?" he corrected. "You seem almost pleased by this."

"Amused," Savahn corrected.

"Her parents are important to us. What will they think of this?"

"I am sure that if Breezy ever tells them, she won't care what they say," Savahn replied. "Is there, after all, a greater statement she might make to them that she is not a child anymore?"

Perrywinkle Shin rubbed his chin and muttered under his breath.

"Laugh about it, my friend," Savahn said. "Get past your jealousy!" She chuckled heartily at her own joke, which had Perrywinkle Shin harrumphing repeatedly.

"When you think about it, it is the perfect ending of Breezy's time in our Order," Savahn went on. "When we two are long gone, there will probably be a new tradition in the Monastery of the Yellow Rose: the Way of Breezy."

Despite himself, the crotchety old master couldn't suppress a smile at that.

Savahn laughed again, considering her own words. She thought that she should have predicted Breezy going to Gregory as her last act of defiance. She was indeed amused and admiring of the fiercely independent young woman, and she took hope that Breezy would find her way out from under the smothering wings of her many protectors onto a stage of her own making.

Savahn knew then without doubt that she had been correct in listening to Jarlaxle.

Andahar skidded hard on the sloping grass of the mountainside and reared when the great beast landed on the wide trail before them, rearing and roaring, spreading its leathery wings wide to block the way and sending its overwhelming trumpet out across the miles to warn every person, every animal, that a dragon had arrived.

The dragon's breath rolled over unicorn and rider.

Breezy tried to hold her seat, grasping the mane in both hands, but for some reason, she found herself moving more slowly. The surprised unicorn kept slipping and twisting, and finally, Breezy gave up and threw herself out wide to avoid being crushed under her mount. She hit the ground awkwardly, but recovered quickly and sprang right back to her feet. She lifted not her scimitar but her fist, and called not upon the belt buckle that would bring Taulmaril to her hand, but upon her voice.

"Tazmikella!" she yelled, and her voice was drawn out as her vocal muscles battled against the dragon's breath, a magical mist that slowed the movements of those it caught. "Did you have to do that?"

The dragon came down to all fours, tucked her wings in tight, and replied with a look that was truly toothy and terrifying—but that Breezy recognized as a smile.

"Where is he?" Breezy asked.

Tazmikella lifted a foreleg and began casually picking at her teeth.

"Jarlaxle!" Breezy yelled.

The trees lining the wide and sloping mountainside glade began to rustle. A moment later came the sister dragon, Ilnezhara, settling down gently on the field, Jarlaxle sitting astride her.

"You called?"

"What are you doing?" Breezy demanded.

"I? What are you doing? The trail to Sudrav is on the other side of this mountain, is it not?"

Breezy glared at him. She wanted to ask how he might know she was heading to Sudrav, or that she would be out at all today, but she dismissed the question.

He was Jarlaxle.

He would know.

"Why should I follow the commands of the Grandmaster who evicted me from her Order? Any authority Savahn had over me ended yesterday."

"Indeed, and does that trouble you?"

"It thrills me," she said, sarcasm dripping on every word.

"I think it does. Or think it should, at least. Did you really hope to spend the next years of your life trapped within that dreary monastery, focusing all your learning, all your training, all your improvement into such a narrow path?"

"I found a different path," she reminded. "And yes, one that interests me."

"And you think the Monastery of the Yellow Rose the best place to explore it?"

Breezy started to respond, but held back, caught by that question. She stared hard at the drow rogue.

"Have you ever met Lady Avelyere?" Jarlaxle asked.

Breezy considered it for a moment. "I think so, briefly, but even if not, I have heard of her."

"Your mother trained with her, indeed, perfected many of her wizardly skills from the lessons of powerful Avelyere."

"Yes," Breezy agreed, recalling that tale.

"She is not a shade, but she is Shadovar," Jarlaxle explained. "A Neth, who lived and taught at the Shade Enclave before its fall. She has traveled through the Plane of Shadow many times. She has breathed this substance you so long to explore."

"The Way of Shadow?"

Jarlaxle shrugged.

"To what end? I am no longer a monk."

"You have just illustrated why you are no longer a monk," said Jarlaxle. "You viewed your time there as a goal, not a journey."

Breezy spent a moment digesting that. "Goals are important."

"The journey is your life. That is more important. Now, dismiss Andahar and go to Tazmikella."

"Why would I do that," she impertinently replied. "I am now on a journey I choose."

"Because Lady Avelyere has agreed to teach you, and that is no small thing, and will be commenced at no small expense. The sooner you get to the Host Tower, the sooner you will begin the next part of your greater journey. As wondrous as Andahar might be, a unicorn is not about to match the speed of Tazmikella."

Breezy paused and looked around. She dismissed Andahar and moved to Tazmikella deliberately, looking back and locking stares with Jarlaxle every step of the way.

"No small expense?" she echoed, trying to focus her thoughts here.

Jarlaxle had already arranged all of this, but how?

It had been less than three days.

12

THE STUFF OF SHADOWS

Lady Avelyere was in her eighties, she had been told, and so Breezy was quite surprised when the woman who greeted her and Jarlaxle at the Host Tower of the Arcane in Luskan introduced herself as Avelyere. She looked no older than fifty, if that, with light gray eyes and brown hair, rich and dark and lustrous, and she moved with the limberness of youth.

"Is something wrong?" she asked, obviously noting Breezy's failing composure.

"I thought you were old," Breezy blurted.

Avelyere fell back a step. Jarlaxle laughed and said, "I told you."

"I mean . . ." Breezy fumbled, trying to recover.

"I am old, in the reckoning of human years," Avelyere said with a sly grin. "But I have breathed the shadows."

"The shadows?" said Breezy. "So, this . . . this youthful appearance, is not just some illusion, some trick of magic?"

Avelyere's eyes widened again, and Jarlaxle said, "I warned you."

"I would have thought that the granddaughter of a king, the daughter of nobility would have learned more tact," Avelyere said, and when Jarlaxle tried to intervene, she held up her hand to silence him.

"You do speak your mind," the veteran wizard added.

Breezy shrugged. "Jarlaxle intends to leave me here," she explained, "and does so with the permission of my parents, who are disappointed, I expect, from my failure at the Monastery of the Yellow Rose. He says you're going to teach me, and that I'll be with you for a long while."

"That is the agreement, yes," Avelyere confirmed. "The first part, at least. We shall see about the second."

"And only because of Lady Avelyere's great generosity in agreeing to the arrangement," Jarlaxle said pointedly, nudging Breezy with his elbow.

"I do not want to waste your time or my own," Breezy declared. "So yes, I do speak my mind, and I hope for the same from you."

"Humility, girl," Jarlaxle whispered, though of course Avelyere, too, could hear him.

"You may go, Jarlaxle," Avelyere said. "I do not wish to waste any time with this young woman."

"Reconsider, I beg," Jarlaxle said. "There is much here of substance in Breezy Do'Urden. She is worth your time."

Avelyere's face screwed up in puzzlement. "Oh, I see, you misunderstand me. *You* may go. Leave this one here in my care. I find that I am already quite fond of her."

Now it was Breezy's turn to widen her eyes in surprise.

Jarlaxle laughed, kissed Breezy on the cheek, bowed to Lady Avelyere, and left the private quarters of the Neth mage.

"Always tell me the truth, and I will return that respect," Avelyere told Breezy when they were alone. "I will show you to your chamber. It is modest, but comfortable. Organize it as you will. If you need anything, simply ask."

"When do we begin?"

"We already have. Your formal training will commence in a few days, after I have determined your present understanding of the shadowstuff."

Breezy waited a few moments, studying the woman, trying to wrap her head around the momentous events in her journey that had occurred so quickly and so unexpectedly. Just a tenday before, she had expected to defeat Brother Gregory Antoine and continue at the monastery as one of only three Masters of Dragons, only to find a flying elbow waiting for her as she stepped out her great play for victory.

"Do you know of the Way of Shadow in the great traditions of the monks?" Breezy asked.

"Not the particulars, but there is nothing regarding the shadow-stuff within that tradition that I wouldn't understand, I am sure. In the end, the monks perform with their will and determination the same actions that wizards perform with magic, and that clerics perform with the gifts of their respective gods. We are all wound into the same fabric, after all."

Breezy found herself quite intrigued by that last notion, one that she had entertained privately many times. She let Avelyere have the last word and followed the accomplished woman to her assigned quarters.

LIKE MOST PRIVATE QUARTERS OF the many wizards residing in the Host Tower, Lady Avelyere's consisted of a modest trio of rooms on one of the tower's tree-like branches, but with a door that led to a much larger extradimensional suite.

Avelyere showed Breezy the portal, and promised great things beyond, but explained that Breezy wasn't ready for that adventure yet. And so the eager young student spent many hours in a small study, hunched over spellbooks and scribing scrolls, and reading texts that attempted to explain the depths and substance of the Plane of Shadow.

Half of each day was dedicated to physical training, similar to her monk studies, followed by hours of practice in casting a simple cantrip, which Avelyere taught her to grant her insight into an opponent's defenses.

A noted practitioner of the wizardly School of Divination, Avelyere brought an entirely new perspective to Breezy's magical repertoire, and in an area of great utility in both combat and life. She learned to see the glow of magic, to smell the presence of poison or disease, to sense nearby fiends or undead or other creatures not natural to the Material Plane of existence.

Schooled by her mother in the arcane spells of evocation, Breezy had never given much thought to the insights of divination magic, but the sheer utility of Avelyere's lessons truly intrigued her, so much so that the tendays flew past, and indeed, Breezy was shocked to realize that more than two full months had elapsed, the summer half gone, before she finally moved through the tempting magical doorway into Lady Avelyere's true abode.

Gromph Baenre's extradimensional mansion was the largest and most magnificent home she had ever seen, of course, for Gromph was one of the most powerful wizards in the Realms. Breezy had visited that mansion twice, once with her parents and once with Jarlaxle, and had been delighted by his translucent magical servants, dressed in finery, serving conjured food that would make the greatest chefs of the lands proud. But for all the fine food, magical tricks, and sheer opulence, the expansive and decorated ceilings, Breezy found herself more enchanted by far with Lady Avelyere's comparatively modest extradimensional home. For this magical place was not a typical concoction of a pocket secluded in the multiverse. Avelyere's was a replica of—and was connected to—the Plane of Shadow.

Breezy loved the gloom and inhaled the shadowstuff with relish.

She was surprised at how much greater her understanding of shadow had become, and she could only imagine how much better she could utilize that understanding in a battle.

She thought of ways to foil Gregory and take him down but quickly dismissed that line of thought.

She wasn't a monk anymore. There would be no rematch. She grabbed at her thick hair, trying to digest all these dramatic changes. It wasn't frustration that came to her as she considered the loss of the Monastery of the Yellow Rose, however. She missed Gregory and some of the others, missed making Master Perrywinkle scrunch his face up in, by now, resigned disapproval. She missed the sparring sessions, the common meals—particularly those in which she could begin a food fight.

Yes, those memories were fond ones, but strangely, Breezy was no longer lamenting her expulsion. Grandmaster Savahn had been correct, she now believed, particularly since this new phase of her life with Avelyere held such promise, with goals attainable in the near term and not after she had spent her entire life climbing a single stair up Savahn's metaphorical mountain.

When she left the shadow pocket for the first time and retired to her small private room for the night, she was still considering those past days at the monastery, and recalling so vividly and pleasantly the night she had spent with Gregory. Breezy fell fast asleep with a warm smile on her face. Such pleasant dreams became a part of her routine. During the day, she worked with books, with ink and quill, and on her balance, striking, and tumbling. But all this she did for shorter periods now, as Avelyere took her into that shadow pocket more frequently and for longer durations, teaching her.

"Shadows across the world are not of shadowstuff except to those who understand the connection of those shaded areas to the Plane of Shadow," Avelyere explained when they entered the pocket dimension one day. "When you execute your monkish shadow step, you are really stepping into and out of the Plane of Shadow. It is a minor teleport, more a Blink or Dimension Door or Misty Step, to be sure, but that is essentially the magic you are using."

"Every time I do it, I grow more at ease with it," Breezy replied.

"Of course, but what you do not gain is a better understanding of the actual stuff of shadow, how to shape it, how to call its creatures to your side. This is the destination I intend for you in our lessons."

The lady stood very still and cast a spell, which Breezy recognized as some sort of detection magic. A moment later, Avelyere cast again, this time very clearly a spell of summoning.

Out of the gloom came a large hound, its shoulders nearly as high as Breezy's head, its form blurring with every movement as it shed shadows from its powerful frame. Breezy wasn't sure if it actually voiced a growl or if that was just some expectation being realized in her own thoughts, but either way, she found herself irrationally afraid.

The black dog walked up to Avelyere and sat obediently.

"The mastiff wants to know if I have brought you to it as a meal," Avelyere remarked, and only her lighthearted tone kept Breezy's knees from wobbling at the mere thought.

On Avelyere's whispered command, the dog moved over to Breezy and sat very still beside her.

"A diligent sentry when you sleep upon the open road, yes?" the lady asked.

Breezy thought of her beloved Guenhwyvar. How many times had she slept soundly under a starry sky, comfortable in the knowledge that Guen was standing watch? If she could call and control such beasts as this . . .

She nodded in agreement.

With a clap of her hands, Lady Avelyere sent the shadow hound bounding away, melting back into the gloom.

"Shadow has substance," she said.

"Was that creature a creation of shadow by you?"

"No. The mastiffs are quite common in the Plane of Shadow, and so they flitter about the Material Plane, their existence essentially the reverse of we who inhabit the Material Plane. They do not know how to cross those dimensional boundaries on their own, as you do with your shadow step, but they can come to a call. I sensed this particular hound nearby and bade it to my side. With my spells, I find allies in the darkness, and so will you."

Breezy nodded again, but couldn't keep the disappointment off her face.

"What troubles you?"

"Shadow has substance," Breezy answered. "To create such a companion from seeming nothingness . . ." She shook her head. "I thought that you meant that shadow had substance you could mold, not that there were beings within the shadows that you could summon."

With a grin, Lady Avelyere began casting once more. She reached her hand out into the darkness and began clenching and unclenching her fist, rolling her hand as if bringing more and more shadow-stuff into her grasp, the darkness deepening all about her hand.

Breezy blinked and fell back a step, startled, for Lady Avelyere was suddenly holding a sword that appeared to be fashioned wholly of shadowstuff.

"You have never seen this?" Avelyere asked, seeming surprised.

Breezy shook her head.

"It is not so difficult a dweomer," Avelyere explained. "Even a relatively inexperienced wizard—a conjuror or a theurgist—could create one. It is lesser used, I admit, for while it is a fine weapon, it is one for physical combat, and not one many mages, even those who sometimes engage in physical combat, would favor. I'm surprised that your mother has not shown you the Shadow Blade dweomer."

"This is the first I've seen of it," Breezy said, shaking her head but with her eyes never leaving the sword-shaped collection of deep shadow in Lady Avelyere's hand. "May I hold it and feel its balance?"

"You cannot," Avelyere said. "It is a creation of my magic and bound to me and my continuing magical attention. I could throw it at you, but you would catch it quite painfully, perhaps even mortally."

Breezy sighed but nodded, understanding.

"Again, it is little used, and it requires the full concentration of the wielder. As such, only a wizard interested in melee combat . . . or . . ." Avelyere reshaped the sword into a spear with a thought and launched it across the room.

Breezy watched it, her eyes sparkling even in the shadows, and then even more when she looked back to see the weapon re-created in Avelyere's hand.

"Or throwing as a missile," Avelyere finished. "And of course, there are better evocations to deal pain to your enemies."

"This is an evocation spell, then."

"No, an illusion, but an undeniable one. The shadow blade strikes with the fierceness of a mighty sword and the mind of the victim turns its psychic sting into physical trauma without fail. And woe to one battling this weapon in an arena of shadows, for they'll not see it coming half the time, offering great advantage to its wielder. It is far more difficult to block or parry a blade you can hardly locate!"

"It sounds marvelous on so many levels," Breezy said. "Yet little used? I do not understand. My mother is a fine warrior. Why would she eschew such a—"

"Because she is also a mighty priestess, and many of her greatest advantages in battle would come from the utility of divination to reveal weaknesses in her enemy. Or to grant added magical armor, or resistance to various elemental weapons like lightning or fire. The magical attention demanded by a shadow blade is complete. The wielder cannot maintain other spells which also would require such attention.

"Or perhaps Catti-brie simply never learned this one," Avelyere said with a shrug. "There are vast numbers of dweomers, after all. But this is one I think you will find most useful, so I will teach it to you in time, and you may share it with your mother."

"You said a beginning mage, even a mere conjuror, could cast it. I have achieved at least that much knowledge already."

"The more powerful you are, the more powerful your shadow blade can be," Avelyere explained. "I will show you, if and when I believe you are ready for it. Not before. You have much work to do."

"You tease me, then."

"I offer the secrets of creating a shadow blade as a reward for your efforts."

Breezy smiled, her gaze still locked upon the weapon her teacher held, which then winked out, though from the limit of the dweomer's duration or from its dismissal by Avelyere, she could not tell.

"Come," Avelyere said, leading her back to the door that would take them into the Host Tower on the Material Plane. "Your next lessons will be in divination magic that will allow you to sense the presence of creatures from the Plane of Shadow." She paused and smiled wickedly. "But I warn you not to experiment with such summoning. Shadow mastiffs are always hungry."

From her many months in the Ivy Mansion of Longsaddle, Breezy was quite familiar with the tedium involved in learning spells, particularly those dweomers which were not in her school of greatest proficiency.

She reminded herself constantly that Jarlaxle had brought her to this mentor, and he wouldn't have done so if he didn't see the value.

Value like creating a shadow blade.

The mere thought of the shadowy, malleable weapon brought a grin to Breezy's face. She had several spells, arcane and divine, in her repertoire, and she had found a couple to be quite useful and expedient. She could throw missiles of pure magical energy that would unerringly strike and sting a foe. She could produce balls of flame that she could hurl at enemies or at flammable items to ignite them. She could add a bit of shocking energy to her hand, even, to slap and sting an opponent.

But none of them, nothing she had learned, had ever tickled her imagination like that summoned sword of shadow.

Breezy did not want to be a wizard, standing back behind the heat of battle, launching magical bombs. She did not want to be a cleric, moving to heal fallen comrades while the battle still raged—and also because, like her father, she wasn't sure there was a god among the pantheon worth worshipping. She greatly doubted that she could ever bring herself to believe in the gods as anything more than meddlesome higher beings.

No, Breezy loved the smell of the fight, the confusion and immediacy of melee. While she hadn't much enjoyed killing a reasoning being like the drow she had shot with a hand-crossbow on her way to Icewind Dale, she held no such reservations about the many monsters of the world, creatures she had battled even years before when she had secretly slipped away from her teachers at the monastery and gone out on the road of adventure.

The only thing that had kept her sane in the Monastery of the Yellow Rose, she now understood with that experience forever behind her, was the promise of challenging a higher master to take their rank.

She returned her thoughts to the present. A shadow blade would put her in the heat and frenzy of the fight, where she belonged, where her instincts would give her the biggest chance of victory.

So, she worked. So, she studied. So, she practiced Avelyere's dweomers repeatedly and with all her heart until the lady nodded in satisfaction and moved on to the next one. Breezy wasn't happy, though, with the sheer amount of time involved—hours that she couldn't spend in training her fighting techniques.

Breezy began getting up earlier in the morning and falling right into her monk practice, maintaining that muscle memory of striking and blocking, turning her tight-muscled frame with grace and speed. She took care to hide this from Avelyere, though, for the great lady was a wizard, just a wizard, and though Avelyere could bring forth the shadow blade, in watching her movements with it, Breezy had come to understand that Avelyere wasn't very good at wielding it. Breezy saw that clearly on the first occasion, particularly when Avelyere had thrown the improvised weapon across the room.

"But I will be," she told herself every day, chasing away the exhaustion building from her secret double training.

Driven by the belief that she could someday make a weapon suitable to her skills instead of borrowing Icingdeath or Twinkle, Breezy flourished. The tendays flew by, so quickly that she was truly surprised when she learned that the autumnal equinox was nearly upon them.

"Your parents wish for you to return to Gauntlgrym in five days' time," Avelyere informed her one late summer day. "I do believe that they are traveling north for some event. I have heard the name cazz-something."

"Cazzcalci," Breezy explained, nodding. On the one hand, she was excited by the thought of returning to Callidae, and even more so of seeing Grandda Zaknafein again. He would fight in that blood-sport event, no doubt, along with his beloved Azzudonna, an aevendrow woman Breezy truly admired. But on the other hand, Breezy didn't want to be away from her studies. Not now. Not when she felt like she was finally breaking through the milestones Avelyere had set for her in order that she might gain her reward.

She smiled, then frowned, but a moment later, Lady Avelyere handed her a scroll tube that took the frown away.

"Scribe this into your spellbook," she said.

Breezy held the tube in a hand that began to tremble.

"A new cantrip?" she asked.

Avelyere laughed. "You have all the cantrips you need, and all the minor dweomers that you'll ever use."

"Is this . . . ?" Breezy asked.

"I promised to teach you the Shadow Blade spell when you were ready. You are ready. Now, go and take your time—my servant brought the ink and quills to your room while we were here training. Take your time. Let not one symbol be entered in less than a perfect manner. This will be among your most-treasured dweomers, my dear Breezy. Of that, I am certain."

"When can I first attempt to create a shadow blade?"

"Not until you have shown me the completed page in your book. It is not so powerful a spell, and I see the gleam in your purple eyes, so I expect that you will work straight through the day, and I will see you again at suppertime, spellbook in hand."

"You are going to Callidae with them?" Braelin Janquay asked Jarlaxle that very same day.

"Cazzcalci alone is worth the journey," Jarlaxle answered. "No matter how many times I see it, I find it hard to catch my breath with the onset of each match."

"Perhaps Jarlaxle should join a team, then," Braelin teased.

"It is an all-encompassing endeavor. Zaknafein and Azzudonna train with the other members of the Whitebears throughout the year, and all for one moment of glory under the Merry Dancers as the north's single day turns into a half year of night."

"It is hard to imagine, all of it," said Braelin.

"I also wish to look in on the udadrow refugees from Menzoberranzan who have thus far been allowed passage to the aevendrow enclave," Jarlaxle explained. "All is well, from what I have heard, and it is possible that our friends in the far north will accept as many as a hundred new refugees before the end of this year. The physical borough of Cattisola is nearly fully reclaimed from the ice now, and our friends in the northland city have more room. Indeed, this very year will be the first in memory where the borough of Cattisola enters a team into the Cazzcalci competition, and many of our kin and kind, I am told, will fight for that team."

"I would love to witness such a thing."

"Oh, did I not tell you? You will. I need you there. The Companions of the Hall are all coming, along with some select others, including Breezy. I want you with her up there. I want to know her every movement."

Braelin leaned back and studied his boss carefully. "You fear that she will decide to stay," he said at length.

Jarlaxle laughed at that, but nodded. "Such unexpected moves by that one are always to be feared. And I'll not have it. I have spent too many favors and too much politesse in bringing dear little Breezy to this point."

"If her parents knew of your machinations . . ."

"They do not, and they won't. But they know that I am guiding her, or at least that I am aiding her on her journey, as her heart leads her. They know that she is happy and trust me enough to make sure that she is properly looked after."

"You will always keep her under your protective wing?"

"She wouldn't be much use to Bregan D'aerthe were that the case, would she? And Breezy—ah, Breezy—would hate me if I tried, and hate her parents if they made me try. She is going to make her way, and woe to any who stand to block her."

"You truly believe that she is a special one, don't you?"

"I couldn't love her more if she were my own daughter, Braelin Janquay—and that is something you should always keep in mind when you're dealing with her, particularly on those long tendays when you might find yourself alone with her."

That set Braelin back on his heels, but just for a moment, when Jarlaxle's grin showed him that his fatherly warning was more bark than bite.

"If you fear that I would take advantage of the young woman, remember that we're speaking of Breezy here. Perhaps you should be worrying that she will take advantage of me. After all, she is more like you than she is her own father."

"I suspect that she will surpass us both, in skill and in audacity. When we return from Callidae, remind me to tell you of poor Master Gregory."

"Gregory? The monk who defeated Breezy?"

"So he, so we, believed," Jarlaxle said with a chuckle.

Braelin's face screwed up with confusion at that, which made Jarlaxle chuckle again and shake his head.

Braelin had seen that expression of helpless exasperation so many times in conversations regarding the daughter of Drizzt and Cattibrie.

So full of life, that one, he thought and sighed.

Lady Avelyere had finished her supper by the time Breezy walked into the dining area.

"I took my time," the student said. "It wasn't easy, but I took my time."

Avelyere wiped her lips with a napkin, then prompted, "And?"

Breezy took a deep breath and quietly began whispering as she held out her right hand toward the nearest shadow. She called to the shadowstuff and brought it streaming to her hand, bit by bit.

She felt the darkness growing there, elongating, taking shape to her call.

She held a sword, a sword of shadow, a shadow blade.

"Well done!" Avelyere congratulated and clapped her hands.

Breezy smiled, but only briefly, as she moved this initial shadow blade about. "It feels strange."

"A shadow blade is all but weightless, and you are used to swinging a scimitar. Icingdeath, I believe, and even with its enchantments and magical balance, a metal scimitar weighs a pound or two more than that which you now hold."

"But this lighter weapon doesn't feel as powerful."

"Its power is psychic, as I told you," Avelyere reminded. "If you strike someone with that weapon, they will be viciously wounded, I assure you, even if the cut shows only as a shadow across their skin."

Breezy nodded, having no choice but to take Avelyere's word for it. "It does not feel as powerful as Icingdeath or Twinkle," she did mutter, disappointment evident.

"As you become more powerful, you will be able to upcast the dweomers and inject more magic into the blade. Practice and study, Breezy. As in martial training, as in monk training, there are no shortcuts in wizardry. But now you have reached a tangible goal—you hold it in your hand. You have learned a truly brilliant spell that may well follow you through your life journey, serving you ever more powerfully at every point along that trail."

Breezy nodded, though her thoughts were moving to a different place as the shadow blade demanded her concentration. She thought of other spells she might use in a fight, like magic armor or dweomers of heroism. She couldn't maintain the enchantment of either of those with a shadow blade in her hand.

She wondered the value of this prize then, but only briefly.

For then she looked at the sword of darkness in her hand. Her creation, *her* weapon, and she thought it a beautiful thing.

PART THREE
DANCING ON THE EDGE OF DISASTER
LATE SUMMER, DALERECKONING 1509

He couldn't fathom it.

For all the goodness within his heart, and it is considerable—truly, my grandda Bruenor is one of the warmest, kindest, most generous people I've ever known— he simply could not anticipate, comprehend, or accept the choices made by the people of Icewind Dale, even though to me, with far less worldly understanding and experience, the reaction from the folk of the dale seemed rather obvious and predictable. Grandda Bruenor has his own perspective, and I think he was all too quick and self-centered to judge the people of Ten-Towns without really seeing the other side of it.

Their side of it.

Perhaps this strange and unexpected clarity was precisely because of my lack of experience. Perhaps it was because I didn't just know the way things had to be—and had to be simply because that was the way they always had been. So, seeing the resistance in Icewind Dale wasn't as steadfastly against the normalcy ingrained in me.

Those in the dale didn't want to be ruled. Not by him,

a kind and generous and benevolent king, and not by any-one. Almost all of the people living in Icewind Dale are there by choice. Only the Reghedmen tribes have true roots there. Whatever the reasons varied folk have had for traveling to and making their homes in Ten-Towns, the common cause is freedom. Freedom that is nearly complete. Existence in a place where the only real rules of governance are to not impinge upon, to not hurt, others. And the only duties are personal, or at least, personally chosen.

They are under no obligation for even common defense, although, as with the Callidaeans in the farthest north, when you live in a land that wants to kill you, you usually come to understand the personal benefits of such a community mindset when it's truly needed.

They can hunt, fish, and grow their own food if they so choose, and be completely self-sufficient—many are! Or they can work some trade they love to barter, or earn gold, to take care of their basic needs.

There is no MUST to the settlers of Ten-Towns.

I do not say this wistfully, or with any longing to live my life there, though I hope to visit often. The other side of that philosophy is that there is no Feather Fall to catch you when you plummet. Most people who die in Icewind Dale do so alone and are found later, sometimes much later. Oftentimes not at all.

Those who live there, even the dwarfs of Clan Battle-hammer who choose to stay at Kelvin's Cairn, value above all else their own choice in every matter. Not all of them, of course, but surely enough of them to reject the notion of a magical gate that could bring an army so quickly to their homeland, even a force that could support them.

I wonder if this is the distinguishing feature of all cities and all lands and all cultures. They are a spectrum of authority, either through religion or system of governance, or tradition. A king or a council can both be tyrannical, of course, though I believe the former more likely than the latter.

I imagine that more of the dwarfs here in Gauntlgrym would prefer to live in Gauntlgrym as opposed to Icewind Dale. Clearly, they see the world differently than Stokely Silverstream and Holiday and the like, for if not, Grandda Bruenor would certainly allow them to leave, to Icewind Dale to go wherever they so chose.

Perhaps the biggest decisions before me as I shape my own way of things, then, is to find where on that spectrum of commitment, allegiance, community, and individuality I most comfortably, and most happily, fit.

Now that the embarrassment of my defeat is gone, I am truly glad to be out of the Monastery of the Yellow Rose and the rigid Order of Saint Sollars. So glad! I was suffocating there. I was studying in anger as much as joy, because what I really wanted to do was beat the monks at their own way of life. What a terrible Grandmaster of Flowers Breezy Do'Urden would have been. Saint Sollars, whoever they might have been, would have come back from their resting place and punched me in the nose, I'm sure!

Maybe that's why I felt so entranced by the Way of Shadow tradition. It was starkly different from the traditions of my monk brethren, and a place for me to hide away from their demands.

The monks always speak of discipline.

I speak of joy.

And this need for resolute dedication goes far beyond the monks, I know. They all speak of discipline—the monks, the priests, the wizards, the warriors. Discipline, training, order, practice, repetition.

Do they ever have time to live, I wonder?

—Breezy Do'Urden

13

TOP OF THE WORLD

Breezy's heart soared when her group exited the huge building dominating the Mona Chess borough in Callidae. She stepped into the brilliance of the ice canyons. They were under the low-riding sun of mid-Eleint, the ninth month of 1509. Eleint the Fading, this time of transition was commonly called, with the autumnal equinox fast approaching.

"There is something so wonderful about the cold air and brightness, but I do look forward to the change," Breezy said to the aevendrow beside her, the young but accomplished wizard Allefaero, who had teleported the eight visitors from Gauntlgrym to the appointed reception room in the heavily guarded bowels of the Siglig, the glacier city's seat of power. "But I do look forward to the sunset."

"That solemn moment when the sun goes to her winter's sleep," Allefaero happily and wistfully agreed. "The one true sunset of the year. Quista Canzay, we call it, and for we who witness this transition only once a year, it is a time of great reflection."

"And a time to beat each other senseless, eh?" Bruenor interjected, drawing a laugh from Regis and Wulfgar.

"Cazzcalci reminds us that we live on the edge of disaster and must be ever vigilant," Allefaero told the dwarf.

"Aye, and it's load o' fun, no doubt," said Bruenor. "Yerself and yers should really let me bring a team o' Pwent and his boys up here to show ye what real mayhem's lookin' like."

That brought chuckles from the others of the group, Drizzt, Catti-brie, Jarlaxle, and Braelin Janquay, and wary looks and resigned sighs from the nearby Callidaeans.

"That'd be worth a watch," Bruenor declared.

"Someday, then, perhaps," Allefaero replied.

"Oh, don't give him hope, young fool," said Jarlaxle. "Callidae would never be the same, even if it somehow managed to survive."

"Aye, that crew'd crack the glacier," Bruenor said with a hearty howl.

"Where might we find Zaknafein?" Drizzt asked as his own laughter subsided. "Will he be at his training?"

"You won't find him for much of the day, I am sure," Allefaero replied.

"When Cazzcalci is this near, the warriors seclude themselves," Jarlaxle agreed. "I expect that Zak will find his way to the Temple of Eilistraee in the borough of Scellobel at some point."

"He will certainly remain in Scellobel," Allefaero said. "The members of each fighting team do not venture out of their home boroughs this near to the grand melee."

"To the temple, then," Catti-brie said.

"To the inn of Ilbistato first," Jarlaxle suggested. "Let us secure our rooms and drop our traveling gear. It would not be friendly of us to parade about this wondrous city carrying weapons."

"So says the rogue who'll be carrying the most weapons and tricks of all, and hidden away for none to see, don't ye doubt," said Bruenor.

Jarlaxle tipped his hat at that compliment.

"I'm guessing ye could put a pile o' catastrophe to bury me axe and shield, Drizzt's blades, Wulfgar's hammer, and Rumblebelly's rapier and dirk, eh? But I'm bettin' more that ye won't."

"You wound me, good dwarf."

"Many's the times I've wanted to."

The good-hearted banter continued all the way out of the borough of Mona Chess and down the long ice tunnel that would bring them to Scellobel, the largest and most populous of the city's five boroughs.

Breezy walked near Allefaero, occasionally engaging him in some small talk, but more just listening to the back-and-forth among the other seven of their party. Despite her determination to strike out on her own and make her own way in the world, she understood that there was something quite special about the friendship among her parents and their three longtime adventuring partners, Bruenor, Regis, and Wulfgar. These five, the Companions of the Hall, had so many tales to tell, could finish each other's sentences, and would, any of them, die for another of the group. Even with that, however, they were more than happy to fully let Jarlaxle into their circle, and even Artemis Entreri, who had been invited, but had decided not to make the journey north.

She knew a lot of that acceptance and trust had to do with the influence of her parents. Drizzt and Catti-brie cared only about the content of a person's character, believed in redemption and second chances, and gave great trust when trust was earned.

She tried to see them in that light now, to give them due credit, and not to judge them under the cloud of protectiveness they had used to smother her.

She knew that they loved her.

But how they annoyed her!

Breezy viewed the aevendrow beside her, however, in a very different light. She was always happy to be around the awkward Allefaero, a man so brilliant in his books, yet quite clumsy in his interactions with other people. She knew that he fancied her, for she could make him blush with the slightest of winks.

"I've learned a new spell," she told him after an hour of walking in the tunnel, still a long way from Scellobel. Breezy had slowed her pace, Allefaero staying with her, and the others moving many strides ahead at this point.

"Have you?" Allefaero replied.

Breezy could see that the wizard was trying very hard to sound impressed. Allefaero could learn a new spell every hour of every day if he so desired, she knew.

"Yes, my favorite of all," she said.

That seemed to pique the wizard's interest.

Breezy rubbed her hands together and began calling to the nearest shadows. She grabbed at their substance and shaped it in her thoughts, bringing forth a dark sword a few heartbeats later.

"Shadow Blade," Allefaero said immediately, and Breezy's smile disappeared, though when she thought about it, she realized that his familiarity with a supposedly rare dweomer should not have surprised her.

"A fine spell," the wizard quickly added.

Quickly, she realized, because Allefaero had recognized that his lack of surprise had disappointed her.

"Few can cast it," Allefaero stuttered, trying too hard.

"Few choose to cast it," Breezy corrected. "And fewer still bother to scribe it into their spellbooks and waste the precious ink and pages."

"Well, it is a bit of a specialty spell," said Allefaero. "A lightning bolt can be thrown at a great distance from the danger of sword fighting, and that removed position is where most wizards prefer to stand."

"To hide, you mean," Breezy teased.

"But it is a fine spell, nonetheless," Allefaero went on, "and one that will grow more powerful as you grow more—"

"I know," Breezy interjected.

"And you like it?"

"I do indeed," Breezy admitted, and, strangely, she realized, as much to herself as to him. "It fits me. It fills in well with the Way of Shadow, the monk tradition I was studying at the Monastery of the Yellow Rose."

"Ah, even better for you. Do you wish to follow more your mother, then, and become a great wizard? I had thought you more in the way of your warrior father."

Breezy shrugged. "Yes, both of them, I guess," she said. "When battle is joined, I expect to be in the melee, not standing behind the line of warriors throwing bolts of lightning and the like."

"In the melee, shadow blade in hand," Allefaero said with a smile.

Breezy shrugged again. "Perhaps. I am sure that you could create one far more powerful than I."

"I cannot cast the spell."

"You knew of it."

"I know almost all of them, I believe. Or at least, *know of* almost all of them. I have not scribed this one in my book." Allefaero grinned sheepishly. "I throw lightning bolts."

Breezy laughed.

"But you," the wizard continued, "for all of your martial training, you still study the arts arcane?"

"There is great utility there, even for a swordsman or a monk, I believe."

Allefaero nodded with every word. "Moreso, perhaps, than you truly understand," he said, but waved his hand when Breezy moved to dig down deeper on the promising remark.

"There is . . ." Allefaero then said, "there is possibly something much more to this combination of melee and arcane." His gaze seemed to drift off into the distance and he unintentionally chewed his lip.

Breezy studied him curiously. "What do you know?"

"Perhaps nothing," Allefaero replied. "But let me check my sources, and if I find something which might be of value to you, I will most assuredly bring it to you."

Breezy kept staring.

"Will you be going to Cazzcalci to watch Zaknafein's battles?" Allefaero asked, clearly trying to change the subject. His sudden fidgeting that accompanied the question hinted at something more than simply a deflection. And as soon as he had completed the ask, the wizard seemed to emotionally deconstruct, just for a few moments. It was, after all, a fairly stupid question, since he had teleported Breezy and the others to Callidae for exactly that reason.

He was trying to segue the question to another one, Breezy knew, although the thought of continuing down this line was obviously terrifying to him.

"I was considering it, yes," she said dryly, and before Allefaero could more completely decompose, she added, "Would you go with me and sit with me and explain the battle on the rink below us?"

Allefaero stuttered many times.

"I haven't watched this strange bloodsport for several years," she continued, "and the rules remain rather . . . abstract. I could use a guide, and more than that, I would welcome a companion."

Allefaero nodded.

"Good!" Breezy said. She nodded her chin ahead—the others were now out of sight around a bend far ahead.

She grabbed Allefaero's hand. "Come, let us catch up."

And she led him away.

She thought to kiss him, but figured that if she did, he'd probably faint away and she'd have to carry him all the way to Scellobel.

"Shouldn't you be training and sweating with your fellow Whitebears?" Jarlaxle asked from behind the kneeling Zaknafein, startling his friend from his prayers. They were in the circular gazebo of the temple to Eilistraee, the Dark Maiden. More a sculpture than a structure, it was set against the canyon wall in Scellobel, open and inviting to all, though few Callidaeans accepted that invitation. Fewer now, given the losses among this group in the war in Menzoberranzan, and the loss, most of all, of Holy Galathae, who had been Eilistraee's most prominent missionary in the city.

The weapons master looked up, staring straight ahead, sighed and chuckled, then slowly turned to regard the rogue.

"So, you decided to join us for the celebration this year," Zak said. He stood up and stretched—clearly, he had been in that kneeling, head-down position for some time—then turned about and moved to join Jarlaxle in a great hug.

"I had other business up here," Jarlaxle answered.

"Causing trouble, no doubt."

"My reputation precedes me," Jarlaxle said with a bow. "That can be an advantageous thing or a troubling one, but in this case, it is simply incorrect."

"You would claim that in any case."

"Not with you, old friend. Were I here to cause trouble, I'd have long ago enlisted your aid."

They both smiled at that.

"Just to watch me and Azzudonna reclaim the title we lost last year, then?"

"Other business," Jarlaxle repeated. "Though, yes, I was surprised to learn that the Whitebears had been dethroned."

"We suffered injuries to some important teammates, including Azzudonna," Zak explained with a shrug. "And we lost three members of our team to the new participants from Cattisola, for they traced their family histories back to that long-lost borough."

"I had wondered if you, too, might join that borough. Most there are udadrow, and from families you knew well from your days in Menzoberranzan."

"This is my home," Zaknafein insisted. "Perhaps the first true home I have ever known. Azzudonna was born in, raised in, and has always lived in Scellobel, and she would no more fight against Biancorso than you would fight against Bregan D'aerthe. Aside from all of that, there is a member of House Do'Urden fighting for Cattisola."

"Dinin, yes," Jarlaxle said.

"I have no desire to see him or train beside him," Zak admitted. "There are too many terrible memories there. He is changed, yes, but I do not need that constant reminder of a time I prefer to forget."

"Drizzt feels the same way," Jarlaxle noted.

"And my temple is here, in this borough," Zak added. "And here I belong."

"Never did I expect that Zaknafein would fall under the spell of a goddess," Jarlaxle said, almost snorting as he spoke the last word.

"Lolth is a demon, nothing more. Eilistraee—"

Jarlaxle held up his hands to stop Zak. He patted them in the air, formulating his response, then simply said, "I am truly happy for you."

Zak's smile was sincere. "Fear not, my friend. I'll not proselytize to you."

"To me?"

"To any," Zak clarified. "You find it in your heart or you do not."

Jarlaxle let it go.

"What other business brings you so far north?" Zak asked.

"Your family. I have been quite involved in redirecting your granddaughter, you see, after the disastrous loss that she suffered."

"Her loss, yes. I have heard a bit of it. She is out of the monastery forever, then?"

"So it would seem, and yes, forever, if I have any say. Breezy was never meant for the life of a monk."

"Breezy?"

"Breezy. That's her name now, given by Pikel Bouldershoulder as *Bweezy,* I believe."

"I remember, and yes, I think it was Pikel," Zak said. "The nickname of a child, though."

"Where her heart will ever remain."

That made Zak smile even wider. "She's here in Callidae, I am told, but I haven't seen her yet."

"You'll be proud. The promise is . . . great."

Zak nodded. "Do you intend to leave her here with the aevendrow?"

"No, not for now, at least. She has come to Callidae to simply relax and enjoy Quista Canzay and Cazzcalci. To watch you and Azzudonna lead Biancorso, the famed Scellobel Whitebears, to glorious victory," Jarlaxle said dramatically. "But there are a few pieces of business for me here as I help guide her along the next steps in her most interesting journey, I expect."

"You guide her, yes. Always some gain in it for Jarlaxle, I suppose."

Jarlaxle didn't fully deny that, but said, "I guide her because I love her as if she were my own daughter."

"And manipulate her for her own good?"

"You have grown more cynical in your newfound faith, I see."

"I knew these truths of Jarlaxle long before I had ever heard the name of goddess Eilistraee. You have plans for Brien . . . Breezy, no doubt, and those would involve serving you."

"I have opportunities for Breezy," Jarlaxle corrected. "And I will present great gifts to Breezy." As he finished, he nodded toward the large blue-white sword in Zaknafein's hand. "Bluccidere, is it?"

"Bluccidere the Avenger," Zak said. "A holy sword, and a finer weapon than anything I have ever held."

"A bit too large to be paired with a second weapon," Jarlaxle observed. He knew that Zak had been using this sword as companion to the light blade he had given to his friend, a marvelous combination of sword and whip—and a whip so powerful that it could cut lines into the elemental Plane of Fire! Allefaero had informed Jarlaxle that Zaknafein was no longer using that magnificent weapon, which he had named Soliardis.

In response, Zak grabbed the bracer on his left arm and turned it, which unwound it into a glowing, shimmering buckler that seemed to be made of magical energy alone. Zak then lifted Bluccidere in both hands, which comfortably and easily fit on the leather-wrapped long grip of the weapon.

"You've changed your fighting style," Jarlaxle remarked.

"A bit. The monsters I battle up here, frost giants and slaadi, hit rather hard. The shield is heavily enchanted and a most welcome mitigation from the weight of those strikes."

"You might still use Soliardis, which weighs little."

"Yes, but I have unlocked Bluccidere's true powers, and the sword itself wishes for no second."

"The sword told you to get rid of that glorious weapon I gave to you?"

Zak laughed at the bluntness. "Bluccidere is very convincing, and when I swing it with both hands, I can cut the legs off a frost giant! My enemies feel a bite like no other." He winked at Jarlaxle and lifted his left arm. "And I can carry this buckler, as well, one bearing the symbol of the Dark Maiden and carrying within it the power of Eilistraee."

"The power of Eilistraee channels through your sword, then."

"Wielding Bluccidere with both hands while calling on the power of the Dark Maiden to aid me is a smite quite uncomfortable for even a giant, I assure you."

"Zaknafein the paladin," Jarlaxle said, shaking his head.

"That is no insult."

"It isn't meant as one. I am truly happy for you, my old friend. I have never seen you more at peace. Holy Galathae has proven to be a great mentor."

"And Azzudonna remains the most wonderful partner I could ever have hoped for," Zak said. "I seem at peace because I am at peace. I only wish that Bluccidere was still in the hands of Holy Galathae, but I am honored beyond anything you can imagine that she chose me, that Bluccidere chose me, that Eilistraee the Dark Maiden chose me, to take up her sword."

"I should be wounded, given the trouble I went through to get you the weapon you have discarded."

"You know that I still have Soliardis, Jarlaxle," Zak said, and then he chuckled. "Indeed, Soliardis is most certainly why you have sought me out this day."

"Perhaps I merely wanted a hug from my oldest and dearest friend."

"But you still want the weapon."

Jarlaxle smiled. "I told you that I am guiding your granddaughter. Can you think of a more worthy wielder?"

"She is a monk and thus uses her hands and feet as her weapons, I thought."

"Breezy is so much more than a monk."

Zak eyed him curiously.

"You would not want to suffer a punch from her, trust me," said Jarlaxle. "But those martial studies are but a smattering of the disciplines that one has trained. Soliardis will serve her well."

Zak nodded, then moved over to a nearby bench between two pillars on the side of the gazebo, where he had left his pack. He fumbled about in it for a few moments before producing the hilt of a weapon, a magical hilt that contained both the blade of light and the whip, whichever the wielder demanded.

He flipped it to Jarlaxle.

"If you wish to keep it," Jarlaxle said, holding it up.

"I have my sword."

"Perhaps there will come circumstances where Soliardis would serve you well."

"Bluccidere serves me well."

"Ah, but the unexpected . . ."

"Eilistraee the Dark Maiden walks with me through my sword."

Jarlaxle nodded and let it go. He didn't truly understand this great transformation in his oldest friend, this enlightenment that had befallen Zaknafein. The man had spent the better part of his life killing Lolthian priestesses and had professed complete hatred for the goddess and for all the self-proclaimed gods of the Realms, considering them meddling beings that caused naught but havoc and strife. Jarlaxle would have no more believed that Zak would become a holy warrior than he would himself, or Entreri, even.

But here Zak was, so happy . . . no, *happy* wasn't the right word, Jarlaxle decided.

So . . . content. There was a palpable inner peace emanating from the man, and for all his own doubts regarding Eilistraee or any other god figure, Jarlaxle could not deny his happiness in seeing Zak like this.

"Was it the miracle of that first Quista Canzay which so transformed you?" he asked, then added with a grin, "Perte miye, Zaknafein?"

Zak considered it for a few heartbeats, then shrugged, then nodded uncertainly. "Maybe that was the beginning. I was doomed, we all understood. There was no cure for the disease the slaad had injected into me with its filthy claws, and you cannot begin to understand the pain and the dread of the chaos phage. Even mighty Catti-brie, a Chosen of a god, had no hope of curing my affliction. Yet here I am, whole of body and clear of mind."

"But the magic of that night, the chanting from all the folk of Callidae with one voice, was aimed to the Merry Dancers, not to the Dark Maiden. Even Azzudonna, your beloved, the one who began that call to the dancing lights, was not of Eilistraee."

"She still isn't," Zak explained. "And yet, she accepts my choice without question and supports me in my prayers."

"As do I."

"You question."

"I try to understand," Jarlaxle corrected. "I accept it, and I am quite pleased for you."

Zak's smile was warm. "Perhaps someday we will pray together."

Jarlaxle highly doubted that, but he took Zak's hope in the kind spirit with which it had been offered.

"Are you praying for victory?" he asked.

"No, of course not. Cazzcalci is of no concern to Eilistraee, and if it were, I would question the point of my faith. It is a game, important to the people of Callidae as a matter of unity, of borough pride, and as a contest proving our readiness. We win or we lose of our own accord, and I don't thank Eilistraee in the former event, nor feel abandoned by her in the latter. I pray, as always, for the well-being of those around me, for those I love but too rarely see. For you, for my son and his wonderful family."

"You've become quite serious."

That gave Zak pause, but then he burst out laughing, collected his bag, and said, "Only because you haven't bought me a drink."

"Is that wise with the important battle only a few days before you?"

"I'm going onto an ice rink to get my face bashed in," Zak deadpanned. "I could use a drink."

"Going in by choice!"

"You see?" Zak said. "Becoming a paladin was only the second stupidest thing I've done up here in Callidae."

They moved down the steps of the gazebo. At the base, Zak grabbed Jarlaxle by the arm to stop him.

"Do you know the way from here to Ilbistato?"

"Of course," Jarlaxle answered, pointing out toward the middle of the canyon which held the borough.

Zak smiled slyly and slung his pack tightly.

Then he bolted away, Jarlaxle hesitating only an eyeblink, in fast pursuit. Off they raced, freerunning across Scellobel, leaping fences, scaling buildings to sprint across the roof and flip off the other side to land in perfect stride.

Two old friends, as full of mischief and full of the love of life as they had been in their younger days when they were denying the dread weight of Menzoberranzan with the freedom and joyful spirit of their wild races across the Lolthian city.

"If I win, you must train and join in the next Cazzcalci!" Zakna-fein yelled.

"Never!" Jarlaxle shouted back, and he lowered his head, leaped a fence, rolled over a cart without breaking stride, and tried not to get distracted by Zak's words, by the thought that participating in the Callidaean bloodsport might indeed prove a worthy adventure.

14

BECAUSE THEY SAID NO

Breezy hadn't been to Callidae in years, but the place—at least the four boroughs Breezy was allowed to visit—hadn't changed much in that time. It was enchanting enough in this celebratory season of the autumnal equinox, the sunset to mark the half year of night here at the north pole, fast approaching. There were rousing cheers and clinking mugs in every tavern and common room, and Allefaero, Breezy's constant companion, even took her up the long stair out of the canyons to the top of the Qadeej Glacier where stood the rink and grandstand that had been prepared for the coming battles.

The constant cold wind cut right through her up there, and though the sun was low in the sky, its reflections off this river of ice annoyed her and stung her eyes. Beyond the immediate discomfort, even after the short few days she had been in Callidae, the lack of night grated upon the young woman, and she had to wonder if her training, both at the monastery and then with Lady Avelyere, had somehow changed her very body, acclimating her eyesight, familiarizing her skin with shadows, making her more comfortable in darker times of day. Perhaps she had uncovered a distant part of her heritage, one emanating from the deep Underdark. She vowed that if she ever came back up to Callidae for any extended stay, it would be in the long night of the polar winter, under the beautiful shifting glow of the Merry Dancers.

All of that agitation was minimal, though, compared to the true item nagging at her sensibilities: She had been forbidden by her parents to travel to the fifth and newest borough of Cattisola.

"There are too many refugees from Menzoberranzan there," her mother had explained. "When they know you as the daughter of Drizzt Do'Urden, their reactions will be powerful. Almost certainly in a positive way, but still, that is something you should not deal with at this time."

Even though her parents had promised to take her to Cattisola briefly before they returned to the south, the idea that they had commanded Breezy not to go of her own accord had stayed with her, gnawing at her with every step. Allefaero was explaining the rink, the field of battle, below them. He became quite animated, his voice growing ever more excited, but Breezy was hardly listening, her gaze cast across the glacier sheet to the huge visible holes in the flat ice, the canyons which held the five boroughs.

"There!" she heard Allefaero say quite emphatically, shaking her from her musing to glance over at the tall and lean wizard, who was pointing down and to the left of where they were standing, to a section of the carved ice seats in the grandstand.

"There," he repeated, thrusting his finger a couple of times at a particular area.

"There?"

"Perte miye, Zaknafein," Allefaero explained. "That was where Zaknafein, Jarlaxle, Artemis Entreri, and your mother were sitting when the miracle happened, when the magical power of the Merry Dancers was channeled down through the chants of tens of thousands of Callidaeans to cure your grandfather of the slaadi chaos phage. It was a moment I'll never forget, a moment that none in attendance will ever forget. I expect you'll be sitting there for the coming battles."

Breezy nodded and forced a smile. She didn't want Allefaero to think that she didn't care about that truly marvelous miracle, and the thought of what might have happened to her grandda if it had not succeeded surely filled her with dread.

But she had been but a toddler at that time, and she really didn't know Zaknafein all that well even now, having seen him only a handful of times since her earliest days.

"Do you want to go down to the exact row where the miracle manifested?" Allefaero asked.

"No," Breezy quickly answered. She led Allefaero's gaze across the glacier sheet. "Which canyon holds the new borough, where the Menzoberranzan refugees have settled?"

Allefaero pointed off to the canyon farthest to their right. "Cattisola," he said. "Jarlaxle was instrumental in helping us find a way to rebuild the—"

"I know the story. Did you go below and fight the mighty polar worms?"

"I did, with Holy Galathae. I do not wish to ever do battle with them again."

"They're all gone now?"

"Driven from beneath Cattisola, yes, which is why the warm river again flows and the borough has been reclaimed from the ice."

"Just in time to house the newcomers." Breezy started walking that way. "Show it to me."

"We should start back to Scellobel," Allefaero said, stuttering. "You have a great feast to go to this very night."

Breezy kept walking.

"We should not cross the open glacier," Allefaero warned. "The wind . . ."

Breezy kept walking.

"Your parents told you not to go there!" Allefaero called, and he sprinted to catch up to her.

"I just want to see it," she replied when he arrived at her side. "And I'm going to. The only question is whether you will accompany me, or abandon me out here on this sheet of empty ice. Perhaps I'll become disoriented and not find the stair back down to Scellobel, and when I'm frozen dead up here, you can explain your unfortunate choice to my parents and to Jarlaxle."

"You are truly incorrigible."

"Thank you. Are you coming?"

A short while later, Breezy and Allefaero stood at the northern edge of the indicated canyon, looking down at the reclaimed borough of Cattisola.

"We really should be getting back," the wizard said, and he waved to a nearby scout from the borough who kept a wary eye on the glacier top.

"I can't walk all the way back to the stair," said Breezy. "It's too cold. Cast a spell."

"A spell? One that will take us back to the stair?"

"No, a Dimension Door that will bring us down there. We'll walk across Cattisola and to the tunnel back to Scellobel. You can show me the staging area where you went down to so heroically battle the mighty remorhaz. Tell me of your battles."

"I . . ." Allefaero fumbled for a way to argue, but recounting his heroics to Breezy was truly too tempting.

Just as she had planned it.

"My parents will never know," she said to tempt him further. "And if they somehow find out, then we, or I, will simply remind them that I am an adult and you could not stop me, and so of course you thought it your duty to go with me and protect me. It is really as simple as that."

"You only need me because I can create a magical door to the canyon floor."

Breezy laughed. "I can climb down that wall easily enough, but we haven't the time." The low rays of sunlight sparkled off her mischievous, alluring smile.

Defeated, Allefaero began casting.

THE WHISPERS SPREAD FAST AROUND Cattisola that the daughter of Drizzt was in the borough. Most of the drow here owed a great debt to Drizzt, for he had come to Menzoberranzan twice in recent times, first to serve as the spear of the city in driving out the physical manifestation of the great demon lord Demogorgon, and then more recently to aid the heretics in their escape from Lolth and her vile ways. Many wanted to glance upon the daughter of the great hero, the granddaughter of a great warrior their borough might soon face in the battle of Cazzcalci.

One Cattisolan took even more interest, and found a way to look out upon Breezy as she passed, her mere presence inciting in him a whirling tumult of emotions.

Breezy was his niece, though she knew little to nothing about him, he was sure, for he and his brother had only spoken very briefly those years ago in the escape from Menzoberranzan.

Dinin Do'Urden, who went by Dininae these days, had joined the heretics in that escape from the clutches of the Spider Queen Lolth and her vile matrons. But Dinin, the brother of Drizzt, hadn't gone for that reason, nor had his companion, who herself had once been a matron of a powerful drow house in Menzoberranzan. No, Dinin had been sent away by agents of Lolth to carry out a heinous crime. He would succeed, or he would be eternally tormented, they had assured him.

Now the object of that plot seemed to be delivered to him. He didn't know what to make of this young woman as she danced more than walked her way about the streets. So many emotions and fears twisted through him.

This was Brie. This was the daughter of Drizzt, the child, now woman, Dininae had sworn to kill in exchange for a pardon from Lolth and her priestesses. He would have done anything to escape the torture prison of Matron Zhindia Melarn back in Menzoberranzan. The task of murdering Drizzt's daughter and wife had seemed to him, in that moment, a perfectly acceptable risk compared to the horrors he would most surely face had he refused.

"It's really her," said a voice over his shoulder.

He nodded, and didn't have to look back to know that it was his co-conspirator in Lolth's task, Kyrnill Kenafin, who was once the Matron of House Kenafin, and who, now, like Dininae, was hoping for a pardon.

"That would indicate that Catti-brie has come, as well," Kyrnill went on. "Do you think this our time to strike?"

"Here?" Dininae asked incredulously.

"It has been nearly twenty years," the older woman replied.

"Twenty eventful years, mostly," Dininae reminded. In the first months on the surface, or more accurately, in a cavern near to Gauntlgrym, Dininae and Kyrnill had been invited by Jarlaxle to join Bregan D'aerthe. They had accepted, thinking that becoming members of that group would give them opportunity to fulfill their diabolical mission and be done with Lolth and her priestesses once and for all.

But Jarlaxle had other ideas. He had sent them the length and breadth of Faerûn on many missions, during which the two had become more than traveling companions. Five years before, when they had returned from one such journey, Jarlaxle had informed them that they had been invited by the Callidaeans to journey here to this aevendrow city and help with the resettlement of Cattisola.

It had come as a shock, to be sure, for they hadn't even applied to move to the far north, as had many of the other Menzoberranzan refugees. But when Jarlaxle had informed them, it had been clear from his attitude that it was a great honor and one they should not let pass.

Thus, they had accepted, for to do otherwise would have raised great suspicion. The mere fact that Jarlaxle had been the conduit for this move had convinced Dininae that Jarlaxle might be on to the long game they were playing under the orders of Lolth's priestesses.

Jarlaxle was the most dangerous man Dininae had ever known, with tendrils and networks spread about the whole of the Realms, and probably to other planes of existence as well.

"What should we do?" Kyrnill asked.

"What can we do?"

"These two will be entering the tunnel for Scellobel, it would seem. It is a long and empty walk. It has been nearly two decades, and this is our first chance, my love."

"The man she is with is a noted wizard."

"Allefaero the bookworm. He will prove no match for me, and you can surely dispatch that child. Come, take my hand and we will wind walk ahead of them and prepare an ambush."

Dininae didn't reach back. Instead, he rubbed his face and tried to sort out the swirl within him.

"You hesitate?" Kyrnill asked. "Do you not wish to be done with this?"

"Maybe I already am," he replied, still not looking at her. He almost expected a spider-shaped dagger to dig into his back at that moment, but there was nothing, not a movement, not a sound.

Finally, he turned about to face Kyrnill.

"You vowed," she accused.

Dininae shrugged.

"You promised Matron Zhindia."

"Matron Zhindia is dead."

"But Matron Mother Sos'Umptu Baenre is not, and Lady Lolth is eternal, as is the punishment we were promised if we fail in this task."

Dininae closed his eyes. He thought of his earliest days in the City of Spiders. He remembered when he had stabbed his brother Nalfein in the back, killing him, an act which had elevated him to Elderboy of House Do'Urden.

That act had also meant that Drizzt would be spared from being sacrificed to Lolth, since Drizzt was no longer the third living male child born to Matron Malice Do'Urden. Drizzt's very life, in no small part, had happened because of his brother Dinin's treachery.

What a winding road Dininae's life had been! He had served with Jarlaxle's band long ago, after the fall of House Do'Urden. He had been turned into a drider by his sister Vierna's Curse of Abomination, and soon after he was slain by Drizzt's dwarf friend, King Bruenor Battlehammer.

But death had only sent him to the Abyss, to be tormented and tortured, a seemingly eternal fate. Only the Great Heresy against Lolth had rescued him, when he and so many other undead driders had been sent to serve in the army of Matron Zhindia Melarn. In their initial charge against the forces of the heretical drow, the driders had run through the most magical of webs, and so they had been reborn, regifted life, once again in their natural drow form.

"You will be a drider again," Kyrnill warned, and the words brought cold sweat to the haunted man. "And I will be one!"

Dininae rubbed his face again, harder, trying to push away the truth of it: He didn't want to do this.

"Come!" Kyrnill demanded, holding out her hand, and this time, Dininae took it.

She began to cast a spell to wind walk them into the distant tunnel, but Dininae, looking down the street once more, interrupted her. "Look!"

Kyrnill leaned forward.

Down at the edge of this Cattisolan neighborhood, Breezy and Allefaero held hands, the wizard waving his free hand and gesturing, and then they were gone, simply vanished. Dininae and Kyrnill blinked repeatedly in surprise.

"They teleported back to Scellobel," Dininae reasoned. "Allefaero is known for his expertise in this area—he is the one who brought the whole group up here from Luskan, no doubt."

"Back to Scellobel, I agree, and now we know where they are," said Kyrnill.

"Yes, and we know too that they are with Drizzt and Catti-brie, Jarlaxle and Zaknafein, probably King Bruenor and his insane dwarf bodyguards. And who knows what other heroes accompanied them to Callidae—maybe Gromph Baenre himself. Would you suggest that we walk in and murder Brie in the midst of that group?" He turned and stared hard at Kyrnill.

"It has been nearly two decades since we were tasked with this," she reminded.

"A mere heartbeat for eternal Lolth. What are a few years or even decades more in the counting of the Demon Queen of Spiders?"

Kyrnill huffed indignantly and pulled her hand away, but Dininae was surprised to recognize something other than anger on her face.

She was as relieved as he.

THE HOURS BLENDED INTO DAYS in the unending sunshine and the continual celebration throughout Scellobel. Surprisingly, Breezy found herself drawn into the excitement of the coming celebrations and events. Watching the last parade of Biancorso, the Whitebears, leading the way up the long stairway to the top of the glacier, had her fantasizing that one day she might indeed participate in Cazzcalci.

That urge to join in only heightened as she witnessed the vicious matches throughout the day, the fighting across the rink, the blood, the intensity, and the cheering—mostly the cheering. She would quite enjoy tens of thousands cheering for her, of course.

But what she'd really enjoy was the game itself, this bloodsport of Cazzcalci, so beautiful and so painful and so dangerous. She wanted to run down and leap the rink's border and crash into the nearest player, ally or opponent.

But alas, it was not to be—not this year, at least.

Cattisola was the first team eliminated, followed closely by the reigning champions, the B'Shett borough team of Boscaille.

"Scellobel is sure to win," Allefaero promised when Boscaille went out.

But no, it was not to be, for the Whitebears were defeated next and would not even participate in the final match.

"Zak is sure to press you to join for next year," Breezy heard her mother say to Drizzt.

Maybe it will be me, Breezy mused.

The discussion around her continued and grew with the excitement as two teams of different boroughs entered the final match, neither of whom had been crowned champions in many years.

Breezy wasn't listening. Her attention went to the arena around her, filled with fifty thousand Callidaeans, with more than thirty thousand of them cheering for teams which were eliminated. This included the crowds from Scellobel and B'Shett, who came to the rink this day confident that they would be participating in the championship match.

But no one moved, not a person left, and the palpable tingling of excitement did not diminish.

The cheering did, just a bit at first, but then all of a sudden, the Grande Coliseum went silent, perfectly silent, as if even the unending polar wind dared not disturb the moment.

Breezy looked to Catti-brie, who had a finger over pursed lips and was pointing up with her other hand.

Nightfall.

The stars came into view above Callidae for the first time in six months. Slowly, a chant began around the coliseum, growing as the starlight intensified.

Breezy could feel the magic tingling on her skin, warming her heart. She didn't really remember this celestial event, but she knew what was happening here.

Somehow, she knew.

Fifty thousand Callidaeans and every one of the visitors from the south gasped when a green ribbon appeared above.

"*Alle'Balleri*," Breezy mouthed using her limited understanding of the language of the aevendow. The Merry Dancers.

The sheer spirituality of the moment, the sense of being insignificant and part of something grand and infinite and eternal all at once, overwhelmed her. She felt the tears welling in her eyes and knew that she was not alone here, knew that everyone in attendance was feeling equally overcome.

She understood why no one was leaving, and not just for the power of this transition, no, but because Quista Canzay, the beginning of a half-year night, put the whole of Cazzcalci into proper perspective. For pride and bragging rights, Cazzcalci mattered to the teams and their boroughs, yes, but in truth, it was Cazzcalci, it was the celebration of this day, the reflection of the coming night, the realization of their place in the multiverse, that bound Callidae together as one.

Breezy understood.

And in that moment, she felt almost ashamed that she had so fantasized and cared about others cheering for her.

She was truly off balance in that moment, her mind trying to circle about the truth of meaning and competition and comradery and all the rest.

But more than off balance, she was okay, perfectly so, wrapped in a moment of complete inner peace.

For the first time since she had come up here, she was very glad of making the trip.

Very glad, indeed.

———

Down near the end of the coliseum to the right of Breezy and her troupe, Dininae Do'Urden watched the transition with no less reflection and warmth. Battered from the day's matches, the warrior didn't feel his cuts and bruises then, everything physical taking a distant place in his mind from the magic and inclusion of Quista Canzay, the invitation to something beautiful and forever. He had witnessed this event a dozen times and more, but the feeling had not dimmed one bit.

When the enchanting moment passed and the calls for the final match began, Dininae leaned forward on his icy bench to study the crowd. He sorted out his brother, his father, his niece.

Mostly, he looked at Breezy.

If she hadn't been teleported away earlier in Cattisola . . .

The thought shook him profoundly.

He muttered some curses under his breath.

He aimed all but one of them at the Demon Queen of Spiders, holding a single muttering against Matron Zhindia Melarn.

Truly he hoped that wretched Zhindia was even then being tortured in Lolth's web in the Abyss.

"We are ready to return to Luskan," Jarlaxle informed Allefaero a couple of days later. "Drizzt and Catti-brie are with Zaknafein but should arrive soon with the others."

"Could I trouble you for some of that Luskan gold?" the wizard asked. "A few coins, perhaps, or maybe some other interesting baubles I might use as barter? I have something I would like to bring, but the person holding it will require collateral. The more coin, the longer we will have with this item."

Never one to easily part with treasure, Jarlaxle cocked his eye rather suspiciously at that.

"It's for Breezy," Allefaero explained. "I've been thinking about this for some time. She, and you, will find this a worthwhile investment."

"What is it?"

"Let me surprise you."

"I don't like surprises and rarely entertain them."

"It will surprise you in a good way, on my word. Haven't I earned your trust? Surely you know that I would never hurt Breezy."

Jarlaxle gave a little chuckle and looked to Braelin Janquay. "So we've noticed," he said, and Braelin nodded and smirked at Allefaero, who blushed fiercely.

Jarlaxle tossed him a small pouch that jingled when he caught it. "Be quick. I have a lot to do in Luskan."

Allefaero cast a minor spell to summon a magical steed, a large, long-haired, and huge-horned goat. He leaped upon it and galloped off across Scellobel, straight for the tunnel to Mona Chess. He didn't slow until he reached the Siglig, then ran through that voluminous structure to the library, where he proffered a particular book, large and old and rarely borrowed.

He was back with Jarlaxle and the others soon after, and pulled the mercenary leader aside. Glancing back to make sure no one else was close enough to eavesdrop, he showed Jarlaxle the tome.

"I can translate," Allefaero offered when Jarlaxle reached for it.

Jarlaxle snorted and took the heavy tome. He moved his eyepatch from one eye to the other and deliberately pulled open the thick leather cover.

Allefaero smiled widely when Jarlaxle's uncovered eye popped opened wide. "Truly?" Jarlaxle asked, looking over at him. "This is a school of wizardry?"

"Little used and little known, and almost exclusively practiced at this time by the elves," Allefaero explained. "It was they, the high elves, who perfected it."

"And it is powerful?"

"If used correctly by a person with the correct attributes, then truly so." He shrugged. "I thought that Breezy, with her background, with all that training . . ."

"Interesting," Jarlaxle said.

"You think it worth the coin in the pouch you gave me? We have rented six months with this rare tome."

"Oh, I think we may want it longer than that."

"You saved Callidae," Allefaero said. "I am sure that will be no problem in adding to the bargain."

"Take us home," Jarlaxle said and closed the book carefully, then rubbed his hands reverently over the old leather. He started back toward the others. "We have much work to do."

15

THE SHADOWDANCER OF BLADESINGING

Breezy observed the conversation between Jarlaxle and her parents from afar, trying to read expressions, lips, anything that could give her some hint of what they might be discussing. She had thought that she would return to Longsaddle and the Ivy Mansion with her parents to continue her studies, arcane and divine, as her time here in Luskan with Lady Avelyere was ended.

But Jarlaxle was apparently pushing for some other course, from what little she could garner from the conversation.

She hoped that to be the case.

Perhaps her mother didn't, she noted, as Catti-brie suddenly became more animated and seemed to be scolding Jarlaxle.

Jarlaxle didn't back down, and Drizzt, too, seemed to be countering whatever disagreement Catti-brie had made. A moment later, Catti-brie sighed and shrugged, motioned toward Breezy, then led the others over.

"Jarlaxle has a gift for you," Catti-brie told her as they neared. Even as she finished, Jarlaxle flipped the gift at Breezy.

She caught it, confused for just a moment, until she recognized the item as the hilt of Grandda Zaknafein's magical sword.

"Take care when you ignite the blade," Jarlaxle said.

Breezy stood stunned for a long while. She finally managed to close her eyes and turn her thoughts to the weapon, feeling its power. She brought her arm out wide, clear of the others, and with a thought brought forth the light blade. She felt its balance, felt its magical energy, and felt, too, a bit of ruefulness, which she tried to keep off her face.

Yes, this was a mighty weapon indeed, and she understood that she could call forth a flaming whip instead of a light blade, and wouldn't that be fun when she learned how to use such a weapon as that? She thought of the one time she had seen Zak practicing with it, snapping it from a myriad of angles, leaving red lines, rifts in the Material Plane, in its wake.

But to the Plane of Fire, not Breezy's preferred option.

And with this in hand, what, then, of the shadow blade? What of that marvelous dweomer she had only recently learned?

"You will let me practice with this?" she asked Jarlaxle.

"Practice? Do as you will, young warrior. It is yours. I'm not loaning it to you. It is a gift, and I hope that you will find good use for it as a supplement to all else that you have learned in these many years of training."

Breezy returned that with a smile and a nod, mostly sincere, but with a tinge of regret.

"Back to my practice, then," she said and looked to Drizzt.

"You can get your training with your new weapon in during the days or nights," Drizzt answered that look. "In those times when you're not too busy with your other lessons."

"We're returning to Longsaddle?"

"No," said Catti-brie. "Jarlaxle here has convinced us that you would be better served at the Host Tower of the Arcane here in Luskan."

"With Allefaero and Nvisi," Jarlaxle immediately added.

Breezy looked at him curiously. "Nvisi the Diviner? The strange little man with the round face?"

"Yes, yes, and yes," Jarlaxle replied with a laugh. "Nvisi is all of that and more. You will be amazed, I promise."

"But my ma and Penelope . . ." Breezy started, though she really wasn't trying to argue here, as she found that she didn't want to be under the watchful eyes of her parents at this time.

"You will soon understand," said Jarlaxle. "Now, bid your parents farewell—they will be only a step or two through the gates away from us—and come with me that I can show you your next, and greater, present."

Her curiosity piqued, Breezy was happy to oblige.

THIS WAS BETTER THAN HER life in Waterdeep, Keely reminded herself many times every day. She made it a point to focus on the worst of her experiences in her short life, of the many beatings she had suffered at the hands of troubled men and women. She had attended balls in Waterdeep, which many would have thought attractive—so many wanted to get in to the grand parties of the noble houses of that great city.

But none of those jealous commoners would have enjoyed the experiences Keely had known at those social gatherings. Far from it. The contempt on the faces of everyone there not named Brevindon Margaster had been obvious. Keely had been the butt of many jokes. She had wine "accidentally" spilled upon her often.

She smiled through it, because she had to, and used every opportunity to brush whatever crumbs she could find into a small bag she carried with her so that she might not be quite as hungry the next day. She had been caught with her fingers in the garbage more than once, and had faced humiliation and physical beatings, though not as badly as one cold winter's night when she had tried to steal a dirty tablecloth from the laundry to wrap about her shivering body after Brevindon was done with her and had put her back out on the street. Oh, but the noblewoman had whipped her good for that one!

Yes, life in Manse Dorcrae was better, Keely told herself, but she found herself rubbing her neck as she tried to focus on that thought, her fingers running over the newest punctures from Lady Delilah's fangs. She winced, no less a prostitute now than in Waterdeep, with sessions at least as intimate and invasive as her encounters with Brevindon or any of the others.

These were more pleasurable, at least, and Lady Delilah wasn't whipping her or beating her. But was this service to the vampire really better? Did she believe that or was she simply trying to convince herself?

"No, it is better," Keely told herself through gritted teeth, grunting and shaking her head as she moved alongside a wagon's display of wares.

"Did you see one that was spoiled, then?" asked the merchant, a short woman with dark skin and bright eyes that seemed somehow too big for her face. Her accent was strong, and from the south, far south, Keely knew. Calimport, she guessed, or maybe Memnon, but surely somewhere in the desert lands of southwestern Faerûn.

The fruits and vegetables in the wagon were not from that distant south, though. They certainly weren't the exotic goods that often came up from Calimport. Keely had seen those and stolen more than a few in the streets of Waterdeep. Likely this newly arrived caravan in Westbridge had come from the City of Splendors after debarking its ship, selling its southern wares—valuable because of their rarity— and loading its carts with goods from Waterdeep to transport along the highways.

"No, they are all fine," Keely replied, starting to smile, but cutting herself short before she showed her teeth. She tried to keep her voice steady and her train of thought true, but found herself unexpectedly distracted by the beauty of this southern woman.

She tried to sort that notion out, for really the merchant seemed quite plain, and with some features far from perfect, but still . . .

In that moment and in that light, she was, to Keely, quite beautiful. No, not beautiful, but appetizing.

Ah, to bite this one's thin neck . . .

Keely forced the thoughts away. The urges were growing stronger. She ran her tongue inside her upper lip and felt the points of her front teeth, the smooth edge of the middle four, the sharper points of the canines.

Were they growing yet?

For her hunger surely was.

She wasn't a vampire, of course, and not even a vampire spawn as yet, which was why Lady Delilah had sent her to market, this day and on every daytime journey when the mistress desired some goods, whether to keep up appearances, or for needed supplies like thick linens for the all-important curtains, or hooks to hang them upon.

Keely was the errand girl, because Keely had Delilah's trust, and more so because Keely, unlike most of Lady Delilah's servants, could go out in the sunlight.

She didn't like the shining glare anymore, however, and whenever that infernal orb peeked out from behind the many puffy clouds, she squinted with the pain of a true headache.

I am neither dead nor alive, she lamented, though she knew that the notion wasn't true, of course. She was still very much alive.

Delilah kept her alive, and not only to run these errands for Manse Dorcrae, but to satisfy Delilah's thirst for the blood of a living human being. Keely understood that the arrangement wouldn't last forever, perhaps not even for much longer. She could feel the changes within her body. She was stronger, yet somehow thinner—yes, thinner was the word, as if this mortal coil was being hollowed out with each withdrawal of blood.

Eventually, she would transform.

"Transform," she said aloud and snorted.

"What?" the merchant woman asked impatiently.

"Oh, it is nothing."

"You're touching everything. Do you mean to buy?" The Calimshite put her hands on her hips and stared as sternly as she had spoken.

Keely almost jumped upon her, almost gave in to the urges. She could see the woman's thick artery bulging in her throat as she grew angrier.

One good bite would tear it open, and the fountain of refreshing blood . . .

Only the merchant's eyes, going even wider with obvious fear, clued Keely in to her threatening posture. She backed off immediately—wouldn't Lady Delilah beat her soundly if she caused such trouble here in Westbridge!

Keely shook all the urges out and leaned away from the merchant, but the Calimshite woman kept backing.

"Just take them!" she said. "Aye, a bag of fruit for a pretty lady, yes?"

Keely was shaking her head, but the woman kept stammering, waving her hands in denial as Keely brought forth her purse, sputtering "It's a gift" over and over again.

Poor young Keely didn't know what to do. She glanced all about and noted that many eyes and ears were trained on this suddenly loud exchange at the fruit cart. Panicking, she pulled open her purse, took a few silver coins and placed them on the counter, then turned and rushed away before the Calimshite merchant could protest.

Even though the next cart had a fine supply of fish, and the one after that was stocked with fat roasts—the vampire spawn who live at the house would actually feed on those if they were fresh enough to leak some blood—Keely kept going, her pace swift, never looking back, all the way out of Westbridge.

No footsteps or hoofbeats came behind her, but a jumble of emotions did indeed chase poor Keely out of town.

Fear and dread battled an undeniable sense of power within her. How wide those eyes had gone! The Calimshite probably wouldn't even have found the strength to oppose her if she had attacked.

Power.

And she wasn't even a spawn yet.

Which meant that she wasn't even dead yet.

The euphoria flew away with that realization.

Was she ready to die?

A FEW DAYS LATER, A thoroughly charmed Breezy sat at a desk in the extradimensional training room Archmage Gromph had conjured for her and Allefaero. Before her sat two books, one an ancient tome, the other a small and limited spellbook recently penned by Allefaero and titled *Fighting Enhancements*. Allefaero had instructed her to focus on the second book, the small spellbook, until she had learned to easily cast the spells. She wasn't there yet, but Breezy had already pushed that mundane book aside in favor of the larger, ancient tome.

For this book, *Bladesinging,* described an old elven school of wizardry, one little known now and rarely studied. Allefaero was of the School of Scribes, which gave him access to so many magical spells. Archmage Gromph was an evoker, following the School of Evocation, which made his lightning bolts and fireballs supremely devastating. Allefaero's Ulutiun friend Nvisi, a charming, round-faced man who kept a score of blind arctic lemmings as pets, including one named Doodles that served as his familiar, was of the School of Divination. People would pay Nvisi quite well for his visions and portents.

Breezy hadn't picked any school of specialization, hadn't even given it much thought. Her wizardly studies had been disjointed because of her commitments to the Monastery of the Yellow Rose and all the other side streets of the grand adventure that had thus far dominated her life. With the very notable exception of Shadow Blade, she had only learned how to cast a handful of minor spells, mostly mere cantrips, and those had been learned for everyday situations, like heating a pot of stew, more than for the desperate frenzy of battle. And of course, she had learned magic to better "see" the Plane of Shadow under the dweomers offered by Lady Avelyere. The notion of selecting any school of wizardry, she had believed and witnessed with Allefaero and the Harpells, meant dedicating herself fully to an unappealing desk-bound lifestyle, to hours and hours of studying with her face in a book, and to endless scribing.

But all those preconceptions had washed away the moment Breezy had read the introduction, the overview, of the dusty tome Allefaero had given to her. She pored through the book hungrily, absorbing every word, for the promise of bladesinging called to her heart as surely as the Way of Shadow had lured her from the predominant tradition of the monks at the monastery. She wasn't formally a training monk anymore, but she'd never let go of the Way of Shadow. Similarly, bladesinging showed her a wide web of possibilities, and promised to bring together all her talents and expertise from every area of experience and study.

As soon as she read the introductory synopsis of the practice's goals, she understood why Jarlaxle had guided her to this school of wizardry.

"How is your studying this day?" she heard Allefaero ask, entering the room.

"I will be the Shadowdancer of Bladesinging," Breezy declared with a wide smile. She looked over at him to see him standing with his arms crossed, scowling down at her.

"You have mastered all the spells already?" he asked skeptically, pointing to the small spellbook.

Breezy slowly closed the *Bladesinging* tome, looked to the spellbook, and shrugged. Scribed within it were a handful of wizard spells that could aid a fighter while in melee, like one that would bring forth magical shielding as fast as she could think it, a reflex more than a conscious casting. In a desperate situation where an opponent found an opening in her physical defenses, such a shield could possibly turn a blade and save her life. Another spell would capture a portion of any energy—fire, lightning, cold—thrown against her, even giving to her some of that energy to redirect through her fist or her weapon to pay back her opponent in kind.

"Most seem fairly simple," she said.

"Are you ready to try them?"

Breezy shrugged again, then laughed, and admitted, "No."

"These spells are the entire point of bladesinging," Allefaero insisted. "They are integral to elevating a bladesinger above a simple warrior."

"There is no such thing as a simple warrior," she returned. "A living one, anyway."

Allefaero laughed at that and Breezy just sat staring up at him.

"What would be the point of this particular wizardry school if not to combine the magic and the martial, the power of a spell and the cut of a sword?"

"I know," Breezy admitted. "And I will learn them—I'm sure that I can cast some, at least, with only a bit of practice."

Allefaero stepped over and opened the book, flipping to the last spell of the group. "This might become your greatest advantage," he said, poking the title of the enchantment, one he had harped upon from the beginning of their training. "Speed," he continued. "Speed of movement, speed of action. Learn it, master it, and when you have that mastery, practice with it often, I beg. Become comfortable with the boost in energy, with the fluidity and quickness of your strikes, your parries, your heightened movement.

"Or this one," he said, flipping back a few pages to a spell that would add magical energy to a weapon strike.

"Both of those are more powerful than anything I have learned to cast," Breezy admitted. "I'm not sure that I have the experience yet to even attempt."

"You know Shadow Blade."

"Just the basic version. These two are of higher difficulty than that."

"I have spoken with Lady Avelyere. She has assured me that you have conjured shadow blades of equal power to these spells. Do not be afraid to try! I am certain—"

"It's not that," Breezy said. "Not with these two spells you offer, at least."

Allefaero looked at her curiously.

"I know Shadow Blade," Breezy said. "I love Shadow Blade and am eager at the thought of bladesinging with such a weapon in hand."

"And?" Allefaero seemed at a loss, but then caught on and said, "Oh, you cannot maintain a Shadow Blade with either of these."

"And I do not like the trade-off."

"Weren't you just given a weapon of great power? One you need only call upon and not cast? I was told that Soliardis could . . ."

"Yes, a powerful sword or whip," Breezy admitted. "It is a great gift from Uncle Jax." She stopped and sighed.

"But it does not call to your heart as does Shadow Blade," Allefaero stated, and Breezy shrugged again.

"This cannot simply be about efficiency and power," she said.

"Bladesinging is very powerful for someone of your exceptional physical talents."

"Bladesinging is beautiful," Breezy corrected. "Shadow Blade is beautiful. That is the dance I envision."

"The Shadowdancer of Bladesinging," Allefaero said with a chuckle, echoing Breezy's earlier declaration, and Breezy shrugged yet again.

"I can only tell you that which calls to me."

"And I will help you find it and make it the best you can," Allefaero promised. "But please, learn these spells—I will help you. Options, choices . . . these are how wizards survive in a brutal world, my dear Breezy. You are going to master bladesinging, I promise you, but I will not bring you to that level of mastery until you have learned the reasons for it, and that means the magical accompaniments for such a fighter. I do not know if you have read to this point yet, but the dance of bladesinging, like with most arcane magic use, is not compatible with armor. If you are not good enough, an enemy's sword—"

"You sound like Grandmaster Savahn," Breezy interrupted, and the wizard paused. "Monks don't wear armor, silly wizard. Our armor is here," she said and waved her arms. "And here." She tapped her temple.

Allefaero nodded, accepting defeat, but then said without compromise, "You should be able to master all these spells within a tenday. And they will help you to become a more powerful wizard—"

Breezy started to interrupt, but Allefaero pressed on.

"And a more powerful wizard will cast a more powerful Shadow Blade, yes?"

Breezy was out of arguments. She sighed, she groaned, and she dragged the spellbook before her.

A tenday later, she was ready to try the spell of Haste.

"Relax your mind," Allefaero reminded as she began to cast. "You have the ability and the experience now."

Breezy started to close her eyes, but shook that away. This was a spell for battle! She couldn't ask the melee all about her to pause and let her cast it.

She slapped her left hand across her chest, pressing the root shaving—licorice root, she thought—tightly as she suddenly pumped her legs and sword arm, blinking rapidly and uttering the arcane phrase, "*Facomie-celerit!*"

She felt her heart pounding in her chest, the blood pumping furiously through her veins. She ignited Soliardis in her right hand, holding it vertically.

Even as the light sword appeared, Allefaero thrust the end of his staff at Breezy's chest.

Across came Soliardis to bat it aside—but no!

She was too fast, her parry already across before the tip of the staff got close enough to deflect.

About to get hit, her monk training came into play, her left hand rolling up to slap the rushing staff to a harmless height.

But again, she was too quick.

So as a last resort, she ducked, still with plenty of time to avoid the strike.

Breezy hopped back. "Waitwaitwait!"

Allefaero blinked curiously.

"Thisissoverystrange!"

"Breezy, calm," the wizard said, lowering his weapon.

She let go of the spell and bent forward, hands on thighs and gasping for breath. Though she had been in the thrall of the dweomer for only a few moments, a great weariness came over her. She had expected things to return to normal, but now everything slowed around her, just briefly.

When it all finally settled, she looked up at Allefaero and shook her head.

"It takes getting used to," the wizard explained. "Learning to cast it is the easy part.

"Very strange," she said and took a deep and steadying breath. She closed her eyes and let the last vestiges of the exhaustion flow through her and out of her.

"You seem displeased."

"I am not trying to hide it," Breezy retorted.

"It is a powerful spell."

Breezy started to argue, but bit it back. Her father had told her that it had taken him a lot of time and practice to get used to those speed bracers he wore. This dweomer was even more disorienting, she figured, since it was enhancing everything about her, quickening every muscle. She tried to suppress her distaste for it, silently reminding herself that part of that feeling was her affinity to a shadow blade and her inability to even consider it in concert with this spell, as maintaining either would require her undivided magical focus.

"Practice it," Allefaero instructed. "And do so in earnest. This is the most powerful spell you have ever attempted, I believe, and it will help you grow greatly as a wizard."

"I don't want to be a wizard."

"Do you want to cast Shadow Blade?"

"I could just do that, then. And use the same level of concentration and energy."

"Does the idea of bladesinging still appeal to you?"

"Yes."

"Then cast the spell of Haste and practice your moves in its thrall!" Allefaero sternly replied.

Breezy gave him a sour, almost threatening look.

"You'll want me to tell Jarlaxle of your enthusiasm, I am sure," Allefaero added. "That is, if you expect him to retain his great interest in you."

Breezy's scowl became a glare, but the threat fell out of it. "Have that broomstick you call a staff ready for our morning fight," she said, and she went back to her desk and pulled the other tome, the ancient elven tome, before her.

The next morning, Breezy was truly surprised when Allefaero took her to the extradimensional training gym with an actual broom, not his usual stave, in his hand.

"I borrowed it from Caecilia."

Breezy eyed him curiously.

"The cloud giantess of the Host Tower."

"I know who Caecilia is. You borrowed her broom? And isn't that broom rather small for her?"

Allefaero didn't answer, but just entered the portal into the training gym. "Use Soliardis," he instructed when she went for the training sword. "Cast your spell."

"I'll probably cut you in half," Breezy said. "I cannot fully control . . ."

"Just do as I say."

"Very well, then. I'll make sure that you're sent home for burial," Breezy muttered. She cast her spell, the world around her suddenly slowing down—or no, she was suddenly speeding up. Oh, it was all so confusing!

Then more confusing still when Allefaero threw the broom out in front of her. Instead of falling to the floor, the weapon animated and attacked! And had Breezy not been moving at a faster pace, it would have hit her, and hard.

She brought forth the light blade, kept her spell of Haste running, and waded in, the broom matching her in a furious back-and-forth. She got clipped a couple of times, but she found a rhythm and soon enough gained the upper hand, stabbing and slashing the imaginary wielder of this animated broom.

"Keep going," Allefaero said.

"You're already dead," Breezy insisted.

"Keep going."

So she did, and the broom continued apace. She was long into the spell then, she knew, and its energy was taxing her body to its limits. Her heart pounded in her chest.

Knowing that she was nearing the end of the enchantment, she finished with a flourish that stunned the broom for a moment, then leaped back and took a deep breath.

"Keep going!" Allefaero yelled.

The spell was gone, the weariness, the sluggishness, the sheer exhaustion, coursed through her.

The broom came on.

She held up her hand to call for an end.

The broom whacked her fingers, stinging her.

"Keep going!"

She fought back, took a few hits at first, but then remembered her other spells. She shifted to a defensive posture that she could fend while the wave of weariness washed away. Still the broom got through, but this time, a magical shield intercepted it.

"Keep going!" Allefaero shouted, now with enthusiasm.

The broom swept at her feet but re-angled at the last instant, flipping over into a sudden thrust, and it got through—almost, for a second reflexive magical shield deflected it just past her face. The weariness was gone and Breezy went into her normal battle stance, fighting the broom as she had fought her father and Wulfgar on the way home from Icewind Dale.

The broom had no chance of hitting her.

None.

The broom had no chance of blocking her attacks.

None.

Even without the magical haste, she was too quick, and as soon as she fully understood that, she worked Soliardis brilliantly to force the broom nearly vertical, then leaped upon it and snatched it from the air with the same techniques she had learned at the monastery for catching spears, even speeding arrows.

Allefaero stood giggling, clapping, and nodding.

"We will do this every morning, and you will use every spell in that book and in your repertoire," he explained. "In the next fight, you can even discard Soliardis and bring forth a shadow blade after your spell of Haste expires."

"All of that will be over long before lunchtime," Breezy pointed out. "Then what?"

The wizard nodded toward the desk. "Then spend your hours studying the tome of *Bladesinging*."

Breezy's smile nearly took in her ears as Allefaero's words truly registered, as she came to truly appreciate the potential of the opportunity he had just offered to her. For the first time in so very long a time, Breezy had been offered the chance to pursue her own course, without interference, without disapproval.

And with the promise of the old book lying on her desk, this powerful and rare school of wizardry that seemed as if it had been sculpted exactly for a person with Breezy's many and varied skillsets, the timing of this freedom could not have been better.

She nodded and smiled widely. Yes, she had indeed veered into another of the valleys Grandmaster Savahn had predicted, and oh, but this one was grand, indeed!

———

Keely stood on the path looking up the hill to Manse Dorcrae. The sun was setting behind her, twilight falling fast. Lady Delilah and her closest "friends" would be waking up.

The young Waterdhavian woman took a deep breath. Somewhere deep inside of her came an urge to turn around and walk away. But where could she go? Would Delilah even allow it? Or would she and her spawn go out hunting for her? For she knew the truth of Manse Dorcrae, the awful truth of Lady Delilah. How could the vampire let one with such knowledge simply walk away?

She pushed the thought away. Even if she could walk away, would she want to? Keely's entire life had been a hardscrabble for survival, picking the scraps from dumped garbage in the alleys of Waterdeep, even catching and eating rats. And cockroaches! What misery her life in Waterdeep had been. She had known many sexual partners, but she had certainly never known love. Everything, every action, every moment of her existence, had been a quest for warmth, for food, for shelter, for simple survival. She had never felt safe, not once, or at least, never remembered any feelings of safety, until she had come to Manse Dorcrae.

"But now I am safe," she told herself. "And powerful!"

The conviction in her voice hid the deeper truth of a terrible paradox, though, for how could she feel safe in the house of the vampire who was surely going to kill her?

She thought of the vampire spawn serving Delilah, the wretched, withered, ugly, and vicious creatures.

She loathed them and was repulsed by their mere presence. It was an existence that no one, not even a girl who had to eat cockroaches to survive the filthy streets of Waterdeep, would ever accept.

But Keely had been fed upon by Delilah many times now, and was moving somewhere past life and into undeath. As with the vampire and her undead spawn. The hunger was beginning to call to Keely, undeniably so. In Waterdeep, she had yearned for warmth and trust and love, and she still wanted all of those things, of course. But now there grew within her a different lust.

She knew the intimacy of Delilah's bite. She wanted to know the taste of being the biter.

And so, as much as she loathed the vampire spawn, Keely was growing to envy them.

THE TENDAYS PASSED, THE MONTHS passed, and Breezy found no distractions in her afternoon studies—lessons that often extended long into the night and only ended when Allefaero insisted that she break and eat some food before she retire to her bed.

Never in her life, not in her studies at the Monastery of the Yellow Rose, not in her work with the Harpells and her mother at the Ivy Mansion, not in her fighting lessons with her father and various uncles, had the young woman found anything that so sang to that which was in her heart. In her mind, she compared her studies with this ancient elven tome to her grandda Zaknafein's newfound obsession with the goddess Eilistraee.

Because to Breezy, this particular discipline was more than a school of wizardry, more than just another trick in her bag of options.

This was spiritual.

She worked her routines every morning with a better understanding of the spells involved. The magical shields came to her without error, blocking the broom, and when her hastening spell ended, she learned ways to protect herself until the wave of weariness passed. Then she dropped Soliardis back into its magical hilt and brought forth a shadow blade.

She understood the power of Soliardis, understood the trouble Jarlaxle had gone through in getting the light blade. She knew of the great risk Jarlaxle and Catti-brie had taken, the work they had undertaken in putting the light blade and Zaknafein's magical whip into the Great Forge of Gauntlgrym, calling upon the power of the fire primordial to fuse the magics of the two weapons into this magnificent combination.

But in her mind, she was the Shadowdancer, and the fitting weapon for her was a blade formed of the stuff of shadows.

The concepts of bladesinging began to seep into those morning practices, but it took nearly two months of study before Breezy had her first true breakthrough.

She launched a wild and perfectly aimed flurry at the broom, batting it all about, kicking it, spinning it, catching it, and tossing it aside with a snort.

"How are you doing that?" she asked Allefaero, who sat at the side of the room and seemed to be hardly watching the practice session.

"Doing what? The broom fights of its own magic."

"The music!" Breezy insisted.

Allefaero's face screwed up with puzzlement. "Music?"

"The music," Breezy said. "The heartbeat in the background, the rising melody, the song of the winds and the nightbirds . . ." She began to dance as she rambled on.

Allefaero came out of his chair, moving near to her with his head craned. "I hear no music," he said quietly, but Breezy did not notice and wouldn't have believed him if she had. She danced, she twirled, she moved with great speed, her blade, her legs, her weapons, all in perfect coordination.

Allefaero ran to the side and scooped up the broom, called upon its magic again and flung it into battle before her.

It didn't get near to striking her. She hardly seemed to be looking at it, but she perfectly blocked or dodged its every attack. She worked fast, so very fast, stepped around it with spinning beauty, attacking it from the side, from behind, though the broom had no flanks, of course.

But there was something more here, Breezy began to fully appreciate.

The song guided her—she could almost see the dancing elves, could hear their voices, and in those notes, the patterns.

The patterns.

The movements she would make to counter, to attack.

Deep in her trance, the flow of battle wafted through Breezy subconsciously, her thoughts meshing with her instincts in a way she could never have imagined.

She came out of it later, she knew not how long, blowing a deep and settling breath. Only then did she realize that she had the broom in hand. She turned to the side of the room, to Allefaero, who stood with his mouth agape, his eyes unblinking.

"What was that?" he asked.

Breezy shrugged. She thought of her father and the deeper warrior he sometimes instinctively summoned within himself, another side of his battle lust known as the Hunter.

But that was more of a primal, almost feral alter ego, a side of Drizzt that was purely an aggressor.

This was different. This was not violence, but beauty and grace, song and dance, battle in a way Breezy had never imagined. And there she knew the answer to Allefaero's question.

"What was that?" he asked again.

"Bladesinging," Breezy answered with complete confidence.

16

THE PRICE OF NORMALCY

Brevindon's blood burned her throat, its stinging taste assaulting her sensibilities and turning this great pleasure into something terrible. Dahlia understood her new aversion to alcohol—even fine fey-wine burned at her throat. But this spirit liquor, this grape-skin concoction distilled by the peasants of Westbridge was simply too much for her. She was standing behind the man, so he couldn't see her hateful scowl as she tried to sort out whether any of this was worth the pain this night. Gershwin Caldwell was out of town, and she hadn't given Keely enough time to recover from the last feasting to safely drink of her blood again this night—doing so might finish that one's life, and she would be no further use to Dahlia as a vampire spawn.

But Brevindon simply disgusted her at this moment, and not only because of the alcoholic burn of his blood. He hadn't delivered another victim from Waterdeep as he had promised, and beyond that, simply the man's weakness, his inability to find any purpose in his miserable, privileged life, made him ever more repulsive to Dahlia. She had come from nothing and had suffered the torments of the vile lich Szass Tam and the tiefling brute Herzgo Alegni.

This woman who had reinvented herself as Delilah Dorcrae could not stand weakness, and Brevindon smelled of it.

Worse, her sensitivity to alcohol was apparently growing even more acute, and Brevindon was rarely anything but drunk of late. She needed him, but he was becoming useless to her as a feeding trough.

She had to consciously remind herself that Brevindon, wretched as he was, was a man of great means and thus could bring her other victims from faraway Waterdeep.

It took some effort, but Dahlia resisted the urge to tear his throat out then and there.

"More, more," the drunken fool moaned, cocking his head to the side to better present his neck to Dahlia's fangs.

"I am quite finished," she replied, moving away.

He spun about and grabbed her by the arm, his grip tight, his expression as desperate as a lover jilted at the penultimate moment. "But I'm not."

With strength that clearly frightened the man, Dahlia pried his hand free and shoved him backward, sending him rolling over the side of the bed in his rented room in Westbridge. He tumbled to the floor.

"If you want more, then quit filling yourself with stinging liquors," Dahlia scolded.

"But . . . but, I did not mean to . . ." the nobleman stuttered. "I didn't expect you so soon. I . . . I . . ." Brevindon gave a great wail and began sobbing, to which Dahlia merely sighed, shook her head, and left the room, sweeping down the stairs and out the door of The Happy Halfling, not even bothering to acknowledge the greeting call of Ghaliver Longstocking.

The halfling was probably heading up to Brevindon's room even then, Dahlia thought as she moved along the street, which was nearly empty now as the hour was well past midnight. He knew the truth of Lady Delilah, and he likely worried that she had given in to the urges, at long last slaughtering the idiot Brevindon Margaster.

Ghaliver would be relieved that Brevindon wasn't dead, and perhaps that would give the powerful halfling even more confidence in Lady Delilah's discretion and control.

But while all of that might work to her benefit, it did nothing to alleviate the hunger or the incessant urges. She needed to feed—if it hadn't been so near the dawn, she would have turned into a bat and flown into the forest to hunt a goblin or two—though she knew well that even that would do little to sate her for long, as goblin blood was no more fulfilling than Brevindon's spirit-laced fluids.

She fought again the urge to go back and drink from Keely— where would she be with that one wellspring closed to her?

"Gershwin," she muttered. Why did he have to be out of town? She was going to have to lean on him to start serving her alternate meals, as Brevindon had done in providing her with Keely. Dahlia stopped her frantic walking and took a moment to hold herself calm as she tried to work through the problem. It would be more difficult for Gershwin, of course, for he lived in Westbridge and not some far-off city with multitudes who would not be missed.

But if she could make it work . . .

Dahlia started off again, entertaining the fantasy of having four Keelys at her disposal. Four young servants living at Manse Dorcrae. Survival would be so much easier, and the variety of sweet young blood givers . . .

The vampire had no breath, so she couldn't actually sigh.

All of that seemed such a wonderful possibility, and yes, she'd have to work to make it happen, she decided.

But this night, the here and now, the hunger, the urges.

She was out of the town proper, then, and moving along the more scattered hovels of Westbridge's common folk. The houses were all dark and quiet, which did her no good, for she couldn't enter any home without being invited.

She noticed, then, a light come up in the window of a cottage down a side street. With hardly a thought, she glanced around, then ducked behind one corner to hide from anyone who might be peering out one of those darkened windows. She flipped her cloak up high so that it fell over her, and before it even covered her head,

Dahlia was gone, replaced by a large bat that fluttered up above the rooftops to find that candlelight, then swooped down to land beside the cottage.

She was a woman again as she landed, leaning to the side and peering into a small room.

An old man shuffled about, pouring some tea and starting back for the chair beside the single small table where he had placed a candle.

She didn't know him, didn't know if he was alone.

She rolled from the window and put her back against the wall.

Normalcy, she told herself. That's what Ghaliver wanted from her. The halfling hadn't said it in so many words, but he had made it clear that Westbridge could tolerate Lady Delilah if she could be as any other normal person in the village.

Normalcy.

She looked in the window, studying the platters, the cups, seeking any hints of whether there was another living in the tiny cottage.

Normalcy, her mind screamed at her.

That was the price.

But the hunger . . .

She tapped on the window, lightly and briefly. A part of her wanted the man to not notice.

But he gathered up the candle and moved to her, putting his face nearly against the glass.

She lifted one leg and rubbed her ankle, a pained expression on her face. A few moments later, the cottage door opened.

"Lady Delilah?" the old man asked, candle in hand, peering at her.

"I seem to have twisted my ankle," she lied.

He rushed to her side, such a kind-hearted fool. "Well, come inside, good lady. It's too cold in the night. Let me wrap it and we'll get you to The Happy Halfling and a warm bed. I've a cane—two! One for you and one for me, eh?"

He helped her into the cottage.

Dahlia glanced around one last time before entering, to make sure that no one had noticed.

As soon as the door closed, she pinched out the candle.

"Did you find him this time?" Braelin Janquay asked Jarlaxle when he entered the room.

Jarlaxle was already getting up from his seat in the middle of the small chamber, tossing a cloth over the crystal ball that rested in a specially made base on the pedestal before him.

"I cannot be sure," Jarlaxle admitted. "The longer Kimmuriel is one with the hive mind, the less he resembles the drow I knew."

Braelin grimaced. "Surely he is not beginning to look like a mind flayer."

Jarlaxle gave a little laugh. "No, not physically. There is no physical Kimmuriel anymore. It is merely a matter that he seems to be becoming more akin—no, that word isn't correct. It seems almost as if he's blending into the collective of the illithids, becoming one with all of them, and less the drow I knew."

"That sounds horrific."

"He seems more content than I ever knew him to be," Jarlaxle replied with a shrug. "What have you to report?"

"It is Effron, indeed," Braelin replied. "He has built a tower—a fine one, if the merchant is to be believed—in the village of Westbridge."

That brought a nod from Jarlaxle.

"Do you think she is there?" Braelin asked.

"Possibly. Kimmuriel hinted strongly that Dahlia is somewhere south of here and near to the Sword Coast. There are several places she might be if that is indeed the case."

"Then we'll find her."

"Carefully and in good time," Jarlaxle replied. "Dahlia fled from us in a fit of great rage, and that one, I believe, is known to hold her anger for a long time. In good time."

Braelin nodded and let it drop. He had never been enamored of

Dahlia, though he wouldn't tell that to Jarlaxle, who saw her, of course, as a possibly great asset.

"LADY," GHALIVER LONGSTOCKING SAID QUIETLY, his voice calm, though he was seemingly on the edge of nervousness.

The last part was only partly true, Dahlia expected. A week had passed since she had fed on the old man, who had not survived her excited approach. She had done well to hide the truth of his death, tucking him back into bed with no obvious wounds other than two small punctures. It seemed to any who were not looking closely as if he had just passed in his sleep.

But still, Ghaliver Longstocking would very possibly have looked for those particular punctures, would he not? The halfling reminded her of Jarlaxle. Ever suspicious, always wanting to know everything.

The two were sitting in the common room of The Happy Halfling, at a table tucked in the farthest corner from the bar. The place was nearly empty now, as midnight approached. Or at least, it appeared nearly empty, Dahlia knew.

Ghaliver had a host of halfling bodyguards nearby. She could smell their blood, and he certainly wouldn't be about to make such an accusation without ample backup. He was reputedly formidable all on his own, but he preferred to have others do the fighting for him.

So much like Jarlaxle.

"I . . ." he began and paused. "We had a death in the town."

The vampire shrugged. Westbridge wasn't so small a place that such things should not be expected, of course.

"An old man," Ghaliver went on, seemingly finding his voice as it strengthened with each word. "His name was Mickle Corning. Still tended his farm every day."

"I am sure it was a terrible loss for you," she replied.

"He was a good man."

"An old man, you said?"

"Yes."

"Old men die."

"Lady . . ."

"Take care your next words, Master Longstocking."

"He was a good man," Ghaliver repeated. "Good for Westbridge for many years."

"Am I not good for Westbridge? How fares the purse of Ghaliver Longstocking from his friendship with Lady Delilah, I wonder."

Ghaliver fixed her with a perfectly plaintive look.

"Will you dismiss the good I have brought to you and to Westbridge? Did I not strengthen the bonds between Westbridge—between *you!*—and House Margaster of Waterdeep? When the bandits were spotted on the south road, who was it—"

"I dismiss none of it," Ghaliver interrupted. "That is why I am speaking to you privately, of course. Lady, I saw the body of Mickle Corning."

Dahlia sat perfectly still.

"Only I," Ghaliver assured her. "But we spoke of this."

"Perhaps you should quit pouring so many drinks for Brevindon Margaster."

"Lady."

"It won't happen again," Dahlia said.

"It might."

Dahlia could only shrug in reply.

"Do try to *not* let it happen again, I beg."

"He was old and soon to die."

"I know," said Ghaliver. "And yes, Mickle will not be missed by anyone who can do anything about it, but my dear, this is not our way. It cannot be our way."

"I do not disagree," said Dahlia. "I am determined now to remedy the unfortunate situation. When will Gershwin return?"

Ghaliver gave her a curious look. "Within a tenday, I am told."

"I have a plan to prevent . . ." Dahlia let it drop there, ending with, "Fewer drinks for Brevindon when I am coming to meet with him. None, indeed! After I am gone, pour him into a stupor—I care not."

"What about Mickle?"

"What would you have me say? Am I to pay recompense?"

"He has no family in Westbridge, so, no, no. But what will become of him now? Will he rise to serve you?"

Dahlia put on a perfectly wicked smile.

"We cannot have that," Ghaliver urged.

"I will never send him near to Westbridge."

"That is not enough," said Ghaliver. "I will not have Mickle rise in undeath. Not in any role. You must destroy him before he rises."

"He will remain at Manse Dor—"

"No!" Ghaliver insisted. "Lady, I'll not have it."

"You'll not have it?" Dahlia asked and gave a little laugh.

But Ghaliver held his composure. "Not with Mickle and not with any of Westbridge's folk. This is not a part of our unspoken bargain.

"Stop the rise of Mickle's corpse," Ghaliver insisted. "Or I will have to, and in that event, all of Westbridge will know that we have been assailed by a fiend."

"You will betray me?"

"Never," Ghaliver replied before she had finished the question. "But I cannot keep the secret of a malignant spirit haunting the town if I have to make a public display of destroying the corpse of Mickle Corning, now can I? For it is not something I can do alone, and why else would I ask for such assistance in the grim task?"

"He will not rise," Dahlia promised.

"And this will not happen again," Ghaliver insisted.

"I will try to remedy—"

"That was not a question, Lady Delilah," said Ghaliver Longstocking, and he straightened and seemed quite formidable in that moment. "This will not happen again. There is only so much I can overlook, only so many chances I can offer. Yes, you have been a great boon to Westbridge, and yes, Mickle Corning was a very old man. But . . . no more, Lady Delilah. Not here. Not with the people who entrust me with their safety and prosperity."

"You are the Westbridge burgomeister again, then?"

"I speak for the burgomeister. I speak for Westbridge."

Dahlia just sat and stared at him for a few moments, trying to take a full measure of the halfling. How many others had he told about her? she wondered. What contingencies had he taken should she ever decide to be rid of him?

Thoughts of eliminating this potential problem couldn't take hold, though. Dahlia reminded herself that she really hadn't wanted to kill Mickle Corning, or anyone, for that matter. And Ghaliver was proving himself to her again right now, wasn't he?

She had done well for Westbridge, yes, but she couldn't deny that Westbridge had done quite well for her, too.

"It will not happen again," she said quietly.

"I trust it won't."

17

A TALE OF TWO RINGS

"An amazing ring," Allefaero told Breezy, the two walking the hillsides surrounding the famed Ivy Mansion of Longsaddle. The year had turned to 1510, and the winter had given away early, the forests about them in full bloom already, though the fifth month had barely commenced. "These are rare, and greatly treasured among those who dabble in magic of any kind."

"I'm not really sure how it works," said Breezy. "Penelope Harpell loaned it to me and told me that it would add to my spellcasting energy, but when I put it on, all that I feel is that it is somehow an empty vessel."

"Cast some spells into it—spells that you would likely use."

"Just cast them in?"

"Just cast them in. And they will be there when you call upon them, even if that is days, tendays, months, years later. The ring does exactly as its name implies. It stores the magical energies of spells."

"So I can fill it with my most powerful spells, or I could have you fill it with your most powerful spells."

"Yes, and no. My most powerful spells could not be contained within that ring. The number of spells is not as important as the energy required to cast a spell, you see, and that energy for the greatest spells is surely beyond the capacity of the ring, or of any such ring."

Breezy put on a little smile, seeing how the normally timid Allefaero puffed up when boasting that no ring could hold his greatest powers. She wasn't mocking him, certainly, and found that she rather liked this oft-repressed aspect of the Callidaean.

"But you could put a handful of minor spells in, or one or two more powerful dweomers. Or I could do it for you," he suggested.

"The magical shield I call upon in difficult moments of sword fighting is a minor spell," Breezy said, her face lighting up.

"The ring would hold that five times."

"Shadow Blade," Breezy declared, her purple eyes sparkling.

"It would depend on the power of the blade you wish to create," Allefaero explained. "You could put two in the ring, and even add a single magical shield to the collection, if they were of the weakest form. Or a single Shadow Blade dweomer could fill the ring and bring forth a powerful weapon, indeed. But such a conjuration would be beyond your capability."

"But not beyond yours. Were you to fill the ring with a single powerful Shadow Blade, would I be able to call upon it?"

"Anyone attuned to the ring could, yes, but I don't know the spell."

"But you will learn it for me, yes?" She smiled so sweetly that Allefaero actually laughed aloud.

"Promise me that you will," Breezy said more seriously.

"I will," he said. "But don't forget that Lady Penelope Harpell's ring is just on loan."

"Maybe I can convince Lady Penelope to let me keep it." Her smile was that of a cat with a secret. "I am pretty good at convincing people to do things."

"Like learning how to cast Shadow Blade, I know," Allefaero deadpanned, and Breezy hopped over and kissed him on the cheek. He was right, of course. Breezy could only hope that Allefaero understood that she would do the same for him, and more, if ever he needed her help.

"Why do I suspect that you're going to get me into a lot of trouble someday?"

"Why do I suspect that you're going to like the adventure accompanying that trouble?"

Allefaero sighed and surrendered, and the two continued their walk. Breezy reiterated her hope that Allefaero would learn to cast the Shadow Blade spell when they parted later that morning, for Breezy had a lesson planned with her mother and Penelope Harpell.

ALLEFAERO WANDERED THE GROUNDS OF the Ivy Mansion, loitering about the marble concourse where the Harpell family had paid homage to their most heroic, and oftentimes their most ridiculous, ancestors.

The wizard paused for a long while at the statue of Bidderdoo Harpell, which seemed to him the epitome of Harpell magic gone awry—a story that he had heard much about from his time with Jarlaxle and Drizzt. The other Companions of the Hall had fought beside the heroic, eccentric Bidderdoo during the DR 1358 war between Mithral Hall and Menzoberranzan.

Long previous to that battle, Bidderdoo had trapped himself into the form of a dog. In the first upheaval of magic, the famed Time of Troubles, the Harpell family had found a way to restore Bidderdoo to his human self, but in the stress of the ensuing war with the drow in Mithral Hall, Bidderdoo had given in to the residual animalistic urges. The wizard had raged into battle as a werewolf—indeed, as the warrior werewolf who had slain the great weapons master, Uthegentel Del'Armgo.

Allefaero shook his head, recalling the details, and thinking too of the first sounds he had heard when he and Breezy had come to Longsaddle a few nights earlier: howling in the forests all about Longsaddle.

These were werewolves, the apostles of Bidderdoo, who defended the town from within the shadows of the forests. They posed no threat to the people of the secluded community and were affectionately known by the folk of Longsaddle as the Bidderdoos.

Ah, Longsaddle! Allefaero truly loved this strange, strange place. It spoke of creativity with magic, and it screamed of the sheer love for exploring the greater arcane powers offered by the multiverse.

Longsaddle—or the Ivy Mansion, and these many statues and plaques in particular—also warned of the dangers of such "creative" practice with the mighty arts, the sometimes-fatal consequences of which were on display here in the concourse of the Ivy Mansion.

That warning led him to think of his companion. Had Breezy ever faced consequences for her airy attitude about magic or about the world in general?

Her expulsion from the Monastery of the Yellow Rose had been one consequence, he presumed. Surely, her loss to Brother Gregory had wounded her physically and emotionally. Had there been a lesson there, and if so, was it one that had stuck?

He nodded as he considered it all. Getting kicked out of the Order of Saint Sollars was a necessary thing for Breezy if she meant to continue along her path to achieve such great personal power, he had come to believe. Whether as a warrior or a wizard, or with both through the School of Bladesinging, Breezy was a supremely talented person, both intellectually and physically, and with vast resources at her disposal.

She needed that added emotional talent of caution and humility. Her actions in the future would be consequential, not just to herself, likely, but to many others.

Breezy's heart was good, Allefaero knew, and he had great faith that she'd get there, that she would become a positive force in the world, particularly under the guidance of Jarlaxle, her current and most important mentor.

And in this moment, he, Allefaero, was her most important instructor, he realized, and so he ended his dawdling and headed for the Ivy Mansion's well-appointed scriptorium. He would learn Shadow Blade, and he would put a truly powerful one in the ring Penelope had loaned to Breezy.

"You didn't need to bring Soliardis," Catti-brie said when Breezy entered the room to join her and Penelope Harpell. She wasn't trying to be confrontational. The smile on her face was genuine, as she was quite happy about these sessions in the arts arcane that she and Penelope would offer to the young woman.

Breezy shrugged. "I always wear it. Since there's no blade unless I call upon it, I hardly realize that I have it strapped to my belt."

"And do you call upon it often?" Catti-brie asked.

Breezy chuckled and dryly replied, "Every day in my practice regimen, mother."

"I only ask because I wonder if you have truly come to appreciate this gift from your grandda Zaknafein. The power of Soliardis—"

"It is a mighty weapon, I do not doubt."

"But?" Penelope interjected, and Catti-brie understood that Penelope was hearing the same emotions from Breezy toward that weapon. Not disdain, exactly, but something less enthusiastic than one might expect.

"I prefer the incarnation from the spell of Shadow Blade."

"A fine illusion, yes," Penelope said.

Breezy narrowed her gaze at that. "Illusion?"

"The shadow blade is a trick of the light."

"It seems more a conjuration spell to me."

"It merely gathers shadows to you that allow you to convince—"

"Shadows are more than a trick," Breezy interrupted.

Penelope and Catti-brie exchanged curious looks.

"I suppose that one could view it that way, yes," Penelope agreed. "A shadow blade is a powerful weapon, but it is one that severely limits your other magical options, yes?"

"Whenever I draw a blade, I am more a warrior than a wizard."

"A spell of Haste on the way into combat is a fine option," Penelope pointed out, and Breezy wondered if she had been talking with Allefaero. "As is a curse to slow your enemies, or bringing forth an elemental to join in your battle. I believe that Soliardis can aid in that endeavor. But you couldn't maintain the shadow blade with any of those other choices in effect. And they, too, are powerful options."

"As is a lightning bolt from the back ranks," Catti-brie added, her tone lighthearted.

"I am not that kind of a wizard," Breezy answered very seriously.

"But you are a wizard," Catti-brie replied.

"I have found a school of wizardry that interests me."

"Bladesinging," said Penelope. "Yes, and it is a fine choice for one of your skill and talent."

Catti-brie regretted the sigh the moment it inadvertently escaped her lips. Truthfully, she didn't disagree with Penelope. In looking over the School of Bladesinging, Catti-brie understood immediately that Breezy was as fine a candidate for the little-used practice as anyone she had ever known. She couldn't dismiss, however, her instincts as a mother, and so she couldn't deny that she preferred Breezy engaging in any battle from far behind the lines.

"Is that a problem?" Breezy asked her, responding to the sigh.

"No," she said, trying to find the right way to express herself. "I am glad that you will be prepared if the battle comes to you."

"I welcome the battle."

"I know."

"But you wish me to stay in the back, like you do."

"I only want you to explore all the possibilities before you."

"And you hate that I choose bladesinging. I prefer to spend my days in training physically to sitting at a desk with a pen. I would fight my enemies up close above throwing magic from—"

"Neither Zaknafein nor Jarlaxle would have given Soliardis to you without my express permission," Catti-brie insisted.

"Grudging consent."

"No. That's not it," Catti-brie insisted. "I have watched Gromph lay waste to a crowd of frost giants from across a wide cavern. His power is beyond anything any warrior can replicate. I had hoped the same for you—and yes, I still do!"

"Is that really your objection, mother, or are you just jealous?"

That opened the eyes of Catti-brie, and of Penelope, wide with surprise, but Breezy pressed on. "Are you upset that you did not find bladesinging when you transitioned from warrior to wizard? From all that I have heard of your exploits, the school would have fit you as well as it fits me."

"Even had I heard of it in those long-ago days, I was too injured at that time."

"But you're not now."

"I'm not a young woman now."

Breezy laughed, catching Catti-brie off guard. "I've watched you sparring with Da. You'd still be a great bladesinger."

Then Breezy added something that turned the conversation around and made Catti-brie's heart warm.

"Train with me."

The offer was sincere, Catti-brie knew, and whether she'd even consider it or not, being asked by Breezy to spend more time with her was indeed a gift to her.

"Be careful, I just might do that."

"You can use Soliardis," Breezy said with a wink, drawing another sigh from Catti-brie.

"I know that you prefer the conjured blade," Penelope interjected, "but I have to agree with your ma here. The weapon you now carry is more powerful than any shadow blade you might create. Indeed, it is likely more powerful than any shadow blade even an archmage like Gromph Baenre could conjure. Truly, Soliardis is a work of magical art, a joining of two superbly crafted weapons into a unique form."

"Have you even tried the whip?" Catti-brie asked.

"I've never used a whip."

"You'll pick it up quickly, particularly if your heart is in the practice, and perhaps then you will understand the true power of this weapon Grandda Zaknafein gave to you. Perhaps we can send you back to Callidae to be trained by him, for none are better with a whip than Zaknafein. And the whip contained within Soliardis is . . ." She paused and shook her head in awe. "The wielder can breach the barrier to the Plane of Fire itself! Cut a rift for planar essence to drip through, perhaps even create minor fire beasts at the feet of your enemy."

"I don't know anything about that and am not sure that I want to."

"You shouldn't fear the beasts who may drip through your rift. They will aid you."

"They would aid *you*, you mean," Breezy countered. "You can dominate such creatures easily with your arcane skills, or fully protect yourself from them with your divine skills! I will never be a wizard of your particular powers, Ma. If that is what you expect . . ."

"It isn't," Catti-brie interrupted, not wanting this important exchange to veer into animosity. "I understand. Your mind is marvelous and chasing every squirrel."

"Marvelous?" Breezy snorted. "Discordant, you mean. Unorganized. Confused and scattered! Chasing squirrels, yes!"

Catti-brie winced at hearing Breezy's recognition of her different way of thinking, at her difficulty in focusing and her easy distractibility.

"Hardly," she said sincerely, moving to her daughter. "*Beautiful* is the word I would use. I was a fighter, an archer, and then I wasn't. I had to dedicate myself fully to my tasks to reach any level of proficiency as a warrior and then as a wizard. You invite me to join in your bladesinging, but the mere thought of trying to juggle martial and arcane training overwhelms me. But look at you! You changed your monastic tradition right before your fight for rank!"

"And I lost!"

"You did, but in a well-fought match against a formidable, fully dedicated Master of Dragons who had not strayed at all from the primary tradition of the Order."

"And I was kicked out for my squirrel chasing."

"You were removed by Grandmaster of Flowers Savahn for your own good," said Catti-brie. "We all see that now. I was angry at Savahn—oh, but your da and I wanted to tear the Monastery of the Yellow Rose down to its foundation when we were told of your expulsion. But look at you now, learning with purpose, and in a dozen different directions, as suits your desires. It is a beautiful thing to watch, my love."

"Yet you disapprove."

"No," Catti-brie said. "No. Not at all. I'm just unreasonably afraid. You're my little girl, however formidable or powerful you become. I was glad the monks wouldn't let me watch your fight with Master Gregory—I don't know that I could hold my breath for such a length of time!"

She choked up, sniffled a bit, and looked Breezy in the eye for a few heartbeats, then offered her daughter a hug.

Breezy sighed, but she was obviously grateful and returned the embrace with equal enthusiasm. Catti-brie felt as if she and her daughter had just passed an important milestone in their relationship, and the intensity of the embrace assured her that Breezy felt it, too.

"Give Soliardis a try, I beg," Catti-brie said when they broke the hold.

"You're very proud of your work," Breezy replied with a grin.

"I don't think you quite understand what your mother accomplished with the Great Forge," Penelope interjected. "She coaxed a godlike being to undo and redo magical items that were powerful all on their own."

She would have continued, but Catti-brie put her hand on Penelope's shoulder and bade her to stop.

"Soliardis is composed of a sun blade and a whip of elemental fire," Catti-brie said. "Your da's second scimitar is a blend of the defender sword Twinkle and of Vidrinath, a powerful drow weapon given to the Elderboy of the greatest of Menzoberranzan's houses. Your grandda Bruenor's shield is similarly a combination of two powerfully enchanted shields. They were created by—"

"By you. Yes, I know."

"No, by Maegera," Catti-brie corrected. "The primordial creature of fire held in Gauntlgrym's chasm. Maegera powers the forges of Gauntlgrym, including most especially the Great Forge, and that oven is a marvelous device, indeed. Maegera unbound the magics of the items I fed into that oven, not I, and Maegera rebound them in powerful ways for Twinkle, Soliardis, Bruenor's shield, even the belt buckle which holds Taulmaril."

"Maegera did it because your ma compelled Maegera to do it," Penelope added. "And at the very edge of catastrophe, I am sure. She has gone down to the face of the godlike primordial, below the water elementals that swirl about the chasm and trap the godly being below. Catti-brie dared to stand on the cooling magma and commune with a creature that could snuff out her life with hardly a thought. And she partnered with the primordial in her creations within the Great Forge. These are feats that even Gromph Baenre admires, so do show proper respect here, I insist."

"She's my daughter," Catti-brie deadpanned. "That is a difficult request you make of her."

Penelope laughed at that. Catti-brie watched Breezy's embarrassed blush, her smooth gray skin taking a rosy hue, the violet highlights of her face becoming truly red. Even in blushing, her daughter was a beautiful thing, she thought.

"How does one compel a primordial?" Breezy asked. "Did Grandda Bruenor do it to power the portals?"

"Your mother, again," Penelope said before Catti-brie could explain.

"So, you are the only one?" Breezy asked Catti-brie.

"She is the only one who had the courage to try," Penelope answered.

"There were reasons beyond any of my abilities or courage for that," Catti-brie said humbly.

Breezy seemed perplexed and interested, Catti-brie noted. "Soliardis is a greater gift than you appreciate, I believe. Try it. You wish to be a bladesinger, and I think that you suit the study. But no bladesinger could wish for a better weapon than the one you so clearly take for granted. Give it a true try, I beg."

"I will," Breezy said.

"The whip," Catti-brie said. "Learn the whip."

Breezy was shaking her head. "I don't want to play with fire."

On impulse, Catti-brie reached for a ring she wore, one that seemed like two separate bands connected by a mithral triangle set with a beautiful triangular ruby, so perfectly clear and perfectly cut that any light reflecting off it seemed like it was coming from inside the gemstone. The front band resembled a sculpted and embossed crown of gold, while the base circlet was of a plainer brown metal, the lower edge ringed by more than two dozen small brown gems.

When Catti-brie pulled it from her finger, that crown-like band simply disappeared.

"Here," she told Breezy, handing it over. "Wear it and attune to its powers." She saw the glimmer in her daughter's purple eyes as she rolled the powerful ring over with her fingers.

"And the crown circlet will reappear?"

Catti-brie shook her head. "No, that deeper magic is dependent upon conditions you would have to meet personally to unlock the full power of the band. But even without that, you should feel safe in practicing with that whip, and with any minor elemental beasts that Soliardis can bring forth."

"What conditions?"

"Nothing you need consider!" Catti-brie said adamantly. "I am not gifting you this ring. This is a loan for your practice, nothing more. Perhaps when I am old and feeble and no more interested in adventure, we can consider whether your arcane abilities and understanding are worthy of such a ring as this. But for now, use it to train with that whip and to better understand the beauty and power of Soliardis. Put it on and keep it on—promise me now that you will not allow anyone else to wear it, indeed, that you will not remove it from your finger until I ask for it back."

Breezy stared at her curiously for a long while before saying, "I promise."

"Wonderful," said Penelope, and she cast a wink at Breezy. "Now, get your quill and ink and let us begin your lesson. We will concentrate our efforts this day on spells that will require your focus to maintain."

"Spells that I cannot use with a shadow blade, but can use with Soliardis," Breezy slyly replied.

"Do you want to be a stubborn, and thus dead, warrior, or the most effective bladesinger of all?" Penelope bluntly returned.

Breezy ran her hand over the campfire she and Allefaero had set down by the invisible fence that surrounded the hill of the Ivy Mansion.

"You will burn yourself, silly," the Callidaean wizard said.

"I hardly feel the heat of it," Breezy replied with a grin, and she turned her hand just right to let the triangular ruby of her ring sparkle at Allefaero.

"What is that?" came the predictable question, asked with intrigue.

"My ma's ring. She uses it to dominate beings of fire, even to communicate with and befriend the primordial Maegera."

"A Ring of Fire Elemental Control?" Allefaero gasped.

"You've seen one before?"

"No, we don't get a lot of those particular elemental beings up in Callidae. Or yes, rather, for I recall your mother wearing a similar ring." He paused and seemed a bit confused, then added, "I remember its appearance a bit differently."

"It has a second band, a crown of gold, that appears when she puts it on," Breezy explained.

"Conditional, of course! That is the norm with those powerful rings."

"You just said you've never seen one."

"Not of fire, no, but we have Rings of Air Elemental Control among the very greatest of our heroes, of course. The glacier Qadeej is named after a wind god, and his children often come to play. And also, the greatest of our people can use such rings to commune with Qadeej, or so they claim."

"Like my ma communes with the primordial Maegera, I suppose."

"You understand that there are four types of these rings, one for each element. They all require some condition be met before they reveal their full power for a new wielder, from what I have heard, though even without that, they offer many benefits."

"What is the condition?"

Allefaero shrugged and asked, "Why do you have it?"

"Ma wants me to learn the whip function of Soliardis," Breezy explained. "It can cut into the Plane of Fire, and sometimes little beasties fall out."

"May I see the ring?"

Breezy reflexively reached for the ring, but pulled her hand back and shook her head. "I promised my ma that I would not take it off."

Allefaero nodded, then put a sly grin on his face, cast a quick spell, and stuck his hand into the campfire—a campfire that he had magically created when they had come out to hear the howls of the Bidderdoos.

"Show-off," Breezy grumbled, and she cast a spell of her own, one Allefaero had taught to her, and that dweomer combined with the ring allowed her to reach into the flames and hold his hand. She moved her fingers over his and noted that he, too, was wearing a ring.

"Is that my other ring?" she asked.

Allefaero pulled his hand out and held it up before her. "It might be."

"Did you . . . ?"

Allefaero's smile beamed. He pulled off the ring and tossed it to her.

Breezy had it on her finger in an eyeblink, and she leaped up to her feet.

"Don't you want to save it for the morning practice?"

"You can cast it again," she answered with a wink, and from the Ring of Spell Storing, she brought forth a shadow blade.

And such a shadow blade it was!

She could feel the power brimming within it, and could only imagine the damage she could inflict on a monstrous enemy with a single cut of this beautiful and deadly creation.

There came a howl from the forest, followed by a second.

"The Bidderdoos are not our enemies," Allefaero reminded her.

"I know," said Breezy. "But I wish a troll or an evil giant would come wandering by right now."

She went through a series of movements, then, a deadly dance combining her sword skills and her monk training, striking an imaginary foe repeatedly with the shadow blade, with her open hand, with a straight kick or leaping kick or circle kick.

The fighting routine only lasted a short while, until the shadow blade blinked away.

But Breezy kept going, drawing Soliardis, bringing forth the whip instead of the light blade. She went into a more frenzied dance then, spinning circles, cracking the whip with every turn, snapping it and slashing with it, cutting the air and then creating a small rift.

Globs of liquid fire dripped through, spurring the swordswoman on.

Another rift, this one deeper, brought forth a small living flame that rushed about without apparent purpose or aim and left a glowing and smoking trail in the grass in its wake.

She finished when the little beastie winked out, dismissed the whip and put the weapon away, then clapped her hands and laughed heartily.

"It is a mightily enchanted weapon," Allefaero said.

Breezy stiffened and stared at him, then shook her head. "The shadow blade was better."

"But the shadow blade doesn't last."

Breezy blew a resigned sigh, then looked down despondently at Lady Penelope's ring, which Allefaero would have to recharge.

Then she looked at her other ring and sprouted a wicked little grin.

18

THE PERCEIVED INVINCIBILITY
OF YOUTH

"Well?" Breezy asked when Allefaero returned from a lunch with Dowell Harpell, Lady Penelope's husband and an accomplished enchanter.

"He is a most generous host," Allefaero replied, drawing a huff from Breezy.

"Surely he knows of the ring," she said.

"Surely. And you could have just gone and inquired about it yourself."

Breezy's huff turned into a low growl and muttered curses at Allefaero's teasing. If she could have gone herself, she would have. But if she had, then Dowell might suspect her intentions regarding the powerful ring her mother had given her.

"Are you going to make me pull every word out of you, or should I just bring up the whip?" she asked.

Allefaero laughed. "Master Harpell was quite forthcoming regarding the ring. To open its true powers, you would have to help in slaying a fire elemental—a true one, and not the little sprites of flame that come through from your whip."

"You can summon such a beast."

Allefaero cleared his throat. "Yes, but . . ."

"Let's do it."

"When I summon such a monster as that, it would be within a protective circle and with the expectation that I could control it, not that I would fight it. Have you ever seen a fire—"

"You've defeated polar worms!" Breezy interrupted. "Give me your mighty shadow blade in the other ring and we can win handily."

"You underestimate the fury of a true fire elemental, I fear."

"You always fear—that's why your life is boring."

That brought a laugh, but it was not one without a bit of regret seeping into it. "Breezy, a true fire elemental is not to be trifled with."

"We will have every advantage. We can prepare the battlefield well in advance and you can choose the spells most effective against the beast. And we both have magic to aid in our shielding against their biting flames."

"No!"

"I'll use Taulmaril. Summon it on an island in the small lake in the forest and we'll strike at it from the water! I'll get Guenhwyvar."

"It will burn Guenhwyvar!"

"Guen heals on the Astral Plane."

"And you care nothing for her pains?"

Breezy snorted and cursed under her breath. "Take a risk, Allefaero. We need the ring fully opened to me, we both agree."

"I haven't agreed to anything yet. This whole thing seems absurd."

"Then go back to your books. Bury your face in . . . words, while the world spins with adventure around you."

"That's not fair. This beast could kill us both."

"Your concern is touching," came the sarcastic reply. "Or is it cowardice?"

"Breezy," the Callidaean wizard said helplessly.

"I fought five—five!—tundra yetis in a single battle with Wulfgar. I went into a cave and fought udadrow priestesses and warriors to steal back the primordial essence for King Bruenor's planned magical gate in Icewind Dale. And you . . . you've gone into a hole in Cattisola to a sub-chamber of giant crystals, and there did battle with hordes of polar worms."

"That was different. Those were necessary battles for the cause of good."

"So is this. Think of what we'll create!"

Allefaero couldn't hide his intrigue as he chewed his lip, and that brought a knowing grin to Breezy.

"Out at the small lake?"

"At night," Breezy said. "Tonight."

"The Bidderdoos are out there."

"They're not our enemies."

"But they might take exception to us bringing a fire elemental to their forest!"

"But, but, but," Breezy teased. "It's right here," she said, holding up one hand and rubbing the tips of her fingers together. "Right here, for us to take."

"You don't even know if any of this will work. This seems like the first and easiest step, and this alone could kill us both!"

"And we never will know if it will work unless we try."

"The primordial . . ."

"We're talking about a fire elemental right now. A monster that you can summon and that we can defeat. One fight at a time, yes?"

A long silence ensued. Allefaero closed his eyes and seemed to be taking it all in, weighing the gains and the risk. He took a deep breath and surrendered.

"Tomorrow night, at the lake," he said.

"WE DON'T WANT TO GET in close to the monster," Allefaero explained. He and Breezy stood on the bank of a small pond in the forest west of the Ivy Mansion. A hundred feet or so from them, barely visible in the dim moonlight, sat a small and bare island of stone. "Even with our magical protections, the flames of a fire elemental will curl the skin from your bones.

"It will be destroyed before it gets close enough to harm us," Breezy insisted, but the wizard shook his head.

"This is no yeti. It can move quickly and can take a lot of punish-ment."

"You said merely crossing the water will hurt it."

"Not nearly enough."

"Don't shoot until I return to your side," Allefaero instructed. "Let me begin the battle. And understand that I will have only a single dimensional escape left to get us out of the fight once the elemental arrives before us."

Breezy lifted Taulmaril and set an arrow to the string. "You worry too much."

"You worry not enough."

"Probably true," said Breezy. "But I have more fun."

Allefaero just shook his head. He climbed into a small canoe they had "borrowed" from a nearby dock, and began paddling his way quite unsteadily out toward the island. Once there, he lit a small fire in a brazier, poured in some magical components, and began casting his conjuration.

A minute later, a larger flame appeared near to him, swirling and growing. In moments, it was taller than Allefaero, taking a roughly humanoid shape within its brightly burning flames.

Breezy held her breath as it continued to grow, now twice Allefaero's height, then thrice! Arms of flame reached out from it, but it made no move to attack the wizard.

Still, Allefaero nervously glanced over his shoulder repeatedly when he got back into the canoe and paddled away from the island.

"Are you sure?" he asked Breezy when he neared the shore.

She nodded and smiled, thinking she was doing quite well in hiding her terror.

"We can still change our plans," Allefaero explained, climbing out and coming ashore. "The elemental thinks me a friend now, as it is under the thrall of my spell. Our first strike changes that completely."

"Then make your first shot count."

Allefaero took a deep breath and produced a tiny piece of fur and a small glass rod. He took another deep breath. "Count to five," he told Breezy, and he launched into spellcasting.

Eager Breezy let fly right at five, her arrow leaving a trail of lightning energy as it sped for the stationary monster. A blinding flash and a thunderous crackle came forth from Allefaero's fingertips at almost the same moment.

Breezy kept her calm and set another arrow, lifting Taulmaril and letting fly before the now enraged elemental had even left the island. That one, too, dove into the flames, blasting a gout of fiery red out the monster's back.

A third arrow was set in quick order, and now Breezy had to fight the sensations in her mind, for she could feel the elemental's anger, could hear its crackling protests, could sense its very thoughts.

The ring was serving as a conduit!

Allefaero blasted forth a second lightning bolt, flames spitting out from the diminishing but still formidable monster. Steam rose up from the lake as it charged across.

Breezy shot it again.

"We flee through the gate!" Allefaero cried. "Oh, but too late!" He sprinted back from the beach and began casting desperately.

Breezy didn't set a fourth arrow. Instead, she lifted her hand and stared at the approaching monster over her ringed finger. She marveled at the magnificent creation of fire, at its speed, for it was barely ten yards from her!

"Breezy, run to me!" Allefaero yelled. "Now!"

But she didn't.

Instead, she sent her thoughts, her demands, through her ma's powerful ring, casting a spell of her own from within its powers.

"Stop!" she demanded.

The elemental halted its charge.

The water hissed and stole more of its living flames, steam rising and obscuring the creature.

"Hold!" Breezy demanded. She could feel the monster fighting her domination, and understood that every sting the water inflicted worked against her commands.

"Come here and open a portal back to the island," Breezy told Allefaero. "And when we land there, we hit it again as hard as we can."

"This is madness."

"Hurry."

Allefaero ran up beside her and did as she had ordered. They stepped through the gate onto the stone of the island, and Breezy had Taulmaril up again, another lightning arrow on the way. And another lightning bolt followed.

Breezy almost gasped at the intensity of the hatred she felt in her mind coming from the elemental. She thought to try to dominate it again with the ring, but no, not now. That would be futile, she knew, for all the fire beast wanted was to consume her and the wizard who had summoned it from its fiery home.

She shot it again, then again, confused at the lack of another blast of lightning from her wizard companion.

Instead, Allefaero moved to the edge of the lake and knelt.

On came the greatly diminished but still lethal monster, speeding back across the water.

Another lightning arrow hit it, then another.

Still no strike by Allefaero.

Thirty feet away. Twenty!

Breezy lifted her bow for one last shot, let fly, and dropped the weapon. She reached for the magical hilt of Soliardis, but paused and changed her mind, her eyes going to the ring she wore on her right hand, the ring Penelope had loaned to her and Allefaero had charged with his powerful spell. She could feel the intense heat burning her eyes and nostrils, singeing her hair, even.

The elemental charged faster and would run right through them, igniting them! Breezy tried to dismiss her sudden terror, tried to remind herself to summon the powerful shadow blade.

Too late, she feared, for the elemental monster was right there in front of her.

But the lake leaped up before it, so suddenly, a wall of water immediately in its path. The elemental slammed in with a great hiss and splash, warm water flying over Breezy and Allefaero.

Beyond the wave, nothing.

"We did it," Allefaero said, clearly shocked, his voice shaky.

Breezy thought to summon the shadow blade, but saw nothing to attack. She felt something, then, from a ring—her ma's ring. She lifted her left hand up before her and watched in awe the mystical appearance of a second band, a golden crown, connected to the first.

"Well, you almost wasted my spell, but . . ." Allefaero stopped, jaw hanging open, as Breezy held up that left hand for him to see the transformation of the elemental ring, her fingers waggling.

"We did it," she said with a wide smile, indeed. "Let's go visit my grandda Bruenor."

BREEZY WATCHED WITH DELIGHT ONLY a short while later as Bruenor unwound his shield, the small item widening out like a spiderweb to become a solid buckler.

"How?" Breezy gasped, exaggerating her excitement for Bruenor's sake.

"Bwahaha!" laughed the dwarf king. He reached behind the shield and produced a flagon of ale, handing it to Allefaero, then a second one for himself, which he held up to the wizard in toast.

"None for me?" Breezy asked.

"Yer ma'd kill me to death," said Bruenor.

"I can battle udadrow and yetis, but a beer . . ." She stopped when Bruenor threw a wink at Allefaero, the two of them laughing at Breezy's expense.

"How did ma create that?" Breezy asked, pointing to the shield.

"She throwed me old shield in the furnace along with the web shield we got from the drow, from that Tiago fellow, I think."

"And you hammered the two together when the Great Forge made them malleable?"

"Nah. Yer ma did it all—or she had the primordial thing do it. This one came out o' the forge all ready to strap onto me arm."

"Truly amazing," said Allefaero. "The belt buckle holding Taulmaril, Drizzt's sword, your shield . . . the softer bits, the leather straps and softer metal . . . none of them were destroyed?"

"The fire's not just eatin' in there," Bruenor said. "The primordial thing's doin' the shapin' and the meldin' o' magic and metal, and wood and leather. Aye, but it's a bit o' enchantin' to make old Moradin himself take note."

"And Maegera did it all, with coaxing from Catti-brie?"

"Girl's got a bond with it," said Bruenor. "Through that enchanted ring she wears."

Allefaero noted that Breezy had the hand with the ring to the side, behind the folds of her shirt.

"She even went down the chasm to get Entreri's sword back from the beast, and it let her! She came back up without a burn," Bruenor finished.

"And then she just went to the Great Forge and bid the primordial to improve her items?" Breezy asked breathlessly, trying to coax it as a story from her grandda instead of asking for instructions.

"Blended 'em," Bruenor explained. "Aye. Took a lot o' trust for us to do that. We sent some mighty items into that furnace. Started with yer da's scimitar. Broken, so yer ma sent it in with the one called Vidrinath. And what came out, well, ye seen it."

"Twinkle is a truly powerful blade now," Breezy agreed. "And you've a shield that gives you drink!"

"That's a gift from the throne up in the hall above. Drow shield added the trick o' changin' the size of it. And," he added with a wink, "I can make it sticky. Catch a swinging mace or blade and hold it fast. Aye, a fine shield, she is."

Breezy guided the conversation away from the items then, asking for another description of the battle of the Qadeej Glacier, which Bruenor was always happy to relate. She wanted his thoughts far from her earlier questioning before she and Allefaero took their leave, traveling a roundabout route to the room with the chasm that held the fire primordial captive.

"I can hear its murmur," Breezy told Allefaero as they entered the short tunnel which led to that room, the magical engine of Gauntlgrym.

Allefaero stopped her, then cast a spell.

Can you hear me? he asked, but not aloud. He was in her mind.

Yes. Can you hear the murmurs of Maegera?

I cannot understand them.

Whispers, Breezy telepathically replied.

They entered the large, natural chamber, Breezy moving right to the rim of the chasm, staring down through the mist and the swirls of the water elementals that served as prison bars to the lava face of Maegera.

It is truly beautiful, she heard Allefaero's thoughts in her mind, and she agreed. *What is it whispering to you?*

Breezy didn't know how to answer. She wasn't hearing words from Maegera, but more like feelings . . . hesitance . . . wariness. But not anger.

She was glad of that, for she could sense the power of the being, and she understood in that moment that she had never before been in conversation, telepathic or otherwise, with any creature remotely as powerful as this overwhelming primordial. Not Gromph, not her parents, not even the dragon sisters. She thought of the battle Bruenor had just described in the northern glacier, when so many powerful heroes had gone into that ice cave in the north and waged war on the slaadi and the frost giants, and she knew, she just knew, even that mighty force would be mere insects before the bared power of Maegera.

Come to me.

Breezy thought it was Allefaero, and did as he asked.

But then the wizard's hand was on her, grabbing her by the shoulder and yanking her back forcefully. She felt him tumble to the floor, but she held her footing. Allefaero didn't let go, however, grasping her powerfully by her shirt.

"No, Breezy! No!" he shouted, and she heard the same thing in her mind from him, felt the desperation in his tone, audible and telepathic.

Breezy blinked open her eyes and looked at him curiously, then turned back toward the chasm and the railing set at its edge.

"You were trying to climb over!" Allefaero said. "Take off the ring!"

Breezy glanced back and forth curiously, but she did not remove the ring. Allefaero leaped up and hugged her tight, holding her back.

"Take off the ring, Breezy, I beg!"

She looked at him again, barely registering his words or his obvious terror. He reached for her ring, and she instinctively caught his hand, did a subtle duck and turn, grabbed the shoulder of his robe with her free hand, then sent him flipping over her back as she suddenly ducked, putting him hard to the floor.

Only his cry of pain finally broke the trance, and Breezy quickly pulled off the ring, stilling the voice of Maegera in her mind.

"Wow," she gasped. "By the gods, Allefaero, it is amazing."

"You were trying to go over the rail," the wizard said, awkwardly pulling himself up from the floor. "You were going to leap into the chasm!"

Breezy shook her head—but deep inside, she realized that he was speaking truthfully.

"Let us return to Longsaddle. Get your mother to do this deed. I am sure—"

"No!" There was no debate in her tone. "I can do this. *We* can do this."

"I could barely sense the beast, and understand it not at all."

"No beast. It is a god-creature. We are the beasts to Maegera."

"Let me try the ring."

Breezy started to hand it over, but pulled it back, remembering her promise to her ma. She thought it curious that the promise would hold her back. If her ma and da and grandda or anyone else knew what she meant to do here, that promise would be the least of her restraints.

But there it was, and she shook her head and did not offer the ring to Allefaero.

"We cannot do this," Allefaero said. "You are not ready to ask anything of Maegera."

"Yes, we can."

"Breezy, you almost went over the rail. Were I not here, you would be lying dead atop the lava of the primordial's face. Your parents would never even find—"

"No. You're wrong. It didn't want to kill me, just to know me. I felt it."

"How would you have even descended? You would have fallen, and to your death."

"Monks can fall a long way," she boasted.

"Onto lava?"

"The ring would have protected me!"

"No," he said, shaking his head.

Breezy sighed. "You're right," she said somberly, lowering her gaze and seeming so suddenly defeated and deflated.

Her head came up slowly to regard the wizard, and she blew a long and resigned sigh.

Then she burst into motion, ducking low and sweeping Allefaero's legs out from under him. Before he even began to react, even to call out, Breezy slipped the ring back on and flipped over the railing and the edge, scrambling down the sides of the chasm, half climbing, half falling, through the swirling water of the guarding elementals, then below them, into the true heat above the true face of Maegera.

"SHE WILL COME TO APPRECIATE Soliardis when she learns the whip," Drizzt said to Catti-brie. "If only she becomes nearly as good with it as Zak—and truly, is there anything she has not mastered when she puts her mind to it?"

"That is always the question, though, isn't it?" Catti-brie replied.

"We all have our own ways of learning and of living."

"She seems happier now that she's out of the monastery."

"I should have realized it sooner," Drizzt said.

"We," Catti-brie corrected, but Drizzt shook his head.

"I," he said. "I studied there. I understand the discipline and dedication they demand of their students—even though I wasn't really a student in their conventional terms. But I should have seen this turbulence coming, and should have looked at our decision to place her within the Order of Saint Sollars through Breezy's eyes, not my own."

Catti-brie nodded. "I feel the same about trying to introduce her to Mielikki. She must find her own path. I just wish she was less impetuous and uncontrollable!"

"Indeed!" came a third voice, and the two turned to see Jarlaxle approaching.

"What is Jarlaxle doing in Longsaddle?" Catti-brie asked, her surprise obvious, for it was rare that the mercenary leader would visit the Harpells. "To check on Breezy?"

"Allefaero, actually," Jarlaxle replied. "I want him to speak with Nvisi for me. Have you seen him? I heard that he had gone out into the forest with Breezy to better investigate the Bidderdoos."

Drizzt and Catti-brie exchanged looks at that, both wearing the same query on their faces: Their daughter out in the forest with a young man?

"We haven't seen her in some time," Drizzt replied.

"Not since her last lesson with me and lady Penelope," Catti-brie added. "I assumed that she would be practicing with Soliardis."

"Ah, yes, how fares the young warrior with that most magnificent of weapons?" Jarlaxle asked.

"Her preference is to the shadow blade," Catti-brie replied. "Since she learned the conjuration, she finds it truly fascinating."

"Fascinating and limiting," Jarlaxle said. "Given her relative inexperience in the arcane magics, she could hardly bring forth such a weapon to equal the power of Soliardis."

"Try explaining that to Breezy."

Jarlaxle laughed and nodded his agreement. "I do agree with your last description of that one: uncontrollable."

"It scares me," Catti-brie said.

"You seem to be able to control her," Drizzt remarked. "Better than we two, at least."

"Because you are her parents, and she wants nothing more than to cast a shadow of her own."

"Perhaps a bigger shadow than she is capable of," said Drizzt.

"Perhaps," Jarlaxle replied. "Perhaps not. How is Breezy to find her limitations if you are ever there building walls about her? Is that not the same thinking by the monastery that she escaped, freedom from which now fuels her newfound happiness?"

Catti-brie nodded, thinking it telling that Jarlaxle had used the same term, *happy*, in speaking about Breezy as she and Drizzt had just . . .

Then Catti-brie realized that it was likely no coincidence, and likely, too, that Jarlaxle was listening to them long before he made his presence known. She trusted Jarlaxle, and loved him like a brother now, but that one was ever infuriating!

"She's no child," Jarlaxle said. "She's young, yes, but she's more accomplished and more capable than most others will ever become. She needs to learn her limits."

"She needs to survive the lessons," said Drizzt.

"As in the cave when she rescued the precious essence on your journey to Icewind Dale?"

Drizzt and Catti-brie exchanged looks again.

"Should she have come and asked your permission before sprinting off in pursuit of the thieves?" Jarlaxle continued. "In that instance, we would have lost them, and the essence, and Gauntlgrym would now be in danger, likely, for with that magic it is possible that our enemies in Menzoberranzan would be able to enact a teleportation gate to swarm into Bruenor's home. That is no small achievement by your daughter, no small thing that Breezy did."

"She could have been killed," said Catti-brie.

"Something I could say of you, or Drizzt, or any of us a hundred times over the last centuries. You know it to be true, and you know as well—as I see plainly in your eyes—that if impetuous and uncontrollable Breezy does meet with an untimely death, the pain will be intolerable to you. But that adventure, that risk, is to her what makes life worth living. Would you steal that from her because of your fears?"

"Could we just delay it?" Catti-brie asked with a helpless laugh.

"It would be no easier for you unless you delayed it until after your own deaths," said Jarlaxle. "Eventually, she will have to strike out on her own and truly learn her powers, her limitations. Whether that happens now or a decade from now or two decades from now . . ."

"Doesn't make it any easier," Drizzt remarked.

"She's too stubborn to be herded," said Jarlaxle. "Whether guided to Soliardis above the shadow blade, or indoctrinated into the church of Mielikki, or to the Order of Saint Sollars, or anywhere else. What she wants from all of us is our trust in her. That is why she has come to favor me of late. I trust her. I expect a lot from her, of her own initiative and her own accord. She is not a child anymore. She is a young woman, capable, smart, skilled, and, like her parents, quite deadly when she needs to be—and she knows when she needs to be."

Drizzt and Catti-brie exchanged looks yet a third time, both offering a helpless grin and a nod. "Thank you," Catti-brie said to Jarlaxle. "We're parents. Sometimes we have to be reminded."

"Perhaps we can find a way to ingratiate Breezy to Soliardis," Jarlaxle said.

"Maybe you can use the Great Forge yet again," Drizzt suggested to his wife.

Catti-brie just sighed. "Let's go find her and Allefaero and see what they're up to."

"But let's not come upon them in surprise," Drizzt replied with a wink. "Just in case."

"Bite your tongue," Catti-brie replied. "Hard!"

Breezy jumped down the last thirty feet of the chasm wall, working her hands frantically to slow her descent and to guide her to a block of magma, a dark island in the liquid orange glow of the lava.

It was hot and she was certainly sweating, but the fires under her feet and the simmering waves coming off the primordial did not burn her. She was correct—the ring had communicated to her honestly, and she was wholly immune to the element of fire.

Maegera stirred, a wave of lava climbing before her.

The heat of the fire wouldn't kill her, but she understood, and heard in her mind, that the primordial could bury her in its molten creations, suffocate her, drown her, crush her under a wall of magma.

She telepathically sent forth a respectful greeting, one sincerely tinged with deep respect, even admiring awe.

My ma told me of your beauty. I had to witness it. Please forgive me, mighty Maegera.

The wave came up right before her, towering over her, a wall of molten stone some twenty feet high. Breezy bowed and accepted the judgment of the god-being.

Breezy?

She smiled, thinking it Maegera, and it took her a moment to realize that, no, it was Allefaero with his telepathic bond.

I'm all right, be quiet!

Maegera stirred. The primordial had felt her thoughts, and so she quickly explained that she was getting a bothersome friend out of her mind, and surely offering no commands or requests to a creature as godly as Maegera.

The wall of lava swayed back and forth. Breezy could feel the primordial trying to decide whether or not to bury her where she stood.

You have witnessed, she heard in her head, in some language she didn't know that she knew. The sounds crackled and hissed like a campfire in the rain, but they formed words.

I have, and am full of gratitude. My life is fuller now that I have looked upon the face of a being so great.

No response.

I will leave if you so desire.

The wave of lava flattened suddenly and Breezy understood that the primordial was no longer in her mind. She wasn't sure of her next move, and it wasn't until she turned back to the wall that she realized that coming down was a lot easier than trying to climb up.

She began to pick her way, glancing back often to make sure that Maegera wasn't mad at her.

Can you summon me? she telepathically called to Allefaero.

Levitate, he replied. *There was a dweomer of levitation in the spellbook I gave to you.*

That brought a wide smile to Breezy's face—until she realized that she hadn't prepared the spell. She cursed herself, and Allefaero heard it in his thoughts.

If you thought you were going down there . . .

Get out of my mind! she demanded, her tone reflecting both anger and embarrassment. Breezy began to climb.

A long, long while passed with little progress gained, for the wall had been melted nearly smooth in many places. Several times, Breezy had to backtrack, once all the way down and back to the magma block. Sweat stung her eyes and her fingers, her shoulders, her back, ached from holding on to narrow ledges.

She felt the discomfort and the mounting impatience of the primordial.

Determinedly, fearfully, Breezy leaped back to a higher hold and dragged herself up, hand over hand.

Be gone, she heard in her mind, feeling the god-being's tone of annoyance.

She wanted nothing more than that, but she came again to a dead end. She tried—how she tried!—to find a handhold, but the wall was too sheer.

She felt the heat growing—again, not burning—and glanced down to see a wave of lava, like a primordial tendril, flowing up the wall at her.

She leaped upward, hands scrabbling on the wall. But there was nothing.

She fell.

19

PLAYING WITH CATASTROPHE

Drizzt and Catti-brie found Penelope Harpell instead of Breezy at their daughter's private quarters.

"I feared I was late for the lesson," Catti-brie said.

"You are, and so is your daughter," Penelope replied.

"Have you seen her?" both women asked each other at the same time.

"The last I heard, she went out into the forest with Allefaero to study the Bidderdoos," said Catti-brie.

"I was told they returned some hours ago," Penelope explained. "But I cannot find her."

"Probably the courtyard," advised Jarlaxle, who had followed the couple to Breezy's quarters. "Allefaero has been spending a lot of time out there."

"Or in the library," said Drizzt. "Those two have been working hard on this bladesinging discipline, studying the best spells for such a marriage between melee and magic."

"We'll check the library," Catti-brie said, taking Drizzt's hand. "You two go to the courtyard and we'll circle back to here, Drizzt and I along the back corridors, you two along the front."

They nodded and split up, but only a short distance away, Jarlaxle took his leave of Penelope, explaining that he had to look into something else and promising to meet them all back at the rendezvous point in short order.

Indeed, Jarlaxle beat the other three back to Breezy's room. He met them with a frown when they turned the last corner.

"We haven't found her," Drizzt said, approaching.

"You won't," Jarlaxle explained. "Apparently, she went through the teleportation gates to Gauntlgrym to visit her grandfather."

"She must have forgotten our lesson," said Penelope.

But Catti-brie was shaking her head and muttering.

"What?" Drizzt asked.

"She has my ring."

She needed to say no more, for they all knew Breezy well enough to understand Catti-brie's grim tone. Jarlaxle was the first away, leading the running troupe to the teleportation gates.

Breezy didn't sink into the lava tendril. She lay atop it, floating. She could sense its heat, but it did not burn her—oh, how wonderful was her ma's ring!

She remained deathly afraid, though, for the tendril was descending, slowly, slowly, as if she was about to be fed to the primordial. She still didn't hear Maegera's voice or even feel the being's connection, except distantly—too much so to garner its intent.

Down she went, far below the water elementals now. She could see them spinning around the chasm above her, about halfway to the top, she figured, as they served as the barrier to keep Maegera in its place.

The lava stopped its descent.

What? Breezy telepathically cast through the ring.

Her answer came in a sudden upsurge of the lava, lifting like a spring, hurtling upward toward the water elementals. Then it stopped, so suddenly, but Breezy did not, and she was flung upward, hurled by the power of the primordial. She soared through the splashes, mists, and spits of the guarding elementals, bursting through the other side of the watery wall to continue her speedy ascent.

She saw Allefaero peering over the railing, and nearly laughed aloud at his wide eyes and slack jaw.

He reached for her, and she caught his hand as she came up beside him, catching the railing with her other hand.

Maegera had thrown her to the lip of the chasm, perfectly so.

Allefaero pulled back, and Breezy went with him, pitching over the railing and falling to solid ground once more. She rolled over a couple of times to release the rest of her momentum.

"By the gods!" the wizard exclaimed, patting at her steaming robe and clothing, acting as if he expected her to melt into a lava puddle before him. But Breezy just grinned widely, quelling his alarm.

"What?" he asked.

"We can do this," Breezy answered, her purple eyes sparkling. "We really can!"

They rushed down the short tunnel, back out into the forge room. Several dwarven smiths were there now, beginning their daily orders, and more would be coming soon, likely.

"There you are!" Breezy loudly proclaimed when curious eyes turned upon her and her companion—curious to see them entering from that tunnel, for few people visited the chasm of Maegera, surely!

"Aye, and what're yerselves doin' here?" asked one sooty blacksmith. "And in there?"

"Looking for you, all of you," said Breezy. "My grandda, King Bruenor, has received a tremendous requisition from Icewind Dale. He commanded me to come here and round up all the smiths working this day to send them straight to him in the upper audience hall, so that he can properly divvy up the workload."

The dwarfs all glanced around at each other, confused.

"Go, go, and I will remain here to tell any of your fellow smiths you don't pass in the corridors to hurry up and join you," said Breezy.

"I just got me damned fire burnin'," one dwarf grumped, shaking his hairy head.

"I can keep it going," Allefaero said, picking up on Breezy's plan. "Perhaps even add a little magical assist to the flames?"

"Aye, and nay," said the dwarf. "Keep it goin', aye, but take care with any magic here."

"No magic here," another dwarf agreed. "Ye're in the face o' Maegera, and if yer spells wake it, it'll melt the robe onto yer skin. Ye just turn the rings to let more or less o' the monster into the forge." He pointed to the tangle of pipes and valves which dominated the wall nearest the primordial's chasm.

"Just the rings, then," Allefaero agreed.

The obedient dwarfs all set down their instruments and tools and left the room.

"Well played," Breezy congratulated the wizard.

"You lie so easily and with such quick reaction and wit that it scares me," Allefaero replied, following Breezy to the heavy main door of the room, which led to the wider complex and up to the main areas. Breezy glanced out into the corridor and, noting no movement other than the departing smiths, quietly closed the door.

"Lock it with your magic," she bade Allefaero.

The wizard stared at her. "No."

"Hurry up."

"No, I'm not doing that. They'll be back with King Bruenor and—"

"It will take them half an hour to get to Bruenor's audience room, sort out the lie, and return. We'll be done by then," Breezy assured him. "Magically lock the door."

Breezy moved for the famed Great Forge, large and nearly central to the room. Allefaero watched her go, then glanced at the door. "I won't," he called after her.

"If we have to run, we can go through your enchantment, but any enemy chasing us cannot," Breezy reminded, laughing.

"That enemy would likely be another fire elemental of some sort, and such beasts can flow through the tiniest of cracks."

"So we'll destroy it."

"Or Maegera itself, who will tear the door from its hinges."

"Don't be silly. Maegera would just blow up the entire mountain, and whether or not the door was locked will hardly matter," Breezy said with an impish grin. "And there won't be anyone left to be mad at us, right?"

"Breezy . . ."

"You're wasting time, and we haven't much," Breezy said. "We can't turn back now."

Allefaero blew a resigned sigh and placed an Arcane Lock dweomer on the heavy door. By the time he rejoined Breezy, the gate to the large furnace of the Great Forge was open, and Breezy somehow had a blazing fire going within.

"Maegera has heard me," Breezy whispered to the wizard. When she saw Allefaero falling back, shielding his eyes from the white-hot glow, she nodded and added, "Can you feel the very power and heat of it? It's like we brought the sun itself down into this furnace!" She dropped the hilt of Soliardis on the tray, then licked her lips and pulled Penelope's ring off her finger. "You put the most powerful Shadow Blade spell you could cast into the ring, yes?"

"The most powerful one the ring could hold," Allefaero replied. "I assure you that every bit of storage within that ring is filled with that single spell."

Breezy nodded, took a deep breath, and turned back to the tray, hoisting a mithral tong and laying it on the end of the tray, then a mithral cue stick, used for pushing items into the Great Forge. She marveled at the tools. They had to be mithral here, she realized, or Maegera's power would melt them in short order.

That gave her pause.

Soliardis and Penelope's ring were both valuable items. If this didn't go as planned, how might she explain losing them to the mouth of the fire primordial? She picked up the hilt containing the powerful weapon, which could be brought forth with merely a thought. She didn't call it, though, for she didn't want to reveal to the primordial being which magic within the item she favored, blade or whip.

"You've been in there before," she whispered to the hilt, nodding, and she placed it back down. The ring, though, seemed so much more fragile. The one she still wore, her ma's ring, could surely survive the flame, but this one? She rubbed her finger across the five small gemstones running along the top of its golden circle, each a container for magical energy.

"Maybe we should wait," Allefaero offered from halfway across the room. "You could ask your mother to help."

Breezy snapped a glare at him, and he sucked in his breath.

His suggestion had sealed her decision, surely! She growled, dropped the ring next to the hilt, then took the handle of the cue stick and slowly slid the two magical items into the furnace.

She called telepathically to the primordial as she did, begging Maegera to make something of these items for her—she didn't dare get explicit intentionally, but with this kind of telepathic joining, she was fairly certain that her thoughts were naked to the primordial, and thus Maegera not only knew her wishes, but she couldn't hide them from it if she tried.

The bond grew between the impetuous Breezy and the primordial, and the telepathic communication morphed onto a telepathic confrontation.

Pull me through! Maegera demanded.

Grant me a creation, Breezy ordered.

Free me!

Blend these items I have fed you! Your existence is to create and destroy. I have given you gifts to do this.

She sensed the primordial pause, her mind suddenly still of its intrusion. Only for a moment, though, until a compulsion came over her, along with a complaint: *You used a tool. You do not trust in me.*

"I do!" she yelled out loud.

Breezy was hardly aware that she had moved along the considerable tray table and was standing beside the mouth of the open furnace.

She heard Allefaero shout out her name in alarm, and only then realized that she was reaching into the mouth of the furnace, indeed, into the mouth of Maegera. Her eyes went wide with alarm, but she did not, could not, retract her hand, though every instinct was screaming at her that it would certainly melt away to nothingness, ring or no ring.

But no, she felt no pain.

She heard Maegera's whispers, guiding her, showing her. Her eyes stopped stinging from the intense light of the white fires, and she saw the items as the flames saw them, all about them, every speck. But then she didn't see them, exactly, or rather, she saw through them, saw the various pieces, the magical dweomers, that comprised their true powers. She saw the individual storage of Penelope's ring, the five compartments all swirling with shadow from Allefaero's spell.

She saw the energy of the blade of light of Soliardis, and the strand of fire, primordial-like in its extraplanar power, that was the whip.

And she felt Maegera's thoughts as if they were her own, the god-like being destroying.

The godlike being weaving magic.

The godlike being creating.

And it was a beautiful thing, she thought, and it was a terrible thing, she thought.

And Breezy felt very small, insignificant, an insect crouched before a titan, one with its boot lifted above her. She tried to pull herself past that terror, to focus on the magical creation.

No, she thought, not creation.

Destruction.

The five small gems on Penelope's ring sizzled suddenly and melted, and Breezy gasped, the heat stinging her throat.

Soliardis hissed and sputtered, smoked and melted, and Breezy gave a soft whimper.

What had she done?

Panic filled her. She felt a line of fire race past her, into the room, suddenly, violently, like the arm of Maegera itself punching forth from the mouth of the Great Forge of Gauntlgrym.

The floor shook, the mountain shook.

Somewhere far away, Allefaero cried out.

"Ye don't think she'd . . ." Bruenor said, or started to say, to the four who had just come from Longsaddle.

The ground rolled under his feet, a great shudder coursing through the entirety of Gauntlgrym.

"Me King!" cried Thibbledorf Pwent, stumbling into the room. "The smithies, the smithies're here as ye asked."

"As who asked?" Bruenor roared, and the room shook again. As soon as he saw his blacksmiths stumbling in, though, he knew that Catti-brie's fears about Breezy were true. He started to turn back to his dear friends, but they were already running past him, sprinting for the door and the corridors that would lead them to the source of the earthquake and, they all knew, to the young woman who was tempting such catastrophe.

"Bah, but she's just like her ma," Bruenor grumbled, taking up the chase, and pausing only long enough to grab his shield and his many-notched silver axe.

Thibbledorf Pwent rumbled along behind him, yelling out for the Gutbusters to come to the aid of "me King!"

THE ROOM'S SMALLER DOOR, THE one to the primordial chamber, blew off, flying across the room, slammed a forge and flipped over it with such force that when it hit the opposite wall, it drove its edge into the stone and stuck there.

Breezy watched in horror as blocks of magma bounced and rolled out of that open tunnel—no, not blocks, not separate thrown boulders, but a single entity, an elemental monster of fire and stone. It stood up on two flaming stone legs, heavy arms waving, a gaping, fiery maw belching smoke and flames in rage.

"Allefaero!" she cried, looking to the wizard—but not seeing him. For the line of fire that had flowed out of the Great Forge like a living tendril of flame had snaked across the floor to form a tight semi-circle about her companion, locking him against the wall. She could hear him back there above the crackling and roaring of the fires, calling for her to help him.

Earn it! came a stabbing telepathic demand from Maegera.

Breezy didn't even know what that meant. She slapped her hand around inside the forge, hoping against hope to find the hilt of Soliardis.

Her fingers closed around something much smaller, disk-like, and she pulled it forth, falling back as the magma beast rushed forward and swung a heavy arm at her.

Breezy sprinted away, leaping clear over the tray of the nearest forge, falling into a roll and scrambling behind the next forge in line.

She heard the monster coming for her and peeked out through the legs of the tray table.

Then she used her monk training and stepped into a shadow back across the room, behind the monster, and there examined her prize.

In her hand was a ring, somewhat Penelope's ring, but instead of the five individual stones, it had a single setting, a disc-shaped gemstone perhaps an inch in diameter, orange in hue and shot with lines of black.

Without thinking further, she slipped the ring on her finger, then rolled it under so that she could close her hand about the disc.

She thought of the belt buckle that held Taulmaril. She thought of the hilt of Soliardis.

She felt, keenly, the dweomer of Shadow Blade that Allefaero had put into Penelope's ring. Breezy called to it, and a shadow blade materialized in her hand. And such a blade—she could feel its power!

But there was more.

The floor shook with the heavy footsteps of the magma monster as it came for her.

Breezy called upon the ring again and watched, mesmerized, as a thin line of the brightest orange climbed up the edge of the shadow blade, reflecting varying splays of colors back along the flat of the magical weapon, the sheer beauty of the display reminding Breezy of the very last moments when the sun would set below the distant horizon of the ocean beyond Luskan.

"Twilight," Breezy whispered, and to her surprise, she noted that elusive green flash sometimes seen in the setting sun, and she took that as an affirmative response from the sword.

The table of the forge nearest her went flying away, swatted by the magma monster.

Breezy didn't hesitate, leaping forward and stabbing hard, then diving aside to avoid the swing of a heavy arm. She took satisfaction from the monster's vibrating roar—her weapon had indeed hurt it, though how much so, she couldn't begin to guess.

Now she squared up with it, using her speed to duck and dodge, to stab and slash. She scored small hits, yes, but knew it would never be enough.

And the monster was not stupid, she realized to her horror, for its every step was designed to cut down her escape routes, to corner her, and if it did so, it would kill her before she could possibly strike it enough to destroy it.

She changed tactics when the arm swiped at her once more. Instead of simply dodging, she dropped under it onto her back and cut her sword to intercept. The impact nearly took the weapon from her hand, but she held on and rolled herself into a backward somersault that brought her to her feet, leaning forward then charging forward to stab her weapon hard into the magma monster's side.

The creature's arm swung in a stinging backhand that clipped Breezy and took her breath away, launching her toward the center of the room. The fire of the monster didn't burn her, but the sheer weight of the behemoth's swing had her lurching in pain, making it hard for her to draw breath.

So too did the monster roar—the stab had hurt it profoundly. A line of molten stone poured out its side, and more dripped from its arm.

The monster charged and leaped, trying to bury her beneath its bulk where she stood, arms wide to prevent her escape to either side, and its bulk flying far enough over her so that she couldn't possibly back away.

So she dove forward and to the ground instead, trying to dodge the heavy legs, and mostly succeeding, except for a deep and painful pinch on her right thigh.

She ignored the considerable pain, spun about, and leaped over the thing, stabbing and slashing wildly.

The magma monster turned its head to face her as it began to stand, and breathed forth a line of brilliant white fire.

That would have been the end of Breezy were it not for her mother's ring—and were it not for the fact that she had unlocked the ring's true powers by defeating the elemental. She didn't feel the fire, but within the vomit were bits of stone, battering her, stabbing her, slashing her.

Right in the middle of the barrage, Breezy kept her wits enough to shadow step out of it, coming to a perch directly behind the monster, to the tiniest of shadows up in the corner above one of the pipes along the ceiling of the forge room.

She clutched the pipe with one hand, bracing her feet against the wall.

The magma elemental was still breathing its destruction where she had been, fully engaged and looking away from her.

Above the tumult, she heard screaming from the room's main door, heard her father's voice, her grandda's voice, heard the violent pounding of her allies trying to get in past Allefaero's Arcane Lock dweomer.

Breezy grimaced when she glanced that way, for between her and the main door loomed the wall of fire that had come forth from the Great Forge, now fully against the wall where her friend had been standing, and with no sign of Allefaero.

What had she done?

She thought to leap down to the side and run to the door for help, but her rage overwhelmed her fear.

She sprang out straight ahead instead, coming down from on high, taking up the shadow blade in both hands and using her descent to put every bit of her weight, every ounce of her strength, into the blow as she drove the weapon straight down upon the back of the magma monster's rock skull.

Right *through* the magma monster's rock skull.

Breezy came down hard to the floor, and the monster came down hard all about her and over her, the elemental falling apart, tumbling and bouncing blocks of stone.

The room fell quiet so suddenly.

Maegera's wall of fire fell to an orange line on the floor, then disappeared altogether.

"Breezy!" she heard her parents and allies screaming, followed by a heavy thud on the door.

Battered, Breezy tried to rise, but cried out in pain to learn that her left leg was certainly broken.

You are worthy, she heard Maegera whisper into her thoughts. *You are brave.*

She tried to stand again, but the pain dropped her back down. She had to crawl to the door, she thought, but she paused and stared dumbfoundedly as a rope appeared, falling from emptiness, so it seemed, near where Allefaero had been standing.

She gasped a grateful expression of relief when Allefaero began to appear, bit by bit, as he wiggled out of an extradimensional space and clumsily onto the rope, then half climbing, half falling down to the floor. Wisps of smoke wafted off his robes and hair, and every bit of his skin that Breezy could see was bright red, as if he had fallen asleep on the sand under a high desert sun.

He started for Breezy, but turned and sprinted to the door instead, pulling it open, then crying out and leaping aside as a barreling Thibbledorf Pwent, a living battering ram, came roaring by.

Breezy kept herself propped on one arm, staring at the weapon— the weapon that remained even though she was not concentrating on it. She knew she could keep it open as long as she wanted, and she surely knew its power.

Thank you, godly Maegera, she thought, and hoped the primordial would know her true gratitude.

"Solsecur," she stated, naming her new weapon with the Callidaean word for twilight.

20

NO MORE A CHILD

Breezy tried to appear calm as she sat on a chair before the desk of King Bruenor. Pwent and Athrogate had come in with Fist and Fury, Bruenor's queens. The four dwarfs huddled about Bruenor now, detailing the damage to the forge room.

Breezy could only hear bits of their conversation, and couldn't maintain her focus, for standing behind her and to both sides were her parents and Uncle Wulfgar, along with Jarlaxle and Penelope Harpell. Donnola Topolino was there, too, but Uncle Regis was away at the time, riding with some friends.

The door opened, and Breezy craned her head about to see Allefaero enter the room, his face still bright red from the heat of Maegera's wall of fire. She offered him a sheepish and apologetic smile and shrug, and took heart when he returned a wide grin and a wink.

Her smile disappeared as her gaze followed him to the side of the room, to be intercepted by the scowls of Catti-brie and Drizzt.

This would be one of many inquisitions, she feared.

"Well, good enough, then!" Bruenor announced suddenly, startling her and everyone else. Queens Tannabritches and Mallabritches Fellhammer-Battlehammer took their thrones beside him, his generals Pwent and Athrogate moving to stand behind him.

"Four tables to be rebuilt," he said. "And a new door to the primordial chamber—we're not even yet able to get th' old one out o' the durned wall!"

Breezy could feel the judgmental gazes weighing upon her.

"One forge'll need fixin', and a few pipes need replacin', to be sure," Bruenor continued. He paused and looked to Penelope, all eyes following. "Yer ring's gone." Then to Jarlaxle, "And whate'er that weapon o' yers was melted full, eh?"

"It was no longer mine, good King Bruenor," Jarlaxle said with a bow. "I gave it to Princess Breezy. The loss is hers."

"Aye, and how're ye feelin' about that, girl?" Bruenor demanded.

Breezy started to respond, but had to stop and swallow the lump in her throat. "I'm not seeing it as a loss, Grandda . . ." She stopped in the face of Bruenor's scowl. "Er . . . good King Bruenor," she corrected quickly.

"Ye're meanin' this?" Bruenor asked, holding up the newly fashioned ring with the flat orange-and-black gemstone disc.

Breezy nodded and looked over to the Callidaean wizard. "Allefaero can recharge it, and I can show—"

"It doesn't need to be recharged—ever," Penelope Harpell interrupted. "The blade within—shadow blade and whatever else it might be—appears to be a permanent enchantment now."

"Solsecur," Breezy mumbled quietly.

"Oh, ye think ye've the right to name it, do ye?" Bruenor said.

Breezy's first instinct was to shake her head deferentially, but she resisted. She gathered up her courage. "I do," she said steadily. "I made it. Or Maegera made it for me, at my request, and because I proved myself worthy in the mind of the primordial."

"Ye made it out o' her ring," Bruenor reminded, pointing to Penelope. "I'm thinkin' ye might be owin' Penelope Harpell more than ye know."

"I didn't know it would destroy—"

"Ye didn't know!" Bruenor shouted, slamming his fists on his desk. "Ye didn't know! Ye didn't know if yer gibberbouncin' scheme'd set Maegera free in me home. Ye didn't know that, did ye?"

"No, Grandda," Breezy replied quietly, lowering her gaze.

"Last time that one got out, it melted the city of Neverwinter to the mudsill! Did ye know that? Ye might've killed to death every Battlehammer in Gauntlgrym and wiped out Weeping Vines as well, aye! Ye might want to be apologizin' to Lady Donnola there, I'm thinkin'!"

Breezy looked the halfling's way, but before she could begin to mouth any apology, Bruenor brought her back with his roaring.

"Yer friend the wizard almost got cooked good, didn't he?" Bruenor growled and slammed his fist on his desk again. "Did ye know that? Did ye?"

"No," she admitted. "But I trusted . . ."

"Trusted what?"

"Maegera!"

"Ye trusted Maegera?"

"I went down to the lava," Breezy blurted. "I spoke to Maegera. I asked, I offered. I didn't think the primordial would . . ."

"Ye could've stopped yer talkin' at the word *think*! Ye didn't think!"

Breezy didn't look up as Bruenor fell silent for a long while.

Athrogate began to giggle.

"What'd ye know?" Bruenor demanded.

"She'll be ridin' a dragon with a keg o' flamin' oil on her back one day soon, me King," the dwarf replied.

"Well, she'll be wantin' her da's scimitar, then," Thibbledorf Pwent added.

Snorts and chuckles came from all around, other than Breezy and King Bruenor, and Breezy's parents, who sat grim-faced.

"This one's got spunk!" Queen Mallabritches said.

"Pwent should put her in the Gutbusters, aye!" agreed Queen Tannabritches.

"Ye're makin' it hard on me," Bruenor complained, and they laughed all the louder.

"She could have been killed!" Drizzt said, silencing them.

"She's the daughter o' a durned elf who walked out into the Underdark alone," Bruenor reminded.

"And the daughter o' the girl ye called nothin' but trouble from the day ye called her yer own daughter," Mallabritches said to Bruenor.

"Really, me King, might we'd've expected less mischief from this one?" said Athrogate, and he bounded over between Breezy and her parents and burst into rhyme. "Well, hey-ho, but their girl's a spitfire! A clever young lass and a bit of a liar." He looked to Jarlaxle as he continued, "With proper taste and a feathery flair, that's sure to land her in a mad dragon's lair!"

"Might that that'll get them two ma and da out and fightin', eh me King?" asked Pwent, nodding toward Drizzt and Catti-brie.

"Nah, but what old stodges they've become," Athrogate teased.

"She could have been killed," Drizzt stated.

"I've said the same about yerself a hunnerd times," Bruenor said. "And a hunnerd more than that about me girl there beside ye. Aye, and it's as true now as 'twas true then. That spirit!" He came around his desk and walked up right before Breezy. "Ye went down to the lava?"

"Aye."

"Ye're sure to turn this set o' me hair gray, girl," he said. "Ye don't do anything like this again!"

"No, King Bruenor," Breezy said quietly.

"Not unless ye're askin' meself to stand aside ye!" Bruenor finished.

Breezy's face came up fast, eyes wide. She looked from Bruenor to her parents. She couldn't read their expressions. She looked to Penelope and said, "I'm sorry."

"I'm a Harpell, dear," Penelope replied. "We have more baubles than we know what to do with, and which usually bring us to some catastrophe or another, anyway. We're known for, shall we say, taking chances."

"Usually with disastrous results," Wulfgar added.

"Well, then," declared Donnola, "it would seem like this new hero of ours is already ahead of many of the Harpells."

Breezy wasn't quite sure what was happening here.

"The durned primordial did her biddin'!" Bruenor roared, turning to Catti-brie and Drizzt, who were both looking to Jarlaxle.

"I told you so," Jarlaxle said to them. "Your little girl is no more a little girl."

"It's harder than I thought," Drizzt admitted.

"Pride and terror," Catti-brie agreed. "Do not believe that you are escaping this without a punishment," she said to Breezy. "You'll be working for Jarlaxle until you've repaid Penelope Harpell and Gauntlgrym for the damage you've caused."

Breezy fumbled for some words, so shocked was she—and more shocked still when Bruenor tossed her the ring with the flat disc. "Solsecur?" he asked. "Twilight, eh? Good name, girl."

A second ring flew over to her. She caught it and stared at it. Her mother's ring.

"I can protect myself well enough with my own spells," Catti-brie explained. "If I know Jarlaxle, you'll be in some difficult places soon enough. But if you have the desire to speak with Maegera again, promise me that you'll do so from the lip of the chasm instead of sitting in the monster's durned lap."

LATER THAT NIGHT, DRIZZT AND Catti-brie sat side by side, leaning on each other for support.

"She's not a child anymore," Drizzt said. "At all. When we try to protect her, she'll just ignore us more."

"She could have asked me to create this new weapon with her," Catti-brie replied, and added a helpless laugh. The two were alone now in their room at Gauntlgrym, expecting Breezy to join them soon.

"I'm terrified of it all," Drizzt admitted.

"I have to keep reminding myself that she's older than I was when we two and our friends found ourselves in one desperate situation after another."

"It's different when danger comes to you and you must fight," said Drizzt.

"And when you go looking for trouble to find Mithral Hall?"

"We didn't bring you," Drizzt reminded her. "Entreri did, and in no good way."

"And I resented you for leaving me!" Catti-brie replied, her voice rising as the epiphany hit her fully. "I was much less accomplished than Breezy, with few fighting skills and little experience. I grew up quickly on that journey with Entreri. I learned what it meant to feel the blood of an enemy flowing from your blade and onto your hand."

"Breezy already learned that terrible lesson."

Catti-brie nodded.

"She's not a child anymore," Drizzt reiterated after a moment of reflection.

"I wouldn't have given her my ring if I didn't agree," said Catti-brie. "Or this." She held up the belt holding Taulmaril.

"I don't know whether I should be afraid for her or for Faerûn itself," said Drizzt.

PART FOUR
SHADOWDANCER
SUMMER, DALERECKONING 1510

They complained that I lack focus, that my mind will not allow me to remain faithful to a path. Grandmaster of Flowers Savahn pressed this point repeatedly when she kicked me out of her monastic order.

While I applaud her decision—it truly was what was best for me, I know already—I know too that she was wrong about what I could do within the monastery. It wasn't my inability to discipline myself enough to climb the ranks, no, but rather, it was . . . boredom.

Or are these things two sides of the same gold piece?

Does one, boredom, precipitate the distraction? Am I doomed to lose focus, to walk a path of side trails and meandering valleys as I make my way up the mountainside of my life, as Grandmaster Savahn claimed at our last meeting?

I've thought a lot about it, and about the challenge I waged to become a Master of Dragons and the fallout of that fight. I don't like losing. Even, as in this case, for me

losing meant winning a better road to my future pursuits—
and indeed, there will be more than one!

To the question of boredom versus a simple inability
to find the persistent discipline to complete these seemingly endless tasks, I have no answer, and I fear that I
never will. I know that I could have climbed to the very
top ranks of the Order of Saint Sollars. I know it! But
there is, I admit, a place deep within me where I wonder
if I'm just lying to myself for the sake of foolish pride. Is
this distractable manner I possess as much a weakness
as a physical inability? Or am I right in my stubborn
belief that I could do it, could do anything, if I truly
wanted to?

Doesn't everyone who fails make such claims?

But here is what I do know about me: I am a half-elf.
If I don't get myself killed (as everyone around me seems
to fear is inevitable), I may live through two centuries,
twice the lifespan of a full human, perhaps a quarter of
the potential lifespan of a drow.

It's not enough. Even were I a full drow who lives
through eight or nine centuries, it would not be enough!

There is too much magic to study, too many monsters
to vanquish, too many friends to cheer, too much beauty
to see and hear and smell and touch and taste, and too
many lovers to know.

I want it all!

Life is a great feast to me. Some people might prefer
to choose a favorite food and eat it throughout the meal
with perhaps a few complementary side dishes.

But for me, I'll walk—nay, run!—the length and width
of the vast smorgasbord of life, and take a bite out of
every choice.

Maybe that seems a weakness to some, a lack of focus,
a constitutional deficiency of discipline.

Perhaps they're right, and in the end, I'll not be a

Grandmaster of Flowers, or an archmage, or the champion of weapons masters, or the Chosen of a goddess.

But I won't for a moment think I'll be somehow lesser for that truth.

As a bladesinger or, as I have titled my curious combination—monk, priest, warrior, wizard—following that ancient elven school of magic, a shadowdancer, I will bite of every fruit, martial and magical, and will use those delicacies to improve the combination. Anything that bores me will lead me to something else, and that something else will come back to the whole, and the whole will grow stronger.

I won't defeat Grandmaster of Flowers Gregory Antoine (should he ascend to that rank) by fighting him with the weapons of monk tradition, but if we find occasion where we have to do battle, I will destroy him. I will hit him from every angle with so many more tools than he can bring to bear.

I will never rival the great wizards of the Realms in sheer spellpower, of course, but when I step out of the shadows unexpectedly close, I'll take their tongues before they can cast their spells.

I want to taste it all. I want to turn wherever my heart takes me whenever my heart asks me. That is my joy, and because it is my joy, it is my strength.

Uncle Jax sees it, and indeed, lives it. Grandda Bruenor, often bored with the duties of the throne, understands it, and judging from his verdict in my reckless act, accepts it with a lifted mug.

And most importantly, now, finally, my parents see it.

They do. I am certain of it every time I glance at the ring my ma gave to me, or feel the belt buckle containing another great present: Taulmaril. When my ma and da look at me now, I see no disappointment—quite the opposite.

Above all else, they want me to be happy.

And I am. I am the Shadowdancer of Bladesinging, ready for adventure, ready to run the buffet of magic and monsters, of friends and lovers, to taste it all. I don't want to die, certainly, but if I do not do this, if I do not live this, then in my soul, I am already dead.

—Breezy Do'Urden

21

DARK SHADOWS

THEY RODE INTO WESTBRIDGE TO THE CHEERS OF THOSE FOLK OUT ON THE streets this day, all splendid in their fine polished armor, some with plumed helms, shields and barding shining in the sun. The Grinning Ponies were well known here and much loved, for the halfling patrol band had many times rid the region of highwaymen, of monsters, and even, on occasion, of entire troublesome crime organizations.

Most splendid of all this fine spring day was an infrequent participant in the patrols, a most notable halfling who served as first-husband to the governor of the halfling village of Bleeding Vines, just outside of Gauntlgrym. There, he was known as Regis, Companion of the Hall, but when he rode with the Grinning Ponies, he did so as Spider Parrafin, and he rode in splendor upon his blue-eyed pinto pony, Rumblebelly—a magically summoned creature of spirit, of course, though any looking upon the rider and his horse would have a hard time realizing that. Spider's long and curly brown locks bounced about his shoulders, and he wore a red neckerchief pulled up over his mouth, covering his goatee, though it had slipped enough to show much of his neatly trimmed mustache.

A bold blue beret capped the hero, matching perfectly with his blue riding gloves and the broad blue sash that traveled down diagonally from his left shoulder to his right hip. A black, sleeveless leather vest over a puffy-sleeved white shirt, black leather breeches, and high black leather boots completed his outfit, all reflecting the highest quality and perhaps a bit of magic—for though Spider's cloak showed the mud of the road, not a speck of it was to be seen on his clothing beyond the soles of his boots. Indeed, this was an outfit one might expect of a Waterdhavian Lord attending a ball, and anyone could be forgiven for their surprise in seeing such finery on a halfling who barely topped three feet in height, riding a pony in need of a bath on a long and muddy road.

But while the vanity seemed obvious, none looking carefully would confuse Spider Parrafin as a fop. He wore a fabulous rapier easily on his left hip, an exquisite dirk with sculpted snakes for a crosspiece on his right, and a hand-crossbow set in a holster on his blue sash for easy retrieval.

To say nothing of the rather famous company he kept. Several of the original Grinning Ponies had retired, several others had been killed over the years, but they carried themselves with the confidence of heroes, and with the reputation of such well earned.

The troupe of a dozen and one pulled up before Ghaliver Longstocking's Happy Halfling inn, a place well known and often visited by the band.

"How long?" asked Doregardo, the founder of the troupe, who was nearing the end of his first century of life, and who had been riding and fighting since his days with the famed Kneebreakers in the faraway Bloodstone Land, several score years before.

"A meal and a drink and off you go," Spider replied.

"Off we go, you mean," said Doregardo's second, Showithal Terdidy, another of the original members of the band.

"I've a bit of business here," Spider explained.

"Then we've a bit of business here, eh?"

"No," Spider replied. "Regis has business here, not Spider. And business that does not and must not involve the Grinning Ponies." Regis gave a wink and added, "For the sake of our reputation, of course."

"He's spitting about Bregan D'aerthe again," Doregardo said, relaying that wink over to Showithal. "Ah, but for the days when Spider knew his place."

"Good enough, then," said Showithal. "We were tasked with escorting this Jarlaxle scout up and down the Trade Way, it would seem, which means that this one here, this Regis fellow, should be paying for the meal."

That brought a laugh from all who heard.

"I insist, of course!" Regis replied, throwing a leg over Rumblebelly's back and dropping to the dirt, falling perfectly into a low and graceful bow. "It is the least I could offer in exchange for the protection of this most marvelous troupe of heroes."

"But you mean to be without our protection, and we're a long way still from Bleeding Vines," Doregardo said somberly, his tone ending the moment of levity.

"My business won't take long," Regis explained. "I'll likely catch up to you long before we near the Crags."

"Then we'll wait."

"No," Regis curtly replied, shaking his head emphatically. "This is no business to be connected to the Grinning Ponies in any way. Indeed, I'll ride out with you until we're out of sight, and return inconspicuously." He tapped his magical beret as he finished, reminding them that he could appear very different from the foppish-looking noble fellow who would share their meal this hour.

Later that same day, half a dozen miles along the road north of Westbridge, the company parted ways.

Regis slipped down from Rumblebelly and waited until the others were out of sight, then dismissed the mount, sending its spirit into a second pendant he now wore, a scrimshaw miniature of his precious pony. As far as the Grinning Ponies and pretty much everyone else knew, Rumblebelly was a real pony, flesh and blood, but alas, Regis's dear mount had passed away years ago. After enlisting Gromph Baenre to create the pendant summoning a spirit into Rumblebelly's form, Regis had told everyone that his new mount was the son of the original blue-eyed brown-and-white pinto.

He liked to believe that the spirit infusing the magical pendant was that of his dear Rumblebelly, and perhaps it was, for certainly this Rumblebelly seemed more akin to Guenhwyvar than to a simple magical item, full of personality, and one that reminded him of his dear lost pony.

He tucked the pendant back under his shirt, then tapped his blue beret, changing his appearance to that of a dwarf, sturdy and a foot taller than his true form, and wearing a bundle of hides as armor instead of his fine leather vest, and a weatherbeaten hat with a wide brim instead of his beret. His blue sash appeared as a thick rope wound about him, and the holster and hand-crossbow now looked much more like a drinking skin.

It was all illusion, of course, and would not likely withstand a close inspection, but it didn't matter, for it was just to get him inconspicuously through Westbridge center and down the long and lonely side street to the house of the man he had been asked to interview. Indeed, when he arrived at the doorstep of Donjon Syn'dalay, the dark tower of Effron the Twisted, he dismissed the disguise. No need to try to hide from this warlock, an old acquaintance and one he knew would see right through, and likely take offense at, his magical disguise.

The two met for more than three hours, through most of the afternoon, and it was pleasant enough, if rather disappointing to Regis, who felt that Effron was being a bit cautious, even evasive, in answering the questions he had come to ask regarding the whereabouts of two different magical cloaks. The warlock had no reason to be suspicious here, Regis believed, and yet the perceptive halfling couldn't shake the feeling that Effron wasn't happy to see him, and was answering in such a way as to close off the discussion with prejudice.

Maybe it wasn't about the items at all, Regis wondered. Perhaps Effron simply didn't want him there in Westbridge.

But why?

Regis's intuition and experience had him on high alert then. He had wondered from the time Jarlaxle had asked him to come here whether the request was sincere, or at least, if a pair of magical cloaks was all this side-excursion was about.

Still, Effron fed him well, which was always appreciated, and even offered him lodging in the tower for the evening.

"Another day, perhaps," Regis declined, then explaining that he had to catch up to the Grinning Ponies and be on his way back to Bleeding Vines. "I'll likely be riding right through the night," he explained, and with a tip of his beret, he was gone.

He had studied Effron's nonverbal response throughout that last bit. A flicker of relief that he had declined? The slightest wince at the notion of a return visit?

Long down the road, Regis went back into his disguise, called the spirit pony Rumblebelly to his side, and moved into the woods to sit and wait, playing a hunch.

Sure enough, Effron's coach rolled by soon after.

Regis followed, far behind and out of sight, using the newest wheel ruts in the muddy ground as his trail.

He dismissed Rumblebelly and crept from shadow to thicket to blocking stone up the bare, rocky hill, up toward the huge and palatial house nearing construction atop it. They were a few miles out of town, he knew, and wondered why anyone would build such a mansion so far from the main roads.

He got his answer soon enough, when an elven woman met Effron at the door

Regis paused, recognition sparking as he looked upon the tall and slender elf. Her red-and-black hair, thick and bouncing about her shoulders was very different from the topknot she had worn when he had known her, but there was no mistaking that initial recall.

It was Dahlia, certainly. Dahlia Sin'felle.

She was alive!

Jarlaxle had sent him here to gauge Effron, he knew then, and so the mercenary leader suspected that Dahlia would be nearby. No doubt Jarlaxle was catching two fish with one hook, as the old saying went, for he probably did want a suitable cloak for their new protégé, Breezy. So, Dahlia's presence made sense, but still it came as a shock. As far as Regis knew, Jarlaxle, and mainly Artemis Entreri, had given up the search for her, accepting that she was almost certainly dead, since Regis had found her prized tri-staff lying with the flotsam and jetsam among the ruins of a pirate ship he had helped Jarlaxle and crew blow apart, sending it to the bottom of the sea.

Yet there she was, in the light of the lamp burning beside her doorway in this most magnificent house.

Regis started from the shadowy cover, but paused, wondering his move here. He considered his sense of trepidation—the hairs on the back of his neck were surely tingling—but then dismissed it. Yes, Dahlia had left the companions on less-than-ideal terms those many years ago, but she and Regis had forged a special bond in their travels together during the war. Or so the halfling believed.

He dismissed his disguise and came out of the brush, moving openly for the porch of the house, his smile wide. "Dahlia!" he cried when she noticed him. "It is so good to see you alive and well!"

She fixed him with a stare that sent a chill through him, but Regis kept approaching, kept smiling.

"Go home, Effron," he heard her whisper to her son.

"Mother, no."

"Now. Go home." Her voice was low and more than a little baleful, Regis noted, but it changed considerably when she looked up and replied to him. "Halfling Regis, is it you? After all these years, is it really you?"

The sudden reversion to charm, or any charm at all for that matter, seemed a bit out of character for Dahlia, truly, but Regis pressed forward. By all superficial markers, Dahlia looked quite the same as he remembered, other than the change in hairstyle, but with every step he neared, there seemed to be something . . . different. Some aura, perhaps. Or maybe the tone of her skin.

"You should not have followed me here," he heard Effron warn, but distantly, for Regis found his focus inextricably fixed upon Dahlia, just Dahlia.

Fully fixed. Magically fixed. Helplessly fixed.

"Go home," Dahlia demanded of Effron, who gave a little growl and began to shamble down the stairs, moving past Regis at the bottom and turning for the carriage house, where his coach awaited.

Regis hardly noticed.

He could only look at Dahlia, beautiful Dahlia, alive and well.

Or maybe not, he realized somewhere deep in the back of his mind. Something was different. Something more than her hair.

Something more than the fangs . . .

"IF YOU DON'T TRULY BELIEVE in Mielikki, then you won't be granted greater spells of healing or anything else from her," Jarlaxle explained. "But if you don't believe in your heart, you can't will it to be."

"Where then does that leave me?" Breezy asked.

"You are an exceptional warrior, a powerful monk, a bit of a priestess, and a budding wizard," Jarlaxle replied with open astonishment. "What more could . . ."

He stopped when he saw the pained look on the young woman's face.

"You mean after all of this," he said. "When you die."

Breezy nodded.

"You ask the greatest question of all, my dear. The biggest fear and the biggest hope, all tied into that one answer, whatever it might be. Or might it be more than one answer? I do not know."

"The unanswerable question," Breezy lamented.

"You're too young to consider such issues."

"My intended journey could lead to a short life," she reminded him.

"There are clues, or maybe there are only deceptions."

"You're not making it better."

Jarlaxle laughed at that. "There are only two groups of people who know the answer to your question," he explained. "Those who have passed, or nobody."

"Grandda Zaknafein was dead."

"He remembers nothing."

"My ma, Grandda Bruenor, Uncle Regis, Uncle Wulfgar . . ."

"Were they dead? Truly? Or did Mielikki simply interfere on the timeline of their journey?"

Breezy gave a heavy breath of exasperation. "Kimmuriel, then," she said. "Or Grandmaster Kane, or even my da, who transcended."

"Clues, I hope," said Jarlaxle.

"But maybe deceptions."

"Who can know?"

"Only two groups of people," Breezy replied, and Jarlaxle smiled wide.

"You ask the most common and important question among all reasoning beings—the mortal ones, at least," said Jarlaxle. "And surely, the most frustrating question of all."

"It instills fear."

"Churches depend upon that fear. The gods need that to curry their followers, which gives them power. The matrons of Menzoberranzan exploit the promise of eternal torment—the driders served Lolth in the Abyss in conscious undeath, so there is certainly some state beyond this mortal coil we all wear. Have faith."

"You might've said that first," Breezy dryly replied.

"If I had, you would not have explored your own thoughts through the length of this conversation. And who really knows where life ends and death begins, or where delusion plays its role. You spoke of Wulfgar. Did you hear the tale of the journey he took to the Abyss very early in his first life?"

Her furrowing brow and expression showed that she had not.

"He was lost to a yochlol, a handmaiden of Lolth," Jarlaxle explained. "We thought him dead. But no, he was taken to the lower planes to be tormented with true delusions by a mighty balor. I won't go into more detail—that is for Wulfgar to explain if ever he chooses. And you should not ask him of that part of his life, I think. He would not enjoy reopening such wounds."

"I'll coax it from him without ever asking," Breezy replied, and Jarlaxle smiled.

He was teaching her so very well, he knew, but only because he was tapping into that insatiable inquisitiveness that was already within this wonderful and accomplished youngster.

He realized then that he would not be surprised if their next conversation on this subject offered him more insight from Breezy than the reverse.

———

"DAHLIA, WE HAVE BEEN SEARCHING for you since you left those many years ago," Regis said, finding that he had to consciously focus on every syllable to properly get the thoughts into words. "I found your . . ." He stopped as she moved nearer.

"Come inside," she said.

Regis knew that he should not, but he found himself walking up the stairs beside her, then through the door, which he heard close, as if of its own accord, as he and Dahlia continued through the foyer and into a lavishly appointed sitting room.

"Searching for me, so you claim," she answered, taking a seat on a luxurious divan. "It seems quite strange, then, that none of you, none of Jarlaxle's vast spying network, ever found me."

"Well, we didn't begin searching immediately," Regis explained. "We respected your wishes to be done with us." Her doubting laughter interrupted him for a moment, but he pressed on. "Until I discovered something that led us to believe that you had met your death."

"As if any of you would care."

"We did care!"

"Drizzt?" Dahlia scoffed. "He cast me aside like the rotting husk of a Memnon melon."

"This isn't . . ." Regis stammered. "I mean, this is not the reason . . ."

"Why are you here?"

"I came to speak with Effron."

"But then you followed him, surreptitiously."

Regis fell silent.

"That was your mistake."

"I will leave you in peace, then, good lady."

Dahlia scoffed again and nodded her chin to indicate an area back by the sitting room entrance.

Regis slowly turned his head.

A handful of people had walked—no, not walked, but floated—into the room behind him. That realization, along with their pallor, told him that these were not *living* people, surely. He shook away whatever remnants of his old companion's charm, finally admitting to himself, all doubt removed, that Dahlia was a vampire.

A vampire!

He understood that now, and knew, too, much of what that meant, for Regis had some experience with that particular type of undead monster—Thibbledorf Pwent had been cursed with vampirism decades before.

And these were her spawn, vampire spawn.

Regis rolled his fingers, taking measure. His hand-crossbow was loaded, and with an explosive dart that could cause tremendous damage, perhaps even enough to take down Dahlia, which he most certainly did not want to do.

His heartstrings tugged at him. He and Dahlia had spent a lot of time together on the road in the war against Lord Neverember and his demonic allies. They had worked together extensively and with great effect, and had, indeed, saved Artemis Entreri from an eternity of horrific torture.

The spawn were not approaching, though he could see them licking their lips with the obvious anticipation of feasting upon him.

"Dahlia," he began.

"Delilah," she corrected, confusing him.

"Dah . . . Delilah, you know me. We're friends."

"Are we, then?"

"We saved Artemis Entreri only through our teamwork and trust."

"Artemis Entreri, who betrayed me? That ungrateful fiend."

"No, he didn't. It doesn't have to be like this. Not at all. He wants to know that you're well."

"To assuage his own guilt, no doubt."

"No," Regis stuttered many times. "Your . . . affliction. It can be cured. I've seen . . ."

"Cured? Stolen, you must mean. This is no *affliction*. I choose this life."

"Life?"

"Existence!" she corrected angrily. "This is no curse. Look around you, foolish Regis. I am finally livin—" She paused and sighed, which seemed weird to Regis, for no breath came forth. "I am finally graced with the existence I deserve. This is no curse. Not to me.

"I know what you're thinking," she continued. "But you cannot defeat me, even without my children surrounding us. And there is no escape. You are caught. If you surrender, perhaps you are worth a bargain to me with your friends, or perhaps I will even bless you with a better existence. If you fight or flee, my children will tear the skin from your bones and drink deeply of your blood. There will be only pain, and you will pray for death long before you find it."

"Dahlia . . . Delilah, we were friends."

"And thus you are still alive, but my patience grows thin."

JARLAXLE LOOKED TO THE SOUTH as he walked from the House Topolino in Bleeding Vines, leaving Donnola with Doregardo and Showithal of the Grinning Ponies. He had left them with assurances that Regis had many duties to perform and would likely be away another tenday, at least.

But it was all a lie, and Doregardo's concern that Regis had not caught up to them on the road was well placed, Jarlaxle feared, for it was very unlike his associate to change course in the middle of a mission.

He should have returned by now.

Jarlaxle moved fast to Whistle Whetters, a large inn serving as the local headquarters of Bregan D'aerthe. It was located at the southern end of the halfling village, very near to the tram down to Gauntlgrym, and had proven very profitable in coin, if not in information. The evening tram inevitably delivered a horde of dwarfs to the common room, filling every seat not occupied by the halflings of the town, to be served by the brothers Bouldershoulder, or more particularly, by the conjured animals of the druid Pikel.

Ivan Bouldershoulder, sitting at the bar with some Battlehammer friends, nodded to the drow mercenary when Jarlaxle entered, then quickly excused himself to meet briefly with Jarlaxle in his office.

"I'll send yer boy Braelin yer way, and I'll be back with the girl in an hour," Ivan promised, departing.

Jarlaxle nodded and waited, sitting on the edge of his desk, tapping his fingers together and concentrating his thoughts, convincing himself of this new plan.

He spoke with Braelin only briefly before sending him out, then summoned another associate and waited some more, until Breezy Do'Urden at last knocked on the door.

"I was preparing to return to Longsaddle," Breezy told him when she entered. "Ivan found me on my way to the portal."

"Ah, well, I did not mean to interrupt."

"No trouble, of course," Breezy said. "I've needed some respite from my repairs to Grandda Bruenor's forge room."

"The cantrip of Mending which Penelope taught you is working well, then?"

Breezy laughed. "Not well enough. I'm wielding more wrenches and hammers than magical spells."

"I hope that you're incorporating them into your training dances, at least."

Breezy laughed again.

"Do you think King Bruenor will give you some time free of your punishment?"

"He did. That's why I was going to Longsaddle."

"I might have a better course," Jarlaxle said. "I've been pondering your interest in the deeper truths of this existence. I think I know a good next step for you."

Breezy collapsed into a comfortable chair set before the desk. "Do tell."

"Perhaps it is nothing, but there is a man I know, a necromancer— a warlock—of great renown and great power. He is well versed in the line between life and death, and even in ways to circumvent it. Witness the rebirth of Gromph Baenre into a prepared simulacrum after the battle in Menzoberranzan, one planned and prepared before he traveled back to the city of his birth."

"Then I should speak with Gromph Baenre."

Jarlaxle laughed at the thought of his brother spending time with one who, by Gromph's reckoning, would be but a mere child. "The warlock I speak of showed Gromph the way to his planned rebirth. He might have some interesting tidbits to offer to you."

"And to you?"

Jarlaxle shrugged. "Perhaps I am too set in my knowledge and beliefs at this point to benefit as much as you might from a conversation with my warlock friend. His name is Effron the Twisted, and he has built a wondrous tower not far from here, in the city of Westbridge."

"I know the name, I think," Breezy said.

"He is known to your parents and their friends. Much of his story has been told in these regions, in Neverwinter Wood and thereabout."

Breezy shrugged and nodded.

"Go see Braelin Janquay down in the common rooms. He will help guide you on your way and provide you with a horse. And have Pikel and Ivan give you enough supplies for a pair of tendays. Effron will not be hard to find in Westbridge, and he will receive you, I expect. He owes me many favors—including information regarding an enchanted cape that will fit your interests quite well, I think." Jarlaxle nodded to the door. "Be off this very night," he said. "I know you prefer the darkness."

Breezy came forward and gave Jarlaxle a big hug. She fell back with a smile as wide as Jarlaxle had ever seen from her.

His expression, though, grave and serious, dimmed the young woman's light.

"What is it?" Breezy asked hesitantly, obviously caught off guard by this sudden shift.

"I know what happened on your journey to Icewind Dale," he said. "I know what it did to you. Are you sure, my dear, dear Breezy, that you are ready for this adventure?"

She stared at him with plain confusion. "You said I was going to see an acquaintance . . ."

"Yes, along dangerous roads, thick with monsters."

"I killed yetis," she said, biting it off sharply.

"And thick with bandits," Jarlaxle continued. "Sometimes human bandits, elven bandits, halflings, and dwarfs. You cannot deal with them with half measures."

"I know," Breezy growled, but she swallowed hard at the implication, that awful moment replaying in her mind as clearly as if it had happened only a few moments ago.

Bruenor's caravan from Luskan to Icewind Dale had been way-laid in the pass through the Spine of the World. While the battle had raged outside the defended wagons, infiltrators had snuck in to steal the magical essence of Maegera. From the safety of a wagon where her parents had left her, Breezy saw it all. She witnessed the murder of dwarfs and the theft of the essence, and, with no time to seek help, she gave chase.

The pursuit of the precious item landed her in a cave, cleverly hidden behind the very thief, a drow woman. She hoped to pilfer the essence back and make an escape, but she couldn't grab the coffer that held the precious item, for she couldn't reach it from her con-cealment. So, she had snatched the drow's loaded hand-crossbow from its holster and shot the woman in the back of the head. She only meant to drop the woman with the sleeping poison that was surely coating the bolt, but she was close—very close, too close—and the hand-crossbow proved more powerful than she had expected.

The crunching and tearing sound echoed in her mind. She felt the warmth of the woman's blood and likely other fluids pouring out onto her hand.

And the woman dropped, straight down, and Breezy knew—she just knew—that she had killed her.

She was lost in that memory then, almost wholly unaware of her surroundings, and didn't even really register the touch of Jarlaxle as he brought his hand up and behind her head, grabbing her thick hair, so much like her mother's with just a hint of violet highlighting the auburn waves.

She didn't *let* herself cry. She just couldn't help it.

She felt Uncle Jax tightening the hug then, pulling her close, holding her steady.

"I'm sorry," she managed to whisper after a while, adding a sniffle.

"Breezy," Jarlaxle whispered back. "My dear, dear Breezy. I am quite proud of you in this moment."

"Crying like a child."

"Feeling empathy and remorse like a good-hearted person," Jar-laxle said. "Do not ever lose that. Do not ever become numb to the tragedies of the things you must sometimes do, no matter how much your enemy deserves it. You are not crying over a demonic gnoll here, nor any other monster. You took a life—well, perhaps you took a life. There were likely powerful priestesses in the troupe with these agents of Menzoberranzan. You did what you had to do."

"It hurts."

"Good."

"I know I had to, I mean," Breezy said, pulling back to look Jarlaxle in the eye. "If they got away with the primordial essence . . ."

"They would have used it to create and open a gate into Gauntlgrym to bring an army against your grandfather and his clan. Your head knows this. Your heart will catch up. But let it hurt, Breezy. Feel the pain as a reminder that you fight only when you have to fight, and kill only when you have to kill. It is an ugly and dangerous world we live in."

"That doesn't make me feel better."

"Is your father a bad person? Your mother? How about your grandfathers?"

"No, of course not."

"Trust me when I tell you that your grandfather Zaknafein has killed more drow than you've met. He did not become a legendary weapons master by killing monsters. No, unless when we refer to monsters, we mean the drow monsters who served as Lolth's priestesses. And indeed, they were and are serving as little more than Lolth's instruments of terror and cruelty."

Breezy stepped back and composed herself with a deep breath.

"Are you ready for this adventure?" Jarlaxle asked her again.

Breezy nodded.

"You will do what is necessary?"

Another nod, followed by a pause, and a third nod, this one with conviction.

"You have wanted your adventure," Jarlaxle said. "Here it is."

Breezy stared at him for a few moments, the enormity of it all freezing her in place. A smile melted the pause. She leaped over and kissed Uncle Jax on the cheek, then bounded out of the room.

Jarlaxle watched her go with mixed feelings, though he kept his smile wide until the door was closed behind her—closed by a man who had been hiding within a secret closet set to the side of the room.

"You take a great chance," Entreri told him.

Jarlaxle shrugged. "She is ready."

"Using the daughter of Drizzt and Catti-brie like this?"

"Shh," Jarlaxle said. "There is a lot at stake here if our suspicions are correct. I only hope we won't be too late."

"We could go in with a powerful force to find our missing halfling."

"We are. I have faith in Breezy. And in Braelin Janquay."

Entreri didn't seem convinced.

"And in Artemis Entreri," he added. "Give her room, but not too much, yes?"

Jarlaxle could see the conflicting emotions running across his best friend's face. Hope and anticipation shifted to sheer dread and back again repeatedly. Entreri held a great fondness for Regis, and his concern had been no less than that of his friend when Jarlaxle recounted to him Doregardo's tale of the last parting with Regis.

"Perhaps Effron gave him the information he needed to find this cape you so desire," Entreri remarked, and Jarlaxle nodded—though both of them knew well that Regis, while capable and dependable, rarely took initiative to go beyond the boundaries of his given mission.

With the slightest of nods, Artemis Entreri left the room.

22

THE HUNTRESS

Breezy walked her horse off to the side of the main road and into a small clearing beneath a wide-spreading oak tree. She didn't bother tethering the animal as she set her camp—her last camp before entering Westbridge, she believed—for she had come to know the mare well enough to trust that she wouldn't run.

She brushed aside the acorns in one area and lay out her bedroll, then went into the woods to gather enough kindling for a campfire. The air was soft and warm enough, with fewer insects buzzing about now as winter approached. Many leaves had turned, and more were on the ground now than on the trees. They had piled about at the bases of ridges and against fallen logs, thick enough for Breezy to smile and remember how many times she had played in piles of leaves through her childhood, in Bleeding Vines, in Longsaddle, where they gathered against the invisible wall at the base of the Ivy Mansion's hillock, and even at the Monastery of the Yellow Rose.

Truly, she loved this time of the year, the smells, the cool winds, the falling leaves dancing their way to the earth.

So many people thought of the passage of autumn as a time harkening the onset of death, but not Breezy. To her, this was a time of reflection and peace, a time to appreciate the simple pleasures of friends and warm hearths.

And now, thanks to Jarlaxle, of adventure. .

She had been out of Bleeding Vines for four days, riding little-used trails and open pastures southeast, using the Sword Mountains as her guide and crossing due east before them. She had avoided the growing town of Phandalin altogether, both to keep her journey quiet, as Jarlaxle had instructed, and simply to enjoy the solitude. Her horse was named Windy, which Breezy found so appropriate in the blowing leaves and the chilly bite of the northern blow.

Windy was quite enough companionship for her in this cool night and in her solitary musing.

It was more than simple solitude and peace that had kept Breezy avoiding Phandalin and other house clusters she had passed. She felt mysterious, and important. Jarlaxle had sent her on a mission—yes, it was one for her benefit, but still, they had trusted her. All of them—her parents, her grandda Bruenor and her protective uncles, Jarlaxle, all of them—had trusted her to work with him in Bregan D'aerthe, and now Jarlaxle had sent her alone on a journey of well over a hundred miles into barely-tamed regions south of the Crags. She had no recall or teleport spell, not even a magical mount, which meant that so many things could go wrong.

But she would make do and make her way, Jarlaxle and the beloved Bouldershoulder brothers and Braelin Janquay had all trusted.

It took her a while to come to terms with the wave of good feelings that she had carried out of Gauntlgrym. Was it vindication? Responsibility? A combination of both? Along with perhaps a bit of sadness, because along this ride, Breezy had come to understand that she had crossed a threshold here, had left a part of her life behind.

Reflexively, she felt the powerful ring her mother had given to her.

Was it possible that they were all coming to accept at long last that she was no longer a little girl who needed protecting?

Perhaps. It seemed as if Jarlaxle was, at least.

Breezy nodded, reminding herself that she had crossed a threshold. Now she had to live up to it.

She eschewed the rations in her pack this night, likely her last for a while on the open road, and instead foraged for her dinner, taking great pride in a rather tasteless and sloppy stew she managed to brew.

She set a magical alarm along the approach from the road and lay back under the stars—so many stars this moonless and cloudless night. She let them take her up into their realm, so she imagined, and looked back on the world and on her life as if she were a million miles and a million years removed. Who was she and who were they all?

What would people think of her long after she was gone? Would they remember her? And truly—and this surprised her—she found that she didn't really care. Her ma and da had always told her to do what she believed to be right and let everything else fall where it may, and now as Breezy considered that advice in the new light of her new standing, she was beginning to understand it.

Somewhat.

"They will remember me," she whispered to the stars behind her sly grin.

She wasn't sure if she was awake or dozing or in a deep sleep when the magical alarm began clanging in her head. It took her a few moments to even decipher what the sound might mean, until it was accompanied by the shriek of her horse.

Yes, a shriek, not a whinny or a neigh.

Breezy leaped up, flipped her ring, and pressed the flat disc to activate Twilight before she even had a clear picture of what was transpiring.

Windy bolted, galloping away and carrying a pair of riders.

No, not riders, and not carrying. They hung from her sides, claws slashing at her hide as she bucked and sprinted and tried to shake them.

Breezy started in pursuit, but only took a step before realizing to her horror that poor Windy hadn't taken all the attackers with her as she fled.

———

REGIS PACED HIS SMALL CELL in the bowels of Manse Dorcrae. He was stripped down to his breeches and undershirt, all his weapons, armor, supplies, and items taken from him. He was hungry, though of his own accord, for he dared not touch the many plates of seemingly delicious food that Dahlia's vampire spawn had brought to him, always leaving their delivery with a feral snarl—a constant reminder to Regis that these lesser vampires surely wanted to eat him.

But they wouldn't—couldn't—defy Dahlia, and she had prohibited any harm to the halfling, at least for now. She was protecting him, perhaps out of their shared experiences together, when they had each relied upon the other to survive. Or maybe it was from simple practicality. Regis understood that Dahlia feared retaliation from Jarlaxle and the others, and that made him a valuable bargaining chip.

Slanted rays streamed in the one small window at the top of the wall of this mostly subterranean cell, catching the halfling's attention. He stopped his pacing and stared at the opposite wall, watching the light climb it as the sun descended to the horizon.

Nightfall fast approached.

Regis hated the darkness—not usually, but certainly so in here, in this place of vampires. Unless Dahlia allowed them out to hunt, the vampire spawn would come to this room and stare at him through the bars. Sometimes it was so dark that all he could see were their eyes, shining infernally red with bloodlust and hatred.

He took some comfort that Dahlia had given him this room with some access to the daylight, though only for a short period in the late afternoon for any direct sun. But at least it offered some respite from the visits of the slavering spawn creatures.

The sunlight traveled up, up the wall and was gone, the room growing very dim and the twilight fast dissipating into darkness.

Regis went to his cot on the back wall of the cell. He climbed onto it, but not to lie down—no, there was no way he could hope to sleep at night in this place. Rather, he crouched with his back against the wall, staring back at the cell door, waiting for the eyes to appear.

Instead, though, this night he saw the flickers of a torch in the outside hallway, and then the torch itself, held by Dahlia.

She swept into the room, a pair of spawn coming in behind her, but waiting obediently at either side of the open exit door, while Dahlia approached the locked cell.

"They say that you are not eating," she scolded, glancing around to see the plates piled with food. "Are you trying to get skinny enough to slip through these bars?"

Regis didn't answer, didn't blink.

"Don't be a stubborn fool. You have to eat," Dahlia said.

"Fattening me up for your feast?"

That brought a laugh from Dahlia, though no reaction at all from the vampire spawns, staring at him, licking their fangs.

"What purpose is served by you refusing fine food?" Dahlia asked. "And I assure you, it is very fine food, prepared by the best cooks of Westbridge."

"And laced with what poison?"

Another laugh from the vampire. "If I wanted to kill you, do you think I'd need to do it that way?"

"Potions, then. Perhaps an elixir to charm me."

"I am a vampire, silly halfling, and quite aware of my own charms. Besides, I have your ruby pendant, and I know well its properties. If I wanted to charm you, then . . ."

"Then a potion to turn me into one of them!" Regis said, stabbing a finger at the vampire spawn.

Dahlia smiled and tapped one of her fangs. "That is done with these, not with any potion."

"But you haven't. Why?"

"I thought we were friends," she said, her genuine tone catching Regis by surprise. "Even when it all fell apart between me and your companions, you never seemed to hold any ill will."

"I never did, and don't," Regis said, coming forward to stand close to Dahlia, close enough that she could have reached through the bars and throttled him. "When you left, I felt a great loss. When we thought you dead, it saddened me deeply. When we began to suspect that perhaps you were still alive, I came here full of hope."

"Good."

"And you threw me into a dungeon."

"For your own protection," Dahlia said and glanced back at the spawn. "They are mostly obedient, but to have one with such tender flesh as yours moving about might be more than some of them could resist, whatever my orders."

"Then just let me leave."

"You know I cannot."

"But we're friends," Regis said dryly.

"It is a conundrum, I admit. But I do not wish for the others to find me."

"My word—"

"Is not enough. They would not understand. They would not accept."

"They could cure you."

"There is nothing to cure. This is my choice," Dahlia declared, her tone reminding Regis that there was no space for debate here.

"Why? Why would anyone choose such a thing?"

"I am immortal—as long as I am clever and careful. Think about that, Regis. When you turn to dust, I will remain."

"By killing others."

"No. No, it doesn't have to be like that. I control this condition, it does not control me!"

"Then what of them?" Regis asked, motioning to the spawn. "Where did they come from if not . . ."

"From the vampire who tried to make of me a spawn."

"All of them?" He noted Dahlia's slight wince.

"Most."

"The one who first brought me a meal?" he demanded, for a young female had come to him with food the first day of his imprisonment, and she had entered before the room had gone fully dark. She had seemed to Regis then—and he had not seen her since—very different from the others. She didn't carry the scars of the spawn, like the two now in the room, and her skin was not as set in its rot.

She barely growled at him and hadn't even bared her fangs. It had been too light, perhaps, but he had not noted that red glow of undeath in her eyes.

"Keely," Dahlia explained. "Just Keely, and she has no surname and doesn't even know where her name came from. She had no life before she was brought to me that she would care to remember, I assure you, and she would have died soon anyway. A lost soul. Sickly, debasing herself for crumbs. She is happy now."

"That is not your choice to make!"

"Why not? Would those around her allowing her to wallow in misery until she met her end be less guilty? Would you point your judgment at them, the nobles of Waterdeep, I wonder?"

"Then why not me, Dahl . . . Delilah? Why are you allowing me to remain alive, instead of either being torn apart as a meal or turned into one of your spawn?" To his surprise, Regis felt a great pang of sympathy at the look Dahlia then gave him.

"I remember our time together on the road. Do you? When we battled that strange little Sharon creature . . ."

"The personification of conscience," Regis said, for that is what they had agreed regarding that very unnatural childlike being.

"Yes."

"And we saved Entreri from the cocoon," Regis said.

Dahlia snarled. "Had I known he would then betray me, I'd have left him inside that wasp nest to atone for his sins throughout eternity."

"He didn't betray—"

"He did! The choice was to stay loyal to me or to stay with Drizzt Do'Urden, curse his name! Artemis Entreri knew that I could not remain with them."

"He believed that you could, that they would accept you. And he knew this after being more of an enemy to them than you could ever be."

Dahlia stared at him hard. For a moment, he thought she would strike out at him.

"You clearly do not begin to understand the depth of the shared hatred between myself and that vile wife of Drizzt," she said, and hissed. "But you should fear not my wrath—unless you earn it. However great my hatred for Drizzt, curse his name, or that prancing wife of his, however simmering my feelings toward Artemis Entreri for his betrayal to me, you are the one—perhaps the only one of them—I truly do not wish to harm."

"Then let me help you."

"Help me? You do not begin to understand. I am a valued member of Westbridge. I am invited to all the balls, to all the social gatherings. I am Etriel Ath Tel'Daoine, the Lady of the Stars, to the folk of the region, mysterious and delightful—and envied. Look around you! You saw Manse Dorcrae when you arrived. Does it look like I need help? Or your salvation?"

"Not until they discover the truth."

Dahlia's laughter surprised him. "They already know. Many of them, at least, though they wouldn't admit it, probably not even among themselves. They don't care, and why should they? I pose no threat to the folk of Westbridge, certainly not to the important ones! I am a valued member of the Westbridge community and society, and I am hardly the only one of my kind to be accepted in such a manner around Faerûn. When I lived in Thay those many years ago, I knew of several vampires, and even had one as a lover—and he never once tried to enslave me or make me of his kind. We coexist with reasonable folk, as dwarfs coexist with elves."

"If all that is true, then why not let me go?"

"How could I until all of this is all settled? You have powerful friends who will look for any excuse to bring retribution upon me."

"No, no, that's simply not true. Jarlaxle would likely find a way that you and he could become great allies."

"Do not speak his name to me, Regis. Not him, nor any of the others. They are dead to me and I to them, and I prefer to keep it that way."

"And so you will imprison me in here until I die of old age?"

"I will find a way around that, perhaps."

Regis shook his head. "If that is your honest belief of my friends, then this will never be settled, Dahlia."

A sudden change came over the woman, then, dark and menacing, and she rose up high before Regis, staring down at him. "My name is Delilah, and if you continue to try my patience, there will be consequences, I promise you. I remember our time together, yes, but those good memories can be overcome, and if they are, you will not like the result."

She turned and swept out of the room, the vampire spawn pausing just long enough to flash fanged smiles at Regis before going out behind her.

BREEZY SWUNG ABOUT, SLASHING TWILIGHT before her to keep the attacker at bay. She didn't have time to bring the sword back and to bear on a second attacker, so she let the follow-through slash shift all her weight to her left foot and snap-kicked with her right, slamming her enemy in the chest.

The attacker didn't gasp or go tumbling backward, though, but just floated fast back the way it had come.

These were no humans, Breezy realized, or at least, no longer humans, for these attackers were undead things—specters or ghosts or vampires of some sort.

Off in the forest, Windy shrieked again, and whatever hesitation or fear or confusion spinning in Breezy's thoughts disappeared in an eyeblink.

She recovered from the kick, hopped to that right foot, and reversed momentum, darting at the first assailant. Twilight went up over her head in a spin, then came down from on high diagonally, left to right before her, forcing this monster, once a woman, to throw back her reaching arms to avoid losing them.

Breezy kept closing and so did the undead thing, and Breezy's sword arm finished its cut, coming forward in a stab right before she and the monster crashed together.

Clawed hands came in at Breezy, even though Twilight had gone through the monster's torso nearly to its hilt.

The undead thing, in a frenzy, didn't seem to notice the seemingly mortal wound. It reached about Breezy to force her even closer, and opened wide its mouth, showing its fangs.

Something was wrong, Breezy realized in an instant, and reacted by driving her left palm up and under the vampire's chin, keeping the bite at bay for the moment. She had wielded a shadow blade before, of course, but this felt different, as if Twilight, suddenly hot in her hands, was sending her a message.

The fiery line, she thought, and turned the blade to put that thin orange line up, then retracted the blade as she drove it upward, the fire of its edge shearing through ragged clothing, flesh, and bone, so that when it came free near the shoulder of the vampiric creature, it left a foot-long gash front to back from belly to collar.

The monster hissed, keened, and flailed, but Breezy stepped back just out of reach, went into a full spin while taking up Twilight's hilt in both hands. She swept the devastating blade across just above the undead thing's right shoulder, cleanly lopping off its head.

Breezy ended that turn facing the second, returning assailant, windmilling the glowing blade before her in a great flourish that gave her enough cover to drop into a crouch from which she came up with suddenness, and with the full power of both legs, springing forward, angling Twilight upward to stab it under the chin and through the vampiric monster's mouth, brain, and skull.

Breezy didn't slow her rise, driving up and back. Twilight's hilt went right against the bottom jaw of her assailant, and Breezy fell right over the creature, crashing hard atop it on the ground. She scrambled to her feet, tearing her sword free and sprinting away from the two corpses.

She called upon a patch of shadow far ahead in the forest and stepped through it, moving deeper into the forest in search of Windy. So much blood had the poor horse lost that she could feel the slop of the blood-muddy ground beneath her feet.

She was on a small trail, with no obvious turns about, so she shadow stepped again and came out of the darkness almost tripping over the huge mound of Windy, who was nickering pitifully and not quite dead, with two hungry vampires tearing and biting at her flesh.

The only thought that went through Breezy's mind in that awful moment was anger, just a sheer red wall of absolute rage. She fell into a state that she didn't know existed, one beyond thought and planning, a state of the purest primal rage.

All her instincts, all her muscle memory, all her training fell together into absolute harmony and absolute fury. She slashed and stabbed, kicked and punched, spinning, leaping, rolling. She stepped inside the swing of a monster's right arm, inside the reach of the clawed hand, rolling her left arm up and over the extended limb, then turning to throw her back against it, falling back and punching forward with her locking arm, popping the shoulder out of joint.

And she kept going, rolling right behind the creature, turning a full circuit to slash it across the back. It stood there for a heartbeat, right arm out wide, left arm hanging weirdly, and Breezy rammed into its back, launching it forward into its companion and following it in, Twilight's fiery edge glowing as if reflecting its wielder's rage.

Slashing, chopping, stabbing with wild abandon.

Not even bothering to aim, but simply eviscerating everything in Twilight's path.

And screaming, simply because she had to scream.

When at last it ended, Breezy found herself standing in the midst of body parts, looking back at Windy, poor Windy. Off to the side, a form, another humanoid figure, darted away.

Another murderer, Breezy thought, but she hadn't the energy to give chase. On a sudden thought, perhaps inspired by Twilight, she cut the blade across before her, leading with the dark edge. To her surprise, it cut a planar rift—not to the Plane of Fire, as the other edge might do, but to the Plane of Shadow.

Deep black shadowstuff dripped and spread below the gouge.

Breezy reached into it with her mind, calling to the darkness, searching the shadows. A large black hound came bounding out, and she sent it after the fleeing monster.

"Destroy it," she begged.

On the ground behind her, Windy nickered softly, weakly.

Breezy closed her eyes and took a deep, deep breath. She spun about and stabbed hard, knowing the truth, knowing that Windy was beyond any hope of healing.

Windy knew it, too, she realized, when the horse managed to turn her head to lock Breezy's gaze with one eye, and nickered again softly, as if in thanks or apology, or despair, one last time before expiring.

Breezy Do'Urden fell to her knees and cried.

23

THE LESS THEY KNOW

Caught somewhere between anger, horror, and hunger, Keely stumbled away from the gruesome scene. She heard the horse's rider crying. She heard the growls of the shadow mastiff as it bounded off after another of the vampire spawn—and how she was glad that it wasn't coming for her!

But still, what had led to this horrific night?

What humanity had she left? she wondered. She had been so happy when Lady Delilah had at last allowed her to go out with the spawn, to taste the blood so fresh, to revel in a kill for the first time!

Revel?

Watching that poor horse die had brought a sensation of utter revulsion to Keely, had assaulted her sensibilities in ways that she had never imagined.

The wails of sorrow from the rider followed her as she fled. Keely, too, this almost vampire spawn, began to cry as she continued to stumble through the dark forest, running, scrabbling, back to Manse Dorcrae and her master, who would help her to understand, she hoped.

It was all too confusing.

It was all too horrible.

But still, soon after and still running, the young woman who was not yet an undead thing began to feel differently, began to wonder what actually killing that horse might have felt like, what pleasures actually tasting that spurting blood might have brought to her.

Angry and dirty, her clothes covered in blood, Breezy walked into Westbridge late the next morning. She wore the suspicious stares of the folks going about their day as a badge of honor. Battle-tested and tough, angry and spitting venom, she was more than ready to stare down (at least) any who scoffed at her or turned their noses up at her.

She carried no weapon openly, for Taulmaril was tucked into the belt buckle and Twilight waited in her ring, but she was clearly part drow, of course, and so she accepted the suspicion, even fear, she noted on some.

She cast return gazes to play on that obvious fear, using her appearance, her heritage, to her benefit.

She noted the town's inn, The Happy Halfling, and pushed in through the swinging door.

The common room, thick with patrons, fast fell into a hush at her arrival. She scanned the gathering with a scowl, settling on an old halfling sitting alone at a table right beside the main bar. His hair was gray, but thick, and he sported an impressive mustache, waxed and twirled at either end. Unlike the others, he met her look with a wide smile and waved her over to him, indicating the empty chair across from his seat.

As she approached, the mustachioed halfling motioned to a fellow tending the bar, who immediately began filling a glass with water, then cobbling together a plate with bread and cheese and a small cup of beer.

"Ghaliver Longstocking at your service, traveler," the seated halfling said, then hopping to stand and bow as she neared. "Welcome to Westbridge, though it would seem as if your journey was fraught with undesirable circumstance."

"Your roads are not as secure as one might wish," Breezy replied, and she took the offered seat. She left it at that, having no desire to give out too much information to strangers in these dangerous lands.

"Are you wounded? Shall I call a priest?"

"It's not my blood," Breezy said, then added with a scowl, "it never is."

That caused the halfling to pause as he moved to sit back down, so much so that he overbalanced and plopped down into the chair awkwardly.

"Well," he stammered. "That is a good thing, I suppose."

Breezy nodded.

The plate and drinks were placed before her.

"No charge, of course," said Ghaliver. "We are a village welcoming to visitors, and truly I am sorry to hear that you were assaulted on roads nearby. We do patrol, but the lands are full of dangers, and so we mostly spend our sentry patrols about the town's perimeter. We are a small village and would lose many if we ventured too far out from our walls. Again, I welcome you to Westbridge and to The Happy Halfling, my establishment. We've comfortable rooms, though of course, for those, there will be a fee—a fair one, I assure you."

"Perhaps," Breezy said and took a long draw of the water.

"Passing through? If you are in need of a horse . . ."

Breezy's grimace stopped him. She hadn't meant to scowl directly at this welcoming gent, but the mention of a horse threw her thoughts back to the dying Windy's side.

"I have come from Gauntlgrym and Luskan as an emissary to one who resides in this region," she explained. "A small man, a warlock by trade."

"Effron the Twisted, of course," said Ghaliver, who relaxed then, which clued Breezy off to the fact that Effron was a citizen of good standing. "Yes, yes, his tower is just outside the edge of town. Easy to find."

Breezy nodded. She had seen such a structure on her way into the village.

"Gauntlgrym and Luskan?" Ghaliver asked. "Officially? That would be King Bruenor and High Captain Beniago, yes?"

Breezy nodded, seeing no need to correct the latter guess. High Captain Beniago, of course, answered directly to her real boss.

"How are the High Captains of Luskan?" he asked.

"I don't go there often," she replied.

"King Bruenor, then? What a wonderful dwarf! A hero of the north, he and his friends."

Breezy understood that he was playing her with the praise, though he seemed sincere enough. Ghaliver knew of Bruenor's friends, of course, and could see that she was half-drow—which was a quite rare heritage. He had probably already guessed her identity.

"And what may I call you?" he asked, and she smiled knowingly.

"I am known by Breezy," she replied. She took note of his obvious momentary confusion. That Drizzt and Catti-brie had a daughter was common knowledge throughout the north—she was a princess of Gauntlgrym, after all—but her nickname seemed not as widely disclosed. She thought of the many things Jarlaxle had taught her, particularly his repetition of *the less they know of you, the better.*

"Well, enough then, Miss Breezy, and I am glad that you managed your way to us," he said. "Enjoy your breakfast, or perhaps it is your lunch, or pre-lunch, as it were. As you are an emissary of the leaders of the north, I offer you again lodging, should you require it, and will of course waive our fees. Stay as long as you like, ask of me and my staff whatever you may need, and I will escort you personally to the tower of Master Effron when you wish to go. It is not far."

"Then soon," she said, beginning her meal.

"Perhaps a bath first?" Ghaliver offered. "A change of clothing?"

"I would just get dirty again when I am back on the road," she replied.

"But the blood . . ."

"A reminder to always hold strong my guard."

"Yes, yes, of course," he stammered. "I will leave you to your meal. Again, with any needs, just ask."

He really didn't know what to make of her, she noted.

Jarlaxle would be proud.

"WHAT HAPPENED?" DAHLIA DEMANDED OF her newest addition, whose cheeks were streaked with lines of tears shed—something that should not be. Dahlia had come home to Manse Dorcrae just before sunrise to discover that most of her children had not returned from their nighttime hunt—she had allowed them out into the Kryptgarden, where they were free to find an animal to hunt and slaughter to sate their bloodthirst. Or perhaps they might happen upon a stray goblin or an orc, or someone or something else that no one would care about.

"They . . . attacked," Keely said quietly, fearfully. "Attacked her."

"Her?"

"A rider on the road."

Dahlia hissed, eyes going wide.

"They were just after . . . just the horse!" Keely quickly explained. "But two of them saw her. Two wanted her flesh. Tender, sweet. Elf blood."

"An elf?"

Keely shifted and shrugged. "Drow."

Dahlia's eyes widened. "You attacked a drow on the road outside of Westbridge?"

"A horse!" Keely insisted. "Only the horse! And I got none of it, because . . . too late! I found the horse in the woods, but she was there! The drow girl was there! She . . . she . . . she killed. Killed, yes, or destroyed . . . or, or, ruined. Cut them, cut them apart, your children!"

Dahlia took a long pause to compose herself and sort through this startling news—startling and concerning, given the recent visit and capture of a certain halfling known to be close associates with the drow gang that had commandeered so much of the northern Sword Coast.

"You attacked a drow rider . . ."

"Camping. They . . . they, not Keely. She . . . she was camping."

"You attacked her?"

"They," Keely corrected again, desperately, Dahlia noted. "And her horse. Just her horse for three, but two for her. But she heard and woke up. She did not flee."

"And this rider, this drow girl, destroyed some of the others, but you got away?"

"All of the others," Keely admitted.

Dahlia's eyes popped open wide with shock. A single warrior had destroyed a handful of vampire spawn?

"She didn't see me," Keely said, her gaze cast to the floor in shame. "I hid." She looked up. "I wanted to tell you. Someone had to get away and tell you."

Dahlia was no longer even listening, her thoughts stuck on the reporting of so many vampire spawn killed by a single drow. It sounded like Drizzt to her, but Keely had said that it was a girl.

"A girl?" she asked the spawn. "You are certain?"

Keely nodded. "Young. Sweet."

"Go to your sleep," Dahlia instructed, waving Keely away. She wasn't going to get anything more of any value from this one, she knew. Perhaps she would have to pay Ghaliver Longstocking a visit, or maybe, she hoped, a certain halfling presently under her control would know something of this mysterious drow traveler.

She moved to the stairs leading down to Regis's guest quarters. She changed her mind, though, and glanced out the window. She didn't have much time before sunrise.

She nodded and leaped out a window, using her powers to become a large and fast bat, speeding for Westbridge.

She could leverage the life of Regis here, she believed, and get herself an invitation long overdue.

24

THE WEB OF CONFLICTING EMOTIONS

"Vampires? You are certain of this?" Effron asked the road-bloodied Breezy when she arrived at his tower the next day.

"Quite certain, though lesser creatures, I believe, than those true vampires I have read about." She sat in a comfortable chair in a circular sitting room that took up the entirety of the second level of the tower. An animated butler—a zombie bugbear, she believed—had delivered some tea and biscuits, placing them on the small table between her seat and Effron's, and even pouring for them before silently departing.

"Spawn," Effron replied. "Vampire spawn, they are called. Foul and bloodthirsty, and truly a nightmare for those less skilled in battle. But yes, your observations are correct. They are nowhere near as formidable as a true vampire."

"From all that I have heard of Effron the Twisted, I figured you would have the answer," Breezy said, with just enough suspicion in her tone to make the warlock lift an eyebrow.

"I am no vampire," he stated flatly.

"You wear a skull on the end of your stave," Breezy noted. "Am I to believe that you are not versed in the ways of raising the dead into an undead state to serve you? I have met your butler and your two doorway sentries."

"Indeed," the warlock admitted. "But these animations of mine are simple zombies, mindless and fully under my control. Only a true vampire can create vampire spawn."

"Then your village has a bigger problem than the few lesser beings I battled on the road."

Effron considered it, shrugged, and shook his head. "Likely not. Vampire spawn will live on long after their master is destroyed, and in such a state, they roam as pack creatures and travel far and wide, as they are wise enough to kill and move on in order to evade the retribution from their murders. And they can travel great distances through a single night. That was likely what you encountered, a vagabond and leaderless band, perhaps long last escaped from some ruins in the deepest Kryptgarden shadows, where vampires were once well known and thick. Unless more reports come in of attacks in the region, it is probable that you did Westbridge a great service, Breezy Do'Urden, and for that, I thank you."

"You cannot know that they were wandering beasts, or unguided."

"Give me directions to the place of your encounter. I will go out and speak with the destroyed corpses. The dead cannot lie to me."

"I will take you there, posthaste."

Effron laughed at her. "You destroyed them," he said calmly. "There is no urgency, and I have little desire to travel at this hour. Vampire spawn hunt in packs. The pack is destroyed—and won't your parents and the others in the north be proud to hear of your heroic victory?"

Breezy smiled widely, but it was a fake look, for she understood that this warlock was flattering her to gain some advantage. By all that she had heard, Effron had spent decades near the most powerful heroes of the Realms, had worked with Jarlaxle and with Gromph and her father. His compliment was surely gratuitous.

Still, it did feel good.

"So, what has brought you to Westbridge, young Do'Urden?" he asked. "And to my humble tower?"

"Humble?"

"I have seen grander. So have you."

"But you are doing quite well for yourself," Breezy said.

"I am."

"Jarlaxle will be glad to hear that. As will my father. Many of those in the north are quite fond of you."

"Hmm," mumbled Effron, seeming less than convinced.

"I am here from Jarlaxle," Breezy explained. "He said that you might have some information regarding a magical cloak."

"I know of many magical cloaks. Are you working for Jarlaxle now?"

"I am a scout of Bregan D'aerthe," Breezy said—more proudly, she noted, than her explanation of destroying the vampire spawn on the road. "And this cloak is one suited to my skills and my training in the monk tradition, the Way of Shadow."

"Ah, yes," said Effron. "I believe I know the item to which he refers. The Billowing Cape of Shadows, it is called."

"And you have it?"

"Oh no, no, no. But I have an idea of where information regarding it might be found."

"Jarlaxle will pay for that knowledge, of course," said Breezy.

"He must really care about you," came another voice, a woman's voice, and Breezy turned to the side to see a graceful elven woman with black and red hair, pushing open one of the room's windows and hovering there, some ten to fifteen feet above the ground.

"Now, why might that be, I wonder?" the elf said. "Why would Jarlaxle care so much about a half-drow waif, unless she is his own daughter?"

"I am no daughter of Jarlaxle."

"No, I see that now. I understand it all now."

"Mothe—" Effron started, but bit it back as he came out of his chair. "Lady Delilah, well met. I did not expect you."

"You are hosting the daughter of Drizzt Do'Urden and Cattibrie, and you thought I would stay away?" Dahlia said.

She locked stares with Breezy as she slowly floated in through the window, settling on the floor with such grace. Breezy couldn't take her eyes off the willowy elf, thinking her the most beautiful creature she had ever seen.

"Mother!" Effron said, coming from his chair and stepping between Breezy and Dahlia.

Mother? Breezy thought, the notion reverberating in her mind just enough to pull her from the charm spell for a moment. Effron's mother was Dahlia, she knew, and Dahlia was . . .

What was Dahlia? *Only a vampire can create vampire spawn,* she heard in her mind, but the warnings were far away, pushed back by the sheer magnificence of this newcomer to the conversation.

Now her thoughts were spinning, and she closed her eyes and recalled all that she could. Dahlia had been the Avatar of Lolth, once battling Catti-brie, the Avatar of Mielikki. Dahlia had been her father's lover in those years when Catti-brie was thought dead, and Dahlia had nearly killed him when they had parted.

But she was not a mortal enemy of Catti-brie or Drizzt, Breezy remembered. Her ma had little use for the woman and always soured when Dahlia's name came up, but there were many complications involving Athrogate and Jarlaxle and Artemis Entreri, or so Breezy had been told.

She blinked open her eyes and looked up at Effron and the woman he had intercepted, the one he had called Lady Delilah.

How easily Dahlia picked up the small, twisted man with one hand and placed him off to the side, letting Breezy see her brilliant smile.

Her shining fangs.

"The daughter of Drizzt, correct?" the vampire asked.

"You're Dahlia."

The elf blinked and fell back a step. "A perceptive and presumptuous child, are you? I am Lady Delilah—did Effron not just tell you that?"

"Effron's mother is Dahlia. You're Dahlia."

"And child, what does that name mean to you?"

Breezy shrugged. "Lots and nothing. I've heard stories of you. I know that some—Entreri and Jarlaxle, to name two—have been searching for you for a long time."

"And here I am."

"Dahlia."

"Dahlia, who was loved by your father," Dahlia replied.

"I know the story. Some of it, at least, and enough to not care."

The vampire laughed.

"Should I tell them you're alive, and here?" Breezy asked. "Or do you wish to remain . . ."

"Do you think I would trust you to hold silent?"

"Do you think I care?"

Dahlia clapped her hands together and turned to Effron. "Oh, such a spirited one!"

"Mother, enough. Just be gone."

"Yes, do," said Breezy. "Perhaps you should go and infect some more victims to replace your servants I slaughtered on the road."

"Breezy!" Effron said with a warning hiss.

The vampire's face went stone cold. "Perhaps I should," Dahlia said. "And why wouldn't I start with you?"

"Stop it, both of you!" Effron demanded.

"You stay out of this!" Dahlia yelled at him, and she pressed forth her open palm, and magic came from it that shoved Effron skittering backward, sending him falling against the far wall. "This is none of your affair!"

Slowly, Dahlia turned her head to glare back at Breezy, and before it even lined up with her, there came a puff of black smoke, and the vampire was gone.

And Breezy dove forward into a roll, her instincts warning her of the attack, for Dahlia appeared right behind her and lashed out, clipping her on the back of her shoulder. The claws dug in a bit but didn't do much damage as Breezy sped away.

Breezy came up and around, showing her hands in a monk fighting stance, keeping her sword tucked into the magical disc to use as a most unpleasant surprise when Dahlia got close.

"Do you really want it to be like this?" Dahlia asked her. "We could be friends."

"You knew that when you came in here, but you came in to fight. Your mistake."

"I am merely defending myself against your intent—and oh, how I see it so clearly," Dahlia said. "You see me as a threat to your mother."

"You already had that fight. You lost." She noted a bit of a sneer on Dahlia's face, just for an instant.

The vampire replied with a laugh, "Oh, not in that way, silly child. You know that your father loved me, and could again, and that terrifies you."

The idea seemed utterly preposterous to Breezy—for a moment. Images of Drizzt embraced with Dahlia filled her mind, confusing her, sickening her. Somewhere deep inside, she knew it to be a trick, a vampire's otherworldly persuasion, but the notion was simply too deep and too thick in her mind for her to completely dismiss it.

"Our lovemaking was truly a beautiful thing, you see," Dahlia continued. "A sharing of fears and hopes, a sating of desires. That is why your mother is afraid of me, though she has no need, I assure you. Ever will I cherish my time with Drizzt . . ."

"Stop!" Breezy demanded, and she closed her eyes to block out the images, which of course she could not, for they were in her mind, planted by the magical suggestions and charms of the vampire.

She blinked her eyes open to see Dahlia standing right before her.

Breezy snapped her right arm up vertically to forearm block a heavy swing—so very heavy, indeed. Dahlia's punch drove the blocking arm back against Breezy and sent her staggering to the side, so that her own left hook fell far short of Dahlia. She called upon the disc in her right hand, and Twilight came forth with a sizzling sound.

But Dahlia was close, too close, and Breezy couldn't get a solid stab. She traded punches with Dahlia, heavy hits coming from both, with Dahlia's weighted by the strength of vampirism and Breezy's backed by the power of ki.

Finally, Breezy managed to take a quick hop backward and slash Twilight across, digging a line into Dahlia's left shoulder.

But for all the damage she inflicted, it was matched and exceeded by Dahlia's simultaneous strike, a slipped punch to Breezy's jaw that snapped her head to the side and sent her quick-stepping backward, trying hard to hold her footing.

What a hit! Breezy had terrible flashbacks to the sudden image of

Gregory's elbow when she had tried to trick him in their fight, and while she wasn't about to fall just yet, she knew that she hadn't much time before the vampire swooped upon her and sank fangs into her neck.

The room swam, and she blinked hard to try to shake the fogginess from her eyes and mind.

Breezy flashed Twilight across in a desperate attempt to fend, but she held it too upright, and Dahlia got under it with a grasping hand. Again with frightening strength, the vampire pulled the blade from Breezy's hand, pulled the ring from Breezy's finger.

Twilight winked out.

Breezy countered with a snap kick to drive Dahlia back, but the vampire accepted the blow and didn't move at all, the impact instead sending Breezy tumbling backward.

"You will make a fine child of mine," Dahlia teased, tossing the disc ring aside and flashing her fangs.

Then she jolted in surprise, and Breezy did too, as a metallic clang sounded right between them.

Dahlia gasped. Breezy looked to the floor to see three separate metal poles. No, she thought, not separate, but chained together.

A tri-staff . . .

"So, it would seem that you have only grown fouler in your time away," Breezy heard to the side, a voice she knew.

Dahlia hissed at Artemis Entreri.

Breezy struggled to her feet, but Entreri waved her aside as he circled Dahlia. "This is my responsibility," he said.

"Kozah's Needle?" Dahlia remarked while telekinetically willing the staff into her hand. "It has been so long."

"If only that would remind you of who you are," Entreri said.

Dahlia worked the tri-staff with ease, gracefully swirling it about her turning form.

Near the far wall of the room, Breezy watched her with mounting concern. The vampire was powerful enough without the enchanted weapon.

Dahlia brought the staff in close, holding the middle piece and pumping her hand repeatedly so that the other two lengths of metal clanged together—and with each collision, there came flickering sparks of mounting lightning energy.

"I am finally at peace, Artemis," she said. "Perhaps it is that I've finally come to terms with who I actually am."

"A vampire?" Entreri asked.

"A murderer," Breezy said from the side of the room, drawing a feral growl from Dahlia.

"That one is every bit the wretch as her mother," Dahlia said, casting a threatening stare at Breezy.

"You'll not harm her," Entreri warned. "Ever."

Dahlia scoffed at him. "Who will protect her when I am finished with you?"

She flipped her staff, let go of the middle length and caught it on one end, and in the same fluid motion, sent it out whip-like at Entreri.

Entreri hopped over the swinging tri-staff and flipped backward, landing a couple of strides farther from Dahlia. Out came his trademark jeweled dagger in his left hand, with Charon's Claw, his devastating red-bladed sword drawn by his right hand. He didn't slow the movement when Dahlia suddenly advanced, instead sweeping Charon's Claw before him and releasing a wall of obscuring ash from the trailing edge of the blade to hang in the air in its wake, visually separating him and Dahlia.

The vampire reacted by blasting through it, scattering the hanging ash with a flurry of whipping swings of her tri-staff.

But Entreri was no longer behind that visual barrier, and from the side of the room, Breezy marveled at his speed and cleverness, using Dahlia's forward aggression against her as he slipped out and around. For a moment, Breezy thought Entreri had her, so quickly, so cleanly, but Dahlia's recovery was equally impressive, somehow turning her tri-staff into two separate staves, like the jo sticks Breezy had trained with at the Monastery of the Yellow Rose. Dahlia spun the cudgels independently with great speed as she turned about to relocate Entreri and keep him at bay.

And so began a wild back-and-forth, sword and dagger, matching jo sticks, slapping and banging in rapid succession, and with a crackle of lightning pouring forth onto Entreri every so often, stinging him and drawing snarls of protest.

He needed to score a hit, and soon, Breezy believed, but it did not seem forthcoming, for Dahlia was pressing him hard.

Breezy looked all about, spotting her ring at the base of the perpendicular wall. She rushed for it—or tried to, but a wave of necrotic power blew through her, chilling her bones and drawing a gasp as she fell back. She looked over to see Effron shaking his head, warning her away, the eyes of the skull atop his bone staff glowing with dark power.

Rage swept through Breezy. She glanced over at the frenzy of Dahlia and Entreri, then back to the warlock, trying to decide which to attack.

She straightened with surprise and took heart, then, when Entreri's red-bladed sword created another wall of ash between him and Dahlia.

Dahlia measured her response, as if waiting for Entreri to slip around.

He came straight through the ash instead, sword backhand slashing, driving the vampire's jo sticks aside, then following with a thrust of his dagger that stabbed Dahlia in the side. But the blow was brief, as she disengaged her twin weapons underneath Charon's Claw, attached them somehow into a singular staff, then stamped it on the ground right before Entreri brought the sword back in to bear, blasting a pulse of lightning that flowed out from her with such power that it nearly knocked Entreri's feet out from under him.

He stumbled badly to his left, and Dahlia came on, but not before yet another wall of ash was brought forth by an upward horizontal sweep of Charon's Claw.

Dahlia skidded to a quick stop, taking up her long staff like a spear and stabbing through once and again, then spinning about, the staff coming up, over, and around her head to create a full perimeter around her, coming through the ash wall once again and with Dahlia pushing through behind it.

She hit nothing. She saw nothing.

Nor did Breezy, who had no idea of where Entreri had gone.

Around Dahlia spun again, swinging, stabbing, reducing the ash wall to nothingness in her flurry.

Then she stopped, so suddenly, and Breezy, still not understanding, saw a look of sudden resignation come over the vampire.

Across the way, Effron yelled out.

Above Dahlia, hanging by his bent legs from a crossbeam to which he had leaped when he created this last wall of ash, Artemis Entreri dropped and struck.

Dahlia stumbled away, collarbone cleaved, left arm hanging limply.

Entreri, having landed hard at the end of that descent, popped back to his feet and stalked for the kill.

But Dahlia became a cloud of gas, nothing more, and that cloud flowed fast to the room's outside wall and through a crack that sent the gaseous vampire out into the open night.

Entreri, just a step behind that departure, bashed his sword against the wall in frustration, then turned angrily on Effron.

Breezy didn't know whether to go for her ring again or to simply charge at the warlock. When Effron turned his attention to Entreri, she chose the ring.

"She is my mother," was Effron's only answer to Artemis Entreri. "And yet, I did not help her."

"You stopped me from joining the battle," Breezy stated.

"Their conflict is more complicated than that," Effron answered.

"And if she had defeated Entreri, she would have turned again on me!"

"I would not have allowed it." There was little strength in his voice at that point. He cast his gaze to the floor. "Earlier this day, I invited her into my house," he admitted.

"Knowing that she is a vampire," Breezy accused.

"Why would you do that?" Entreri demanded.

"Dahlia . . . Delilah is a well-respected woman in Westbridge, and many know her secret," Effron explained. "This is not a unique situation in the cities of the Realms."

"Yet you admit that you only invited her into your house today," Breezy said. "And you knew that I was attacked on the road by her . . . what did you call them? Her children?"

"Vampire spawn," said Effron. "And yes, because of that. I was trying to mitigate, to steer her away from her determined course."

"Her course of killing the daughter of Drizzt?" Entreri said incredulously.

"No!" Effron replied. "I did not even know that she knew of Breezy's appearance in Westbridge. But when I heard of her spawn attacking Breezy on the road, I feared for another and knew that I had to act, for his sake and for Dah . . . my mother's. I don't want this fight, not for you and not for her."

"Who?" Entreri demanded.

"Who?" the warlock echoed in puzzlement.

"For whose sake? Who is 'he'?"

Effron swallowed hard and whispered, "Regis. Dahlia has Regis."

"Then you should hope he is still alive," Entreri warned. "Let us go, all of us." He pointed a threatening finger at the warlock. "You will lead us to Dahlia, right now. And I warn you, Effron, you will be incurring the wrath of Jarlaxle and Gromph Baenre himself if you hinder us in any way."

Effron matched the drow's stare for a few moments, then nodded, clearly defeated.

EVER THE ARBITER

Dahlia held no illusions when she entered Manse Dorcrae.

They would follow. Or at least, he would. Artemis Entreri would surely come looking for her in her home. Even if the child of Drizzt did not accompany him, Dahlia was not confident in battling Entreri again.

She had to heal. She had to regroup. She had to, perhaps, use her prisoner to bargain.

Though how could she trust a bargain with the likes of Artemis Entreri, who was considered among the most deadly of assassins in all Faerûn?

Her coffin and the dirt therein would speed her healing, she thought, so she moved straight for the secret stairway that would lead her to that hidden corner of the third level of the building's substructure floors.

How she wished she still had her spawn to protect her, and not just the cowardly girl from Waterdeep!

Yes, she would have to finish turning Keely very soon. She so loved the girl's sweet blood, but she needed defenders. She needed vampire spawn.

Leaning heavily on the wall for support, Dahlia shifted the appropriate three panels in the wainscoting to unlock the secret stair-well. A moment later, she spoke the triggering word, and the section of wall before her slid aside, revealing a narrow descending stair.

And revealing, to Dahlia's shock, a figure, a drow, leaning against the wall some three steps down.

"I wasn't sure if you would be heading down or heading up, and I did not wish to disturb your sleep, Lady Delilah," said the drow, and he tipped his wide-brimmed plumed hat and gave a short bow.

Dahlia fell back, suddenly very afraid.

"How?" she stammered.

Jarlaxle came out of the entryway, Dahlia giving ground before him, and with his softly-glowing driftglobe trailing. He tapped the three tiles perfectly and spoke the words to close the door.

"You are wounded," he noted when he saw the vampire fully in the light, saw the cleave gash that had nearly severed her arm above the shoulder.

She felt Jarlaxle's stare boring into her. Had she been fully healed, she would have leaped upon him then, taking her chances, however small, in this clearly desperate situation. If Jarlaxle was here, she knew, so were some of his deadly associates.

"Entreri?" Jarlaxle asked, moving forward, crowding her. "Breezy?"

Dahlia matched his stare, or tried to, at least.

"Why are you here? I have no business with—"

"But you might, after you hear what I have to say," Jarlaxle inter-rupted. "Though I assure you, if either Artemis Entreri or Breezy Do'Urden is dead or . . . infected, our deal will come to a sudden end."

"We have no deal," Dahlia replied with an animalistic hiss.

She heard a click behind her and recognized it as that of a small crossbow, a hand-crossbow, perhaps.

"Are you sure of that?" Regis asked.

"Come," Jarlaxle bade her, stepping out of the stairwell to lead the way to the sitting room, where the mercenary leader, predictably, took Dahlia's own seat. "Let us discuss the possibilities—I could use eyes among the society of Westbridge—and the conditions."

"I am well known and beloved . . ."

"Etriel Ath Tel'Daoine," Jarlaxle finished.

"My people exist in many cities."

"Your people? Vampires, you mean."

"There are many in the Realms, coexisting with the mortal races."

"Of course! I did not come here to kill you, Dahlia."

"You sent Entreri for that purpose."

"Not for that, no. I wasn't even sure you were here." He paused and studied Dahlia, his gaze settling on the garish wound. "You have met up with him, it would seem. Am I wrong to believe that you did not fare the better?"

Dahlia's scowl confirmed it all.

"I did not send him to kill you, in any case."

Dahlia led his gaze to her wound, turning her shoulder just a bit to better display it.

"We will hear his side of the incident," Jarlaxle promised. "Tell me now if you reject my offer of a continued relationship and we can be done here."

Dahlia understood the implied threat.

"No?" Jarlaxle asked after a moment of silence. "You wish to hear my bargain, then?"

Dahlia didn't answer.

"Well, then, to the agreement, and the conditions."

She kept a sour look on her face, to be sure, but Dahlia was listening.

BLADES STILL IN HAND, ARTEMIS Entreri turned toward Effron. Seeing the small and twisted man's obvious despair, he did not immediately advance.

"He stopped me!" Breezy shouted, and brought forth Twilight, striding across the room toward the warlock.

Entreri didn't turn to regard her, but heard her approach and held out his hand to stop her.

"He prevented me from helping you!" Breezy elaborated, but her words were not accompanied by footsteps.

Entreri fully fixed his glare on Effron.

"She's my mother," the warlock answered that glower, his voice barely a whisper.

Entreri straightened, then sheathed his sword and dagger.

"I didn't help her in her fight with you," Effron noted.

"You held me back!" Breezy said again.

Entreri waved Breezy to silence. If she and Effron had both entered the fight, the gain would have been Dahlia's and not his, he knew. Effron looked so weak and pitiful, but Artemis Entreri had seen the warlock in deadly action, particularly in a notable battle in Neverwinter Wood.

Effron's unbridled power had indeed given Artemis Entreri pause. And that fight in the forest was decades before, and warlocks, unlike warriors, almost always grew more powerful with age.

"Take us to Dahlia's home," Entreri demanded.

Effron tilted his head, almost a shake. He seemed to be mulling it over, but finally nodded. "She has Regis, unharmed. Or at least, he was unharmed. But that is her lair, a vampire's lair. She is far more powerful there."

"Less powerful without her spawn," Breezy quietly and sinisterly remarked.

"I will show you, but I'll not go in with you," Effron said. "And you would be wise to lead with negotiations instead of blades, for Regis's sake, if not your own."

EFFRON'S COACH SLOWED TO A stop before it reached the trailhead at the base of the hill leading up to Manse Dorcrae. The eastern sky had brightened, but the sun had not quite yet made its morning appearance.

Entreri stood and pushed open the coach door, leaning out and looking ahead. He gave a little laugh, hardly of surprise, then hopped out, Breezy and Effron following.

Down the hill before the stopped coach came Regis, splendid in his fine attire and sitting astride Rumblebelly. Beside him, dwarfing him, rode Jarlaxle on his own magical steed, a nightmare summoned from an onyx figurine. It snorted fire, its mane was fire, and every stamp of its hellish hooves sent a circle of flame out like a ripple in a pond.

"Ah, well met, my friends," Jarlaxle greeted.

"You were up there?" Entreri asked.

Effron pushed past him, shambling so quickly that his dead arm behind his back swayed like a pendulum. "What have you done to Lady Delilah?" he demanded.

"Ah yes, I see that I arrived just in time to prevent a needless tragedy."

"Not so needless," Entreri replied.

"And hardly a tragedy," added Breezy, and Effron's head snapped around and he shot her a hateful look, one that she accepted with a derisive snort.

"You haven't all the information, of course," said Jarlaxle. "Neither of you."

Effron turned back on him quickly. "Where is Lady Delilah?"

"The Lady Dahlia is resting, and as Delilah is her sobriquet, I would assume that Delilah is resting as well, or should I say regenerating her health. Be at ease, Effron, I have not harmed your mother. Quite the opposite! I have shown to her opportunities for great gain."

"What are you talking about?" Breezy shouted. "She's a vampire!"

"No, my dear Breezy. She is *my* vampire."

Breezy just stood shaking her head, her jaw hanging open as she bit back the torrent of curses that threatened to spew forth.

"Come along, then," Jarlaxle instructed. "Effron, turn your coach about, and I and my halfling associate here will follow you to your tower, where we can better discuss the possibilities that have been presented to all of us. Ah yes, and speak about the Billowing Cloak of Shadows, as well."

Entreri moved next to Breezy and nudged her. He took out an onyx figurine and dropped it to the ground, calling for his own hell-steed. He went up easily, offered his hand to Breezy, then pulled her up behind him.

Effron stood on the road, staring at Jarlaxle, then past him and up the hill to his mother's mansion. Finally, he motioned to his drivers, ordered them to turn the coach around, and slowly climbed back inside.

"Just think of Dahlia as I might consider my hellsteed," Entreri advised Breezy as they made their way back toward Westbridge. "It is a demonic thing, chaotic and murderous if set loose. But under my hand, it is just a mount, or even an ally, if necessary, should I find myself in a fight."

Breezy didn't answer. Just chewed her lip and thought of Windy.

A wave of guilt accompanied the images of the poor horse lying in the forest, shredded and gasping its last agony-filled bits of life. She should have accepted Andahar those days ago when her father had offered the unicorn. She could have ridden that magical steed to this place, for it could not die, could not be shredded and eaten by the children of a vampire. Windy would still be alive, and the vampire spawn posed no threat to the magical Andahar—indeed, Andahar probably would have dispatched the attackers before Breezy ever came out of her reverie.

She was still mulling over that battle, that pain and guilt, when they arrived at Effron's tower, and all through the lunch the warlock offered while he, Jarlaxle, and Entreri discussed many events that simply didn't interest her at that time, not even when the discussion went to the magic item, the Billowing Cloak of Shadows, that Jarlaxle had marked for her.

She did get some time with Regis, who tried to reassure her, telling her that he had been treated well by Dahlia and that the vampire would be controllable by those whom she feared.

"And those she does not fear?" Breezy asked.

"That will be a challenge," Regis admitted.

"I met her spawn and destroyed them."

"Most of them. There are others—one at least who is not quite turned, but surely doomed."

"And Jarlaxle will allow that?" Breezy asked with a sneer. "He will sacrifice this . . ." She paused and considered Regis.

"A young woman from Waterdeep," the halfling explained. "Her name is Keely."

"And she is not yet an undead thing?"

Regis shook his head.

"And Jarlaxle will allow Dahlia to murder her and enslave her in a state of undeath?"

Regis held up his hands helplessly. "Jarlaxle always looks to the greater gain and always accepts that some will be sacrificed to get there."

"This . . . no!" Breezy couldn't even finish the denial past the bile that rose in her throat. She ended up just shaking her head in surrender and changing the subject to the coming plans for Regis and Donnola to step back from the lead in their halfling village of Bleeding Vines.

She kept the rest of their discussion away from the unnerving subject of Lady Delilah of Westbridge.

Several more Bregan D'aerthe scouts arrived at Effron's tower as the afternoon wore on, including Braelin Janquay and the dwarf Athrogate, who rode a magical summoned hellboar beside the nightmares of the half dozen drow scouts.

It was late in the afternoon when the group broke to begin their ride back to the north. Again, Entreri summoned his magical mount and offered his hand to Breezy, but this time, she refused.

"I will make my own way back," she told him.

"I don't think I'm going to leave you here after what we've been through," Entreri replied, pumping his hand toward her more forcefully.

But Breezy didn't take it, and resolutely shook her head.

Noticing the argument, Jarlaxle walked over.

"We're not leaving her here," Entreri said to him.

"No, of course not."

"I wish to ride alone," Breezy said. "Er, or walk. I care not."

Jarlaxle glanced up at Entreri, who shook his head.

"A deal then, good lady," Jarlaxle said. He reached into his pouch and produced his onyx figurine. "Ride with us upon your own mount this night. Prove to me that you can control the hellsteed. If you can, I will have Gromph Baenre fashion you one."

Breezy hesitated and didn't blink. "Prove to you?" she asked incredulously. "Is that the journey of my existence now, to prove myself worthy in the eyes of the great Jarlaxle?"

The sarcasm in her voice was wrought of anger, but Entreri laughed anyway, and Jarlaxle managed a smile as well.

"Just ride with us the remainder of this night," Jarlaxle explained. "Then we will continue, and you can follow at your leisure, or ride swiftly ahead of us, if that is your wish. You need your privacy, it would seem, and so I grant it to you. Can you really say no to this bargain?" As he finished, he wagged his hand up and down, showing off the tempting magical mount.

Breezy took it and brought forth the nightmare. She felt its resistance when she began to mount it, and in truth was more than a bit afraid. She wouldn't let Jarlaxle see that, however.

"Are you going to ride behind me, then, or behind Artemis Entreri?" Breezy asked.

Jarlaxle gave a somewhat pitiful shrug and expression, and lifted his hand toward her. Breezy took it and helped him up behind her on the nightmare, suspecting more than a little that Jarlaxle was doing this for her benefit as anything else. He feared that she would not be able to maintain control of the hellsteed.

She tried not to be angry about his doubts—likely he did this with many of his associates. These horses of the lower planes were not to be taken lightly, after all.

They rode easily through most of the night, set camp before dawn, and readied to leave again when the sun passed its zenith.

"You wish to ride alone now?" Jarlaxle asked.

"That was our bargain," Breezy replied, not even trying to hide the bile that remained.

"So it was, and I know now that you can properly control the hellsteed. But do take care of my pet, I beg." He started away.

Breezy shook her head with typical resignation (where Jarlaxle was concerned) to learn that her suspicions were correct.

"And how will Jarlaxle ride?" Breezy called after him. "Behind Entreri?"

"Dear young lady, you do so wound me," Jarlaxle said with a bow and a tip of his great cap. He pulled yet another wondrous onyx figurine out of his pouch, summoned another nightmare, and so easily went up to his seat. With a tip of his great feathered hat, Jarlaxle gave a whistle to his associates and led the group away, only Entreri lingering behind.

"He has dragons and Lolthian drow, demons and nightmares, illithids and the ghost of Kimmuriel Oblodra," the assassin explained to Breezy. "Dahlia the vampire won't be the worst of his associates, I assure you."

"Is that your idea of comforting me, Artemis?"

The assassin laughed. "Just offering my vision of the world."

"Your dark vision."

Entreri gave a shrug and a nod. "Keeps me alive, aye?"

For the first time in a long time, Breezy laughed and agreed. "Aye."

She watched Entreri galloping hard to catch up to the others, her thoughts already drifting back to that terrible night on the road. And to the fight with Dahlia.

There was no way for her to escape the truth that Artemis Entreri had saved her life.

So be it.

"You're taking a great risk," Entreri said to Jarlaxle when he arrived at the head of the procession. "You know that."

"I know that Breezy is her own person, with her own needs and with her own demands of conscience," Jarlaxle replied. "She will have to decide her course, none other."

"I can guess that course," Entreri dryly replied, more than a hint of skepticism in his voice. When, after all, did Jarlaxle Baenre ever let others truly decide their own course?

Jarlaxle didn't disagree.

"A great risk," Entreri said again.

"Accepting great risks and greater challenges is the life I expect of the daughter of Drizzt Do'Urden and Catti-brie Battlehammer."

"If . . ." Entreri let the grim alternative hang there.

"If," Jarlaxle agreed.

"Risks can be mitigated," Entreri said.

"Of course."

The two stared at each other for just a moment. Jarlaxle cocked an eyebrow and gave the slightest of nods.

Artemis Entreri turned his hellsteed aside.

26

A QUESTION OF MORALS

Dahlia rode in her fancy coach toward Westbridge early that night, hoping to find Brevindon Margaster about. The very substance of her game, her existence, had changed before the dawn, she knew. She had made a pact out of sheer necessity and under duress—had she not agreed, Jarlaxle and his band would surely have ended her!

Now she had to play by their rules, or at least, to work around them to get the sweetness she so desperately craved.

She was going to have to rely upon Gershwin Caldwell or Brevindon to provide her with waifs and urchins no one would miss, or, absent that, she was going to have to travel far from this place, far from Jarlaxle's influence and seat of power. She even briefly considered a return to far-off Thay, but the thought of being discovered by Szass Tam had stopped that notion short. Being found by the archlich would inevitably result in something worse than anything Jarlaxle might do to her.

She could flee to Calimport, perhaps, so far to the south. What pasha wouldn't want a beautiful vampire as his consort?

Or, maybe, she could just do as Jarlaxle demanded and become a benign scout, she thought as the coach pulled up before The Happy Halfling.

The thought brought a scowl to her face as she exited the coach, hoping that Brevindon was about. Because, no, such an existence as Jarlaxle was forcing upon her wouldn't do.

Brevindon would find a way to bring her more victims beyond the eyes of Bregan D'aerthe.

He had to.

And soon, she hoped, because she knew that she wouldn't be able to keep Keely alive much longer. The transition into a vampire spawn was imminent, perhaps even this very night. She needed the taste of blood from a living person, but she needed, too, guards upon whom she could depend. She was vulnerable, so very vulnerable.

And she was hungry, so very hungry.

KEELY HISSED AND FELL BACK, lifting one arm defensively.

But the intruder didn't advance, just motioned to a chair and commanded her to go and sit.

The terrified Waterdhavian woman hesitated, her gaze locked on the thin line of deadly fire waving barely inches before her face. So quickly, it could strike, she knew.

For she had seen this opponent in battle before and knew that she would have no chance against her.

Perhaps that would be preferable.

She pushed aside the thought, too afraid. Too final, that end. There was no escape.

Trembling, she moved to the chair.

THE VAMPIRE SAT ON THE roof of The Happy Halfling, staring down at the street, cursing her fate. She watched a pair of young lovers dancing along, arm in arm, sharing kisses and sweet talk.

She knew where they were headed. She could almost taste their blood.

The vampire growled.

Too risky. Too soon.

Ghaliver's warning echoed in her thoughts. If she gave in to the hunger now, she would have to leave Westbridge, quickly and forevermore.

"You'll never have a better situation," she whispered to herself.

But the hunger . . . it would not let her go!

"Damn you, Brevindon," she muttered, for he was not there, was not in Westbridge, and was not expected back for a tenday or more. Even then, it would take a month for him to find her some new blood from the streets of Waterdeep and secretly deliver it to her at Manse Dorcrae.

The lovers moved out of sight. Dahlia's thirst did not diminish.

Another patron exited the tavern. The vampire leaned forward, nearly pitching over to drop upon him. She caught herself at the last moment.

Jarlaxle would learn of it. He would find her and destroy her.

"Keely," she decided and gave a growl. So be it. Dahlia turned into a bat and flew down to the alleyway, then assumed her elven form again and returned to her coach, ordering her drivers to take her home.

She was going to have to ration Keely so very carefully, she knew. The girl's blood was already beginning to lose its sweet taste, but she had not yet turned. Dahlia had to try somehow to keep it that way until she had new victims in hand, for the fluids of a full spawn were no good to her.

By the time the coach had pulled up before her door, her hunger had surged to near desperation, and she had to remind herself many times that finishing with Keely would mean roaming the Kryptgarden like an animal, hunting for goblins and their unpleasant blood for many days simply to survive.

She caught the scent as soon as she entered the house and followed it along the corridors to her sitting room, the thought of it, the smell of it, driving her more urgently.

She went through the doors, saw Keely sitting at the side of the room.

The young woman recoiled for only a moment, only until Dahlia flashed a bright smile and strangely brighter eyes.

Keely relaxed with acceptance, even gratitude, and the vampire approached and bared her fangs.

Dahlia tried futilely to remind herself again that she had to ration this one. The scent was so inviting, so sweet, so irresistible.

"Hello, Dahlia," came a woman's voice even as she bent to feed on Keely.

The spell broken, the vampire snapped up straight and spun about.

Breezy Do'Urden walked out from behind the heavy drapes at the back of the room.

"Already breaking your agreement with Jarlaxle, I see," Breezy said. "Of course you are. You are a lost wretch and cannot be redeemed or controlled."

Dahlia turned and stared hard at the young woman. From low to the side, she waggled a finger.

The vampire's eyes seemed to almost animate, sparkling like twin stars on the darkest night, and the smile, fangs hidden, beamed brightly.

She wasn't Dahlia, Breezy suddenly realized, and she returned the smile. She was Lady Delilah, a valuable asset, a welcomed member of Westbridge societ—

Breezy didn't change her expression at all as she recognized and mentally defeated the magical manipulation. Dahlia—Dahlia, not some alias!—had put her off balance with her charms once before, but not this time. Not now.

She noted that Keely flinched. *A vampire can only charm one person at a time,* she understood from her studies. That recollection confirmed the current mental attack on her and also gave her hope that Keely, reacting unpleasantly now to the nearness of the monster, might not be too far gone.

Which would matter not at all if she could not succeed here.

"Jarlaxle is only concerned with those I have not yet graced with immortality, of course," the vampire told Breezy. "He has to take care of the reputation of his band. My dear child here is already transforming." She cupped Keely's chin with her hand and tilted the young woman's head back to look into her eyes—into Keely's once more glassy eyes, Breezy noted.

The eyes of a thoroughly charmed victim. How easily Dahlia had turned the spell back on her victim.

Breezy began to cast a spell of her own, a dweomer that had been her favorite until Maegera had gifted her Twilight. She didn't call upon the disc ring. Not yet.

"If you would like to watch our lovemaking, we'll not object," Dahlia said, and bared her fangs. She turned Keely's head to the side and bent to feed.

"Don't," Breezy warned.

Dahlia paused and turned to regard Breezy, her eyes glowing red now, and still showing her fangs as her lips went from a smile to a snarl. "Would you have me starve?" she asked. "Is that your idea of mercy and compassion?"

"You chose your fate."

"Hardly! I was a victim, of course—or so I thought until I felt the power of this existence. You judge me because you do not understand."

"I understand that you mean to harm others, as you are about to do right now. You are a predator."

"And you are not? You work for Jarlaxle. Do you think he acts in kindness and goodness as he takes over entire cities?"

"The people of Luskan—"

"Were conquered," Dahlia insisted. "Subtly, to be sure, as that is Jarlaxle's way, but they did not choose to be ruled by him."

"That is . . ." Breezy shook her head, trying to get the confusing notions out of her thoughts, and trying even harder not to reveal the sting of Dahlia's words. She couldn't help but think of the drow woman in the cave, of the hand-crossbow, of the blood spewing from the mortal wound.

"No!" she insisted. "You prey on the weak and the innocent. You are destroying this woman, Keely, even now!"

"Am I?" Dahlia gave a little laugh. "Do you know this poor girl's history, of how she has been used and tossed into the gutters for all of her short life?"

"She is still alive."

"Alive and without hope," Dahlia insisted. "Without power, without influence. Her lot would revert to that which she knew before she came into my home. Do you really think Keely would prefer that fate?" She looked to the girl. "Would you, Keely?"

Breezy couldn't deny the obvious look of confusion on Keely's face, and Keely wasn't even being magically charmed by Dahlia at that time.

"You could be so much more," Dahlia promised Keely. "Do you wish the life you had before, or would you choose to be as I, a being of the night, indeed, but eternally so! Immortal, without fear, and with true power? What person would try to force Keely the vampire?"

Breezy tried to ignore the look Keely was returning to Dahlia, the slight nod, the hopeful glint that came suddenly into her eyes. Perhaps it was true, Breezy thought. Perhaps Keely would be better off as a vampire—Dahlia seemed to be holding a fine existence here. She couldn't deny that.

"But you must kill to survive," she said, because she had to say something even if the conviction was fading from her voice.

"That is not true," Dahlia answered without hesitation. "Not if I have enough servants upon which to feed."

"You hurt people," Breezy retorted, and she wanted to take back the seemingly childish response even as the words left her mouth.

"We all hurt people, dear," said Dahlia. "As I have already told you: Do you think Jarlaxle's hands clean of blood? Artemis Entreri's? Your father's? Your mother's?" Her chortle at the end of that last pronouncement and the ensuing laugh cut into Breezy's heart, and not just because of how venomously it had been aimed at her mother. She envisioned her hand lifting before her, the hand-crossbow so near to the back of the drow woman's head. In her mind, she felt the vibration of the shot, then the warmth of the blood flowing over her hand as the drow fell to the stone.

"You will be as I am," Dahlia said to Keely. "Strong. In command of your existence. No more a victim."

Keely craned her neck, presenting it for the bite. Breezy could not deny the logic.

But something—the look in Dahlia's eye, perhaps—incited a flicker of clarity. So sly was that look, that of a hunting beast about to make a kill.

Dahlia wouldn't make Keely a vampire, Breezy realized. Surely not! To do so would create a threat, and that was something Dahlia could not, could never, tolerate. She was going to make a wretched spawn of Keely, like those Breezy had destroyed on the road. She would make more of them, many of them and, with Keely, send them out to hunt and murder people and horses.

"Don't!" Breezy yelled at Dahlia. "You're lying! She won't turn you, Keely—not into a true vampi—"

Just before her fangs could sink into Keely's neck, the woman jerked away and Dahlia snapped her head around, glaring at Breezy.

"You're a liar," Breezy said. "You'll just murder her, or make her into one of your slave spawns."

"Would you like to be first?" Dahlia asked.

"Oh, then you would kill me as well, it would seem," Breezy said, working very hard to keep her voice from cracking in the face of this formidable monster. "Would Jarlaxle approve?"

"For you, I would not care what Jarlaxle might think," Dahlia said, flashing the most awful grin, and oh so easily shoving Keely back and to the floor, where the confused young woman curled up defensively. "And your fate will not be immortality, as I offered dear Keely here. No, you will simply disappear, your bloodless corpse fed to the animals in deepest Kryptgarden."

Dahlia kept her gaze on Breezy as she moved over to Keely and hoisted her by the hair, bending her head to the side. She offered Breezy one wicked smile, then slowly opened her mouth and turned back to feed on Keely's long, skinny, naked, irresistible neck.

"Do not!" Breezy loudly growled. "Last warning! Prove now, in this moment, that you are worthy of Jarlaxle's faith in you."

Dahlia hissed, her mouth going wide.

The shadow blade appeared in Breezy's hand, the bladesinger shaping it as a small javelin in her conjuration. As the vampire moved to feed, Breezy let fly the missile of psychic energy, catching Dahlia just inside her nearest shoulder.

With a howl, Dahlia stumbled back from her intended victim, who cried out in horror and scrambled to the side.

Breezy stared hatefully at the vampire, who stood grimacing in pain, her hands on either side of her head, spewing a long, feral growl. After a moment, Dahlia snapped her tightly clenched hands down by her sides, violently shook her head to throw aside the psychic pain, and focused fully on Breezy.

"Leave the poor woman alone, and I will take her and go," Breezy told her, though she really had no intention of doing any such thing.

"No, daughter of Drizzt," Dahlia answered. "Keely is going to see what I do to you, and she is going to then beg to become my full child."

Before the vampire had finished the threat, Breezy, holding her focus on the continuing spell, brought another javelin of shadow energy into her hand.

Dahlia rushed forward.

Breezy cocked her arm to throw.

Dahlia disappeared!

Breezy brought her arm forward, but did not let fly, instead using the momentum to throw herself down and forward. She turned out toward the left as she descended, tucked her right shoulder to land on that shoulder blade, and as she came rotating around just before she hit the floor, threw the javelin out behind where she had been standing.

But the vampire wasn't there, coming at her instead from the side of the room, flying, not running, at remarkable speed.

Breezy went into her roll, desperately kicking out with her legs to hold the fiend at bay. Long claws raked one shin, tearing her breeches and her skin. She tried to scramble back, but Dahlia clamped a powerful hand on her ankle and would not let go, her grip as strong as that of a giant!

Breezy kicked at the vampire's hand and arm repeatedly and began to squeal in terror and gyrate wildly as if trying to break free. She twisted at the waist, facedown and scrabbling desperately to crawl away.

So, she wanted her enemy to believe.

For she called upon her disc ring now to enact the powerful Twilight within, spun back, and reflexively enacted a shield of magical energy to deflect Dahlia's free hand as the vampire tried to rake again at her trapped leg. Breezy swept the mighty Twilight across at the vampire's arm. Dahlia retracted fast enough to miss most of the fury, but that finest edge of living flame bit at Dahlia's forearm, slashing through the sleeve of her blouse, the fabric's rip widening as it was devoured by consuming lines of glowing fire.

Dahlia fell back, grabbing at her forearm, tamping the flames on her shirt, and judging by the pained look on her face, the biting flames on her skin, too.

Breezy pulled her feet in and up, throwing her legs over her into a fast spin that brought her back to a crouch. She didn't steady herself as she rose, instead halting the movement while still leaning forward, and using the tilted posture to hurl herself back the other way, Twilight stabbing as she tried to score a sudden and decisive victory.

Dahlia was too fast for that, but Breezy put the vampire on her heels and pressed the attack with a series of short cuts and thrusts.

Still, Dahlia had another trick, pulling Kozah's Needle from some holster she had fashioned on her back, hidden beneath her cloak. The weapon came out as a pair of jo sticks, as Breezy had seen in the battle with Entreri, and the vampire wasted no time in smacking them together to build a lightning charge after every parry of Twilight.

They fell into a rhythm—one that Breezy feared. Even before she had become a vampire, Dahlia was, by all accounts, formidable and full of tricks, and her weapon, that lightning energy stave that could take many different forms, might well be Twilight's equal or better.

And Dahlia worked it so fluidly, so beautifully. Both hands, both jo sticks, went up over her right shoulder as she jumped back from a sidelong slash of Twilight, and then came forward again, not as jo sticks, but as a tri-staff, three lengths whipping out and across with a reach to far exceed Breezy's sword.

Had Breezy not seen this before, her fight would have ended there, but as soon as she realized that Dahlia had let go of the weapon with her left hand, she went into a leap and backward somersault, the crackling whip of metal and lightning sweeping beneath her.

Breezy felt the stings of that energy on her bottom and back as she went over, and those were enough to tell her that she didn't want to suffer a direct hit.

Dahlia completed the swing by spinning a complete circuit, and she came back facing Breezy with the solid quarterstaff version of Kozah's Needle presented diagonally before her.

A series of buttons controlling the weapon? Breezy wondered. A manner of silent spellcasting similar to her disc ring? A bit of both?

The thoughts roiled within her, but most of all came her sheer awe at how smoothly Dahlia transitioned the weapon, for she had made Kozah's Needle's various forms a part of her battle dance, an extension of her limbs and martial desires. Even before her descent into vampirism, Dahlia was a skilled and deadly fighter, no doubt, one to rival many of the champions in Breezy's circle.

On Dahlia came, punching her fists forward alternately, driving the left and right ends of the quarterstaff in at Breezy in rapid succession and boring ahead so determinedly that she had the younger warrior on her heels almost immediately.

Breezy worked her sword to block right, block left, block right, each collision of the magical weapons sending licks of flame, balls of shadow, and sparks of lightning energy flying about the combatants. The room danced in a macabre strobe of flashes and darkness and poor, overwhelmed Keely began to scream as she covered and cowered at the base of the wall.

Knowing she had no chance to riposte, and running out of room, Breezy shifted the fourth block, back to the left, by stiffening her left forearm vertically to intercept the staff's swing.

And she reacted to the strike with a spell—not a magical shield this time, for her forearm could handle the physical hit, but a dweomer to absorb the lightning energy, some of it at least, and redirect it.

She halted the swing, rolled her arm fast over Kozah's Needle to prevent Dahlia from retracting it and swinging out with the right-side end. She rolled Twilight horizontally, stabbing ahead, a thrust that was strengthened by that redirected lightning energy.

Dahlia yelped in surprise and clear pain, the tip of Twilight barely penetrating, but the unexpected lightning jolt making the jab hurt.

Breezy, meanwhile, managed to hide her own surprise when, despite her absorbing spell, the sheer power of the staff's lightning racked her, burned her flesh red, and sent stunning jolts racing up her arm. She fell back as Dahlia, too, retreated.

"Clever play," Dahlia congratulated with a grin. "But your spells are limited. Note how much of the energy got through to you! You have no chance here, foolish child."

The last part carried magical enhancement, a wave of coercing despair designed to break Breezy's will.

But the Superior Master of the Monastery of the Yellow Rose knew how to avoid such unwanted mind attacks and intrusions. If ever Breezy had regrets or notions of dismissing her time at the monastery as a waste of years, she knew differently in that exact moment. Without the mental training she had received, that would have been the end of the fight.

Dahlia didn't know that, of course, and Breezy wasn't about to let on as she tried to turn the magical suggestion back against the vampire. "I will leave," she begged plaintively, pitifully.

The vampire saw right through the lie and charged ahead, growling, staff swinging.

Breezy called upon her monk training once more, reached into her ki, and shadow stepped to a patch of darkness over by the draperies to Dahlia's rear left flank, coming out of it facing back at the vampire, rushing for a quick kill.

She had to skid to a stop and leap back, though, as Dahlia came whirling about, that deadly staff sweeping a wide circuit. Breezy started an advance in behind the cut, but Dahlia reversed her weapon deftly and immediately.

Breezy threw her shoulders back and rotated backward, right to left, ducking the blow. She came out with a great leap, turning almost horizontal as she climbed into the air, her right foot coming around in a circle kick that snapped just short of the vampire's face, followed by a left-footed kick as she continued her rotation.

Dahlia turned her head to avoid that one, too, and rushed in behind it.

But Breezy wasn't done. All the training, all the years of learning to find her center, her balance, her innermost strength, kept her aloft just a bit longer, rotating yet again. Twice around in that single leap, the monk executed her actual intended strike, right leg coming around a second time in the nearly horizontal spin, right heel cracking against the side of Dahlia's jaw. And in that collision, Breezy reached so very deeply into her life energy, throwing forth her ki, multiplying the strength of the impact.

She crouched as she came around and dropped, pulling her feet under her as Dahlia's head snapped violently to the side.

And up Breezy sprang—a great leap.

THE POWER OF THE KICK surprised Dahlia. She felt her jawbone shatter and knew it would take some time for it to mend. She didn't feel pain from such wounds as a living creature might, but she feared that she wouldn't have the jaw strength to properly feed any time soon.

So be it, she decided. She would take this half-drow creature down and imprison her and take her time in feasting before she tore the little whelp apart.

She snapped back at her attacker and hissed.

Drizzt's spawn wasn't there!

Dahlia spun about, eyes darting to every shadow as she turned, before she realized too late that Breezy had witnessed her disastrous fight with Entreri.

She looked up as the young half-drow creature descended from the leap, that strange dark sword with the fiery edge leading.

She couldn't dodge.

She couldn't bring Kozah's Needle up in time to block the strike.

She became instead a cloud of gas.

But not quick enough, with that oh-so-awful fiery tip diving into her collarbone, the edge slashing downward until she became insubstantial.

BREEZY REACTED INSTANTLY AS THE vampire dematerialized beneath her. She tucked sword, arms, and head, hitting the floor in a fast roll and spinning back with Twilight slashing across, back and forth, whipping through the gas cloud that was floating away from her—but not moving fast enough to leave her behind. Every slash ignited sparks in the mist, wisps of black flame as Twilight bit with both of its magical energies.

"It's still hurting you, vampire!" she yelled, taking up the sword in both hands and cutting it wildly back and forth with even more force.

Dahlia became corporeal again, suddenly and cleverly, driving Kozah's Needle across to slam Breezy's shoulder. She followed with a devastating overhead chop calling upon the lightning charge, but the young warrior stumbled to the side ahead of the strike, and Dahlia's lightning staff crashed instead atop a serving table, exploding it down the middle, splinters flying everywhere.

Breezy roared and shrugged off the burning pain in her shoulder with a growl, coming right back into the fray.

The vampire had missed that second, killing strike, and had released all the stored lightning energy, but she had bought herself just enough room to transform again, this time into a bat, and one flying away from Breezy too fast for the warrior or her sword to catch up.

But Breezy didn't hesitate, dismissing the sword as her right hand went up over her shoulder, her left hand going to her belt buckle, twisting it, releasing the latch, and coming up with Taulmaril. She returned the right hand holding an arrow from the magical Quiver of Ehlonna.

Up, leveled, and off went the lightning arrow, catching up to the bat right before it exited the room's door. It impaled Dahlia in the right wing and redirected her course, slamming her to the wall, pinning her there.

Breezy was already running in pursuit, slowing only to grab one leg of the destroyed table, bracing a foot against its base and tearing it free. She skipped forward, hands wide on the table leg, snapping it in half across her knee. Throwing aside one piece and taking up the second, she slid her left hand halfway along its length, right hand set firmly over its end as she went into a sudden, full sprint and a somewhat reckless leap.

Dahlia returned to her elven form and yanked herself free of the arrow, but she never turned about, never saw it coming, as the living missile that was Breezy rammed into her, crushing her into the wall—and the table leg, the wooden stake driving into the back of the vampire.

Breezy shoved and let go, leaped into a circle kick, and smashed her heel into the butt of the stake. She heard the thud of the tip bursting through Dahlia's chest and thumping into the wall.

Dahlia shrieked, a horrid, otherworldly sound unlike anything Breezy had ever heard before or wanted to hear again. She rolled about on the wall, staring hatefully, her mouth opened wide in a terrible strain of every muscle within her, fighting, fighting, the mortal blow.

Breezy fell back, mesmerized and horrified, telling herself over and over again that this was a monster, a vampire, and not anything like the drow she had killed back in the cave in the pass to Icewind Dale.

Still, pangs of guilt stabbed at her—but only until she was able to summon enough rage to bury them.

With a growl, she brought forth Twilight once more. That growl became a roar of defiance as she swung it wide—not at Dahlia, but across the drapery covering the east-facing window beside the door. The fiery edge easily slashed right through the heavy velvet, leaving burning embers at the cut edges. The bottom half of the drapery fell to the floor in a heap, thin lines of smoke wafting, occasional flames flickering. Beyond the glass, the sky was still dark, but hints of the dawn were beginning to appear.

The vampire continued to roll about the supporting wall, groaning, finally managing to clench her teeth, her trembling hands trying futilely to grab at the impaling stake, front and back. Then she stopped, suddenly, back to the wall, and began to shake violently. Her hands tremored, her eyes bulged, her mouth opened wide again, straining, but now in a silent scream of denial and terror.

Breezy stood transfixed at the gruesomeness of the decaying creature. Part in mercy, part in simple denial of such a spectacle, she swept Twilight across, taking Dahlia's head from her shoulders, where it flipped and fell beside the slowly igniting pile of velvet.

Breezy noted the smoking bundle and nodded. She put her thumbs tip to tip, extending the fingers of her free hand and calling upon the magic of her mother's ring.

A cone of flames burst forth, engulfing the velvet and feeding the blaze. Not even feeling the heat of it, Breezy reached down and grabbed the burning pile of cloth, carried it to the broken table, then tossed the nearby wooden chairs atop it. She moved about the room, slapping Twilight down on the tablecloths, across other drapes— anything that could burn.

Then, on sudden intuition, or perhaps it was the magic of Twilight calling to her, she held the sword out before her and reached more deeply into its connection to the Plane of Fire. With a sudden and violent movement, she slashed that finest edge across the air before her, cutting a planar tear to the fire domain, much as Zak had done with that most marvelous whip that was now within this weapon of combined power. The rift held open in the air for only a moment, but long enough for small drips of flames to fall from it, and those fires, Breezy knew, were alive.

She dominated them through the ring, ordering them to eat, to burn.

Breezy felt a different call from her sword, and she looked to it curiously for a moment. Her eyes went wide, and she cut the blade across, tearing the fabric of the Material Plane, and kept going, turning Twilight over in the strike so that its dark shadow edge was then leading.

And cutting a second rift, this one to the Plane of Shadow.

Out dripped the shadowstuff, living, tiny versions of the mastiff she had summoned in the forest.

Destroy! she telepathically commanded them.

The pack rushed for Keely, but Breezy turned them immediately away from the whimpering woman.

Breezy walked over to her, extending a hand.

"Come with me. My mother will help you."

The young Waterdhavian, still curled defensively and so obviously terrified, shook her head.

"Dahlia isn't going to rise, and these fires aren't going to diminish, and these shadow hound . . . pups are going to devour everything in their path. Would you stay here and be horribly consumed, by fire or by beast?"

Keely didn't move—indeed, didn't seem able to move.

Breezy reached her hand down emphatically. "If I wanted to hurt you, I would. But I don't. Trust me, I beg. Come with me. I know people who can help you."

She saw the fear holding steady on Keely's face. She had heard enough from Entreri and learned enough from Jarlaxle to recognize the source as a life of misery and exploitation.

With a thought, she dismissed Twilight, then bent low to look Keely in the eye, very close. "You're not too far infected," she said softly, and she hoped it was true. "Have you ever been given a chance, Keely? Have you ever been given an opportunity to live your life as you choose, and not how others who would harm you chose for you? Come with me, I beg. I'll show you a better place, a better way, and one where the master of Keely will be Keely alone. On my word. And should anyone try to deny you that, I, Breezy Do'Urden, solemnly vow to destroy them as I destroyed the vampire Dahlia."

She motioned with her hand again, and this time, Keely's hand came up, ever so slowly, and accepted it.

Breezy pulled her to her feet, then looked around to see that the tiny elementals and shadow pups were having a grand time igniting linens and wood and chewing at the table legs, the chair cushions, the baseboards of the room—anything they could find.

Out came Twilight again, and Breezy cut the air again and again, laughing as she created a small army of tiny elementals and shadow pups to swarm and bite at every corner and everything in Manse Dorcrae. She paused only long enough to pick up Kozah's Needle.

By the time she had ushered Keely outside, the eastern sky was clearly lightening.

Breezy dismissed Twilight and called up the hellsteed from the onyx figurine Jarlaxle had provided her. The nightmare snorted and pawed the ground, bringing a frightened wail from Keely, who tried to pull away from Breezy.

Up went Breezy into the saddle, never letting go of Keely's hand, and to Breezy's relief, Keely did come up behind her with very little resistance.

The nightmare reared and leaped away, galloping down the hillside on fiery hooves, Breezy riding tall and proud as the eastern sky brightened with the impending dawn.

Soon after, the pair raced along the road to Westbridge until Breezy paused and turned the horse about to regard her handiwork.

The sun had not yet peeked above the horizon, and in the dim light, the roaring flames of Manse Dorcrae leaped into the sky. There were many trees between the riders and the burning mansion, but somehow the sheer power and brilliance of the fire all but eliminated the obstruction of the view, making that blaze on the hill seem even larger and greater. And glorious, Breezy thought.

"I'm going to help you," Breezy said again to reassure the young woman, who was still trembling in fear.

Her hellsteed snorted, but when she heard the snort of a second nightmare, Breezy turned back to the road.

Artemis Entreri walked his mount up beside her. He nodded his chin toward the fire. "Dahlia?" he asked.

Breezy nodded. "Yes. Destroyed even before the fires began."

"You killed her?"

"She was already dead," Breezy reminded rather sharply, her tone designed to remove any twinges of guilt she might feel for the act. She paused a moment, then, and regarded the man, somehow knowing that he was asking questions to which he already knew the answers.

"You destroyed the vampire?" Artemis Entreri clarified.

Breezy nodded and didn't blink, studying him. Was it possible that he had been there, outside a window, perhaps, watching her, guarding her? She couldn't sort it out—even if Entreri wasn't going to let her be killed, would he have allowed the destruction of Dahlia, of Lady Delilah, Jarlaxle's new recruit?

"And who is this?" Entreri asked.

"Her name is Keely."

"Spawn of Dahlia?" Entreri arched an eyebrow skeptically.

"Not yet, but nearly. My mother can help her, I am sure. Or Jarlaxle."

Entreri's obvious doubts did not diminish.

"We have to try," Breezy told him. "I'm going to try, whether you'll help me or not. That's why Jarlaxle sent you back, right? To help me? To rescue me?"

Entreri gave a little laugh. "No."

"No? You and Jarlaxle knew my desires, obviously."

"We thought to go and stop you, yes."

"But you didn't."

"If Dahlia was true to her word to Jarlaxle, she would have stopped you, with words."

"She might have killed me."

Entreri shrugged. At first, Breezy took that to mean he didn't care, but what she realized was that he, and by extension Jarlaxle, believed in her.

"You knew I was in there."

"Yes."

"Tell me true, Artemis Entreri, did you see the fight I waged with Dahlia?"

"No. Jarlaxle sent me back to learn of the outcome if you acted as we suspected you might. Nothing more. Well, if Dahlia had harmed you, she would have answered to me for it, yes."

The information had Breezy truly off balance because she found that she believed him. She felt as if she had just climbed a sheer cliff with no rope or pitons. For an instant, she found herself so suddenly terribly afraid, and when it passed, she felt a moment of anger at Jarlaxle. If he knew that she was going to do this, why had he bargained with Dahlia? Why had he pretended that all was in control? And why hadn't he sent someone—Entreri or Regis or even Braelin Janquay—to help her finish the deed?

"It was your decision to make," Entreri said as if reading her mind. "Your battle to choose or to defer."

Breezy rubbed her face and ran her hand through her thick auburn hair.

"Will Jarlaxle be mad at me?"

"No."

"Disappointed?"

"No."

"Are you? Dahlia was important to you."

"Lady Delilah was not the Dahlia I knew. She was a vampire, a monster, who killed innocents to sate her thirst."

"She broke her promise to Jarlaxle . . ." Breezy stammered, indicating Keely. "She was still going to feast upon—"

Entreri held up his hand to silence her.

"We have a long ride," he said. "Better for us to be away before Effron and the people of Westbridge learn of these dramatic developments, and better for us to stay away until they can properly digest the news."

"I just want to explain . . ."

"Why?"

That gave Breezy pause. That simple question struck her like a thunderbolt and forced her to truly examine her choice. She closed her eyes and took a deep breath.

She had done the right thing here, and not just because of Keely, she truly believed. Vampire Dahlia was going to continue to inflict misery on innocents. She thought of Windy, poor Windy!

And she thought of Jarlaxle and Entreri.

They had let her do this.

They had let her be an adult, with all the pain and responsibility and difficult decisions and possible remorse that came with it—and for a full member of Bregan D'aerthe, with all the danger that came with it, as well.

Breezy Do'Urden put her head up, urged her hellsteed forward, and did not let Artemis Entreri lead the way back to the north.

She didn't need him to.

EPILOGUE

"Truthfully?" Jarlaxle asked, standing atop the sooty remains of a foundation, the rising sun behind him. "Were it me, I would have less concern and more pride. You have given the world a daring hero. We can never have too many of those."

He went back to his wand, casting another spell from it to detect magic, then continued his pacing about the smoldering ruins of Manse Dorcrae. In his other hand, he held Kozah's Needle.

"And if she had failed and been killed?" Catti-brie asked.

"Would that be my fault, or yours?" Jarlaxle was quick to respond. "The morals and courage of your teachings and your examples brought your daughter back to this place. Breezy's conscience—not mine, I assure you—demanded that Lady Delilah, the vampire Dahlia, could not be allowed to continue. And Breezy, not I, chose to fight her alone."

"You let her take quite a risk," said Catti-brie.

"Does it matter that she saved—or at least, perhaps saved— a young woman victimized by Dahlia?" Jarlaxle asked.

"Hopefully saved," Catti-brie agreed. "I'll not know until I meet this Keely and begin my healing spells."

"Removing the vampiric infection would be but half the task of saving that poor young woman," Jarlaxle reminded.

Catti-brie nodded and looked around. "Thank you for sending Allefaero to me and bringing me here with you," she said.

"And thank me for letting Breezy come back to this place to satisfy the demands of her conscience?"

"That one will take longer to decide," Catti-brie replied.

She looked around at the ruins of Manse Dorcrae, shaking her head that her little girl had caused such destruction. Her emotions continued to swirl tumultuously, leaping back and forth from the perspective of her role as a protector to Breezy and the undeniable pride that she felt for Breezy's choices.

"Destruction?" she whispered.

No, not destruction, she decided.

Cleansing.

Creation.

ACKNOWLEDGMENTS

I want to say thanks to Paul Morrissey at Wizards of the Coast for supporting me along this continuing journey.

To my agent Paul Lucas of Janklow/Nesbit for guiding me through these tumultuous times in publishing.

And to all the folks at Random House Worlds who are supporting this next chapter of my journey through the Forgotten Realms, especially to my new editor, Elizabeth Schaefer. You had big shoes to fill, and you did it.

Read on for an excerpt from

DUNGEONS & DRAGONS

THE LEGEND OF DRIZZT

HOMELAND

R.A. SALVATORE

THE LEGEND BEGINS!

Briza placed the newborn on the back of the spider idol and lifted the ceremonial dagger, pausing to admire its cruel workmanship. Its hilt was a spider's body sporting eight legs, barbed so as to appear furred, but angled down to serve as blades. Briza lifted the instrument above the baby's chest.

"Name the child," she implored her mother. "The Spider Queen will not accept the sacrifice until the child is named!"

"Drizzt," breathed Matron Malice. "The child's name is Drizzt!"

PRELUDE

Never does a star grace this land with a poet's light of twinkling mysteries, nor does the sun send to here its rays of warmth and life. This is the Underdark, the secret world beneath the bustling surface of the Forgotten Realms, whose sky is a ceiling of heartless stone and whose walls show the gray blandness of death in the torchlight of the foolish surface-dwellers that stumble here. This is not their world, not the world of light. Most who come here uninvited do not return.

Those who do escape to the safety of their surface homes return changed. Their eyes have seen the shadows and the gloom, the inevitable doom of the Underdark.

Dark corridors meander throughout the dark realm in winding courses, connecting caverns great and small, with ceilings high and low. Mounds of stone as pointed as the teeth of a sleeping dragon leer down in silent threat or rise up to block the way of intruders.

There is a silence here, profound and foreboding, the crouched hush of a predator at work. Too often the only sound, the only reminder to travelers in the Underdark that they have not lost their sense of hearing altogether, is a distant and echoing drip of water, beating like the heart of a beast, slipping through the silent stones to the deep Underdark pools of chilled water. What lies beneath the still onyx surface of these pools one can only guess. What secrets await the brave, what horrors await the foolish, only the imagination can reveal—until the stillness is disturbed.

This is the Underdark.

THERE ARE POCKETS OF LIFE HERE, CITIES AS GREAT AS MANY OF those on the surface. Around any of the countless bends and turns in the gray stone a traveler might stumble suddenly into the perimeter of such a city, a stark contrast to the emptiness of the corridors. These places are not havens, though; only the foolish traveler would assume so. They are the homes of the most evil races in all the Realms, most notably the duergar, the kuo-toa, and the drow.

In one such cavern, two miles wide and a thousand feet high, looms Menzoberranzan, a monument to the other worldly and—ultimately—deadly grace that marks the race of drow elves. Menzoberranzan is not a large city by drow standards; only twenty thousand dark elves reside there. Where, in ages past, there had been an empty cavern of roughly shaped stalactites and stalagmites now stands artistry, row after row of carved castles thrumming in a quiet glow of magic. The city is perfection of form, where not a stone has been left to its natural shape. This sense of order and control, however, is but a cruel facade, a deception hiding the chaos and vileness that rule the dark elves' hearts. Like their cities, they are a beautiful, slender, and delicate people, with features sharp and haunting.

Yet the drow are the rulers of this unruled world, the deadliest of the deadly, and all other races take cautious note of their passing. Beauty itself pales at the end of a dark elf's sword. The drow are the survivors, and this is the Underdark, the valley of death—the land of nameless nightmares.

PART ONE
STATION

Station: In all the world of the drow, there is no more important word. It is the calling of their—of our—religion, the incessant pulling of hungering heartstrings. Ambition overrides good sense and compassion is thrown away in its face, all in the name of Lolth, the Spider Queen.

Ascension to power in drow society is a simple process of assassination. The Spider Queen is a deity of chaos, and she and her high priestesses, the true rulers of the drow world, do not look with ill favor upon ambitious individuals wielding poisoned daggers.

Of course, there are rules of behavior; every society must boast of these. To openly commit murder or wage war invites the pretense of justice, and penalties exacted in the name of drow justice are merciless. To stick a dagger in the back of a rival during the chaos of a larger battle or in the quiet shadows of an alley, however, is quite acceptable—even applauded. Investigation is not the forte of drow justice. No one cares enough to bother.

Station is the way of Lolth, the ambition she bestows to further the chaos, to keep her drow "children" along their

*appointed course of self-imprisonment. Children? Pawns,
more likely, dancing dolls for the Spider Queen, puppets on
the imperceptible but impervious strands of her web. All climb
the Spider Queen's ladders; all hunt for her pleasure; and all
fall to the hunters of her pleasure.*

*Station is the paradox of the world of my people, the
limitation of our power within the hunger for power. It is
gained through treachery and invites treachery against those
who gain it. Those most powerful in Menzoberranzan spend
their days watching over their shoulders, defending against
the daggers that would find their backs. Their deaths usually
come from the front.*

—Drizzt Do'Urden

1

MENZOBERRANZAN

To a surface dweller, he might have passed undetected only a foot away. The padded footfalls of his lizard mount were too light to be heard, and the pliable and perfectly crafted mesh armor that both rider and mount wore bent and creased with their movements as well as if the suits had grown over their skin.

Dinin's lizard trotted along in an easy but swift gait, floating over the broken floor, up the walls, and even across the long tunnel's ceiling. Subterranean lizards, with their sticky and soft three-toed feet, were preferred mounts for just this ability to scale stone as easily as a spider. Crossing hard ground left no damning tracks in the lighted surface world, but nearly all of the creatures of the Underdark possessed infravision, the ability to see in the infrared spectrum. Footfalls left heat residue that could easily be tracked if they followed a predictable course along a corridor's floor.

Dinin clamped tight to his saddle as the lizard plodded along a stretch of the ceiling, then sprang out in a twisting descent to a point farther along the wall. Dinin did not want to be tracked.

He had no light to guide him, but he needed none. He was a dark elf, a drow, an ebon-skinned cousin of those sylvan folk who danced under the stars on the world's surface. To Dinin's superior eyes, which translated subtle variations of heat into vivid and colorful images, the Underdark was far from a lightless place. Colors all across the spectrum swirled before him in the stone of the walls and the floor, heated by some distant fissure or hot stream. The heat of living things was the most distinctive, letting the dark elf view his enemies in details as intricate as any surface-dweller would find in brilliant daylight.

Normally Dinin would not have left the city alone; the world of the Underdark was too dangerous for solo treks, even for a drow elf. This day was different, though. Dinin had to be certain that no unfriendly drow eyes marked his passage.

A soft blue magical glow beyond a sculpted archway told the drow that he neared the city's entrance, and he slowed the lizard's pace accordingly. Few used this narrow tunnel, which opened into Tier Breche, the northern section of Menzoberranzan devoted to the Academy, and none but the mistresses and masters, the instructors of the Academy, could pass through here without attracting suspicion.

Dinin was always nervous when he came to this point. Of the hundred tunnels that opened off the main cavern of Menzoberranzan, this one was the best guarded. Beyond the archway, twin statues of gigantic spiders sat in quiet defense. If an enemy crossed through, the spiders would animate and attack, and alarms would be sounded throughout the Academy.

Dinin dismounted, leaving his lizard clinging comfortably to a wall at his chest level. He reached under the collar of his piwafwi, his magical, shielding cloak, and took out his neck-purse. From this Dinin produced the insignia of House Do'Urden, a spider wielding various weapons in each of its eight legs and emblazoned with the letters "DN," for Daermon N'a'shezbaernon, the ancient and formal name of House Do'Urden.

"You will await my return," Dinin whispered to the lizard as he waved the insignia before it. As with all the drow houses, the insignia of House Do'Urden held several magical dweomers, one of which gave family members absolute control over the house pets. The lizard would obey unfailingly, holding its position as though it were rooted to the stone, even if a scurry rat, its favorite morsel, napped a few feet from its maw.

Dinin took a deep breath and gingerly stepped to the archway. He could see the spiders leering down at him from their fifteen-foot height. He was a drow of the city, not an enemy, and could pass through any other tunnel unconcerned, but the Academy was an unpredictable place; Dinin had heard that the spiders often refused entry—viciously—even to uninvited drow.

He could not be delayed by fears and possibilities, Dinin reminded himself. His business was of the utmost importance to his family's battle plans. Looking straight ahead, away from the towering spiders, he strode between them and onto the floor of Tier Breche.

He moved to the side and paused, first to be certain that no one lurked nearby, and to admire the sweeping view of Menzoberranzan. No one, drow or otherwise, had ever looked out from this spot without a sense of wonder at the drow city. Tier Breche was the highest point on the floor of the two-mile cavern, affording a panoramic view to the rest of Menzoberranzan. The cubby of the Academy was narrow, holding only the three structures that comprised the drow school: Arach-Tinilith, the spider-shaped school of Lolth; Sorcere, the gracefully curving, many-spired tower of wizardry; and Melee-Magthere, the somewhat plain pyramidal structure where male fighters learned their trade.

Beyond Tier Breche, through the ornate stalagmite columns that marked the entrance to the Academy, the cavern dropped away quickly and spread wide, going far beyond Dinin's line of vision to either side and farther back than his keen eyes could possibly see. The colors of Menzoberranzan were threefold to the sensitive eyes of the drow. Heat patterns from various fissures and hot springs swirled about the entire cavern. Purple and red, bright yellow and subtle blue, crossed and merged, climbed the walls and stalagmite mounds, or ran off singularly in cutting lines against the backdrop of dim gray stone. More confined than these generalized and natural gradations of color in the infrared spectrum were the regions of intense magic, like the spiders Dinin had walked between, virtually glowing with energy. Finally there were the actual lights of the city, faerie fire and highlighted sculptures on the houses. The drow were proud of the beauty of their designs, and especially ornate columns or perfectly crafted gargoyles were almost always limned in permanent magical lights.

Even from this distance Dinin could make out House Baenre, First House of Menzoberranzan. It encompassed twenty stalagmite pillars and half again that number of gigantic stalactites. House Baenre had existed for five thousand years, since the founding of Menzoberranzan, and in that time the work to perfect the house's art had never ceased. Practically every inch of the immense structure glowed in faerie fire, blue at the outlying towers and brilliant purple at the huge central dome.

The sharp light of candles, foreign to the Underdark, glared through some of the windows of the distant houses. Only clerics or wizards would light the fires, Dinin knew, as necessary pains in their world of scrolls and parchments.

This was Menzoberranzan, the city of drow. Twenty thousand dark elves lived there, twenty thousand soldiers in the army of evil.

A wicked smile spread across Dinin's thin lips when he thought of some of those soldiers who would fall this night.

Dinin studied Narbondel, the huge central pillar that served as the timeclock of Menzoberranzan. Narbondel was the only way the drow had to mark the passage of time in a world that otherwise knew no days and no seasons. At the end of each day, the city's appointed Archmage cast his magical fires into the base of the stone pillar. There the spell lingered throughout the cycle—a full day on the surface— and gradually spread its warmth up the structure of Narbondel until the whole of it glowed red in the infrared spectrum. The pillar was fully dark now, cooled since the dweomer's fires had expired. The wizard was even now at the base, Dinin reasoned, ready to begin the cycle anew.

It was midnight, the appointed hour.

Dinin moved away from the spiders and the tunnel exit and crept along the side of Tier Breche, seeking the "shadows" of heat patterns in the wall, which would effectively hide the distinct outline of his own body temperature. He came at last to Sorcere, the school of wizardry, and slipped into the narrow alley between the tower's curving base and Tier Breche's outer wall.

"Student or master?" came the expected whisper.

"Only a master may walk out-of-house in Tier Breche in the black death of Narbondel," Dinin responded.

A heavily robed figure moved around the arc of the structure to stand before Dinin. The stranger remained in the customary posture of a master of the drow Academy, his arms out before him and bent at the elbows, his hands tight together, one on top of the other in front of his chest.

That pose was the only thing about this one that seemed normal to Dinin. "Greetings, Faceless One," he signaled in the silent hand code of the drow, a language as detailed as the spoken word. The quiver of Dinin's hands belied his calm face, though, for the sight of this wizard put him as far on the edge of his nerves as he had ever been.

"Secondboy Do'Urden," the wizard replied in the gestured code. "Have you my payment?"

"You will be compensated," Dinin signaled pointedly, regaining his composure in the first swelling bubbles of his temper. "Do you dare to doubt the promise of Malice Do'Urden, Matron Mother of Daermon N'a'shezbaernon, Tenth House of Menzoberranzan?"

The Faceless One slumped back, knowing he had erred. "My apologies, Secondboy of House Do'Urden," he answered, dropping to one knee in a gesture of surrender. Since he had entered this conspiracy, the wizard had feared that his impatience might cost him his life. He had been caught in the violent throes of one of his own magical experiments, the tragedy melting away all of his facial features and leaving behind a blank hot spot of white and green goo. Matron Malice Do'Urden, reputedly as skilled as anyone in all the vast city in mixing potions and salves, had offered him a sliver of hope that he could not pass by.

No pity found its way into Dinin's callous heart, but House Do'Urden needed the wizard. "You will get your salve," Dinin promised calmly, "when Alton DeVir is dead."

"Of course," the wizard agreed. "This night?"

Dinin crossed his arms and considered the question. Matron Malice had instructed him that Alton DeVir should die even as their families' battle commenced. That scenario now seemed too clean, too easy, to Dinin. The Faceless One did not miss the sparkle that suddenly brightened the scarlet glow in the young Do'Urden's heat-sensing eyes.

"Wait for Narbondel's light to approach its zenith," Dinin replied, his hands working through the signals excitedly and his grimace seeming more of a twisted grin.

"Should the doomed boy know of his house's fate before he dies?" the wizard asked, guessing the wicked intentions behind Dinin's instructions.

"As the killing blow falls," answered Dinin. "Let Alton DeVir die without hope."

DININ RETRIEVED HIS MOUNT AND SPED OFF DOWN THE EMPTY corridors, finding an intersecting route that would take him in through a different entrance to the city proper. He came in along the eastern end of the great cavern, Menzoberranzan's produce section, where no drow families would see that he had been outside the city limits and where only a few unremarkable stalagmite pillars rose up from the flat stone. Dinin spurred his mount along the banks of Donigarten, the city's small pond with its moss-covered island that housed a fair-sized herd of cattle-like creatures called rothe. A hundred goblins and orcs looked up from their herding and fishing duties to mark the drow soldier's swift passage. Knowing their restrictions as slaves, they took care not to look Dinin in the eye.

Dinin would have paid them no heed anyway. He was too consumed by the urgency of the moment. He kicked his lizard to even greater speeds when he again was on the flat and curving avenues between the glowing drow castles. He moved toward the south-central region of the city, toward the grove of giant mushrooms that marked the section of the finest houses in Menzoberranzan.

As he came around one blind turn, he nearly ran over a group of four wandering bugbears. The giant hairy goblin things paused a moment to consider the drow, then moved slowly but purposefully out of his way.

The bugbears recognized him as a member of House Do'Urden, Dinin knew. He was a noble, a son of a high priestess, and his surname, Do'Urden, was the name of his house. Of the twenty thousand dark elves in Menzoberranzan, only a thousand or so were nobles, actually the children of the sixty-seven recognized families of the city. The rest were common soldiers.

Bugbears were not stupid creatures. They knew a noble from a commoner, and though drow elves did not carry their family insignia in plain view, the pointed and tailed cut of Dinin's stark white hair and the distinctive pattern of purple and red lines in his black piwafwi told them well enough who he was.

The mission's urgency pressed upon Dinin, but he could not ignore the bugbears' slight. How fast would they have scampered away if he had been a member of House Baenre or one of the other seven ruling houses? he wondered.

"You will learn respect of House Do'Urden soon enough!" the dark elf whispered under his breath, as he turned and charged his lizard at the group. The bugbears broke into a run, turning down an alley strewn with stones and debris.

Dinin found his satisfaction by calling on the innate powers of his race. He summoned a globe of darkness—impervious to both infravision and normal sight—in the fleeing creatures' path. He supposed that it was unwise to call such attention to himself, but a moment later, when he heard crashing and sputtered curses as the bugbears stumbled blindly over the stones, he felt it was worth the risk.

His anger sated, he moved off again, picking a more careful route through the heat shadows. As a member of the tenth house of the city, Dinin could go as he pleased within the giant cavern without question, but Matron Malice had made it clear that no one connected to House Do'Urden was to be caught anywhere near the mushroom grove.

Matron Malice, Dinin's mother, was not to be crossed, but it was only a rule, after all. In Menzoberranzan, one rule took precedence over all of the petty others: Don't get caught.

At the mushroom grove's southern end, the impetuous drow found what he was looking for: a cluster of five huge floor-to-ceiling pillars that were hollowed into a network of chambers and connected with metal and stone parapets and bridges. Red-glowing gargoyles, the standard of the house, glared down from a hundred perches like silent sentries. This was House DeVir, Fourth House of Menzoberranzan.

A stockade of tall mushrooms ringed the place, every fifth one a shrieker, a sentient fungus named (and favored as guardians) for the shrill cries of alarm it emitted whenever a living being passed it by. Dinin kept a cautious distance, not wanting to set off one of the shriekers and knowing also that other, more deadly wards protected the fortress. Matron Malice would see to those.

An expectant hush permeated the air of this city section. It was general knowledge throughout Menzoberranzan that Matron Ginafae of House DeVir had fallen out of favor with Lolth, the Spider Queen deity to all drow and the true source of every house's strength. Such circumstances were never openly discussed among the drow, but everyone who knew fully expected that some family lower in the city hierarchy soon would strike out against the crippled House DeVir.

Matron Ginafae and her family had been the last to learn of the Spider Queen's displeasure—ever was that Lolth's devious way—and Dinin could tell just by scanning the outside of House DeVir that the doomed family had not found sufficient time to erect proper defenses. DeVir sported nearly four hundred soldiers, many female, but those that Dinin could now see at their posts along the parapets seemed nervous and unsure.

Dinin's smile spread even wider when he thought of his own house, which grew in power daily under the cunning guidance of Matron Malice. With all three of his sisters rapidly approaching the status of high priestess, his brother an accomplished wizard, and his uncle Zaknafein, the finest weapons master in all of Menzoberranzan, busily training the three hundred soldiers, House Do'Urden was a complete force. And, Matron Malice, unlike Ginafae, was in the Spider Queen's full favor.

"Daermon N'a'shezbaernon," Dinin muttered under his breath, using the formal and ancestral reference to House Do'Urden. "Ninth House of Menzoberranzan!" He liked the sound of it.

HALFWAY ACROSS THE CITY, BEYOND THE SILVER-GLOWING BAL-cony and the arched doorway twenty feet up the cavern's west wall, sat the principals of House Do'Urden, gathered to outline the final plans of the night's work. On the raised dais at the back of the small audience chamber sat venerable Matron Malice, her belly swollen in the final hours of pregnancy. Flanking her in their places of honor were her three daughters, Maya, Vierna, and the eldest, Briza, a newly ordained high priestess of Lolth. Maya and Vierna appeared as younger versions of their mother, slender and deceptively small, though possessing great strength. Briza, though, hardly carried the family resemblance. She was big—huge by drow standards—and rounded in the shoulders and hips. Those who knew Briza well figured that her size was merely a circumstance of her temperament; a smaller body could not have contained the anger and brutal streak of House Do'Urden's newest high priestess.

"Dinin should return soon," remarked Rizzen, the present patron of the family, "to let us know if the time is right for the assault."

"We go before Narbondel finds its morning glow!" Briza snapped at him in her thick but razor-sharp voice. She turned a crooked smile to her mother, seeking approval for putting the male in his place.

"The child comes this night," Matron Malice explained to her anxious husband. "We go no matter what news Dinin bears."

"It will be a boy child," groaned Briza, making no effort to hide her disappointment, "third living son of House Do'Urden."

"To be sacrificed to Lolth," put in Zaknafein, a former patron of the house who now held the important position of weapons master. The skilled drow fighter seemed quite pleased at the thought of sacrifice, as did Nalfein, the family's eldest son, who stood at Zak's side. Nalfein was the elderboy, and he needed no more competition beyond Dinin within the ranks of House Do'Urden.

"In accord with custom," Briza glowered and the red of her eyes brightened. "To aid in our victory!"

Rizzen shifted uncomfortably. "Matron Malice," he dared to speak, "you know well the difficulties of birthing. Might the pain distract you—"

"You dare to question the matron mother?" Briza started sharply, reaching for the snake-headed whip so comfortably strapped—and writhing—on her belt. Matron Malice stopped her with an outstretched hand.

"Attend to the fighting," the matron said to Rizzen. "Let the females of the house see to the important matters of this battle."

Rizzen shifted again and dropped his gaze.

DININ CAME TO THE MAGICALLY WROUGHT FENCE THAT CONNECTED the keep within the city's west wall with the two small stalagmite towers of House Do'Urden, and which formed the courtyard to the compound. The fence was adamantine, the hardest metal in all the world, and adorning it were a hundred weapon-wielding spider carvings, each ensorcelled with deadly glyphs and wards. The mighty gate of House Do'Urden was the envy of many a drow house, but so soon after viewing the spectacular houses in the mushroom grove, Dinin could only find disappointment when looking upon his own abode. The compound was plain and somewhat bare, as was the section of wall, with the notable exception of the mithral-and-adamantine balcony running along the second level, by the arched doorway reserved for the nobility of the family. Each baluster of that balcony sported a thousand carvings, all of which blended into a single piece of art.

House Do'Urden, unlike the great majority of the houses in Menzoberranzan, did not stand free within groves of stalactites and stalagmites. The bulk of the structure was within a cave, and while this setup was indisputably defensible, Dinin found himself wishing that his family could show a bit more grandeur.

An excited soldier rushed to open the gate for the returning secondboy. Dinin swept past him without so much as a word of greeting and moved across the courtyard, conscious of the hundred and more curious glances that fell upon him. The soldiers and slaves knew that Dinin's mission this night had something to do with the anticipated battle.

No stairway led to the silvery balcony of House Do'Urden's second level. This, too, was a precautionary measure designed to segregate the leaders of the house from the rabble and the slaves. Drow nobles needed no stairs; another manifestation of their innate magical abilities allowed them the power of levitation. With hardly a conscious thought to the act, Dinin drifted easily through the air and dropped onto the balcony.

He rushed through the archway and down the house's main central corridor, which was dimly lit in the soft hues of faerie fire, allowing for sight in the normal light spectrum but not bright enough to defeat the use of infravision. The ornate brass door at the corridor's end marked the secondboy's destination, and he paused before it to allow his eyes to shift back to the infrared spectrum. Unlike the corridor, the room beyond the door had no light source. It was the audience hall of the high priestesses, the anteroom to House Do'Urden's grand chapel. The drow clerical rooms, in accord with the dark rites of the Spider Queen, were not places of light.

When he felt he was prepared, Dinin pushed straight through the door, shoving past the two shocked female guards without hesitation and moving boldly to stand before his mother. All three of the family daughters narrowed their eyes at their brash and pretentious brother. To enter without permission! he knew they were thinking. Would that it was he who was to be sacrificed this night!

As much as he enjoyed testing the limitations of his inferior station as a male, Dinin could not ignore the threatening dances of Vierna, Maya, and Briza. Being female, they were bigger and stronger than Dinin and had trained all their lives in the use of wicked drow clerical powers and weapons. Dinin watched as enchanted extensions of the clerics, the dreaded snake-headed whips on his sisters' belts, began writhing in anticipation of the punishment they would exact. The handles were adamantine and ordinary enough, but the whips' lengths and multiple heads were living serpents. Briza's whip, in particular, a wicked six-headed device, danced and squirmed, tying itself into knots around the belt that held it. Briza was always the quickest to punish.

Matron Malice, however, seemed pleased by Dinin's swagger. The secondboy knew his place well enough by her measure and he followed her commands fearlessly and without question.

Dinin took comfort in the calmness of his mother's face, quite the opposite of the shining white-hot faces of his three sisters. "All is ready," he said to her. "House DeVir huddles within its fence—except for Alton, of course, foolishly attending his studies in Sorcere."

"You have met with the Faceless One?" Matron Malice asked.

"The Academy was quiet this night," Dinin replied. "Our meeting went off perfectly."

"He has agreed to our contract?"

"Alton DeVir will be dealt with accordingly," Dinin chuckled. He then remembered the slight alteration he had made in Matron Malice's plans, delaying Alton's execution for the sake of his own lust for added cruelty. Dinin's thought evoked another recollection as well: high priestesses of Lolth had an unnerving talent for reading thoughts.

"Alton will die this night," Dinin quickly completed the answer, assuring the others before they could probe him for more definite details.

"Excellent," Briza growled. Dinin breathed a little easier.

"To the meld," Matron Malice ordered.

The four drow males moved to kneel before the matron and her daughters: Rizzen to Malice, Zaknafein to Briza, Nalfein to Maya, and Dinin to Vierna. The clerics chanted in unison, placing one hand delicately upon the forehead of their respective soldier, tuning in to his passions.

"You know your places," Matron Malice said when the ceremony was completed. She grimaced through the pain of another contraction. "Let our work begin."

LESS THAN AN HOUR LATER, ZAKNAFEIN AND BRIZA STOOD TOgether on the balcony outside the upper entrance to House Do'Urden.

Below them, on the cavern floor, the second and third brigades of the family army, Rizzen's and Nalfein's, bustled about, fitting on heated leather straps and metal patches—camouflage against a distinctive elven form to heat-seeing drow eyes. Dinin's group, the initial strike force that included a hundred goblin slaves, had long since departed.

"We will be known after this night," Briza said. "None would have suspected that a tenth house would dare to move against one as powerful as DeVir. When the whispers ripple out after this night's bloody work, even Baenre will take note of Daermon N'a'shezbaernon!" She leaned out over the balcony to watch as the two brigades formed into lines and started out, silently, along separate paths that would bring them through the winding city to the mushroom grove and the five-pillared structure of House DeVir.

Zaknafein eyed the back of Matron Malice's eldest daughter, wanting nothing more than to put a dagger into her spine. As always, though, good judgment kept Zak's practiced hand in its place.

"Have you the articles?" Briza inquired, showing Zak considerably more respect than she had when Matron Malice sat protectively at her side. Zak was only a male, a commoner allowed to don the family name as his own because he sometimes served Matron Malice in a husbandly manner and had once been the patron of the house. Still, Briza feared to anger him. Zak was the weapons master of House Do'Urden, a tall and muscular male, stronger than most females, and those who had witnessed his fighting wrath considered him among the finest warriors of either sex in all of Menzoberranzan. Besides Briza and her mother, both high priestesses of the Spider Queen, Zaknafein, with his unrivaled swordsmanship, was House Do'Urden's trump.

Zak held up the black hood and opened the small pouch on his belt, revealing several tiny ceramic spheres.

Briza smiled evilly and rubbed her slender hands together. "Matron Ginafae will not be pleased," she whispered.

Zak returned the smile and turned to view the departing soldiers. Nothing gave the weapons master more pleasure than killing drow elves, particularly clerics of Lolth.

"Prepare yourself," Briza said after a few minutes.

Zak shook his thick hair back from his face and stood rigid, eyes tightly closed. Briza drew her wand slowly, beginning the chant that would activate the device. She tapped Zak on one shoulder, then the other, then held the wand motionless over his head.

Zak felt the frosty sprinkles falling down on him, permeating his clothes and armor, even his flesh, until he and all of his possessions had cooled to a uniform temperature and hue. Zak hated the magical chill—it felt as he imagined death would feel—but he knew that under the influence of the wand's sprinkles he was, to the heat-sensing eyes of the creatures of the Underdark, as gray as common stone, unremarkable and undetectable.

Zak opened his eyes and shuddered, flexing his fingers to be sure they could still perform the fine edge of his craft. He looked back to Briza, already in the midst of the second spell, the summoning. This one would take a while, so Zak leaned back against the wall and considered again the pleasant, though dangerous, task before him. How thoughtful of Matron Malice to leave all of House DeVir's clerics to him!

"It is done," Briza announced after a few minutes. She led Zak's gaze upward, to the darkness beneath the unseen ceiling of the immense cavern.

Zak spotted Briza's handiwork first, an approaching current of air, yellow-tinted and warmer than the normal air of the cavern. A living current of air.

The creature, a conjuration from an Elemental Plane, swirled to hover just beyond the lip of the balcony, obediently awaiting its summoner's commands.

Zak didn't hesitate. He leaped out into the thing's midst, letting it hold him suspended above the floor.

Briza offered him a final salute and motioned her servant away. "Good fighting," she called to Zak, though he was already invisible in the air above her.

Zak chuckled at the irony of her words as the twisting city of Menzoberranzan rolled out below him. She wanted the clerics of House DeVir dead as surely as Zak did, but for very different reasons. All complications aside, Zak would have been just as happy killing clerics of House Do'Urden.

The weapons master took up one of his adamantine swords, a drow weapon magically crafted and unbelievably sharp with the edge of killing dweomers. "Good fighting indeed," he whispered. If only Briza knew how good.

2

THE FALL OF HOUSE DEVIR

Dinin noted with satisfaction that any of the meandering bug-bears, or any other of the multitude of races that composed Menzoberranzan, drow included, now made great haste to scurry out of his way. This time the secondboy of House Do'Urden was not alone. Nearly sixty soldiers of the house walked in tight lines behind him. Behind these, in similar order though with far less enthusiasm for the adventure, came a hundred armed slaves of lesser races—goblins, orcs, and bugbears.

There could be no doubt for onlookers—a drow house was on a march to war. This was not an everyday event in Menzoberranzan but neither was it unexpected. At least once every decade a house decided that its position within the city hierarchy could be improved by another house's elimination. It was a risky proposition, for all of the nobles of the "victim" house had to be disposed of quickly and quietly. If even one survived to lay an accusation upon the perpetrator, the attacking house would be eradicated by Menzoberranzan's merciless system of "justice."

If the raid was executed to devious perfection, though, no recourse would be forthcoming. All of the city, even the ruling council of the top eight matron mothers, would secretly applaud the attackers for their courage and intelligence and no more would ever be said of the incident.

Dinin took a roundabout route, not wanting to lay a direct trail between House Do'Urden and House DeVir. A half hour later, for the second time that night, he crept to the mushroom grove's southern end, to the cluster of stalagmites that held House DeVir. His soldiers streamed out behind him eagerly, readying weapons and taking full measure of the structure before them.

The slaves were slower in their movements. Many of them looked about for some escape, for they knew in their hearts that they were doomed in this battle. They feared the wrath of the dark elves more than death itself, though, and would not attempt to flee. With every exit out of Menzoberranzan protected by devious drow magic, where could they possibly go? Every one of them had witnessed the brutal punishments the drow elves exacted on recaptured slaves. At Dinin's command, they jumped into their positions around the mushroom fence.

Dinin reached into his large pouch and pulled out a heated sheet of metal. He flashed the object, brightened in the infrared spectrum, three times behind him to signal the approaching brigades of Nalfein and Rizzen. Then, with his usual cockiness, Dinin spun it quickly into the air, caught it, and replaced it in the secrecy of his heat-shielding pouch. On cue with the twirling signal, Dinin's drow brigade fitted enchanted darts to their tiny hand-held crossbows and took aim on the appointed targets.

Every fifth mushroom was a shrieker, and every dart held a magical dweomer that could silence the roar of a dragon.

". . . two . . . three," Dinin counted, his hand signaling the tempo since no words could be heard within the sphere of magical silence cast about his troops. He imagined the "click" as the drawn string on his little weapon released, loosing the dart into the nearest shrieker. So it went all around the cluster of House DeVir, the first line of alarm systematically silenced by three dozen enchanted darts.

———

Halfway across Menzoberranzan, Matron Malice, her daughters, and four of the house's common clerics were gathered in Lolth's unholy circle of eight. They ringed an idol of their wicked deity, a gemstone carving of a drow-faced spider, and called to Lolth for aid in their struggles.

Malice sat at the head, propped in a chair angled for birthing. Briza and Vierna flanked her, Briza clutching her hand.

The select group chanted in unison, combining their energies into a single offensive spell. A moment later, when Vierna, mentally linked to Dinin, understood that the first attack group was in position, the Do'Urden circle of eight sent the first insinuating waves of mental energy into the rival house.

Matron Ginafae, her two daughters, and the five principal clerics of the common troops of House DeVir huddled together in the darkened anteroom of the five-stalagmite house's main chapel. They had gathered there in solemn prayer every night since Matron Ginafae had learned that she had fallen into Lolth's disfavor. Ginafae understood how vulnerable her house remained until she could find a way to appease the Spider Queen. There were sixty-six other houses in Menzoberranzan, fully twenty of which might dare to attack House DeVir at such an obvious disadvantage. The eight clerics were anxious now, somehow suspecting that this night would be eventful.

Ginafae felt it first, a chilling blast of confusing perceptions that caused her to stutter over her prayer of forgiveness. The other clerics of House DeVir glanced nervously at the matron's uncharacteristic slip of words, looking for confirmation.

"We are under attack," Ginafae breathed to them, her head already pounding with a dull ache under the growing assault of the formidable clerics of House Do'Urden.

A second signal from Dinin put the slave troops into motion. Still using stealth as their ally, they quietly rushed to the mushroom fence and cut through with wide-bladed swords. The secondboy of House Do'Urden watched and enjoyed as the courtyard of House DeVir was easily penetrated. "Not such a prepared guard," he whispered in silent sarcasm to the red-glowing gargoyles on the high walls. The statues had seemed such an ominous guard earlier that night. Now they just watched helplessly.

Dinin recognized the measured but growing anticipation in the soldiers around him; their drow battle-lust was barely contained. Every now and then came a killing flash as one of the slaves stumbled over a warding glyph, but the secondboy and the other drow only laughed at the spectacle. The lesser races were the expendable "fodder" of House Do'Urden's army. The only purpose in bringing the goblinoids to House DeVir was to trigger the deadly traps and defenses along the perimeter, to lead the way for the drow elves, the true soldiers.

The fence was now opened and secrecy was thrown away. House DeVir's soldiers met the invading slaves head-on within the compound. Dinin barely had his hand up to begin the attack command when his sixty anxious drow warriors jumped up and charged, their faces twisted in wicked glee and their weapons waving menacingly.

They halted their approach on cue, though, remembering one final task set out to them. Every drow, noble or commoner, possessed certain magical abilities. Bringing forth a globe of darkness, as Dinin had done to the bugbears in the street earlier that night, came easily to even the lowliest of the dark elves. So it went now, with sixty Do'Urden soldiers blotting out the perimeter of House DeVir above the mushroom fence in ball after ball of blackness.

For all of their stealth and precautions, House Do'Urden knew that many eyes were watching the raid. Witnesses were not too much of a problem; they could not, or would not, care enough to identify the attacking house. But custom and rules demanded that certain attempts at secrecy be enacted, the etiquette of drow warfare. In the blink of a red-glowing drow eye, House DeVir became, to the rest of the city, a dark blot on Menzoberranzan's landscape.

Rizzen came up behind his youngest son. "Well done," he signaled in the intricate finger language of the drow. "Nalfein is in through the back."

"An easy victory," the cocky Dinin signaled back, "if Matron Ginafae and her clerics are held at bay."

"Trust in Matron Malice," was Rizzen's response. He clapped his son's shoulder and followed his troops in through the breached mushroom fence.

HIGH ABOVE THE CLUSTER OF HOUSE DEVIR, ZAKNAFEIN RESTED comfortably in the current-arms of Briza's aerial servant, watching the drama unfold. From this vantage, Zak could see within the ring of darkness and could hear within the ring of magical silence. Dinin's troops, the first drow soldiers in, had met resistance at every door and were being beaten badly.

Nalfein and his brigade, the troops of House Do'Urden most practiced in the ways of wizardry, came through the fence at the rear of the complex. Lightning strikes and magical balls of acid thundered into the courtyard at the base of the DeVir structures, cutting down Do'Urden fodder and DeVir defenses alike.

In the front courtyard, Rizzen and Dinin commanded the finest fighters of House Do'Urden. The blessings of Lolth were with his house, Zak could see when the battle was fully joined, for the strikes of the soldiers of House Do'Urden came faster than those of their enemies, and their aim proved more deadly. In minutes, the battle had been taken fully inside the five pillars.

Zak stretched the incessant chill out of his arms and willed the aerial servant to action. Down he plummeted on his windy bed, and he fell free the last few feet to the terrace along the top chambers of the central pillar. At once, two guards, one a female, rushed out to greet him.

They hesitated in confusion, though, trying to sort out the true form of this unremarkable gray blur—too long.

They had never heard of Zaknafein Do'Urden. They didn't know that death was upon them.

Zak's whip flashed out, catching and gashing the female's throat, while his other hand walked his sword through a series of masterful thrusts and parries that put the male off balance. Zak finished both in a single, blurring movement, snapping the whip-entwined female from the terrace with a twist of his wrist and spinning a kick into the male's face that likewise dropped him to the cavern floor.

Zak was then inside, where another guard rose up to meet him . . . but fell at his feet.

Zak slipped along the curving wall of the stalactite tower, his cooled body blending perfectly with the stone. Soldiers of House DeVir rushed all about him, trying to formulate some defense against the host of intruders who had already won out the lowest level of every structure and had taken two of the pillars completely.

Zak was not concerned with them. He blocked out the clanging ring of adamantine weapons, the cries of command, and the screams of death, concentrating instead on a singular sound that would lead him to his destination: a unified, frantic chant.

He found an empty corridor covered with spider carvings and running into the center of the pillar. As in House Do'Urden, this corridor ended in a large set of ornate double doors, their decorations dominated by arachnid forms. "This must be the place," Zak muttered under his breath, fitting his hood to the top of his head.

A giant spider rushed out of its concealment to his side.

Zak dived to his belly and kicked out under the thing, spinning into a roll that plunged his sword deep into the monster's bulbous body. Sticky fluids gushed out over the weapons master, and the spider shuddered to a quick death.

"Yes," Zak whispered, wiping the spider juices from his face, "this must be the place." He pulled the dead monster back into its hidden cubby and slipped in beside the thing, hoping that no one had noticed the brief struggle.

By the sounds of ringing weapons, Zak could tell that the fighting had almost reached this floor. House DeVir now seemed to have its defenses in place, though, and was finally holding its ground.

"Now, Malice," Zak whispered, hoping that Briza, attuned to him in the meld, would sense his anxiety. "Let us not be late!"

BACK IN THE CLERICAL ANTEROOM OF HOUSE DO'URDEN, MALICE and her subordinates continued their brutal mental assault on the clerics of House DeVir. Lolth heard their prayers louder than those of their counterparts, giving the clerics of House Do'Urden the stronger spells in their mental combat. Already they had easily put their enemies into a defensive posture. One of the lesser priestesses in DeVir's circle of eight had been crushed by Briza's mental insinuations and now lay dead on the floor barely inches from Matron Ginafae's feet.

But the momentum had slowed suddenly and the battle seemed to be swinging back to an even level. Matron Malice, struggling with the impending birth, could not hold her concentration, and without her voice, the spells of her unholy circle weakened.

At her mother's side, powerful Briza clutched her mother's hand so tightly that all the blood was squeezed from it, leaving it cool— the only cool spot on the laboring female—to the eyes of the others. Briza studied the contractions and the crowning cap of the coming child's white hair, and calculated the time to the moment of birth. This technique of translating the pain of birth into an offensive spell attack had never been tried before, except in legend, and Briza knew that timing would be the critical factor.

She whispered into her mother's ear, coaxing out the words of a deadly incantation.

Matron Malice echoed back the beginnings of the spell, sublimating her gasps, and transforming her rage of agony into offensive power.

"Dinnen douward ma brechen tol," Briza implored.

"Dinnen douward . . . maaa . . . brechen tol!" Malice growled, so determined to focus through the pain that she bit through one of her thin lips.

The baby's head appeared, more fully this time, and this time to stay.

Briza trembled and could barely remember the incantation herself. She whispered the final rune into the matron's ear, almost fearing the consequences.

Malice gathered her breath and her courage. She could feel the tingling of the spell as clearly as the pain of the birth. To her daughters standing around the idol, staring at her in disbelief, she appeared as a red blur of heated fury, streaking sweat lines that shone as brightly as the heat of boiling water.

"Abec," the matron began, feeling the pressure building to a crescendo. "Abec." She felt the hot tear of her skin, the sudden slippery release as the baby's head pushed through, the sudden ecstacy of birthing. "Abec di'n'a'BREG DOUWARD!" Malice screamed, pushing away all of the agony in a final explosion of magical power that knocked even the clerics of her own house from their feet.

CARRIED ON THE THRUST OF MATRON MALICE'S EXULTATION, THE dweomer thundered into the chapel of House DeVir, shattered the gemstone idol of Lolth, sundered the double doors into heaps of twisted metal, and threw Matron Ginafae and her overmatched subordinates to the floor.

Zak shook his head in disbelief as the chapel doors flew past him. "Quite a kick, Malice." He chuckled and spun around the entryway, into the chapel. Using his infravision, he took a quick survey and head count of the lightless room's seven living occupants, all struggling back to their feet, their robes tattered. Again shaking his head at the bared power of Matron Malice, Zak pulled his hood down over his face.

A snap of his whip was the only explanation he offered as he smashed a tiny ceramic globe at his feet. The sphere shattered, dropping out a pellet that Briza had enchanted for just such occasions, a pellet glowing with the brightness of daylight.

For eyes accustomed to blackness, tuned in to heat emanations, the intrusion of such radiance came in a blinding flash of agony. The clerics' cries of pain only aided Zak in his systematic trek around the room, and he smiled widely under his hood every time he felt his sword bite into drow flesh.

He heard the beginnings of a spell across the way and knew that one of the DeVirs had recovered enough from the assault to be dangerous. The weapons master did not need his eyes to aim, however, and the crack of his whip took Matron Ginafae's tongue right out of her mouth.

Briza placed the newborn on the back of the spider idol and lifted the ceremonial dagger, pausing to admire its cruel workmanship. Its hilt was a spider's body sporting eight legs, barbed so as to appear furred, but angled down to serve as blades. Briza lifted the instrument above the baby's chest. "Name the child," she implored her mother. "The Spider Queen will not accept the sacrifice until the child is named!"

Matron Malice lolled her head, trying to fathom her daughter's meaning. The matron mother had thrown everything into the moment of the spell and the birth, and she was now barely coherent.

"Name the child!" Briza commanded, anxious to feed her hungry goddess.

"It nears its end," Dinin said to his brother when they met in a lower hall of one of the lesser pillars of House DeVir. "Rizzen is winning through to the top, and it is believed that Zaknafein's dark work has been completed."

"Two score of House DeVir's soldiers have already turned allegiance to us," Nalfein replied.

"They see the end," laughed Dinin. "One house serves them as well as another, and in the eyes of commoners no house is worth dying for. Our task will be finished soon."

"Too quickly for anyone to take note," Nalfein said. "Now Do'Urden, Daermon N'a'shezbaernon, is the Ninth House of Menzoberranzan and DeVir be damned!"

"Alert!" Dinin cried suddenly, eyes widening in feigned horror as he looked over his brother's shoulder.

Nalfein reacted immediately, spinning to face the danger at his back, only to put the true danger at his back. For even as Nalfein realized the deception, Dinin's sword slipped into his spine. Dinin put his head to his brother's shoulder and pressed his cheek to Nalfein's, watching the red sparkle of heat leave his brother's eyes.

"Too quickly for anyone to take note," Dinin teased, echoing his brother's earlier words.

He dropped the lifeless form to his feet. "Now Dinin is elderboy of House Do'Urden, and Nalfein be damned."

"DRIZZT," BREATHED MATRON MALICE. "THE CHILD'S NAME IS Drizzt!"

Briza tightened her grip on the knife and began the ritual. "Queen of Spiders, take this babe," she began. She raised the dagger to strike. "Drizzt Do'Urden we give to you in payment for our glorious vic—"

"Wait!" called Maya from the side of the room. Her melding with her brother Nalfein had abruptly ceased. It could only mean one thing. "Nalfein is dead," she announced. "The baby is no longer the third living son."

Vierna glanced curiously at her sister. At the same instant that Maya had sensed Nalfein's death, Vierna, melded with Dinin, had felt a strong emotive surge. Elation? Vierna brought a slender finger up to her pursed lips, wondering if Dinin had successfully pulled off the assassination.

Briza still held the spider-shaped knife over the babe's chest, wanting to give this one to Lolth.

"We promised the Spider Queen the third living son," Maya warned. "And that has been given."

"But not in sacrifice," argued Briza.

Vierna shrugged, at a loss. "If Lolth accepted Nalfein, then he has been given. To give another might evoke the Spider Queen's anger."

"But to not give what we have promised would be worse still!" Briza insisted.

"Then finish the deed," said Maya.

Briza clenched down tight on the dagger and began the ritual again.

"Stay your hand," Matron Malice commanded, propping herself up in the chair. "Lolth is content; our victory is won. Welcome, then, your brother, the newest member of House Do'Urden."

"Just a male," Briza commented in obvious disgust, walking away from the idol and the child.

"Next time we shall do better," Matron Malice chuckled, though she wondered if there would be a next time. She approached the end of her fifth century of life, and drow elves, even young ones, were not a particularly fruitful lot. Briza had been born to Malice at the youthful age of one hundred, but in the almost four centuries since, Malice had produced only five other children. Even this baby, Drizzt, had come as a surprise, and Malice hardly expected that she would ever conceive again.

"Enough of such contemplations," Malice whispered to herself, exhausted. "There will be ample time . . ." She sank back into her chair and fell into fitful, though wickedly pleasant, dreams of heightening power.

Zaknafein walked through the central pillar of the DeVir complex, his hood in his hand and his whip and sword comfortably replaced on his belt. Every now and then a ring of battle sounded, only to be quickly ended. House Do'Urden had rolled through to victory, the tenth house had taken the fourth, and now all that remained was to remove evidence and witnesses. One group of lesser female clerics marched through, tending to the wounded Do'Urdens and animating the corpses of those beyond their ability, so that the bodies could walk away from the crime scene. Back at the Do'Urden compound, those corpses not beyond repair would be resurrected and put back to work.

Zak turned away with a visible shudder as the clerics moved from room to room, the marching line of Do'Urden zombies growing ever longer at their backs.

As distasteful as Zaknafein found this troupe, the one that followed was even worse. Two Do'Urden clerics led a contingent of soldiers through the structure, using detection spells to determine hiding places of surviving DeVirs. One stopped in the hallway just a few steps from Zak, her eyes turned inward as she felt the emanations of her spell. She held her fingers out in front of her, tracing a slow line, like some macabre divining rod, toward drow flesh.

"In there!" she declared, pointing to a panel at the base of the wall. The soldiers jumped to it like a pack of ravenous wolves and tore through the secret door. Inside a hidden cubby huddled the children of House DeVir. These were nobles, not commoners, and could not be taken alive.

Zak quickened his pace to get beyond the scene, but he heard vividly the children's helpless screams as the hungry Do'Urden soldiers finished their job. Zak found himself in a run now. He rushed around a bend in the hallway, nearly bowling over Dinin and Rizzen.

"Nalfein is dead," Rizzen declared impassively.

Zak immediately turned a suspicious eye on the younger Do'Urden son.

"I killed the DeVir soldier who committed the deed," Dinin assured him, not even hiding his cocky smile.

Zak had been around for nearly four centuries, and he was certainly not ignorant of the ways of his ambitious race. The brother princes had come in defensively at the back of the lines, with a host of Do'Urden soldiers between them and the enemy. By the time they even encountered a drow that was not of their own house, the majority of the DeVirs' surviving soldiers had already switched allegiance to House Do'Urden. Zak doubted that either of the Do'Urden brothers had even seen action against a DeVir.

"The description of the carnage in the prayer room has been spread throughout the ranks," Rizzen said to the weapons master. "You performed with your usual excellence—as we have come to expect."

Zak shot the patron a glare of contempt and kept on his way, down though the structure's main doors and out beyond the magical darkness and silence into Menzoberranzan's dark dawn. Rizzen was Matron Malice's present partner in a long line of partners, and no more. When Malice was finished with him, she would either relegate him back to the ranks of the common soldiery, stripping him of the name Do'Urden and all the rights that accompanied it, or she would dispose of him. Zak owed him no respect.

Zak moved out beyond the mushroom fence to the highest vantage point he could find, then fell to the ground. He watched, amazed, a few moments later, when the procession of the Do'Urden army, patron and son, soldiers and clerics, and the slow-moving line of two dozen drow zombies, made its way back home. They had lost, and left behind, nearly all of their slave fodder in the attack, but the line leaving the wreckage of House DeVir was longer than the line that had come in earlier that night. The slaves had been replaced twofold by captured DeVir slaves, and fifty or more of the DeVir common troops, showing typical drow loyalty, had willingly joined the attackers. These traitorous drow would be interrogated—magically interrogated—by the Do'Urden clerics to ensure their sincerity.

They would pass the test to a one, Zak knew. Drow elves were creatures of survival, not of principle. The soldiers would be given new identities and would be kept within the privacy of the Do'Urden compound for a few months, until the fall of House DeVir became an old and forgotten tale.

Zak did not follow immediately. Rather, he cut through the rows of mushroom trees and found a secluded dell, where he plopped down on a patch of mossy carpet and raised his gaze to the eternal darkness of the cavern's ceiling—and the eternal darkness of his existence.

It would have been prudent for him to remain silent at that time; he was an invader to the most powerful section of the vast city. He thought of the possible witnesses to his words, the same dark elves who had watched the fall of House DeVir, who had wholeheartedly enjoyed the spectacle. In the face of such behavior and such carnage as this night had seen, Zak could not contain his emotions. His lament came out as a plea to some god beyond his experience.

"What place is this that is my world; what dark coil has my spirit embodied?" he whispered the angry disclaimer that had always been a part of him. "In light, I see my skin as black; in darkness, it glows white in the heat of this rage I cannot dismiss.

"Would that I had the courage to depart, this place or this life, or to stand openly against the wrongness that is the world of these, my kin. To seek an existence that does not run afoul to that which I believe, and to that which I hold dear faith is truth.

"Zaknafein Do'Urden, I am called, yet a drow I am not, by choice or by deed. Let them discover this being that I am, then. Let them rain their wrath on these old shoulders already burdened by the hopelessness of Menzoberranzan."

Ignoring the consequences, the weapons master rose to his feet and yelled, "Menzoberranzan, what hell are you?"

A moment later, when no answer echoed back out of the quiet city, Zak flexed the remaining chill of Briza's wand from his weary muscles. He found some comfort as he patted the whip on his belt—the instrument that had taken the tongue from the mouth of a matron mother.

3

THE EYES OF A CHILD

Masoj, the young apprentice—which at this point in his magic-using career meant that he was no more than a cleaning attendant—leaned on his broom and watched as Alton DeVir moved through the door into the highest chamber of the spire. Masoj almost felt sympathy for the student, who had to go in and face the Faceless One.

Masoj felt excitement as well, though, knowing that the ensuing fireworks between Alton and the faceless master would be well worth the watching. He went back to his sweeping, using the broom as an excuse to get farther around the curve of the room's floor, closer to the door.

"You requested my presence, Master Faceless One," Alton DeVir said again, keeping one hand in front of his face and squinting to fight the brilliant glare of the room's three lighted candles. Alton shifted uncomfortably from one foot to the other just inside the shadowy room's door.

Hunched across the way, the Faceless One kept his back to the young DeVir. Better to be done with this cleanly, the master reminded himself. He knew, though, that the spell he was now preparing would kill Alton before the student could learn his family's fate, before the Faceless One could fully complete Dinin Do'Urden's final instructions. Too much was at stake. Better to be done with this cleanly.

"You . . ." Alton began again, but he prudently held his words and tried to sort out the situation before him. How unusual to be summoned to the private chambers of a master of the Academy before the day's lessons had even begun.

When he had first received the summons, Alton feared that he had somehow failed one of his lessons. That could be a fatal mistake in Sorcere. Alton was close to graduation, but the disdain of a single master could put an end to that.

He had done quite well in his lessons with the Faceless One, had even believed that this mysterious master favored him. Could this call be simply a courtesy of congratulations on his impending graduation? Unlikely, Alton realized against his hopes. Masters of the drow Academy did not often congratulate students.

Alton then heard quiet chanting and noticed that the master was in the midst of spellcasting. Something cried out as very wrong to him now; something about this whole situation did not fit the strict ways of the Academy. Alton set his feet firmly and tensed his muscles, following the advice of the motto that had been drilled into the thoughts of every student at the Academy, the precept that kept drow elves alive in a society so devoted to chaos: Be prepared.

THE DOORS EXPLODED BEFORE HIM, SHOWERING THE ROOM WITH stone splinters and throwing Masoj back against the wall. He felt the show well worth both the inconvenience and the new bruise on his shoulder when Alton DeVir scrambled out of the room. The student's back and left arm trailed wisps of smoke, and the most exquisite expression of terror and pain that Masoj had ever seen was etched on the DeVir noble's face.

Alton stumbled to the floor and kicked into a roll, desperate to put some ground between himself and the murderous master. He made it down and around the descending arc of the room's floor and through the door that led into the next lower chamber just as the Faceless One made his appearance at the sundered door.

The master stopped to spit a curse at his misfire, and to consider the best way to replace his door. "Clean it up!" he snapped at Masoj, who was again leaning casually with his hands atop his broomstick and his chin atop his hands.

Masoj obediently dropped his head and started sweeping the stone splinters. He looked up as the Faceless One stalked past, however, and cautiously started after the master.

Alton couldn't possibly escape, and this show would be too good to miss.

THE THIRD ROOM, THE FACELESS ONE'S PRIVATE LIBRARY, WAS the brightest of the four in the spire, with dozens of candles burning on each wall.

"Damn this light!" Alton spat, stumbling his way down through the dizzying blur to the door that led to the Faceless One's entry hall, the lowest room of the master's quarters. If he could get down from this spire and outside of the tower to the courtyard of the Academy, he might be able to turn the momentum against the master.

Alton's world remained the darkness of Menzoberranzan, but the Faceless One, who had spent so many decades in the candlelight of Sorcere, had grown accustomed to using his eyes to see shades of light, not heat.

The entry hall was cluttered with chairs and chests, but only one candle burned there, and Alton could see clearly enough to dodge or leap any obstacles. He rushed to the door and grabbed the heavy latch. It turned easily enough, but when Alton tried to shoulder through, the door did not budge and a burst of sparkling blue energy threw him back to the floor.

"Curse this place," Alton spat. The portal was magically held. He knew a spell to open such enchanted doors but doubted whether his magic would be strong enough to dispel the castings of a master. In his haste and fear, the words of the dweomer floated through Alton's thoughts in an indecipherable jumble.

"Do not run, DeVir," came the Faceless One's call from the previous chamber. "You only lengthen your torment!"

"A curse upon you, too," Alton replied under his breath. Alton forgot about the stupid spell; it would never come to him in time. He glanced around the room for an option.

His eyes found something unusual halfway up the side wall, in an opening between two large cabinets. Alton scrambled back a few steps to get a better angle but found himself caught within the range of the candlelight, within the deceptive field where his eyes registered both heat and light.

He could only discern that this section of the wall showed a uniform glow in the heat spectrum and that its hue was subtly different from the stone of the walls. Another doorway? Alton could only hope his guess to be right. He rushed back to the center of the room, stood directly across from the object, and forced his eyes away from the infrared spectrum, fully back into the world of light.

As his eyes adjusted, what came into view both startled and confused the young DeVir. He saw no doorway, nor any opening with another chamber behind it. What he looked upon was a reflection of himself, and a portion of the room he now stood in. Alton had never, in his fifty-five years of life, witnessed such a spectacle, but he had heard the masters of Sorcere speak of these devices. It was a mirror.

A movement in the upper doorway of the chamber reminded Alton that the Faceless One was almost upon him. He couldn't hesitate to ponder his options. He put his head down and charged the mirror.

Perhaps it was a teleportation door to another section of the city, perhaps a simple door to a room beyond. Or perhaps, Alton dared to imagine in those few desperate seconds, this was some interplanar gate that would bring him into a strange and unknown plane of existence!

He felt the tingling excitement of adventure pulling him on as he neared the wondrous thing—then he felt only the impact, the shattering glass, and the unyielding stone wall behind it.

Perhaps it was just a mirror.

———

"Look at his eyes," Vierna whispered to Maya as they examined the newest member of House Do'Urden.

Truly the babe's eyes were remarkable. Though the child had been out of the womb for less than an hour, the pupils of his orbs darted back and forth inquisitively. While they showed the expected radiating glow of eyes seeing into the infrared spectrum, the familiar redness was tinted by a shade of blue, giving them a violet hue.

"Blind?" wondered Maya. "Perhaps this one will be given to the Spider Queen still."

Briza looked back to them anxiously. Dark elves did not allow children showing any physical deficiency to live.

"Not blind," replied Vierna, passing her hand over the child and casting an angry glare at both of her eager sisters. "He follows my fingers."

Maya saw that Vierna spoke the truth. She leaned closer to the babe, studying his face and strange eyes. "What do you see, Drizzt Do'Urden?" she asked softly, not in an act of gentleness toward the babe, but so that she would not disturb her mother, resting in the chair at the head of the spider idol.

"What do you see that the rest of us cannot?"

ABOUT THE AUTHOR

R.A. SALVATORE's books have sold more than forty million copies and been translated into numerous languages. When he isn't writing, Salvatore chases after his Japanese Chin, Pikel; takes long walks; hits the gym; and coaches/plays on a fun-league softball team that includes most of his family. His gaming group still meets on Sundays to play D&D or DemonWars or whatever the Sadist . . . err, Game Master, decides.

rasalvatore.com

ABOUT THE TYPE

This book was set in Caslon, a typeface first designed in 1722 by William Caslon (1692–1766). Its widespread use by most English printers in the early eighteenth century soon supplanted the Dutch typefaces that had formerly prevailed. The roman is considered a "work-horse" typeface due to its pleasant, open appearance, while the italic is exceedingly decorative.